UNBOUND BY SHADOWS

AVALON GRIFFIN

WILD
CLOVER
INK

Published by Wild Clover Ink

UNBOUND BY SHADOWS/Avalon Griffin

Paperback Edition ISBN: 979-8-9866766-1-6

Digital Edition Edition ISBN: 979-8-9866766-0-9

First paperback edition February 2023

Edited by Ellen Margulies and Bethany Seabolt

Cover art by Enchanted Ink Publishing

Map by Cartography Bird

Printed in the United States of America

For Dad

GOBLYN
LANDS

QUEEN LILITH'S
CASTLE

HARPY
LANDS

SNOWMELT

N AELLO'S
ASTLE

IRISWOOD

LKINA
NDS

NEREID LANDS

QUEEN CEBNA'S
CASTLE

THE GREAT QUEENDOMS OF

AURELIA

CHAPTER 1

Nashville, Tennessee, United States
The Gaia Plane

S elene Riley looked down at a new text message on her phone and rolled her eyes. She glanced over at her sister and said, "So apparently, not only are there ghosts where we're going but Bigfoot too."

"Perfect," Cass said as she eased her car onto the congested interstate. "I'll get a photo of him, and we'll be millionaires."

Selene took a sip of her Grande sugar-free vanilla latte and held it tightly as Cass tapped the brakes. Even on a Saturday, Nashville traffic was a nightmare, so Selene was glad her sister was driving for their impromptu road trip to the tiny town of Rugby, Tennessee. It was the least she could do, after all. Selene was only partially functioning after being woken up an hour ago by a knock on her apartment door, followed by her sister's voice squealing, "Road trip!"

"He's lured by the smell of bacon, according to Evan," Selene said as another text about Bigfoot sightings in East Tennessee popped up from her younger brother, Cass's twin. "Thank goodness we're not camping. Wait... we are sleeping *indoors,* aren't we?"

"Of course. But I want to do a little hiking tomorrow morning. You're up for that, right?"

"Do I have a choice?"

"Not really," Cass chirped.

"Great," Selene sighed. She began twirling the ends of her shoulder-length brown hair between her fingers. With her boyfriend out of town, Selene had been looking forward to a weekend of lounging by the pool and reading. But apparently, her plans weren't as important as her sister's desire to enter a photography contest. Cass had argued that the historic buildings of Rugby were the ideal subject, and the June weather was perfect for a little sisterly bonding trip. Selene had protested but quickly gave up. It had always been easier to go along with the plans her family made.

"You're lucky I love you," Selene said, stifling a yawn.

Cass gave her a worried look. "Are you mad at me? I thought you'd always wanted to go to Rugby to see the library."

The anxiety in her younger sister's face made Selene feel instantly guilty. She dropped her eyes to her lap. *Stop acting so spoiled,* she told herself. What was so great about staying home alone when Cass was generous enough to take her on a weekend getaway? After growing up with a small-minded mother and living with a boyfriend who hated flying, most of her time was spent dreaming about faraway lands rather than visiting them. Reaching over to squeeze Cass's elbow, she said, "I'm not mad, and you're right. I have always wanted to visit Rugby. This was a great idea. I'm just sorry Evan couldn't come too."

When Cass beamed, relief flooded through her. Selene had spent so many years trying to shield the twins from difficult emotions that offering reassurance was practically a reflex. And her words weren't a complete lie; Rugby had been on Selene's travel radar for a long time.

With a population of only seventy-five, Rugby was a tiny place with a fascinating past. It was founded in 1880 as a utopian community by upper-class English colonists and boasted over three hundred residents at its peak. Although sickness and poor management caused the social experiment of Rugby to fail, Cass was planning to photograph the handful of Victorian buildings that still stood today. Among them was the oldest preserved historical library in America, complete with all 7,000 books from its original collection.

Selene's phone chimed with another message from her brother. "Here he goes again. Do you know what a Wampus Cat is?"

"Another story Evan made up to scare us when Dad was out of town?"

"No, this seems real," Selene said, squinting at her phone. "Well, as real as any of Evan's stories are. He says the Wampus Cat is a cryptozoological creature with bright yellow eyes and huge paws. If you hear her cry, you will die in the next three days. There was a sighting recently in Rugby, near the woods by the cemetery."

"By the river? That's where I want to do a few sunrise shots tomorrow."

"It doesn't say exactly. The headline is, 'Monstrous Cat Spotted Near Rugby.' It goes on to say a few people saw a huge gold cat limping around some empty bear traps."

"Yikes."

"But if Bigfoot is there with the cat, maybe that's to our advantage," Selene joked. "They'll be too busy fighting over their territory to bother with us."

Cass laughed, and Evan began to entertain them with texts about Rugby's most famous ghost legends. He'd always had a keen interest in the supernatural and was a wealth of information on that sort of thing. Selene, on the other hand, preferred to dwell in reality.

The sisters giggled about the stories, but once they left the interstate and began traveling along the small roads leading into Rugby they grew quiet. The overgrown fields and rugged forests of the Cumberland Plateau echoed with loneliness as the number of cars sharing the road dwindled until they seemed to be the only ones left.

3

They passed several empty churches, barns decorated with folk art, and an old gas station turned general store. Once they reached the ancient sign announcing their entry to Rugby, the sisters cheered even as a prickle of unease crawled down Selene's spine at the sight of the village.

Selene knew Rugby was small, but she didn't expect the town to be a handful of buildings scattered on either side of a single road. After driving past the gift shop, historic printing works, and restaurant, Cass pulled into the Rugby Visitor's Center parking lot.

When Selene stepped out of the car, she couldn't suppress a shiver, though it was 70 degrees out. It was like a veil of crushing silence had dropped over them. The air was dead. Oppressive. There were cars in the parking lot, but the town was completely, eerily hushed.

The sound of Cass's car door shutting cracked like a hunter's shotgun, making Selene jump. Cass inhaled deeply. "Wow, it's so peaceful."

"Yeah," Selene replied. Quiet had always been a comfort to her, a soothing companion. But this quiet was unwelcoming.

They walked into the visitor center, which to Selene's relief was buzzing with voices. Children were laughing as families milled around waiting for the next walking tour to start. Selene loaded up on brochures, including a hiking guide to the curiously named Gentlemen's Swimming Hole. After they picked up keys to their historic guesthouse accommodations from the visitor center clerk, they took the last two spots on the tour.

The library was everything Selene had hoped for. From the charming red roof outside to the delightfully musty smell of old books inside, it was like taking a time machine back to 1882. She was even allowed to flip through a few books while wearing cotton gloves.

While Selene was engrossed in an old schoolbook, Cass pointed her camera and called out, "Hold it right there. Smile!" Selene obliged.

But when Cass quipped that she looked like she was in her happy place, her smile fell. Her sister didn't mean to strike a nerve. To Cass and Evan, the library was a fun place their big sister took them on nights and weekends when they were children. They were lucky to grow up with a branch across the street and even more fortunate that it was staffed by kind librarians who didn't comment on their lengthy visits. Selene and the twins all loved reading, but for Selene libraries were also an escape from the chaos of home.

After the tour, Cass and Selene lingered outside each of the historic buildings for more photos. When it grew dark, they went to dinner at Rugby's only restaurant, the Harrow Road Cafe. It was a bright, airy space with dark beams stretching across the peaked ceiling and wooden booths polished shiny as church pews.

Cass looked down at the menu. "Ooo, do you want to split a piece of pie?"

"No, thanks," Selene said. Cass was the type who could eat anything she wanted and stay lithe as a supermodel, whereas Selene had inherited their mother's curves. "I'll just get a salad."

"You've become as boring as Kevin," Cass said before squeezing lemon juice into her iced tea. "What is the great Kevin P. Norton doing this weekend?"

Selene paused. Trying to make her voice sound casual, she said, "He's on tour as the opening act for another band. It's a huge opportunity for him. He's playing all his original songs. Great exposure."

Selene twirled the straw in her ice water, hoping her sister didn't notice she was hiding something. She wasn't ready to tell Cass that after a year of dating, Kevin had told her he wanted to "press pause" on their relationship while he was on tour. He needed a break to refocus on his creativity, he said. It wasn't about her; he just needed some freedom to explore without boundaries. Although Selene was deeply hurt, she agreed because she wanted to support his career aspirations. Also, she didn't like to argue. She had helped Kevin pack up his things and wished him well, assuring herself that things would go back to normal once the tour ended.

"And he didn't drag you along?" Cass said. "How will he survive?"

"Don't start."

"He should pay you to be his manager. How long is the tour?"

"Eight weeks. I'm just managing his social media while he's gone."

"He can't handle all of his 102 followers on his own?" Cass said with a laugh.

"Give it a rest, Cass," Selene said. "Although he doesn't always show it, he is appreciative."

Cass made a dismissive sound. "Except in the bedroom."

Selene's face grew hot, and her mouth tightened. She knew she should never have confided to her sister that her sex life was as exciting as a deflated balloon. "Do we have to get into this now?"

Cass shrugged. "I just don't think he's the best fit for you."

Defensively Selene asked, "Who do you think I should be with then?"

"I always hoped you'd end up with someone more... wild."

Selene shook her head. "No. That's one of the things I like about Kevin. I don't have to walk on eggshells around him like we do with Mom. He's never yelled at me, he doesn't drink, and I always know where I stand with him."

"Yeah, but guys like Kevin are a dime a dozen in Nashville. When we were growing up, you used to always like men who were a bit out of the ordinary. Like, remember how I had a thing for Tom Cruise in the movie *Legend* but you had a huge crush on the devil?"

"His name is Darkness. Lord of Darkness," Selene said, referring to the demonic character in the classic '80s fantasy film. "And so what? Horns are sexy."

"If you say so," Cass said, running a hand through her blonde bob. "I don't know. I just don't want you to be with someone that dulls your sparkle, you know what I mean?"

"I'm in my thirties now. Sparkle is overrated," Selene said. Although she loved reading stories about wild adventures and fascinating people, she liked to keep her life small and manageable. Focusing too much on her own desires had always led to more drama than she cared for.

~

It was just past 4:30 a.m. when Selene dressed in the dark, pulling on jeans, a T-shirt, and a hoodie to fight the slight chill in the air. Cass wanted to photograph the first rays of sun rising over the Clear Fork River, which required a short half-mile hike starting at the Laurel Dale Cemetery. When Selene laced up her hiking boots, she wondered if Rugby's odd quiet would be even more pronounced in the wee hours before dawn. But as they stepped out on the porch to lock up, she realized Rugby after dark was anything but silent.

There was a faint buzzing, like static from a dead phone line. It was not a peaceful chorus of insects and cricket chirps, but a low-frequency drone. Selene turned her head left and right, trying to determine the direction it was coming from, but it draped over the whole area like a shroud.

The treetops swayed in the wind. An owl hooted to her right, and she startled. At her sharp intake of breath, the wind changed direction, marking her with a gust that whipped her hair around her shoulders before she ducked into the car.

Cass insisted she heard no buzzing, and they argued about it as they drove the two-mile journey to the trailhead. The road leading into the cemetery was narrow, and the trees lining the road swayed as the car crunched over the gravel. Eventually, the narrow path opened to a wide meadow and small parking lot.

Although they were deep in the woods, the cemetery was flat and cleared of vegetation. Selene's breath caught when she saw movement in her peripheral vision, but it was the ripple of a small flag planted by a headstone. The eerie strains of a rusted wind chime, another gravesite decoration, sounded as Cass opened her door. Selene climbed out of the car and put on her backpack.

"Do you want to look around the cemetery for a minute?" Cass asked. She shone her flashlight over the headstones, which were a mix of markers, old and new.

"Let's do it later. I'm starting to get creeped out," Selene replied. She didn't want to admit it to herself, but the droning buzz seemed more pronounced.

"We'll be fine," Cass said. "Look, the sky's starting to lighten up."

Cass's flashlight bounced as she walked toward the wooden sign that read "Gentlemen's Swimming Hole—0.4 miles." Selene activated the flashlight app on her phone and focused on Cass's black-and-white striped leggings as she moved into the woods.

The trail started as an easy downhill slope with a few turns. It was a well-maintained path, but Selene grew frustrated as they progressed. She kept getting her hair tangled in branches and her arms scratched by tree limbs. Pausing to untangle yet another spiky branch from her hair, she marveled at how Cass glided ahead of her with ease, unencumbered. Although it was a silly idea, Selene felt like the forest was reaching out to pull her in.

It wasn't until they reached the trail's hairpin turn around a small creek that Selene's vague unease shifted to genuine anxiety. One moment she felt fine, but then she was hit with a sudden headache. It was sharp and intense like someone had inflicted a blow right in the middle of her forehead. The pain made her stumble for a moment and gasp.

Cass stopped to place her hand on Selene's shoulder. "Are you okay?"

Selene pinched the bridge of her nose. "I just had this pain shoot through my head. Did something hit me?"

Cass shone her flashlight over Selene's face. "I don't see any marks. Do you want to sit down?"

"No, maybe it's my allergies. Let's keep going. I can hear water, so we must be close."

The trees that lined the trail behind them gave way to large rocks and stone ledges. They came upon a downward staircase made of strategically placed rocks cut into a hill. Cass slowly descended before shining her flashlight back to illuminate Selene's steps. As she reached the bottom, they paused to take in their surroundings.

Cass studied her map and said, "This must be what they call the Witch's Cave. Not much of a cave, is it? More like a rock shelter. She shone her flashlight around the stone overhang. Craggy stone walls soared above them on three sides, and a small pool of water collected the moisture from the rocks at the bottom. "It has a funny smell. Like printer toner."

"Ozone. It's the smell before a storm." Selene rubbed her hand over her forehead, wincing. "I feel weird. You should go on ahead. I need a second to sit down." She eased herself onto one of the large, flat rocks strewn beneath the overhang.

"Maybe we should go back," Cass said, but then looked toward the horizon anxiously. Sunrise was about to break any minute now.

"No, no, I'm fine. I just need a moment." Selene took a drink from her water bottle then gestured at the sign pointing to the Gentlemen's Swimming Hole. "I don't want you to miss the sunrise, so go on without me. Hurry."

Cass looked uncertain, then said, "I'll just get a few shots and be right back. Holler if you need me."

Selene nodded and watched her sister's flashlight weave down the trail. The humming sound was piercing now, and goosebumps prickled across her arms. She closed her eyes briefly, trying to regain her usually calm composure.

She breathed deeply for several moments and resolved to Google "sound hallucinations" once they got back to the guest cottage. The rock she sat on had been damp with dew, and that moisture was seeping into her jeans. Slowly she stood up, reaching out to the jagged rock wall for support, noting the irony of how even when she traveled she managed to find a way to be stuck in one place—left behind while others got to experience glorious sights and adventures.

Her head continued to throb, but her attention shifted as loud pops like sparks of static crackled behind her. Tentatively, she turned to see where it was coming from.

Please don't be a rattlesnake. Or Bigfoot, or a monster cat...

Her eye was drawn to a dark hollow within the jagged rock. It was a small, square-shaped opening, only about three feet tall. She took a step back and directed her phone's flashlight into the darkness. When the beam of light hit the empty space, the air seemed to shimmer. The darkness pulsed within her phone's pale light, like waves of heat rising from hot asphalt.

Suddenly she realized her headache was gone. She touched her forehead. The pain had disappeared completely. As she wondered what sort of games her body was playing, she was overcome with a new sensation. It started as a tingly warmth in her stomach. Then it burst within her, traveling down her limbs in waves that made her sway on her feet. But this time, it wasn't anxiety. It was a feeling of welcome. Of *rightness*.

The sensation seemed to tug her forward, propelling her toward the glittering mist.

She took one step closer, then another. She watched her legs move as if outside her own body. Her whole being strained toward the opening, as though a tremendous magnetic force was pulling her closer.

The electric smell of ozone hit her so hard her eyes watered. She shook her head to clear it, never dropping her gaze from the mist. The buzzing sound persisted, but now it sounded like hypnotic music.

She reached out her hand, desperate to make contact with the strange haze. But right before she was to learn of the rock's shadowy secrets, her boot landed directly in the puddle of water pooling on the ground. Then, as if something powerful had grabbed her foot, her body was violently jerked downward.

Everything went black as the ozone smell enveloped her—sharp, metallic, and pungent. Her limbs scrambled wildly, and her stomach dropped. It felt like she was falling from a great height, yet she could only grab handfuls of empty space.

Her vision blurred, and she tried to scream. She struggled for air as immense pressure surrounded her. It was so strong she felt like her bones were breaking, dissolving. Her skin felt too tight, like her muscles might burst out of their confines. She tried to call out for her sister, but she couldn't even open her mouth.

She continued to fall farther and farther down, plummeting and writhing until she was certain this must be what it felt like to die.

CHAPTER 2

Malkina Lands

The Aurelia Plane

S am inhaled sharply as the tug of unfulfilled vengeance burned in his chest. He studied the queen as she walked down the main hall of the castle, barely able to keep his demonic instincts in check. She was clad in one of her finest gowns —a voluminous swirl of gold and black lace that sparkled against her ever-present metal breastplate. Her cat-like tail flicked out from the folds of her dress, the hem of which trailed on the stone floor. But although her feet were hidden, Sam could see something was wrong.

A small limp punctuated Queen Thema's normally graceful glide, and it made Sam's vision blur with fury. He clenched his fists and ground his teeth together. Someone had injured the queen. He needed to make them pay.

Curved black claws shot out from under his fingernails, yet he retracted them quickly. Queen Thema did not need him charging through the castle in a frenzy, especially not today. She was expecting her sister and her royal court to arrive soon, and Sam knew she wished to make a good impression. Pressing his back against the cool stone wall, he took three deep breaths to calm himself.

Several courtiers rushed past him, and Sam hoped they hadn't seen how his big hands trembled. They were dressed in colors that complemented Queen Thema's gown, just as she had requested for all the recent meetings with the other queens of Aurelia. There were seven of them altogether, all sisters, each ruling over a specific territory and race in the Aurelian dimension. They were ordained to protect the crossroads between worlds, and over the past few weeks Queen Thema had requested a visit from each of them. One by one, they had come—with the exception of the Goblyn queen, who had gone missing decades ago.

Today's visit from Queen Cebna of the amphibious Nereid court marked the final meeting of the queens. Sam didn't know the nature of these events, nor did he care. He merely wished they would end soon so he could get back to the stack of unread books waiting for him in the library.

As Queen Thema came closer, her sharp golden eyes spotted him, though Sam had commanded the shadows to surround him in darkness. She placed her hands on her hips and called out, "Samael, step out of the shadows and come at once. I need all my guards at the ready and looking fearsomely brutish."

Sam frowned as his plan to stay hidden evaporated. Although Queen Thema's people, the Malkina, had grown used to having a demon living among them, his presence always unnerved visitors. He dreaded hearing the horrified gasps once the royal court of the Nereid saw him, but he wasn't going to go against the queen's wishes.

He took up pace behind her. "You're limping. Who has harmed you?"

She looked up with surprise, the top of her head only reaching Sam's elbow. He noted that the black kohl she used to rim her eyes made their wide shape even more striking. Her broad cheekbones were dusted with sparkling powder, intensifying the glow of her lined skin. She patted the tower of black braids twirled into a bun on top of her head. "No one, dear boy. I merely stepped in the wrong place."

"Were you attacked?" he growled, his internal drive for vengeance provoked. Although he had escaped the blood wagons years ago, the volatility of his moods remained.

"Oh no, I was foolish and careless on one of my recent patrols," she said, fluttering her hand. She lifted her skirt to stick out her lightly-furred leg, displaying a jagged cut across the top of her left hind paw. "It's healing nicely."

"This happened on Gaia? At the hand of a human?" Sam didn't know much about living humans, but his experience with their undead had shown them to be a cruel and brutal race.

"It was merely an accident that occurred near one of my portals. There is no one to punish, rest assured." A wry smile curved across her face as she reached up to pat his muscled arm. It was a motherly gesture that spoke of their shared history.

The heaviness of Sam's rage lightened. The throbbing pressure in his horns receded, and his shoulders relaxed. No one had harmed the queen, so there was no need to seek vengeance. He closed his eyes briefly, grateful to feel more in control of himself and his emotions.

"You must be more cautious during your visits," he said.

"I am quite capable of taking care of myself, Samael," the queen snapped. Then, turning her attention away from Sam, she bellowed to the servants and courtiers within earshot. "Everyone in their places! The Nereid court does not trade their fins for legs every day, you know. My sister is a notorious gossip, and I will not have her telling tales that the Malkina's reputation for elegance and beauty is unfounded."

The sound of pounding footsteps echoed through the hall as black-and silver-clad courtiers rushed past them to line up along each side of the hall. Even the roaming band of cats—sacred animal of the Malkina—congregated in one spot at the command of their queen.

"Now Samael, for the welcome ball tonight, you may take the night off if you wish," Queen Thema said. The small orange cat that was her constant companion rubbed against her skirts.

"For what reason?"

"I thought you might enjoy some time to get to know the Nereid people," the queen replied innocently, her tail flicking.

Sam shook his head. "You know how unruly some of your guests can get as the wine flows."

"Yes, yes, but there are no threats. Just a bit of stumbling about and light depravity."

"And why should I not stand guard for that?"

"Many of the females are very beautiful. I thought you might wish to... get to know some of them better."

Realization of the queen's true intentions for him settled like a boulder in his gut. He dropped his chin as a familiar burn of shame rose. Yet again, Queen Thema was trying to play matchmaker and pair him off. But when every female he encountered looked at him with fear or revulsion, the queen's attempts were as futile as they were humiliating.

"That's not going to happen," he said tightly.

"Nonsense," Queen Thema said, then studied his face. "I do not forget the debt I owe you, Vengeance demon, and I wish to see you happy. Why can't you—"

"I will do my duty as a guard, and that's all," Sam interrupted.

The queen arched one eyebrow as the lines around her mouth deepened. Sam jerked a hand through his long, dark hair and glared down at her.

Although he usually appreciated that Queen Thema never treated him differently from the Malkina, this time it angered him. He was not the same as the males of her race or any other males within the realm. He was a demon. And while his people believed all demons had a fated mate, Sam had accepted long ago that he would never find his own. It was yet another birthright taken from him, a destiny destroyed the day he was kidnapped as a boy from the Underworld.

Mercifully, the queen's focus on his loneliness was cut short when trumpets heralded the Nereid court's arrival. The wide castle doors creaked open, and they both stepped forward to peer down onto the grounds. A group of Nereid was moving across the stone bridge that connected the castle to Thema's nearby forests.

As Sam surveyed the court, he caught a whiff of fresh mint in the air, the queen's favorite plant. Rows and rows of the fragrant leaves had bordered the castle for as long as Sam had been living there. The sharp scent made Sam remember with a pang the days when he couldn't smell anything but the sulfur and smoke of the Underworld. He blinked as he relived the days when his eyes didn't hurt from the blinding sunlight streaming through the innumerable castle windows, and his ears weren't pierced with shrieks of delight over the latest castle gossip. The shrieks he longed to hear were those of victory and conquest, and the laughter of vengeances fulfilled.

Will I ever see home again?

He stepped back when Queen Thema moved past him to call down to the group, "Sister! Cebna of the Nereid, welcome to the court of the Malkina."

A creature with blue hair and a crown of coral looked up and waved. "Sister! Thema of the Malkina, the Nereid court accepts your welcome."

Small barnacles clung to Queen Cebna's pale face, and her webbed, fin-like ears twitched. Though they walked on two legs, the Nereid moved with slippery, supple movements much the same as their sacred animal, the fish. Unlike the felinesque Malkina, who had smooth skin save for their furred legs and pawed feet, the Nereid were covered in iridescent silver scales.

Queen Thema turned back to Sam with a smile. "I must begin the customs of welcome, but take heart, demon. I have not been having these meetings with my sisters for nothing,"

"What do you mean?"

She pursed her lips for a moment. It was an expression that Sam had seen her make countless times when she was debating which details to divulge and which to hold back. "We are working on a plan to find our lost sister. There's been a... development recently. I haven't yet collected all the information."

"You know I care little for royal business," Sam said.

"Yes, but this is different. Something has happened that's either a great threat or a great opportunity. Either way, it could help illuminate the secret of Queen Lilith's disappearance."

"And yet you won't tell me what it is?"

"Not until I have a plan. Please don't take offense, but I don't want you charging off to handle things your way. We both know how volatile you can be."

Sam felt the back of his neck warm. "I see."

"This is a delicate matter, one that requires careful planning."

Sam shifted his weight. "May I at least ask how finding the lost Goblyn queen affects me?"

"Yes." She smiled then leaned forward. "I believe the secret of her disappearance may hold the key to sending you home."

After the welcome ball for the Nereid people ended at midnight, Sam gratefully fell into his bed. His puzzlement over what Queen Thema had said about him returning home made it difficult to sleep. His dreams were full of hellhounds, imps, and lakes of fire until he woke abruptly just after the sun rose.

There was a disturbance somewhere in the realm. A tug at the corner of his mind made him glance around the room. He heard no sound, but something felt *different*.

He rose from bed and opened his chamber doors, wondering if someone had dared to make the 1,000-step climb up the tower to approach his sanctuary. There was no one. Crossing the room, he jerked apart the balcony doors and stepped onto the broad terrace.

He rubbed his eyes until they adjusted to the direct sunlight. A breeze blew his hair back from his shoulders, and he relaxed slightly. No matter how sumptuous he made his chambers, he would always feel more comfortable outside than within four walls.

Sam walked around the balcony, scanning for anything unusual. He inhaled deeply but only smelled the usual scents of the forest and castle, plus the light musk of the Malkina people. He had become adept at identifying each of the seven Aurelian races by their scent—Goblyns smelled of oakmoss and Lycah of birch tar, while the Vowa emitted a pungent hay scent. Harpies smelled of fresh air, and water races like the Nereid and Drago smelled of seawater and sand.

Finding nothing unusual, he moved inside when the slightest trace of an unfamiliar aroma wisped past him.

Inexplicably, his heart began to pound with excitement. Anticipation flowed through him, along with pleasant warmth. He stood still, waiting for the aroma to drift by him again. When it came, it was the slightest flicker of a smell he had not encountered since childhood. A fruit that came from trees not found in Aurelia. It only grew in two realms he knew of—the Underworld and Gaia, the human plane.

Pomegranate.

After quickly dressing, he bounded down the spiral staircase. When he reached the first floor, he nearly collided with Arkaya, the castle steward.

"Forgive me, my lady," Sam said, taking several steps backward.

Arkaya's sharp green eyes fixed upon him. "You have scented an intruder too?"

Sam blinked, but then wondered why he should be surprised at her question. Arkaya's sensitivity to threats was nearly as strong as her skill in magic. She was unfalteringly loyal to Queen Thema, and not just because they shared a bed. Sam had always admired how Arkaya understood the value of rules and order, with little tolerance for foolishness.

"Yes," he said. "I don't know what it is, but it's somewhere on the grounds."

"I'll find it," she said and tucked a strand of gray hair back into the long braid stretching down her back. The ring of keys hanging from her hip jangled as she began walking toward the gates.

"I'll come with you," Sam said.

"No. If it's a threat, the Queen would want you here. Stand watch at the gates." Arkaya bent to grasp the middle of her wooden walking stick, and twirled it around three times. Instantly, the ends extended, transforming it into a fighting staff that was only a few inches shorter than she was. The top end had been sharpened into a menacing point.

"Take this," Arkaya said, pressing a polished piece of white crystal into his hand. "If I need help burning a body, I'll summon you through the crystal."

Then she swept ahead of him to open the castle gates.

CHAPTER 3

Something pointy was digging into Selene's arm. She felt around and realized it was the strap of her backpack, which also explained the bulky lump pressed between her shoulder blades. Awareness of other parts of her body came into focus. Her legs were stretched out in front of her, her arms cushioned by grass. Her head felt like she had been beaned with an anvil in a Roadrunner cartoon.

"Cass? What happened?" she called out. Her voice sounded croaky and thin. "Did I faint?" She listened carefully for her sister's response but only heard the gentle rustling of leaves in the breeze.

Selene pulled herself up to a sitting position and opened her eyes. When her head stopped swimming, she felt even more disoriented. She was sitting in the middle of a forest, but it looked very different from the woods of Rugby. The trees surrounding her looked ancient—more than one hundred feet tall with wide, knobby trunks. Smaller trees were intermixed among the colossal ones, with sprawling roots that twined and tangled. Dinner plate-sized white flowers bloomed in mossy patches along the ground, and there was a watery tang in the air, as if a lake or river were close by.

Where am I?

Her water bottle peeked out of her backpack along with a protein bar. She seized upon both, hoping low blood sugar and dehydration were to blame for her disorientation. She must have wandered off the hiking trail. Surely she couldn't have gone far. Maybe she'd hit her head in the Witch's Cave and was dreaming?

While she chewed nervously, she dug through her hiking pack for her phone. When she found it, the screen was black. It had been fully charged a few hours ago, but now it was completely dead—no signal, no battery. Before the reality of being lost in the woods hit her, the sound of footsteps made her turn. A figure stepped out from behind a cluster of bushes.

"Intruder! State your business!" barked a petite woman with unusual features. She had long gray hair swept back over her ears into a thick braid. Bronze skin was creased with age, but she looked about as frail as a machine gun. Her emerald eyes were sharp, but they seemed too large for her face and out of balance with her high cheekbones and pointed chin. Her embroidered green dress skimmed the ground while a ring of keys hung from her hip. In her hands was a wooden staff. The sharpened end was pointed straight at Selene.

"E-excuse me?" Selene stammered.

"How is it that you're out in daylight?" the woman demanded.

"I was hiking with my sister, and I think I hit my head."

The woman frowned and took a step forward, giving Selene a glimpse of the gray-furred boots she wore. "Stand up so that I may see whom I fight."

Selene held up her hands fearfully. "No, no! I don't want to fight. I'm lost!"

"Lost?"

"Yes, I'm from Nashville. Do you have a phone I could borrow?"

"A what?" the woman asked.

"A phone. Mine's dead," Selene said, holding up the dead device. The woman spoke with an accent she couldn't place; perhaps she didn't fully understand English. "I'll be glad to get off your land, but I just need to find my sister."

"*My* land!" The woman laughed without mirth, her eyes flashing. "Why, you trespass in the territory of the glorious Queen Thema—Lady of the Flame. The Devouring One. Mother Protector and She of the Change. I am Arkaya, the Lady's house steward and head enchantress, and I abide no intruders. Now stand!"

Selene swallowed as she tried to make sense of Arkaya's words. Maybe she was having an exceedingly realistic dream? She squeezed her eyes shut and tensed her muscles, willing herself to wake up. She concentrated on Cass's face and the last image she remembered of Rugby.

Wake up, wake up!

Something sharp jabbed her thigh. Selene opened her eyes to see Arkaya poking her with the blunt end of her staff. If this was a dream, it was incredibly realistic.

"I really don't want to fight you," Selene said. "I told you I'm just lost."

The woman helicoptered her staff over Selene's head to strike a different pose. "If you think to glamour me or try to trick me with lies, you will fail. What weapons do you hide in your pack?"

"I don't have anything. Look," Selene shook out the contents of her pack at Arkaya's feet.

"Are they strapped to your body?"

"No!" Selene said. The woman continued to eye her suspiciously, causing Selene to anxiously sweep a lock of hair behind her ear. The movement made Arkaya gasp.

"Your ears," Arkaya whispered and lowered her staff. She stepped closer to Selene and bent to peer closer at the side of Selene's head. "Rounded ears. My word," Arkaya breathed as she ran her hand over the tip.

"What's wrong with my ears?" Selene said. She had many insecurities about her body, but her ears had never been among them. She stared up at Arkaya, who now held the staff loosely at her side.

"Let me see your teeth," Arkaya said. Selene dutifully opened her mouth, allowing Arkaya to peer inside. She tilted her head, then said, "You're not of this world."

Selene frowned. "What do you mean?"

"What are you?" Arkaya asked.

"I-I'm a human resources coordinator."

"Human. I thought so." The suspicion on her face was replaced with joy. "A living human—how marvelous! The queen will be delighted. And what a relief to know vampires haven't found a way to walk in the day."

Okay, so I've officially entered the Twilight Zone.

Her odd remarks made Selene's anxiety churn faster, but also gave her a flash of clarity. "Wait! I'm on a reality show, aren't I?"

The furrow between Arkaya's brows deepened. "What is your meaning?"

"This place." Selene gestured to the trees around them as a smile spread across her face. "Your costume and makeup. This is some kind of prank show, right?"

"I wear no costume!" Arkaya said indignantly.

"But—"

"Do you think me human?" Arkaya interrupted. Selene's mouth went slack as the question shot dread down her spine.

Then Arkaya's eyes twinkled as she deliberately turned her head to pull back the hair covering her own ear to reveal its shape. When Selene saw the pointed tip, her eyes widened.

"I am no human. I am of the Malkina people," Arkaya said, as something long and thin flickered out behind her, like a tail. Selene looked down at the bottom of Arkaya's dress and realized it wasn't strange boots she had seen. Arkaya walked upright on two paws. An image from the old cartoon *Thundercats* sprang to Selene's mind.

Slowly Selene asked, "Where am I?"

"You are in the realm of Aurelia. I imagine you went through a portal, which is very rare."

The memory of a shimmering hole in the rock, plus a mind-scrambling drop, came rushing back. But before Selene could ask more, Arkaya said, "Come. I must take you to our castle to see Queen Thema herself."

Arkaya had a strong gait and moved easily through the forest. Selene trailed behind, her knuckles white as she clung to the straps of her hiking pack. They walked in silence for what felt like miles until Selene felt as if the way her heart pounded in her ears would undo her.

She cleared her throat. "Do we have much farther to go? Not that I mind the walk. It's beautiful here in... I'm sorry, where are we again?"

"We are in Aurelia."

"What is that? Is it a country? A city? A planet?"

"Aurelia is the name of our dimension. It is also known as The Realm of the Seven Sisters. Well, I suppose there are only six sisters now. There are cities and villages throughout the land, but as a whole, it is called Aurelia. Like the chrysalis of a glintfly, this realm is home to our queens when they are not in transformation." When Selene did not respond, Arkaya turned. "I suspect you believed the human world was the only realm, am I right?"

Selene nodded.

"There are many other worlds besides yours and ours."

"Okay."

"You come from the human dimension, or Gaia, as we call it."

"Right."

Arkaya glanced at her sharply. "You sound doubtful of my word."

"No! Not at all. It's just not, uh... it's not something we talk about where I'm from. How many other realms are there besides this one?"

"Nine. But there could be more."

Selene's stomach lurched. Nine. She thought back to the time she got sucked into an old episode of *Nova* on PBS. The topic was string theory, and the physicist interviewed believed there were several parallel dimensions all vibrating at the same time.

Arkaya abruptly stopped walking and held out her staff to block Selene from taking another step. She tilted her head back to sniff the air, and her head whipped from left to right. Selene stood utterly still, even as a small growl sounded from her left.

With her heart beating furiously against her chest, she turned toward Arkaya, ready to take orders to flee or hide. Her eyes widened as she saw how Arkaya's lips were pulled back, displaying two animalistic fangs gleaming among her white teeth. She froze as she realized the growl had come from Arkaya herself.

Just as abruptly as Arkaya's growl had emerged, she relaxed and motioned for Selene to keep walking. They walked for several minutes before Selene could muster the courage to speak. "What happened?"

"Nothing," Arkaya said. "I thought I heard a vampire approach, but I was wrong."

"There really are vampires here?"

Arkaya stopped walking. "Again, you doubt my word?"

"No, no, of course not." Selene shook her head swiftly.

"Odd human," Arkaya muttered. She peered at Selene, seeming to scrutinize her face. Although Selene towered over the woman by several inches, at that moment, she felt very small.

Arkaya's expression softened. "Ah, forgive me. I'm not versed in human ways. I have only read about your kind in myths and legends."

Selene struggled to absorb Arkaya's words. She wanted to ask more, but her mouth had turned dry. *Myths and legends?*

A pang hit Selene in the chest as she thought of her brother, Evan. He would undoubtedly be handling this situation with so much more grace. With his wealth of knowledge about the supernatural, he'd probably know how to go home by reciting a special chant or outwitting a troll. He'd at least know whether it was customary to curtsy or shake hands when about to meet a pointy-eared queen.

When will I see Evan again?

Selene felt nauseous as she realized Cass had probably called both Kevin and the police by now. She might be filing a missing person report at that exact moment. Selene looked up and watched a cloud obscure the sun for a moment. *Focus on the positive.* At least she was in a place where the sun still rose and set.

Arkaya gestured with her staff. "Look ahead. You can see the lights of the castle, ready to welcome us back."

Selene followed Arkaya's gaze and spotted large globes of pink light peeking through the trees. They were perched on wrought-iron poles bordering a path shrouded in fog. Ornate ironwork snaked up the poles in swirls and flourishes. Although it had felt like morning when Selene woke up in Aurelia, the sun was beginning to set.

The forest thinned as they continued to walk, and Selene caught her first view of their destination in the distance. It was set into a hill like a shimmering jewel among the craggy bluffs. Other buildings of various heights ringed a central tower, all with pointed steeples and arched windows. The roofs emitted the same soft glow that Selene had seen from the poles, but the colors varied—pink, yellow, green, blue, and purple. The brilliant white of the stone exterior heightened the effect.

Mist swirled around them, making the ends of Selene's hair curl. It was then she was certain what was happening to her was real. There was no way she could ever imagine something so beautiful.

"Ah, I see Samael waiting," Arkaya said, gesturing toward the castle. "I'll just let him know you're of no threat to us." She reached up to rub her gnarled fingers against a white crystal amulet around her throat. "There. That's done." Selene followed Arkaya's gaze, curious to see this person who needed to know she wasn't a threat.

Standing high up in front of the wide castle gates was a man. Powerfully built and tall, he stood with his arms crossed, dressed in black. His hair was long and dark, and though they were too far away for Selene to make out his features, there was something on the top of his head. She assumed it was a helmet or strange hat, but as she shaded her hand over her eyes to see more clearly, she gasped. Her already jumpy heart began to pound wildly, and she shivered.

He had horns.

CHAPTER 4

O nce Arkaya led Selene through the castle gates, the rest of the evening went by in a blur. Selene didn't see the horned man again but passed several strange-looking creatures as they weaved through the castle. Many shared features similar to Arkaya, but others had feathered wings, green-scaled skin, or ears that stuck out like fish fins. They even passed a large furred being who bore a strong resemblance to Bigfoot. The castle was also filled with bands of cats, roving freely.

After rushing through countless corridors and up two sets of stairs, Selene wondered if Arkaya was deliberately trying to disorient her. Finally, Selene was led into a bedroom. It had beautiful arched windows and was roughly the size of her and Kevin's entire apartment. The rich furnishings made her think of the designs in her father's Art Nouveau coffee table books. She felt very lost in the vast space.

"This will be your room," Arkaya said. "The queen has meetings tonight, but expect a visit from her in the morning."

"And then she'll be able to take me home?" Selene asked, wringing her hands.

"I don't know. Are you hungry?"

The thought of food made the anxiety in Selene's stomach churn even faster. "No, thank you. I feel like garbage. I really just want to sleep."

"Of course." Arkaya frowned as she looked Selene up and down. "But you can't sleep in that. Do you prefer to sleep in a gown that's short or long?"

Selene looked down at her faded jeans. "Long, I guess?" She usually slept in an old T-shirt and shorts.

Arkaya nodded, then disappeared into a closet. She emerged holding a white handkerchief. She lifted it above her head then let it fall while tapping her staff on the ground. Selene watched the fabric drift to the floor, somehow creating a puddle five times its original size.

"Will this do?" Arkaya asked, lifting the pool of fabric to give it a shake. Selene was shocked to see a beautiful white nightgown in Arkaya's hands. It had tiny pearl buttons down the front and lace-trimmed shoulder straps.

"It's wonderful," she breathed. She hugged the nightgown to her chest and swallowed the lump of fear rising in her throat. *There's no need to freak out. So magic exists here. Good to know.*

"Get some rest, and we'll talk more in the morning." Arkaya turned to leave, her gray braid swinging out behind her. "Don't look so frightened, child. No harm will come to you here. Goodnight."

Selene watched Arkaya close the door, then sat unmoving on the bed. She looked down at her trembling hands and tried to steady her breathing. Eyeing the door, she considered pushing a piece of furniture up against it to ward off unwelcome visitors, but all the chairs in the room looked too heavy to move. Deep fatigue washed over her as she pulled off her shoes and socks. If she could just get through the night, she could try to find a way to get home tomorrow.

～

Selene slept fitfully, jumping at every sound outside her bedroom. It wasn't until she began to calm herself by internally chanting, "There's no place like home" that she fully drifted off. A nagging urge to pee woke her after sunrise. When she rolled out of bed, she assumed she was about to have her first experience with a chamber pot. However, she was delighted to find that the door in the corner led into a pleasantly appointed modern bathroom.

The relief at her discovery plus the comedown from yesterday's stress had made her slightly loopy. Flushing the toilet was enough to make her giggle, but she broke into applause when she discovered hot water flowing from the sink. Her celebrations were dashed when a sharp knock from outside her bedroom door made her stomach clench.

She rushed out of the bathroom and saw Arkaya coming through with a tray of food. She set it on the small table in front of the velvet couch and said, "Come and eat. Queen Thema is on her way to meet you."

Selene's fists tightened in the sides of her nightgown. "Shouldn't I get dressed first?"

"In a moment. I'm having Hollen bring—"

Arkaya's words were cut off by a melodious voice that called, "By the silver light of the stars, a living human in my lands!"

Selene turned to see a woman enter the room with flourishing movements. She was petite in stature, but her presence seemed to fill up the whole room. Selene took a step back as she took in the woman's large golden eyes, pointed ears, and towering bun of ebony braids. Although she didn't wear a crown, her identity was unmistakable—this had to be Queen Thema.

"H-howdy," Selene said, then cringed. *Howdy? Was that any way to greet a queen?*

The folds of Queen Thema's yellow gown shimmered as she lowered herself to sit on the couch. Her posture was stately even when sitting, undoubtedly a result of the ornate metal breastplate she wore. An orange cat trotted in to flop at the queen's feet.

30

"Come, human, tell me all about yourself," Queen Thema said, patting the cushion beside her. "Ah, where are my manners? Introductions first!"

Selene tensed as she questioned the correct protocol. She dipped into a clumsy curtsy and said, "Hello, I'm Selene Riley. I'm so pleased to meet you, Your Majesty. I mean, Your Royal Highness?"

Queen Thema looked confused, then laughed. Arkaya smiled too from her position at the end of the couch. "Charming! Simply charming. Arkaya, she's as innocent as you proclaimed. Now sit down. I am Thema, Queen of the Malkina. I welcome you."

"Thank you," Selene said. She suddenly understood what people meant by the term "larger than life." The diminutive queen was like the embodiment of a celebrity icon—glamorous, charismatic, but also incredibly intimidating.

"Please go ahead and eat while we chat," Queen Thema said, gesturing to the tray of food. Selene's eyes widened as she realized the tips of the Queen's fingers ended in pink claws instead of nails. They were dainty, pretty claws, but looked lethally sharp.

The queen seemed to mistake her apprehension as worry about the food. "Fear not, my dear. It's not like you traveled to the fairy world. You can eat and drink here without consequences."

Selene tried to keep her expression neutral. *Great.* So *not* eating foods in another world was a thing? She looked down again at the tray. There was a bowl of what looked like miniature watermelons, a thick cut of mystery meat, a dollop that reminded her of clotted cream, and a basket of bread. Odd, but nothing shocking, like a plate of squirming tentacles or bowl of giant bugs. Tentatively, she bit into one of the baby watermelons and found it delicious.

Queen Thema smoothed the sleeves of her gown then said, "I'm sure you have many questions about where you are, but I have questions of my own. How is it that you came through to our realm?"

Selene wiped her mouth with a napkin. "I don't know. I was hiking with my sister in the forest—"

"Of Tennessee?" the queen interrupted.

31

"Yes, how did you know?"

"No matter. Please continue."

Selene looked at her uncertainly but continued, recounting her story of the hum, her headache, and the puddle. Then how Arkaya had stumbled upon her in the strange forest. When she finished her story, Selene tried not to sound desperate when she asked, "Do you know how I got here? And how I can get home?"

The queen tilted her head. "You came through one of my portals. I was injured in your world and must have failed to close the gateway behind me properly. It was careless of me. Foolish."

"Nonsense! You are never foolish," Arkaya argued.

"No, no. I was," Queen Thema said. "But what's done is done. Selene, my sisters and I have been given a sacred duty. We guard the portals between planes. It's very unusual for someone like you to travel to our world and survive. But now that you're here, fear not. You are welcome and safe."

"I appreciate that, but how do I—" Selene's question was cut off by a loud crash at the bedroom doorway.

She turned to watch as a young Malkina woman with long chestnut-colored hair tumbled into the room with an armful of dresses. Arkaya came toward her, looking irritated, to help gather the fallen dresses from the floor.

"Sorry, Arkaya. Damn, I keep tripping on the belt of this pink one, and I... oh!" The young woman looked startled as she stared at Selene. "Wow! She really is human, isn't she?"

A hot blush settled over Selene's face as the young woman gawked at her like she was an alien. She had the same pointed chin and large eyes as Thema and Arkaya, her wide mouth set into an "O" of surprise.

When her gaze shifted from Selene to Queen Thema, her face changed to panicked. "My queen, I'm so sorry. I didn't know you were in here. I'll come back later."

Queen Thema stood, waving her hand. "It's fine, Hollen. We are done here for now."

Selene leapt to her feet. "But wait! When can you take me home?"

Thema's dress rustled as she turned back. "I'm sorry, but I can't do that."

Selene blanched. "Why?"

"Your world is a harbor realm. This means creatures from different worlds can visit and leave as they please. But Aurelia is closed. What comes in cannot go out again. My sisters and I are the only ones who can breach the veil."

Selene shook her head. "That can't be right. If I came through one way, I'll just go back through the other."

"It doesn't work that way."

"Why not?" She could hardly recognize the tinny, pleading tone of her voice. "I can't stay here! I have a family and a boyfriend and a job. They will all be wondering what happened to me. I left my sister alone in a forest, and she's probably freaking out. The rest of my family is a mess, and at the office they need me to—"

"Hush now. It is the way of things," Queen Thema interrupted. She turned thoughtful for a moment, then snapped her fingers. "Ah, but I may know of someone who can help you get back. Give me a few days to make some plans. I'll know more soon, I promise."

"A few days? I don't want to seem ungrateful, but I need to get back now. There's probably a search party out looking for me, and my mom doesn't cope well with stress. She'll be an absolute monster to my siblings and I... " Selene's voice broke as tears filled her eyes at the thought of all the ways her mother might be self-medicating her feelings.

Queen Thema raised her eyebrows. "Calm yourself, human. Perhaps a ball would cheer you? Yes, let's hold a ball tonight! To welcome our lovely visitor and show her all the wonders of our realm. Arkaya, make the arrangements, will you? Guests and staff of the castle only, no outsiders."

"Certainly," Arkaya said. Hollen had retreated to one corner, but a wide grin spread across her face.

"We'll be off now. Hollen will help you with whatever you need. Enjoy your day, precious Selene," the queen said, turning to walk away.

Selene watched Arkaya and the orange cat follow the queen out the door. Before she could even begin to process the conversation she just had, she was tackled by a hug from the woman with the dresses.

"Welcome! I'm sorry I stared before, but you're just so amazing. Did you actually come through our queen's own portal? Have you been to other realms besides ours? Is Aurelia your favorite? Can I see your round ears? Tell me everything about humans."

Selene leaned back to take in Hollen's frenetic energy. She looked to be about twenty years old, but her face was as excited as a child's.

Hollen continued, "Am I talking too much? Sit and enjoy your breakfast. I'll hang up these clothes Arkaya pulled for you. When she told me last night there was a human living among us, and *I* was to be her lady's maid, I didn't get a wink of sleep. Arkaya said I was to help you with anything else you need. What else do you need?"

"Um... I'm not sure. Did Queen Thema say she wants to throw a ball?"

"Yes! Can you believe it? We just had one last night when the Nereid arrived, but this one will be even better! I'll help you get ready. What sort of dress do you want to wear? I think pink would suit you. Would you like me to show you around the castle? We can get snacks from the kitchens, lounge in the courtyard, play in the game room, visit the library, take a nap... "

"There's a library?"

Hollen nodded. "On the eighth floor."

Selene sat back on the couch, debating how to spend her first day in Aurelia. There was a strong pull to hide away in her room where nothing bad had happened to her so far. But another part of her was curious about what could be found outside her door. She had always dreamt of travel and adventure, and now here she was, a true stranger in a strange land.

I might as well make the best of it.

"Why don't you show me the library first, then we'll figure out the rest," she said.

Hollen flashed a smile so broad Selene could see her small fangs. "As you wish, my lady."

CHAPTER 5

S am descended the winding stairs from his chambers with heavy steps. After being informed there was yet another ball to be held tonight, he was in no hurry to start duty. Unlike other guards who enjoyed a raucous shift, Sam preferred to work quiet evenings where he was less likely to lose control.

He had been about to start a new book when the small Quartz of Transference he kept near the bed displayed a message about tonight's ball. It was surprising since a farewell for the Nereid would not take place until next week, and there were no mating celebrations planned. This was probably a celebration of someone's hat or new advancement in napping practices, he thought wryly. The Malkina loved any excuse for drinking, dancing, and sleeping in the next morning.

When he was a boy, the occurrence of balls and celebrations in the Underworld were rare and all the more special because of it. Demons could be hedonistic and greedy, but they understood the importance of ritual. Rules had to be followed, and they never did anything without deep meaning.

His chest ached as he thought back to the stories his mother used to tell about the ball that honored his own birth. The first-born's arrival in the kingdom of Asmodeus, the Venomous One, was marked with great pride, she had said, with feasts prepared, sacrifices given, and oaths sworn. As a boy, he had begged his mother to recite every detail of the celebration. Patiently, she recounted how his uncles had continuously called for more wine, and his aunts bickered over who'd brought the best gift. His grandmother flapped her great black wings as she flew around the kingdom announcing news of his birth, while all the imps bowed before his crib.

But his favorite part of his mother's stories was how his father had cheered when it was announced that Sam was a demon of Vengeance. The Underworld's mystic had seen it in Sam's aura as a baby, and she was never wrong. King Asmodeus was a Wrath demon, so having a son who would be driven to inflict retribution upon the deserving dead was a source of great pride.

Sam frowned as he realized he had never asked how his mother reacted to the news of his calling. Was she pleased to have a Vengeance demon son? Perhaps she would have preferred him to have been born a demon of Judgment or of Delusions—something less prone to violence. She was a graceful Shadow demon and the only one of her kind. What if she wished her son had inherited more of her nature than just shadow control? They both shared a strong sense of justice, yet his mother possessed different sensibilities than other demons in the court. "My fated mate is too merciful, too generous," his father would scold affectionately.

If only I had asked more, paid more attention. This was the refrain that spun around Sam's head constantly: regret that he had not soaked up more of his history, his family, everything about the Underworld during his eight short years of life before he was kidnapped and brought to Aurelia. Without his father to teach him how to judge what actions deserved pass or punishment, he found his innate drive to punish difficult to control.

Quickly, Sam jerked his head as if he could shake the painful memories away. He had been in Aurelia for over twenty years now and knew there was no use pining for the past.

As he approached the ballroom, he considered how at least tonight there was no impending threat to worry about as he and Arkaya had feared yesterday. Once she had sent the signal that all was well, Sam had gone back inside, putting the pomegranate scent out of his mind. Later, he had overheard two guards mention something about a lost human on the grounds, but he'd dismissed the idea. Both guards were prone to exaggeration, but Rig especially was fond of telling falsehoods—at least he had been until Sam corrected him of the habit.

Perhaps he needs a reminder...

Pulling open the doors of the ballroom, Sam surveyed the room for any signs of conflict. He found none. Everyone seemed to be enjoying themselves as they sipped wine and conversed at tables decorated with clusters of crystal shards.

A small crowd of males gathered around one side of the head table, which sat on a raised platform across from the entryway. This was odd, but not worrisome. However, Sam was surprised to see that Queen Thema was not at the center of the crowd's focus as he expected but was gnawing at a bone several seats away next to Queen Cebna. Standing with his back to the wall, Sam fell into his usual guard posture: wide stance, crossed arms, deep scowl. A few of the castle's resident cats rubbed against his legs, but Sam remained motionless.

After the dessert was served, Queen Thema announced, to Sam's dismay, that the night was about to be ruined by the most pointless of activities: *dancing.* The ballroom was cleared of tables, and servants quickly swept the marble floor. The chandeliers were dimmed, but moonlight streamed in through the tall windows, giving the room a soft glow.

Sam watched another guard help steady a drunken Lycah about to stumble headfirst into a tray of dirty dishes. A group of teenaged Malkina girls giggled as they walked past a group of Nereid boys. An elder Drago banged his cane on the ground to get his mate's attention. Rig wasn't on guard duty tonight, but Sam saw him scurry past clutching two glasses of wine in his fleshy hands.

Sam stifled a groan when the court musicians began to play. They started with one of his least favorite selections from their repertoire—a quick melody paired with the trite refrain of "My love, my love, I've found you at last."

Sam saw the crowd at the head table had thinned considerably. Thema had stepped off the platform to make her rounds while Queen Cebna dozed in her seat. Others had dispersed, until all that was left at the table were three females surrounded by a few males. He recognized Arkaya, Hollen, and—Sam narrowed his eyes to identify the third and blinked.

All his senses sharpened, and his body tensed.

He then heard three sounds—a gasp, a sigh, and a growl. It took several seconds before he realized each sound had come from his own throat.

Arkaya and Hollen sat on either side of a female Sam had never seen. His heartbeat quickened as he stared, and a shiver ran through him.

Who is she? What *is she?*

The stranger's features were balanced in a way that was both pleasing and magnetic. She didn't possess the angular, hard edges of the Malkina countenance. Instead, her face held a sweet roundness. Her skin was smooth, and he could see no fur, fish scales, or feathers to place her as one of the Aurelian races. Sam's claws shot out from under his fingernails with the need to stroke the lock of brown hair tumbling over her shoulder. What was happening to him?

She was the one the crowd was gathered around, he realized. A visitor so beautiful she could pull attention away from a pair of queens. His breath came in shallow pants. Her figure was more lush than lean, and the graceful curve of her neck reminded him of something he couldn't place, a long-forgotten memory rising to the surface. His palms began to sweat.

To his right, he could hear an argument over vampire staking techniques getting heated, but he didn't even turn. Someone could have been setting fire to the castle or committing murder next to him, and he wouldn't have looked away. Hollen leaned in to whisper something in the female's ear, and she laughed, causing Sam's stomach to lurch at the appearance of her smile. She bore no fangs that he could see.

The stranger moved with an otherworldly fluidity; unlike any creature he had ever seen in Aurelia. Although it was considered terribly rude to ask one's race, he wanted to charge toward her and demand it. Yet his feet felt rooted to the floor.

With a jolt of clarity, his eyes widened. He realized why she'd appeared familiar to him. Desire pounded through him so swiftly it made him tremble.

Demon. She looks like a demon.

Female demons were known for their beauty. Most were born as Tempters, using their charms, curvaceous bodies, and enigmatic eyes as a tool to feed on the emotions and actions of mortals. Unlike the Punisher class of demons such as Sam, female demons spent most of their time among the living.

Demon! What was she doing here?

Who sent her?

Why didn't I sense her arrival?

A wisp of the pomegranate scent he caught yesterday breezed past him. It was not unlike the perfume his mother wore, and the realization made his eyes fly open. Of course! It had been this strange, beautiful demon he had scented yesterday morning. He breathed in again, focusing on the essence of juicy red fruits and honey.

He watched the stranger converse with those around her until Rig approached to offer her a glass of wine. When she accepted it, Sam gritted his teeth as white-hot jealousy tore through him. He watched Rig let his hand linger as she reached for the glass, touching her fingers in a clumsy caress. Sam's nostrils flared as he tamped down the urge to run across the room to snap the idiot guard's neck.

Then, as if the stranger could sense Sam's sudden mood shift, she turned to look across the room and froze. A current of energy seemed to pass between them. Hot, urgent, and potent. Everything else in the room, the realm, the nine dimensions of the multiverse fell away.

Sam's rage at Rig dissolved as he stared into her eyes. She tugged at the shawl she wore around her shoulders, her grip on the fabric tight.

Sam was used to females looking at him with revulsion or sometimes pity for his scars, but her expression held neither. Her eyes were wide, her mouth slightly open, and a blush stained her cheeks. She seemed startled, but she held his gaze.

Another demon here in Aurelia. Why hadn't he realized she was here sooner? In the Underworld, family members could easily pick each other out of a horde of demons by scent alone. His mother used to say that even the Underworld's master perfumer could never create a fragrance as alluring as the hearth smoke musk that clung to Sam's father.

The memory of his parents' devotion to each other brought a single word to his mind. One that made his horns flare with heat and his loins stir.

Mate.

He swallowed thickly and fixed his gaze on the female even harder, studying her. He wanted to move closer to get a better look, but his knees were shaking.

Could this demon be my fated mate?

He'd told himself that fated mates were only a legend, a fanciful tale that sentimental elders used to spin for him at bedtime. But... what if it were actually true? It was said that every demon is destined to find a consort—one to magnify the other's power. What other reason could there be for the intensity of his reaction? The corners of his mouth rose in a satisfied smile.

His change of expression had a noticeable effect on the female.

Possessiveness burned in him as he watched the muscles of her throat work. Her pink tongue slipped out to moisten her lips.

She recognizes me. She craves to be claimed.

Heart pounding, Samael took a step to walk across the dance floor to her. He was ready to announce himself as the demon she had come for. Ready to pull her away from the hungry gaze of other males in the room. Ready to fully embrace his violent tendencies instead of holding them back. Ready to claim what he knew was his.

He would destroy anyone who dared to stand in his way.

My love, my love, I've found you at last. Suddenly the refrain of the musician's song didn't seem so trite.

Sam slowed his steps as he watched Rig tap the female's shoulder yet again. As she tore her eyes away, Sam resolved he would not snap Rig's neck but instead tear the guard's head from his body. Demon edicts against killing be damned.

The fool must have asked her to dance because Sam watched his mate rise from her seat and drop the shawl from her shoulders. The sight of all that creamy bare skin was enough to make Sam moan, but when she turned he stopped moving, nearly knocking over a dancing couple. His mouth went dry as he stared at her exposed back. What he saw shocked him.

No wings.

Sam tried to see if the demon had tucked her magnificent wings away or hidden them beneath her dress. Moonlight shone on her hair, and her hips swayed as she walked. But her back was smooth. She had no wings.

Which could only mean one thing...

Not a demon.

He closed his eyes, fighting to control the disappointment that lashed through him like a whip. He watched her smile as Rig placed a hand at her waist. Icy shards tore at Sam's insides as he struggled to control himself.

Male demons were easily distinguishable by their large build, retractable claws, and imposing horns. Those especially prone to beastly drives, like demons of Gluttony, were born with cloven hooves and goat-like legs. Female demons, however, lacked all animalistic features except one—leathery black wings set into their shoulder blades. Their wings were strong, elegant, but easily tucked away under clothing to escape angry mortals if their true identities were discovered.

Where were her wings? Sam squinted to see if he could make out scarring on her back. Maybe she used magic to hide them or lost them in some terrible way. He sniffed the air for traces of sorcery but found only the aroma of dinner and dessert.

And that alluring berry scent.

He clenched his fists as his entire body tensed. How could she smell so good and not be a demon? It didn't add up. Pomegranates didn't grow in Aurelia. He hadn't experienced that smell since he was a boy. Pomegranates grew only on trees that thrived in the Underworld.

And the human realm.

The conversation he had overheard from the guards suddenly came back to him.

Human.

It was true then. Arkaya *had* found a human in the forest. The guards weren't lying or embellishing the story. The blow of realization hit Sam so strongly he almost sank to his knees.

He stared down at the floor. He was so stupid, so naive. He had known that demon females looked similar to human women, but he had never known how much. He had been too young to see their souls within the Underworld. And the only humans he had ever seen among the living were undead—pale, rotting, vicious vampires like his kidnapper, Zaybris.

He was disgusted with himself for becoming enraptured by a weak-minded, fragile human. The easiest of mortal prey. What had possessed him to be so ridiculously hopeful? Claims to any demonic-fated outcomes were lost to him now, especially after all that he had done before coming to serve Queen Thema. He flinched at the memory.

An anguished roar threatened to erupt from deep in his chest. He pushed it down and turned to storm out of the ballroom. Dancing couples yelped as they darted out of his path, terrified of how his eyes glowed red. Sam flicked his hand to command the shadows to surround him in darkness. They swarmed, eager to serve. He let them drape over him, swallowing him up in their black embrace. He stepped into the hall and slammed the ballroom doors shut behind him.

So stupid.

CHAPTER 6

The next morning when Selene woke, she felt a bit light-headed. Giddy, even. But also petrified. Maybe a little aroused. Definitely baffled. All from her encounter with the horned man.

The ball last night had certainly been an experience to remember. She often helped out with parties hosted by her mother's event planning business, yet she'd never attended anything as lavish as Queen Thema's ball. Then while she was chatting with Hollen, a strange feeling overtook her. One minute she was fine, the next she had felt her whole body tremble with awareness. Almost as if someone had whispered her name. Urgently.

She had looked across the room... and there he was. The intriguing horned man she had seen in the distance the day before. Just standing there, watching her.

He was a lot to take in. He towered over everyone else in the ballroom, probably 6'6 at least. His skin was tinged with pearlescent shades of gold, green, and peach with a rakish scar bisecting one eyebrow. High cheekbones cast shadowy indentations on his face, while a black leather vest similar to the guard Rig's was pulled tight across broad shoulders.

He cut such an imposing figure that the presence of 5-inch ridged horns sprouting from the top of his head almost seemed natural. The S-shaped curves gleamed amid his mass of long black hair. Like a god from a heavy metal album, she thought. Ominous, but elegant too.

When his eyes darkened on her and his mouth curved into a sensual smile, Selene felt as though all the air in the room had been sucked out. Suddenly, it became too much—intense and overwhelming. Enthralling and terrifying, especially when he started to walk toward her.

Rig's invitation to dance had come at the right moment to break the tension. But once she got out onto the dance floor, the horned man had disappeared. Later, when Selene asked Hollen who he was, the Malkina's eyes grew large.

"You mean the guard who's massively tall, covered in ugly scars, with huge horns and a terrible temper?" Hollen had asked. "That's Samael, Queen Thema's demon guard. She thinks he's wonderful, but he gives me the shivers."

Selene pulled back the covers and got out of the bed, thinking of about a thousand follow-up questions she'd wanted to ask Hollen but didn't get the chance. Right at that moment, Queen Thema had appeared to introduce Queen Cebna. For the rest of the evening, Selene had met so many new people she gave up trying to recall each of their names. But she certainly wouldn't forget Samael.

She pulled on a gauzy purple dress she found in the closet and wondered if she might see him again today. Did she *want* to see him again? Keeping a healthy distance from an actual creature of hell seemed sensible. But, although the way he stared at her was intense, she didn't feel afraid. There was a vulnerability behind his eyes that made her heart pound.

She straightened her dress and thought about how she would

spend the day. Yesterday, Hollen had tried to show her the library but they kept getting interrupted by courtiers who were curious to meet her. Putting aside her nagging fear and anxiety about her situation, Selene decided to start the day with two simple goals—find the library, and then find Queen Thema to ask her again about getting home.

~

After getting lost twice, Selene finally made it to the library on the eighth floor. As she pulled open the mahogany entrance doors, her jaw dropped. It was a stunning room.

The room was round, and despite its size, unexpectedly cozy. It was probably due to the dark wood and the number of leather chairs scattered around the room. Everything had the same Art Nouveau vibe as her bedroom, with spiral staircases connecting the two levels of bookcases. Small nooks and off-shoot rooms were tucked away at random intervals, while sunlight streamed through leaded-glass windows.

The space was empty when Selene approached the stacks, curious about the kind of books Aurelians enjoyed. The first book she pulled out was a volume of poetry, written in beautifully rendered calligraphy. The second was a travel guide to territory of the Harpies, complete with drawings of a cranky-looking creature guarding the entrance. The third was a thick hardcover detailing ocean tides. She was surprised to find that most books were written in English, then remembered how Hollen told her that the queens adapted to speak the tongue of the human lands they frequented most.

Selene made a full loop of both levels, then explored the small rooms nestled between the stacks. The largest one opened up into a gallery of hanging art. A massive portrait of Queen Thema greeted her as she passed through the doorway.

Selene chuckled softly. The artist had certainly captured the way

Thema could be both glamorous and terrifying. The Queen was depicted standing in front of a stylized sun projecting beams on a jagged crop of rock. Her eyes projected confidence as her cream-colored dress billowed out beneath her breastplate like a superhero's cape. In the background, the image of a mountain lion crept toward her.

Selene began circling the room to admire the other paintings, which were also portraits. A silver frame held the depiction of a short-necked woman with feathered wings and a snarling mouth. A being that looked like a cross between a bear and a woman stood with her arms crossed. A fish-tailed siren had long blue hair that flowed around her like seaweed. One portrait was covered with black cloth. Flowers were strewn across the floor around it.

There were also smaller framed items clustered on the back wall, away from the light. Selene moved closer and saw these frames contained mostly documents. Bold black text set onto white paper, like a newspaper, but the headlines didn't seem to fit together.

Cryptologist Society Meeting Thursday

Conway High School Unveils Wampus Cat Indoor Facility

Beast of Exmoor Terrorizes Countryside

Appalachian Legends and Ozark Monsters

Selene heard a pat-pat-pat sound coming from behind her and turned to see the orange cat that always accompanied Queen Thema trot into the room. He mewed up at Selene then rubbed his cheek against her shoe. As she bent to stroke him, she heard the queen's voice.

"Nim? Where have you gone off to?" Her footsteps echoed closer as she entered the gallery. "Selene! What a lovely surprise. Are you enjoying my portrait collection?"

"Yes, they're beautiful. Who are they? And what are these?" Selene asked, gesturing to the documents hanging before her.

"Ah, it's no surprise that you're drawn to them. Look closer," Queen Thema answered. She waved her hand. Suddenly, each of the documents glowed.

Selene jerked with surprise at the queen's hidden skill, then leaned closer.

"They're from your world." Queen Thema said. She looked as if she were waiting for Selene to solve a riddle. "I collect them, or my sisters bring them to me. Do you see a theme?"

Selene read a document's headline aloud, "Monstrous Wampus Cat Spotted in East Tennessee. Hey, that's... " A rush of homesickness made her pause. She turned to Queen Thema to finish her thought, but all that came out was a shocked, "Oh!"

For one moment, Queen Thema had looked normal, just as Selene had known her. But in the next second, like the flicker in a movie projection, her face had contorted. It shifted and morphed— her nose elongated, fur sprouted from her smooth face, her pointed ears migrated to the top of her head, and her eyes glowed.

Selene gasped as the queen's face shifted back to how it was before. Then Thema began to chuckle, the front fangs of her teeth glinting. "Don't worry. I won't bite."

"How did you do that?"

The queen shrugged. "Perk of demi-goddesshood."

Selene swallowed thickly. "Are *you* the Wampus Cat?"

The queen sighed dramatically. "Your people have many foolish names and myths for The Seven Sisters. In your region, some call me the Wampus Cat. I've also been called the Black Beast of Exmoor, the Cactus Cat, the White Death... the list goes on."

"That was you they spotted in Rugby. With the injured paw," Selene breathed. Just when she thought the past two days couldn't get any weirder, here was a whole new layer. "My brother sent me an article about it."

"My injury made the newspaper?" Queen Thema asked excitedly. "I must try to find it on my next patrol."

"So, the other portraits in the gallery are—"

"The Seven Sisters of Aurelia!" Queen Thema boomed. "Despite our best efforts to look like something of your world when we visit, we don't quite fit. It confuses your kind, and so they make up tales."

"Why do you look so different from each other?"

Thema bent to pick up Nim and nuzzled her face against his furry neck. "We each transform into something closer to our sacred animal... and our true nature. My story is complimentary compared to some legends about us."

"What are they?"

"I don't know them all, but they liken us to terrible things. Devils, monsters, dogs... " Queen Thema turned to walk through the gallery, motioning for Selene to follow.

She stopped at the portrait of the snarling winged woman. "They compare my sister Aello to a moth—a *male* moth—when she clearly has the wings of a Harpy." She waved toward the fish-tailed woman. "They blame Cebna, who you met last night, for poor fishing and shipwrecks. And Yerena!" She pointed to the furry, bear woman. "Her people value privacy above anything else, but humans are obsessed with her movements."

"How so?"

"She has a large province with many different portals. But your kind attributes every rustle in the forest to evidence of her presence. And now she has a terrible insecurity about the size of her feet." Thema made an exasperated sound.

"Her feet," Selene repeated slowly. "As in... they're big?

"Mmm. She has to be very careful on her patrols."

"I see." Selene's head was swimming. *I'm talking to the Wampus Cat. Who is sister to Bigfoot and Mothman.*

"You must understand that we were all given a sacred duty to guard the crossroads between dimensions. I told you the human plane is a harbor dimension, yes? We make sure that any creatures who go through the veil do not stay."

"What sort of creatures?"

The queen smiled. "Your innocence is charming. A non-human in the human realm is like—what would your people call it? A child in a candy store. Dwarves covet your gems. Fairies play pranks. Elves leave gifts for children. Demons feed on your faults. It's all in good fun until it gets taken too far. And then we intervene to send them back home, or kill them." Thema paused at Selene's shocked expression and added, "Perhaps it's more polite to say we send them to the Underworld."

"Is that like hell?"

"There is no legendary place where suffering is eternal. Only the Underworld where all dead go to be judged. If they have lived pure, they go to the Afterworld. If not, they are *punished* until they repent."

The vehemence in Thema's voice at the word "punished" was so unexpected, Selene took a step back. Then she stood motionless, trying to let all that she had been told sink in.

Queen Thema introduced the portrait of a woman with spiky hair and wolfish features as Kebee, Queen of the Lycah people. A woman with eel-like skin posed by a glittering lake bore a plaque below her painting that read, *Delphyne of the Drago.*

"Can your sisters go to any dimension?" Selene asked.

"Any dimension but the Underworld and the Afterworld. However, we are charged to use our powers to protect the human world. So that's where we spend most of our time outside of Aurelia."

"But Aurelians can't leave Aurelia?"

"No. Aurelia is meant to be a sanctuary and refuge from the ills that plague societies like yours. Certain stones allow the bearer to travel to any dimension, though they are very rare. Why would anyone want to leave? Aurelia is a beautiful, peaceful dimension. Everything anyone could ever want is to be found here!" Thema held up her arms to twirl dramatically.

Nibbling on her thumbnail, Selene looked around at the faces in the gallery. This whole thing was a new layer of absurd to already outlandish experience. But also, it made perfect sense—the unreliable sightings, the lack of proof, the conflicting stories. The so-called "cryptids" weren't aliens, failed science experiments, or evolutionary hiccups, they were inter-dimensional guardians. A week ago, she never would have believed there were other dimensions, let alone portals to get to them. Yet here she was.

But she only counted portraits of six sisters. Gesturing to the portrait covered by a black sheet, she asked, "And who's this one?"

Dust swirled as the queen ran her hand down the black cloth. "That's the sister that's lost to us" She looked down at the flowers on the floor and whispered, "I haven't said her name out loud in years. It was Lilith. It is Lilith."

Then she wiped her eyes and abruptly brightened. The sadness of her voice was replaced with a jovial tone. "They call her the Jersey Devil in your world! Or sometimes Ahool or Olitiau. They claim she has the body of a goat, the head of a horse, and sickly little wings. Can you imagine? Humans can be so cruel. She's always had a long face, and her wings are bit bony, but really! "

Selene smiled tentatively. "What are her people like?"

"Ah, she is a Goblyn and ruled the Goblyn race. Then later she took on ruling the vampire race up north, near Drago lands."

"She ruled vampires? But aren't they... dangerous? Arkaya was ready to kill me when she thought I was one."

Queen Thema tilted her head. "They weren't always so troublesome, they were human once. Their kind became very lost in your world once they straddled the line between life and death. Dear Lilith took pity on them and arranged to bring them all to live here instead."

"Why?"

"My sister had a generous nature. At first the vampires were model citizens—grateful and hard-working. But now without their queen, they're like petulant children. Won't listen to their aunties or follow any rules. They are meant to live on donated Aurelian blood, yet they don't thrive on it as we had hoped. Many are bitter about it and get into trouble."

"What sort of trouble?"

"Nothing to worry yourself about," Queen Thema said. "The few that are left are old and weak."

Selene nodded. She wanted to ask more, but Queen Thema seemed to be holding control of her emotions by a thread so she tucked away her questions for another time. "I'm sorry. I hope your sister comes home soon."

"Yes, as do I, my dear. As do I." The queen turned to walk out of the gallery and gestured for Selene to follow. "Many think I am a fool for believing that she will, but I know she's alive."

"How?"

"I still see her in my dreams," Queen Thema said. They stepped out of the gallery back into the library with Nim following. From the corner of her eye, Selene saw a dark figure ahead.

"Ah! Samael, I've been looking for you," Queen Thema called out. "Come! Meet our human guest."

Selene's heartbeat quickened. It was *him*. Samael stiffened, then turned to walk toward them. Selene twirled a strand of hair between her fingers, suddenly feeling very self-conscious.

Nim bounded ahead of them to wiggle his rear end playfully at a gray kitten who had appeared from under a bench. The kitten darted out in a counter-attack but then stopped to stand in front of the demon.

Samuel bent to scoop it up, and Selene was seized with a sudden, irrational fear that she was about to witness a terrible, demonic act like biting off the poor thing's head or tossing it like a football. But he only cradled the tiny ball of fur in his massive hand. Then he began to stroke the kitten's forehead until its eyes slid blissfully shut.

"Did you need me, my lady?"

The deep timbre of his voice made Selene's belly flutter.

"Yes! I want you to meet our guest. Samael, this is Selene. All the way from Gaia!"

Selene smiled politely and tried to keep her eyes off his horns. He was much taller up close, and his body was packed with muscle.

"Hello," she said, trying to appear more confident than she felt.

Samael made eye contact long enough for her to see that red

ringed his black irises. He shifted his weight and mumbled, "Good afternoon."

"Samael is also a stranger to Aurelia just like you," the queen said, touching Selene's shoulder. "He comes to us from the Underworld."

Selene cleared her throat. Her father had always said the trick to meeting new people was to find commonalities, even if it was about the weather. But how could she respond to that? A weak, "Oh?" was all she managed.

"We rely on him to keep us safe. He has an excellent knack for sniffing out trouble," Thema said with a wink.

"Um... t-thank you for your service, Samael," Selene stammered, then cringed at how ridiculous that sounded. What did she think he was, a member of the armed forces?

The glare Samael gave her was unforgiving. "It is my duty! Your gratitude is misguided," he said with such force that Selene rocked back on her heels.

She pressed her lips together into a tight line. Yikes, he *was* terrifying, just as Hollen had said. She glanced at Queen Thema to gauge her reaction, but she seemed oblivious. Gulping hard, Selene focused on the kitten in Samael's hand. It had started to squirm, so he bent to release it onto the floor. Selene watched the kitten zoom away at a breakneck pace, wishing she could do the same.

"Samael, there's a matter I need to speak with you about later," the queen said.

"I see. Shall we arrange a time in your study—"

"I will stop by your chambers later."

"But that's not necessary—"

Queen Thema held up a hand. "I won't stay long. I just don't want any disturbances."

He nodded, looking uneasy. "Is that all, my lady?"

"That's all," Queen Thema said. Samael gave Selene a curt nod, then turned to walk out the library's exit. They both watched his retreating back before Queen Thema stifled a yawn. "I believe it's time for my midday nap. Enjoy your afternoon, Selene—"

"Wait! I wanted to ask about what you said yesterday. There's someone who might be able to help me go home?"

Queen Thema gave Selene an assessing glance. "Yes. I do know of someone. But have patience, dearest." She started to walk away then said over her shoulder, "We'll discuss it tomorrow."

CHAPTER 7

S am was stretched out on his couch reading a book when a knock rapped on his chamber door. He muttered a curse and sat up. He had expected Queen Thema to come up later than this, at least after dinner. His mood had been dark after his encounter with the human in the library, and being disturbed in his private sanctuary was not helping.

What could the queen want that was so important? Perhaps she wanted to admonish him for being so rude to her guest. He hadn't meant to speak to Selene so harshly, but the rush of pleasure he felt at hearing his name spoken in her velvet voice had been... alarming. He didn't want her to do it again.

A second knock came, and Sam frantically shoved the book he was reading into the couch cushions before rising to his feet. He crossed the room to open the intricately carved wooden door.

Thema stood hunched in the doorway, panting. She looked up at Sam with a pained expression. "How do you do this every day? I feel like I'm dying."

"I told you we could meet in your study. The stairwell can be treacherous."

"How many stairs are there? I lost count after 300," Thema said. She tapped a claw against the swirling patterns on the door that Sam had carved years ago. "This is lovely, by the way. You've always had such a talent for woodwork."

He acknowledged the compliment with a brief incline of his head. The queen's habit of applauding his aptitudes was well-intentioned, but sometimes felt like the type of praise a worried mother would give her inept son. A bid to eradicate bad habits by reinforcing the good.

Thema entered the room, gracefully lowered herself onto the couch, then let out a yelp. Digging her hands into the cushions, she pulled out the book Sam had hidden moments before. One eyebrow lifted as she read the title, *Yearning of the Storm's Kiss*. Sam's cheeks flamed.

It was no secret that Sam was a voracious reader. He loved spending hours in the library hunched over historical volumes, science tomes, and texts of mythology. But the bookshelves in his private chambers contained only two types of stories—adventure and erotica.

Thema set the book aside without a word. A small smile touched her lips before she looked up at Sam seriously. "I will get straight to the point. Perhaps you had better sit down."

Sam crossed his arms and stood before the fireplace. "I will stand."

"As you wish." Queen Thema leaned forward. "An old enemy has returned to Aurelia. It's the reason I have been meeting with the sisters these past few weeks."

"Who?"

"Zaybris."

Sam froze. Embarrassment about his explicit book fled upon hearing the name of the vampire who had kidnapped him from the Underworld. Rage, deep and compelling, surged in his chest before a red haze blurred his vision. His stomach tightened as if he were preparing for a blow. Fearing a loss of control with Thema in the room, he began to pace.

"Where is he?" he demanded.

"North. Holed up in what's left of Queen Lilith's castle. He's trying to usurp her throne."

"How do you know?"

"The Goblyns still living there sent word to me."

"Is he harming them?"

"No, but he's waging war. He wants the vampires to rise up and revolt against the queens. He thinks he's charismatic enough to convince them he should be the sole king of Aurelia."

"Why now? Why would he care what happens here when he's been gone for so long?"

"He was always an agitator." Thema said. "He was inciting violence and anarchy even before he stole you from the Underworld. He pushed vampires to flout the rules Queen Lilith set up for blood donation, and encouraged his kind to roam the night in packs, drinking from unwilling victims or draining them to death. I've always believed he knew more about Lilith's disappearance than he would say."

Sam clenched and unclenched his fists. "Where has he been all these years?"

"I don't know. He carries a traveler's stone. He could have gone anywhere with it." Thema tapped a finger against her chin. "But I suspect he's been hiding out in the fairy dimension. Their pretentiousness would appeal to his ego."

Sam slumped into his armchair. He sat with his fingers steepled, imagining all the brutal, painful ways he could exact his vengeance. He wouldn't make it quick with decapitation or staking. No, he wanted to watch the filthy vampire's body rot and decay before his eyes. He would make him writhe in agony, begging for mercy.

"Fear not. I will destroy him," he murmured.

"I know you crave retribution, but I need him alive, Samael. At least for—"

Sam sprang to his feet. "Do not ask that of me!" he thundered.

"You don't know the agony I live with, knowing he remains unpunished! It is because of him that my instincts are disordered, my head in constant chaos. I have to find him."

Queen Thema held up a hand. "I wouldn't dream of denying a Vengeance demon his due. But before you kill him, there is something I need."

"When I see him, I will not stop to perform favors," Sam bit out, now vibrating with pent-up energy.

"I know. But I'm asking you to try. If Zaybris still carries a traveler's stone—"

"It will be mine. When I kill him, it transfers to me!" The full impact of Queen Thema's words shot through him like a lightning strike. "It can take me home."

"Of course, but please listen. Inter-dimensional travel isn't the stone's only sacred property. It can be used as a scrying device to find things. Lost objects." Thema stood and stepped in front of Sam to peer up into his face. "Lost people."

Sam turned his head so Thema couldn't see how his face tightened. His greatest enemy, here within in his grasp and Thema wanted his focus on her sister. He growled. Sam knew very little about the lost sister of Aurelia other than the fact that she was obviously dead—beheaded or incinerated. After over thirty years of no contact, no clues, and no leads on her whereabouts, Queen Lilith's fate was clear. He watched the sun descend on the horizon through his balcony doors and wanted to punch through the glass. Every second delaying his return to the Underworld was a waste.

He turned to snarl at Thema and shout no, he would not grant her this boon. After so many years in exile, nothing would keep him from finally claiming his birthright in the Underworld. Yet he was struck by how small she looked. Her entire body seemed to lean toward him in desperation, her large eyes beseeching. She acted so strong, but in truth, she was quite fragile. A small demi-goddess, centuries old, trying to do her best by her people and those she was charged to protect.

When they met, he knew he had gone a bit mad living alone in the forest. Yet she had accepted him completely, never asking how he escaped the blood wagons. She had taken him back to her castle to give him a job, a home, an identity. She treated him like an equal— an ally and trusted friend. Almost like he was family.

A spike of guilt rose at his selfishness. She only wanted to be reunited with her kin and resolve a decades-old heartache. Wasn't that what he wanted too? He could grant her a final act of kindness after he unleashed all the violence, rage, and fury he'd spent so long holding back.

"Fine," he said. "Whatever you need. After I kill him, I'll use the stone to scry and send word of your sister's fate."

Queen Thema clasped her hands to her chest. "Thank you."

Then, in one of her typical mood shifts, she squared her shoulders. "Now, let's discuss the plan."

"I don't need a plan outside of taking his head."

"Be practical, dear boy. Lilith's castle is well-fortified, and I'm told Zaybris rarely leaves. Therefore, we must go to him. *With a plan.* He has surrounded himself with guards and is testing the loyalty of his former associates. They aren't just going to let a demon walk up to the castle to shake his hand."

"They will if I'm the demon."

Thema gave him an exasperated look. "My sisters and I have discussed many tactics, but after speaking with the Goblyns, we found the perfect enticement. Zaybris knows he can't raise an army of vampires in their current state—many of them are so decayed they're no better than walking corpses."

"True."

"He's seeking a way to regenerate their bodies and restore them to the youthfulness they knew before coming to Aurelia. The only thing that can do that is human blood. So... " Thema paused as if waiting for Sam to guess. When he failed to respond, she murmured, "I brought a human here."

Sam's lips parted. "Selene?"

"Yes! Vampires survive on Aurelian blood, but they don't *thrive* on it like they do on human blood. I set a trap in one of my portals, and miraculously, she came through. She's the perfect offering for him, don't you think?"

Sam didn't respond. A protective urge jolted through him, and his claws extended. He suddenly wanted to hurt Thema for her suggestion and steal Selene away to keep her safe. Disturbing visions ran through his mind. He could lock up Selene in his tower, or take her far away to live with him deep into the forest where he could protect her from the vampires and anyone else that might try to hurt her. He would keep her all for himself, and she would be so grateful. Naked-in-his-bed grateful. Anyone who dared to defy him would be destroyed—starting with the insolent queen sitting in front of him.

Breathe. Focus. Control. The words of his mentor echoed through his head. He reminded himself that he was in control of his instincts; they didn't control him. His anger began to ebb with each exhale.

He lifted his head to meet the queen's eyes. "This is wrong. You are cunning, but I've never known you to be cruel."

"Your meaning?"

"I have lived among vampires in this realm. We would be condemning this human to horrors you cannot fathom. She would be a blood slave—"

Thema perched on the armrest of the couch. "Ah, you think too little of me. Naturally, we won't let Zaybris have her. She'll just be bait. Dangle her in front of Zaybris to get an audience. It's all quite simple. You will pretend to offer Selene to Zaybris, kill him, and return to the Underworld. Done."

"It won't work. Why would the human agree to this plan?" Sam asked.

"She wants to return home. She'll agree to anything."

"So you would trick Selene, then trap her here in Aurelia?"

"Pah! We would be doing her a favor!" Queen Thema said grandly. "Trust me. I've seen the way females are treated in her world. They are dismissed, objectified, silenced, and violated. Why

61

would she want to return to that wretched place when she can live here? She can reside in the castle. Or find a mate and live in another territory if she chooses. She'll have no shortage of fine offers."

The mention of Selene choosing an Aurelian mate caused Sam's vision to flash red. He swiped a hand across his mouth and tried to ignore the cold feeling that had settled in the pit of his stomach. It felt wrong to manipulate Selene so, especially when he knew what it was to yearn for home as she must. Yet Thema knew Gaia better than he did. If she believed Selene could be happier, safer in Aurelia, maybe it was for the best. Plus, could he afford to relinquish his only chance at vengeance? With the stone, he could leave Aurelia for good. Perhaps he could even find his fated mate in the Underworld.

"How do we proceed?" Sam asked carefully.

"You and Selene will leave tomorrow morning to go north. You'll travel by foot—"

"Just the two of us? By foot? But that will take weeks!"

"I know, but it's the best way to keep her safe. A demon and a human on horseback or in a carriage will attract attention. Word will travel, and vampires eager to please their future king will want to bring him such a treasure. You must walk by day, as they sleep, and keep her hidden at night."

The cold feeling in Sam's stomach grew spikes. Traveling with Selene? Alone? The thought of spending his days at her side, talking with her, providing her with food, and sleeping near her made his skin tingle.

"Wouldn't she be more comfortable traveling with another female?" he asked. "Someone like Arkaya or even Hollen?"

"You're the only one strong enough to protect her. We can't take any risks. Not when we're so close to getting what we both want. I trust you. And I know I can tell her to trust you too."

Sam really wished Thema hadn't said that. He barely trusted himself around other Aurelians, let alone a human who made him feel so... complicated.

Thema stood and shook out her skirts. "Now, I'm going to talk to

Selene. You'll leave tomorrow at dawn. Queen Cebna has offered to help disguise her as a Nereid, and I have threatened everyone who's met her at the castle with death if they tell others of her existence."

Sam dropped his head as though he were being sentenced. "How will you send word about your gift to Zaybris?"

"I'll send a message to him once you get close," Thema's eyes gleamed as she walked toward the door. "Males are easy to mislead, so willing to believe in their own grandeur—not you, of course, my dear. But I'll lay it on thick to Zaybris. Tell him the sisters are so pleased by his return. We want to offer him a gift..."

Sam didn't want to hear any more details about the proposed transaction. "Do you need help down the stairs?"

"No need, I'll manage." She touched the doorknob then turned to lay her hand on the leather bracer encircling Sam's wrist. "Thank you, Samael. For everything. Safe travels and bright blessings."

CHAPTER 8

I t was still dark the next morning when Selene hunched over the edge of her bed to tie her hiking boots. She paused, trying to steady her fumbling fingers. A pair of white satin slippers were thrust under her nose.

"What about these?" Hollen asked, hopefully.

Selene wiped her sweaty palms down the thighs of her jeans. She shook her head and gently pushed away the slippers that Hollen held. "No. They're lovely, but Queen Thema said we'll be traveling for weeks on foot. I need things made for hiking, not dancing."

Hollen made a face and pointed to Selene's shoes. "But those are so ugly."

When Selene only sighed, Hollen tossed the slippers over her shoulder. Then she continued to rush around Selene's bedroom, throwing items into a green backpack and muttering to herself, "Breeches *and* boots? Hideous."

Selene was heartened to see Hollen fold a thick wool cloak into the pack, but then cringed as she stuffed a glittering pink ballgown behind it.

Focus on the positive, she told herself. The good news was that

Queen Thema had found someone with a magic stone that could send her home. The fact that he was a vampire was unsettling, but Queen Thema waved away all of Selene's questions, assuring her she'd be safe and welcome in his home. Zaybris owed the queen a favor, she had said, and that debt could be paid by sending Selene home.

The bad news? The only way to get to his home was on foot. Four weeks of travel over God knows what kind of Aurelian terrain. Although she and Cass enjoyed nature trails, Selene had never hiked overnight or stayed in a place without at least a port-a-potty nearby. She was dreading days of trudging through the elements, nights of getting eaten alive by bugs, and sleeping on the ground. And then there was her travel companion...

Last night, when Thema had told her she would be escorted by the demon, Selene's heart pounded so hard it felt like her ribs would crack. Queen Thema must have seen the shock on Selene's face because she had said, "Don't look so frightened. Samael is extremely capable. He will allow no harm to come to you."

A flush of adrenaline coursed through Selene's body. "Isn't there someone else who could take me?"

"There is no one more suitable."

"I see," she said softly.

The queen drummed her fingertips against the back of the couch. "You disapprove of my choice in guardian? Do you not wish to return to your beloved home?"

"No, I do, but... " Selene looked down at her lap, struggling to articulate her reluctance. Just saying *he's a demon*, didn't seem adequate because there was more to it. She hated how risky situations always made her feel torn between caution and freedom. Kevin used to roll his eyes when she would ask him to walk her back to her car after one of his many late-night gigs. He had made her feel so stupid and overreactive, but not stupid enough to stop.

"In my world, being alone with a strange man is—" Selene paused, then said, "Well, it can be risky."

"I know what human men are like," Thema said with a snort. "Are you asking if you can trust Samael?"

"Yes. I know you said he would keep me safe but—" Selene bit her lip. "Will I be safe from *him*?"

Thema's eyebrows rose. "A fair question. Let me tell you how Samael and I met. When my sisters and I go into your world, we aren't there to interfere with humans. It's not our role. We are there to keep the balance, not to right wrongs. But many years ago, I interfered. I was on patrol, and I heard a human woman scream. As I prowled closer, I could see two men attacking the female. Probably attempting to do what you fear from Samael."

The queen went on to tell Selene how she had saved the woman but gotten severely injured by the men before killing them. She had been so hurt that once she was back in Aurelia, she couldn't transform out of her cat form and had collapsed in the woods near her portal.

"I don't know if I stayed there for hours or days. One moment my fur was wet with blood, and the next I was warm and dry inside a cave. My wounds were dressed, and I was now in my Malkina form. A male was in the cave with me," Thema's voice turned playful. "Can you guess who it was?"

"Samael," Selene whispered, ignoring the fizzy feeling that rose when she said his name. The queen described how seeing a demon made her fear she had died and gone to the Underworld, but Samael explained that he had been in Aurelia since he was a boy. He had been living alone in a cave and felt called to care for the badly injured cat he came across in the woods.

"Imagine his shock when I became myself again," Thema said, gesturing to her body. "Yet, he said I reminded him of his mother, so I knew he was very homesick. He showed me a different side of the demonic nature. I had been so sure I knew everything about his kind, about their selfishness, their cruelty. But Samael was neither."

"How long were you with him?"

"Weeks. He dug the bullet from my shoulder while I was in cat form, but it took a long time for the gash on my head to heal. The way I transitioned from cat to Malkina meant my ribs never set right, which is why I must wear this," the queen said, tapping her metal breastplate.

"I'm sorry."

"No need, I rather like the look of it," Thema replied. "When I was fully healed, I asked him how I could repay him. He asked for only one thing. A job. Many were critical of my decision to bring him here, but I have never regretted it."

The queen's face was distant for several moments until Selene said, "What an ordeal to have lived through. You're very brave."

Queen Thema swept a hand over her hair, preening at the praise. Then she turned serious and grasped Selene's hands.

"Listen to me. It is very important that you go on this journey."

Selene nodded, touched by Thema's concern. The queen's hands felt warm and unnaturally strong.

"Samael can be ruthless, but only to those who deserve it. His manners aren't pristine, and he finds many of our customs baffling. But he lives by a code of honor that does not include hurting unwilling females."

Her golden eyes locked with Selene's. "There is no one I would trust with you more."

Selene's memory of the conversation was interrupted when a knock sounded at her door. Seconds later, Arkaya swept into the room, carrying a large basket.

"No, no, Hollen. Necessities only," Arkaya said as Hollen tried to stuff two throw pillows in the backpack. "Pack breeches, under-clothes, and tunics. Did you add the wool cloak? I have her bedding here."

Arkaya settled next to Selene on the bed as Hollen disappeared into the closet. "The queen has told me of the journey you are about to take. As her enchantress, I've prepared a few things."

Arkaya picked up a silver metal flask from the basket. "Water bottle. Fill this up as you need when encountering a lake or river."

"After boiling it," Selene affirmed. At least she knew one of the basics of camping.

"No need, the bottle's enchanted to purify," Arkaya said. Next, she pulled out a fabric tube about the size of a soda can. "Your bedding, which will stay as warm or cool as you need it to be. Here's a compass, a kerchief charmed to keep away insects, gloves, solar-powered lantern, and a few other necessities. Now, let's show you your tent."

Arkaya produced a white vinyl tube that looked like a roll of paper towels tied with a red ribbon. She placed the bundle on the floor in the center of the room and then said to Selene, "Untie the ribbon quickly."

When Selene tugged the ribbon, the bundle began to expand. It made a whooshing sound as it spread, and continued to groan and stretch until it reached nearly past Selene's head, forming a small dome. When it finally stopped expanding, the whole structure seemed to exhale as it settled into the shape of an igloo.

Selene gaped. Her "tent" was a far cry from the miserable dirt bunk she had imagined, and more like a luxury yurt suitable for glamping. Though her insides buzzed with anxiety, she smiled. When she followed Arkaya through the stooped entryway, Selene was surprised to find her feet sinking into a padded floor. She could comfortably stand, and the tent seemed so wide it could fit a king-sized bed.

"Roof vent here," Arkaya pointed up to the ceiling, then the walls. "Pockets are set into the walls for you both to store away items each night."

Arkaya's use of the word "both" jolted Selene. "Samael and I will sleep in here... together?"

"No, he prefers a hammock," Arkaya said.

Some of the tension in Selene's shoulders relaxed, though a traitorous whisper of disappointment blew across her thoughts.

Arkaya motioned for Selene to follow her out of the tent. "When you're ready to pack up, come out and pull the ribbon." Arkaya demonstrated, and the tent began to shrink until it was back to its original shape. "Then tie it up, and you're ready to go."

"Wow, I was so worried about roughing it. I didn't expect anything like this."

"You think us archaic? Not as cultivated as your people?" Arkaya asked dryly.

"Oh no! Where I'm from, castles and queens are from another period in history. A less advanced time, so sometimes I assume... "

Arkaya's eyes twinkled. "Well, we do take some influence from human inventions. When Aurelia's glorious sisters make their patrols into your world, they occasionally bring back things or ideas that spark their interest."

"Like the zipper! And toothbrush! Oh, and plumbing!" Hollen said, popping her head from the closet. "It took the Goblyns years to figure out Queen Cebna's drawings of indoor plumbing, but now I can't imagine life without it."

Arkaya nodded. "When a queen brings something back from Gaia, they first hold a council to make sure the item is suitable for Aurelia. If approved, it's sent to the Goblyns for replication. With a few improvements."

"What wouldn't be suitable?" Selene asked.

"Anything that could foul our lands or corrupt our people. Queen Aello tried for years to get approval on a motorized carriage. She stalked many a human operating one to understand the mechanisms, but the queens ultimately voted it down. Filthy creations. And too isolating."

"I see."

"We must seem very old-fashioned to you to travel by foot and horse. But the sisters pay careful attention to what comes from human inventions—the good and the bad."

Hollen appeared before them and held out the backpack to Arkaya. "For your inspection." She gave an exaggerated salute to the older Malkina.

Arkaya glanced through it and murmured her approval. Then she handed it to Selene. Although the backpack was very full, it felt like it weighed nothing.

"One last thing," Arkaya said, handing her a small blue jar. "This comes from Queen Cebna herself. Apply it to your face, and it will disguise your skin to look like the scales of a Nereid."

"Why do I need it?"

"You won't as you travel through Malkina territory, but put it on when you leave our forests," Arkaya said. "Unless you wish to draw unnecessary attention to yourself."

Selene unscrewed the lid, and a sea breeze aroma drifted up. It looked like a jar of moisturizer, but when she applied some to her hand, sure enough, it made her skin glimmer like a fish.

After she closed the lid, Hollen surprised her with a fierce hug. Gasping for air, Selene tried to lift her arms to return the gesture, but Hollen's embrace only grew tighter.

When Hollen finally drew back, she asked, "Why can't you stay here in Aurelia? Don't you like us?"

The wave of guilt Selene felt at Hollen's words made her wince. She had heard similar words from her family, and they never failed to cut deeply.

Don't be so greedy, her mother once said when Selene was ten and had shown her a stack of summer camp brochures. Someone had to look after the twins while she met with clients, her mother had argued.

You need to think of the family now, her father chided when Selene needed a permission slip signed to go on a high school trip to Paris. The trip wasn't happening for two months, but her mom had just been discharged from the hospital for alcohol poisoning.

We miss you so much, her brother Evan had said when she chose to spend her evenings studying in the campus library instead of doing her coursework at home.

Selene patted Hollen back and said, "I'm sorry, but I have to go."

Hollen gave a distressed cry. "But I'll never see you again and—"

"Stop it, Hollen," Arkaya interrupted. "Goodbyes are meant to be quick."

"All right," Hollen said and released Selene.

"Goodbye, Hollen. Thank you for everything," Selene said. She pulled her backpack onto her shoulders, and snapped the hip belt low on her waist. The sooner she started this expedition, the sooner she would be home.

CHAPTER 9

Selene's hiking boots made squeaking sounds as they thumped along the stone floor. They echoed off the corridor leading to the castle's front gate, while Arkaya walked silently beside her. Up ahead, Selene could see a slice of blue sky through the open gate, the sun high above the bridge leading to the forest. Yesterday, the queen had told her they would leave at dawn, but between Hollen's packing skills and Arkaya's magic tricks, it was nearly midday.

As they got closer, Selene saw the silhouette of a man standing near the gate. He had his back to the castle, with a large pack strapped to his shoulders and a brown satchel slung across his chest. Strands of black hair blew around his shoulders, while sunlight made the ridged tips of his horns gleam. He stood perfectly still, staring out at the bridge that led to the vast forest before him. A lonely presence dwarfed by a towering expanse of the unknown. Waiting. For her.

Samael.

Reality hit, hard and fast as a sledgehammer to her chest. Selene's lips parted, and her mouth went dry. Although brief, her time in the castle had made her forget how big Aurelia was. How threatening the landscape looked and the way the woods pulsed with eerie gloom. And now she was alone with a single lifeline. There was just one man charged to be her guide, protector, and companion. And technically, he wasn't a man at all.

Am I really doing this?

A constrictive feeling seized her chest, causing her to cough. But the dryness of her mouth made one cough turn into another, and then another. Arkaya laid a hand on her arm, looking concerned, but Selene waved her away.

The sound of a deep voice caused Selene to jump.

"You're late."

Selene nearly choked again as she turned to see Samael staring down at her. Tall, grim, and looking very irritated.

His gaze traveled from the top of Selene's head, down to her boots, and back up again. He must share Hollen's disgust of her jeans and boots, she thought. The icy disapproval in his expression was clear.

Well, this is a great start.

She opened her mouth to apologize for her tardiness, but Arkaya cut her off. "The fault is entirely mine, Samael. Packing took longer than we expected." She leaned back to look up at him. "Do you have everything you need?"

"Yes." A small frown pulled at the corners of his mouth.

"Then this is farewell," Arkaya said, pulling Selene into a hug. "Safe travels, dear human. The queen sends her best wishes. If you experience any... unexpected proceedings, you will always have a place here. Remember that."

Selene found Arkaya's phrasing odd, but she dismissed it. "Thank you. I'm so grateful you found me in the woods."

Arkaya smiled back and then turned to Samael. "Safe travels to you too, demon. I hope this journey gives you peace."

He nodded, then Arkaya turned to glide back into the castle. A small lump formed in Selene's throat at the sight of Arkaya's retreating back. Bereft of her friend Hollen and her guide Arkaya, Selene now felt truly alone in Aurelia.

"I trust you are prepared?" Samuel said.

"Yes, I'm ready."

In a voice like gravel, he said, "Let's begin."

As they left the castle behind to journey into the Malkina forest, Sam fought to keep his gaze from raking down Selene's frame again. Every muscle in his body had tightened with want at his first glimpse of her that morning. Last night, he had worried that she would slow their progress by wearing shoes that blistered her feet. He'd been ready to endure complaints about the mud that would surely collect on the hem of her fine gowns and vowed to be patient when she lamented the inevitable damage to the gems she would be draped in. Yet she wasn't outfitted at all as he expected.

Snug canvas breeches hugged every line of her legs. She wore a close-fitting jacket, unzipped just enough to show the comely line of her throat. Her pack was much smaller than his, and the belt clipped at her waist accentuated the curve of her hips. Sam's fingers had itched to tunnel through the mass of hair flowing loosely around her shoulders. He even found her boots admirable—cut high enough to support her ankles and soled with a thick tread.

The dark-clothed woman that had stood in the castle gates looked more like an accomplished warrior than a pampered courtier, and the contrast made his heart pound. He felt so flustered that the only way he could keep from falling at her feet was to lash out at her tardiness.

A pack of wild birds pecking at the ground scattered as they passed. They would follow the dirt path leading out of Malkina territory, which could take a few days. Then Sam would consult a map for appropriate routes to take them to the Goblyn castle.

The forests of Queen Thema's lands were ancient and lush, with canopies of trees offering shade. They walked in silence as the castle grew smaller behind them in the distance. Sam was uncertain of what topics of conversation were appropriate for a human, so he kept quiet.

Eventually, Selene spoke. "L-lovely weather, isn't it? We're lucky it's sunny."

"Yes," he replied.

"Have you traveled this way north before?"

"Not this way specifically."

"But you know where we're going, right?"

"Of course," he said, more harshly than he intended.

"Okay. Are there any dangers I should be worried about? Lions and tigers and bears, oh my?" she said with a small chuckle.

"I do not know of those creatures, but there are no threats for you to worry about."

"Got it."

They didn't speak again for another two hours. The forest grew darker as they ventured deeper inside. Small animals and birds peered at them curiously, then hid. The way Selene watched them made him wonder if she found the creatures of Aurelia intriguing or frightening. He chose not to ask.

When they passed over a tangle of tree roots, Selene stumbled, and instinctively, Sam caught her by the elbow. He could feel the heat of her body through the cotton she wore, and he couldn't help but let his fingers linger, noticing how large his hand looked against her small arm. When she fully righted herself, she looked up at him and said, "Oops, thank you."

Sam nodded, noticing her cheeks were flushed. He quickly pulled his hand back and closed his fist, wanting to preserve the tingly feeling that touching her brought.

Later, after passing a boggy creek, Sam felt the brown satchel slung across his body grow warm. Then the fabric abruptly expanded with a *thonk*, bulging with the weight of its sudden contents.

Selene jumped back and pointed at the pouch. "What was that? Do you have some kind of animal in there?"

"It's our dinner."

"Our dinner is a live animal?"

"No, it's… " Sam looked to see if there was a suitable spot for them to stop. "Do you see those fallen logs? We'll take our meal there."

Selene's eyes darted from his face to the pouch. When they reached the clearing, Sam pulled out two bundles. She eyed it skeptically.

"Is it… alive?"

"Not anymore." Sam said. He heard Selene's small gasp when he extended a black claw from under his fingernail to slice through cloth wrapping of each package. He thrust a bundle into her hands.

She sat on the ground and gingerly unwrapped the contents. "It's some kind of sandwich? And is that fruit? But where did it come from?"

"Thema's kitchens," Sam said. When he saw the confusion on her face, he tugged on the strap of the brown satchel he wore.

"Aurelians call this a switch pouch. They were created to exchange messages and supplies for the sisters when they travel. Each one has a twin—this one is linked to a pouch at Thema's castle. What goes in one bag emerges in the other."

"So, all our meals will just appear?"

"Yes. It will be simple fare, don't expect a feast." Sam eased himself to the ground, unnerved by how charming he found her wonder at this most basic of Aurelian tools. "Do they not have things like this in your world?"

"No," she said. "My sister would kill to have one of these connected to her favorite pizza place."

Sam considered asking what pizza was, but said, "Do you come from a large family?" He found himself craving to know more about her.

"I'm the oldest of three. I have a sister named Cass and a brother named Evan. They're twins. What about you?"

"I have no siblings." *That I know of.* He had often wondered if his parents had more children after he had been taken. Did they wish to replace their missing son with a new child? The wistful ache he felt every time he thought of his parents turned to dread as another question sprang to his mind.

"Are you mated?"

Selene paused. "Do you mean married?"

He didn't respond, just studied how she averted her face.

"I live with my boyfriend, sort of, but we're not married."

Sharp, jagged envy clawed at him. Of course she had a lover waiting for her in the mortal realm. Why was he so surprised? And inexplicably *enraged* by the idea of a faceless man putting his hands on her?

"Are you betrothed to your lover?" he asked.

"My lover? Goodness, that's quite a term."

"You share a bed, don't you?"

"What kind of question is that?"

"Just answer it."

"It's complicated," she mumbled.

The strain in her voice raised Sam's anger up another notch. This man was clearly unworthy of her. "Is he wealthy? What gifts does he bestow upon you?"

"Are all demons this nosy?"

He gave her an assessing look. Most people he had observed became alight with joy when discussing their mates, not fretful and reluctant. He knew he should drop the subject. But there was a question that made his jealousy simmer with primal intensity. Perhaps it wasn't appropriate in human customs, but he had to know.

"Does he satisfy you? Pleasure you as a mate should?"

Selene's eyes widened. "Are you serious?"

"He doesn't, does he?"

Her mouth opened as if she were going to protest, but she didn't.

Only raised her chin and said, "It's none of your business." She took another bite of cavefruit and looked away.

Sam crossed his arms and leaned back against a nearby tree. *He fails to please her.* A small bud of satisfaction rose up within him at the realization. This man was a fool. Selfish, careless, and undeserving. If Sam were a human—one betrothed to someone like Selene, he would shower her with gifts. Vanquish her enemies and indulge her every whim, especially in their bed. She would feel no uncertainty about her satisfaction.

Not that Sam was experienced in the art of pleasuring females, but he'd be a quick study.

He tried to keep his voice neutral as he asked, "What is your beloved's name?"

Her eyes narrowed. "Why do you care?"

"Curiosity."

"It's Kevin," she said, digging her toe into a patch of dirt on the ground. "Kevin P. Norton is how he prefers to be addressed both on stage and in life."

Sam smiled as the perverse pleasure he always felt before exacting vengeance rose.

Kevin P. Norton. When this was all over, and Sam was back in the Underworld, he vowed to put in a word with the Magistrate of Souls. He would tell her to summon him when this human's time had come so Sam could be the first, the only demon to exact vengeance upon him.

Within the Underworld's Sanctum of Agonizing Rectitude, Sam would stand before the human, close his eyes and feel the impact of every wrongdoing he ever committed in life. Hear every lie Kevin P. Norton had ever told. See every act of cruelty and hatred he carried out. Feel how the man's neglectful behavior affected Selene—and know of his spiteful deeds that hurt others.

Then Sam would take all that pain, all the suffering Kevin P. Norton ever inflicted and turn it back upon him. He would make his soul experience the pain he caused in life... and maybe with a little extra before he was allowed to transition to the Afterworld.

They ate in silence until Selene said, "What about you, then? Are you *mated*?"

An unseen spark of energy seemed to course between them as he met her eyes. A current of attraction, of connection—like the one he had experienced in the ballroom—seemed to crackle in the air.

His voice was husky as he said, "I am not attached to anyone... of this world."

~

Selene felt frozen as Samael's eyes locked with hers—like he had pinned her in place with the weight of his gaze.

"We've wasted enough time. Finish your food," he said.

Although it was obvious she had been dismissed, she couldn't look away as he stretched his arms over his head. His body was so big, so powerful. It was distracting. The moment he caught her watching him, she feigned a sudden interest in her shoelace before he could give her another one of those penetrating, toe-curling looks.

Were all demons so *intense*? The way his dark eyes fixed on her was disconcerting. It was like he was looking into her soul, making her feel bare and exposed. It was not like he was imagining her naked; it went deeper than that. It was almost as if he could see inside her, straight to all her secret fantasies. And what was worse? His expression seemed to say that he wanted to fulfill them.

Stop this. You're going home soon.

"How fatigued are you?" Samael asked.

"I feel all right. Better after eating."

"Good. Are you able to hike for a few hours more or do you want more breaks to rest? I assume humans have less stamina—"

"I'm fine," Selene said defensively. She sat up straighter, eager to start moving and stop thinking about betrothals and shared beds. "Let's push through. I feel bad about our late start."

"That's not necessary... "

"No, I insist." She stood and brushed the crumbs from her thighs. Pulling her backpack on, she snapped the clasp at her hips with a *clink*. When Samael failed to get to his feet, she prodded, "Ready, Sam?" Then, she blanched with horror. Did she just say *Sam?* Where had that come from? "I'm sorry. I meant to say Samael."

Samael stared up at her. "What made you call me that?"

"I don't know. It seemed like a nickname for Samael. It—it suits you."

"My mother used to call me Sam."

Selene felt more warmth creep into her already heated face. "Sorry, it won't happen again."

He got to his feet and pulled on his pack. "You may call me Sam from now on." Then without another word, he set off down the path so quickly Selene had to jog to catch up.

CHAPTER 10

Z aybris materialized in the dungeon of Queen Lilith's former castle, feeling hopeful. He also felt slightly dizzy, as he usually did when traveling through dimensions, but in good spirits. His evening in the human world had unfolded just as he'd planned. No one had seen him appear or vanish, and his prey had fallen right into his hands.

Certainly, this time would be different. Fate was cruel, yes, but surely his efforts would be rewarded. He was due.

As he walked toward the cells, his footsteps echoed over mildewed stone tiles. He adjusted the weight of the young man draped over his shoulder.

Dodging a trickle of water dripping from the ceiling, Zaybris saw a small creature dart above his head. A bat, he realized with disgust. The castle was overrun with them. Sacred to Queen Lilith and the Goblyn race, the flying vermin were now colloquially linked to vampires as well. Zaybris hated that. They would need to be flushed out from every corner and destroyed.

Queen Lilith never had any use for the dungeon while she reigned, so the decay in this space was more apparent. The electric lights didn't even function anymore. A broken stone tile caused Zaybris to stumble. Glancing down at the damaged floor, he scowled —another thing for him to manage. The number of tasks that a self-appointed king must oversee was truly staggering.

Heavy is the head that wears the crown.

Anger flared as he realized the Goblyns had neglected to tell him how decrepit the dungeon had become. They had only nodded when he gave them the order to light the wall sconces and prepare a cell.

Zaybris tightened his grip around the human, gratified that he could carry such a load with ease. The boy's blood was potent. Zaybris had felt his strength surge and his entire body sing with life the moment his fangs pierced the boy's flesh. He would enjoy drinking from this vessel each night.

A small part of his mind registered that the boy was no longer struggling, and a tendril of fear curled in his gut.

No. He refused to consider it. This one wasn't like the others. This human was robust and strong. He must have fainted, Zaybris reasoned, when his victim's arms swayed against his back. There was so much about twenty-first century society he didn't understand, but the vitality of a young man in his prime hadn't changed.

Zaybris knew the traveler's stone could take him anywhere he chose, but he always seemed to end up back home in Newark— lurking in shadows of streets he had walked more than a century ago. The train station where he used to pluck victims was long gone. But the dark alleys behind modern drinking establishments had proven quite fruitful.

He had found the boy trailing behind a group of other young bucks wearing sports uniforms. His attempts at combat had been admirable, and his life force was vibrant. It was a struggle for Zaybris to hold back when taking nourishment, but he had managed. The stakes were too high. Every precaution had to be taken to ensure the boy's survival on the journey to Aurelia.

When Zaybris came to the dungeon's first cell, he kicked the steel door open. Once inside, he laid the boy upon a cot, careful not to damage the precious cargo. Glancing around the dim room, he grunted with satisfaction. Besides the cot, there was a small table and chair, chamber pot, and a set of chains bolted to the wall.

He could no longer discern temperature, but he reasoned it must be cold in the dungeon. He would call the Goblyns to bring down tea and hot food for his guest.

"A meal for my meal," he mused, chuckling to himself.

When Zaybris leaned down to remove the boy's shoes, the white stone suspended from a cord around his neck swung out, reminding him to tuck it safely away beneath his shirt's ruffled tie. The stone tingled against his fingers, and he gave a silent prayer of thanks that God had put such a gift in his hands.

While he adjusted the bedding, he murmured, "I think I shall call you Adam, since you are the first." Tugging at the white bedsheets, he smoothed them up over the boy's body. "Fear not, sweet Adam, you will soon have others to keep you company. For it is not good for a man to be alone."

Only after he had the human neatly tucked in and comfortable did he pull a torch from the wall to fully illuminate his prize and savior of his race.

His gaze traveled from the boy's feet then to his broad chest. Adam's collar was ripped, though Zaybris didn't remember being so rough with him. Two ragged holes, brown with crusted blood, marred the side of his neck, but that was to be expected.

Zaybris held the torch closer and frowned as he observed the ashen tint to Adam's skin and the stiffness of the boy's limbs. Gathering his strength, Zaybris leaned back to take in Adam's face.

Dull, glassy eyes stared up at him—void of any light. Mouth frozen in an eternal scream. His chest failed to rise. Zaybris touched his wrist and found no pulse.

He was dead.

Zaybris had failed to bring a living human into Aurelia.

Again.

Blind with rage, he flipped the cot over, watching as the body fell to the floor like a soiled handkerchief. This angered him even further, so he picked the corpse up and threw it against the stone wall. A dull thud echoed throughout the cell as his boot made contact with the dead boy's stomach. Zaybris roared for his servants.

Sinking to the floor, Zaybris looked down at his hands. There was still a bit of Adam's blood crusted under his long fingernails. He licked at it, then watched, ruefully, as three black spots of decay slowly faded from his knuckles. The skin knitted together and became smooth, almost alive-looking. Yet it was bittersweet. For what good was the regenerative power of human blood when he could not secure a continuous source?

He let out a hopeless moan. Since returning to Aurelia a month ago to crown himself king, this was his tenth attempt to bring back a human. Young or old, man or woman, weak or strong—each one had died upon arrival. His problem was something like a riddle. He needed to immobilize a human enough with his bite that he could carry them into Aurelia. Yet by doing so, he drained his victims of the strength necessary to survive the inter-dimensional journey.

After several minutes three Goblyns appeared outside the cell, watching him with big, frightened eyes.

"Take care of this. Burn it," Zaybris said, gesturing to the body. When the Goblyns failed to jump at his command, his melancholy mood turned savage. "What are you waiting for? Clean this cell, clean everything. And how dare you let the dungeon turn to rot? Explain yourselves."

After a heavy silence, one of the female Goblyns stepped forward. "W-when our radiant Queen Lilith disappeared we... "

Zaybris let out a howl that made the chains in the cell vibrate. Pointing an accusatory finger, he said, "I told you never to mention her name in my presence!"

The Goblyns nodded fearfully.

"Your purpose is to serve your vampiric betters. Not reminisce over your lost queen."

"Yes, my king," all three of the Goblyns whispered.

A cruel smile played across Zaybris's face as he rose to his feet. "I should punish you for such disrespect. In fact... " He reached down to grab the Goblyn who spoke by her throat. Pushing her against the wall, he sunk his fangs into her thin neck.

He took only one pull of her blood before abruptly dropping her to the ground. Fighting the urge to spit out the bitter liquid that filled his mouth, he forced himself to swallow.

It was foolish to have drunk so soon after imbibing human blood. Like drinking castor oil after sipping champagne. Damn Aurelians! He wiped the blood from his mouth with his sleeve then reached up to run his fingers through his hair. He felt a clump break off, along with a bit of scalp. Staring at the limp strands in the center of his palm, he cried out in despair.

In life, he had taken great pride in his golden locks. Each morning he would carefully style his hair with a part on the left, with thick blond waves swept back on the right. Sometimes it flopped over his eye, giving him what he believed to be a roguish air. It was his most attractive feature, and he had always been loathe to cover it up under a hat when fashion dictated.

Now it was completely white. It hung in stringy waves, barely touching the shoulders of his velvet frock coat. And each day, there was less of it. *Decomposition.* The word made him shudder. He threw the hair to the ground with a snarl, hating how the magnitude of his failure was symbolized at that moment.

He left the terrified Goblyns to clean up the cell and stormed down the dungeon hall. There had to be another way.

Failure was unthinkable.

CHAPTER 11

Selene had been dreading her first night sleeping next to a demon, but she had to admit that Sam was a perfect gentleman. He helped her expand her tent, then set up his hammock before wishing her goodnight, and that was that. She kept waiting for her intuition to kick in and tell her she needed to keep her guard up around him, but the feeling never came. Her exhaustion and the gentle hum of Aurelia's forest insects made sleep come easily.

The next morning, after eating something that resembled a puffy empanada from the switch pouch, they continued their journey. As big as Sam was, he moved easily over rocks and inclines while Selene struggled with her footing. The outskirts of Queen Thema's forests were not as hospitable as the land closer to the castle. A few times, Selene's slow pace caused her to bump into Sam. He was always ready to catch her arm when she stumbled, but when she tripped on a tree root and fell back against his chest, she hoped he mistook her breathlessness for exertion.

The man—no, demon—felt like a warm brick wall. Solid and unyielding, yet exuding a heat that made Selene want to curl up against him and purr like a kitten. When his arm snaked around her waist to keep her upright, her insides dipped with pleasure. Selene had always thought she preferred men with slim, athletic builds, but there was something very appealing about all the muscle and power pressed against her.

Stop acting like a swooning idiot.

"Are you all right?" Sam breathed against her ear, still holding her tight.

He smelled like pine needles and leather. The close contact made Selene feel slightly dizzy, yet she managed to say, "Yes, thank you. I'm just not used to hiking like this."

Slowly, Sam loosened his arm and stepped back. "You will gain endurance with time."

As they continued at a slow but steady pace, the sky that had been clear that morning darkened with rain clouds in the afternoon. First, a light drizzle dampened their clothes. Then the raindrops grew heavier. After an hour, they were both soaked. Thunder rumbled in the distance.

Selene wiped the rain from her face and said to Sam, "Should we stop and get inside the tent?"

"The winds could destroy it," he replied. "We must keep moving, or we'll sink into the mud. The rain should pass us soon."

Selene trudged next to Sam, keeping her head down in a useless attempt to keep water from running into her eyes. Rain continued to pound at them, and Selene's thighs ached with the effort of pulling her boot out of the mud with each step.

I hate this. I hate this. I want to go home. I hate this.

Carefully, they climbed over slippery rocks and pushed drooping tree branches out of their path. When they reached a fast-moving creek, Sam held out a hand to stop Selene. The stream was about four feet wide and full of sticks, leaves, and other debris.

"There's no way around it. We have to cross," Sam shouted since the rain had made it hard to hear. "I'll go first, then help you across."

Selene watched Sam stretch one long leg across the creek, then the other. Once he had safely crossed, he turned and held out his arms for Selene. Tentatively, she stretched and clasped his hands. But just as she readied herself to leap across, the bank crumbled under Sam's feet. He fell forward into the creek, pulling Selene down with him.

They both floundered in the water and mud for a moment, trying to get their bearings as the rain battered them. The creek was shallow, but water was racing faster over them, making Selene fear a flash flood was approaching. The creek bed was like mush underneath her, making it difficult to stand. Sam was on his back with his head submerged, struggling to sit up. Selene could see that his backpack was hung on a tree branch wedged below the water.

Using all her strength, Selene pulled herself up from the mud. Then she reached through the rushing water to find the branch restraining Sam. She pulled as hard as she could until she felt the wood snap, and to Selene's relief, Sam bolted upright. From there, he quickly shot to his feet. Grabbing Selene around the waist, he lifted her and practically tossed her to the other side of the creek as if she were a ragdoll. He then pulled himself out of the water and onto solid ground.

"Are you hurt?" he shouted at Selene. His palms skimmed down her arms, like he was checking her for injuries.

"Fine. Are you?" she shouted back. When he cupped her jaw to examine her face, she didn't dare meet his eyes. She didn't want him to see how his touch affected her.

"Fine. Let's get to higher ground. It's not safe here."

Selene pushed the muddy strands of hair from her face and wondered why she had ever thought thunderstorms were comforting. Sam extended his hand, and the feel of his solid palm against hers melted away some of the terror she had just felt at being nearly swept away.

Sam led them through the forest until, at last, the rain tapered to a gentle sprinkle. Rays of the late afternoon sun peaked through the trees. When they reached a patch of semi-dry land near a pond, Sam suggested they stop for the night. Selene dropped her backpack to the ground, then tried to stomp off the mud from her boots.

"That was absolutely awful. Does it rain like that often here?"

"Occasionally," Sam said. He grabbed handful of fabric from his tunic and squeezed out a steady stream of water. "Thank you for freeing my pack from that branch."

She smiled, "Thank *you* for pulling me out of the creek. Good teamwork, huh?" She plucked at her filthy clothes and hair self-consciously. "I must look like a drowned rat."

"You don't," Sam replied. He looked as though he was going to say more but stopped himself. After a pause, he said, "Go wash up in that pond. I'll set your tent up so you can change into dry clothes."

Since Selene didn't think it was the best idea to get naked in an open field in a strange dimension, she attempted to give herself a fully-clothed sponge bath. When that went nowhere, she submerged herself in the pond's clear water. Tiny pink fish swirled around her curiously. The air was growing colder as nightfall approached, making her teeth chatter when she emerged. The pond wasn't exactly pristine, but it was wonderful to be free of all that mud.

After sloshing her way back to their campsite and taking her time to change in the tent, she stepped out to see Sam building a fire. His hair and horns were wet, and he was wearing different clothes, which sparked a pang of regret that she'd missed seeing him shirtless. The thought surprised her. She had never been the type to ogle male bodies, especially when it was someone she barely knew.

Who am I turning into?

Sam glanced up at her. "Feeling better?"

"Much. Are you all right?"

"Yes."

Selene settled in by the fire, grateful that the awkward tension between them from yesterday was gone. Apparently, tumbling into a flooded creek together was a great icebreaker. When her stomach growled, Selene asked, "The switch pouch wasn't damaged by the water, was it?"

"No, our meal should arrive soon." Sam said. He seemed to study her face for a moment. "You seem very calm for what we just went through."

Selene gave a little laugh. "You're not the first person to say something like that. Don't worry, all my wild emotions are there. I've just learned to keep them to myself."

"You find it easy to control your emotions?"

"Not always. It's a habit, I guess," she said. Sam looked at her as if he wanted to know more, and unexpectedly she found herself elaborating. "I grew up in a home with a lot of chaos. My dad traveled for work constantly, and my mom... my mom struggled with a lot of issues. She *still* struggles with a lot of issues. If I wanted to get anything done, I couldn't go around acting hysterical."

"Was your mother ill?" Sam added wood to the small fire, making it crackle between them.

"In a way, yes. She found it hard to keep sober while taking care of herself, her business, and her three kids. Since I was the oldest, I ended up doing many of the things she couldn't."

"Like what?"

Selene tapped her chin. "Let's see, I was eleven when I started waking up at 5:00 in the morning to get the twins ready for school. They were late so often, their kindergarten teacher had sent home three notes and called twice. The last phone call triggered a huge fight between my parents, so I took the twins across the street to the local library until the fight blew over."

She swallowed, realizing Sam was the first person she had ever told this story. "Later, after everyone had gone to bed, I moved the alarm clock from the guest room to my nightstand. The twins were never late for school again."

When Sam didn't say anything for a moment Selene asked, "Do they have alarm clocks in Aurelia?"

"No, but I understood your meaning. Eleven is young for such responsibilities."

"I guess so. But I loved my siblings, and it was harder to see them struggle than to just take care of things. They really needed someone in their lives to do that."

A *pop* startled Selene as the switch pouch bulged with food. Sam pulled out a covered dish for each of them, and the aroma of roasted meat and spices filled the air. They ate in silence until Selene said, "Sam, I really appreciate you taking me on this journey. It kills me to think about how my family is coping. They must think I've been abducted or murdered and are completely losing it right now. I'll be so glad to get back to them."

Sam shifted his weight on the ground from one hip to the other. "I'm sorry that Queen Thema could not send you home directly."

"Me too. What do you know about this Zaybris person we're trying to find?"

Sam looked at her sharply. "What did Queen Thema tell you about him?"

"Not much. Just that he's a vampire who owes her a favor. She said she would send him a message to say we are coming, but then she hurried off. We didn't have much time to talk."

Gruffly, Sam said, "He is a vampire who lives in Goblyn lands, and he has a stone that can send you back to Gaia."

"Is it a magic stone?"

"It is enchanted, yes."

"Why does a vampire have something like that instead of one of the queens?"

"I don't know."

"Do you think we'll run into any vampires on our trip? I'd love to see one. They're believed to be a myth where I come from."

"Not if I can help it."

"Should I be scared of them?"

"No, they are all feeble and powerless. Nothing to worry about." Sam began to eat more quickly. "Finish your meal. It's getting late."

Selene took another bite of the stew that tasted like Thanksgiving dinner in a bowl. "How long have vampires been in Aurelia?"

"Many, many years." He cleared his throat. "Do you work a trade in your world? What occupations are common for humans?"

Selene thought it was odd that Sam was changing the subject so abruptly but didn't comment. "I work in an office. We sell medical supplies to healthcare providers. My job is to... " She tried to think of how to explain Human Resources to someone completely unfamiliar with the term. "I deal with a lot of paperwork, and people come to me hoping I can solve their problems. The office is probably such a mess right now. They can barely use the coffee maker without my help."

There was a rustle in the grass behind them. Sam quickly turned and let out a growl that gave Selene chills. A little creature that looked like a rabbit with deer antlers peeked up at them before nibbling on a blade of grass. Sam relaxed. Selene strained her eyes to see in the dark then said, "Is that a jackalope?"

"It is called a brisby in Aurelia," Sam said.

Selene watched the animal hop around for a moment before disappearing behind a tree. "Another thing that's just a legend in my world. I so wish Evan could see this, he'd be absolutely thrilled." A fresh wave of anxiety washed over her, and she rubbed her forehead. "I hope he remembered that his license plate expires this month. He always seems to forget and then gets a ticket he can't afford to pay."

Sam gave her a pointed look. "You don't need to concern yourself with the needs of others right now," he said quietly. "Enjoy the time you have in this realm."

Selene sighed and took the last bite of her stew.

Easier said than done.

CHAPTER 12

On their sixth day of traveling together Sam had to admit to himself that Selene was nothing like he had originally expected. Although she was human, she wasn't fragile. He knew their journey's exertions made her weary, but she never complained. She was conscientious with her gear, and prompt if he gave her a morning departure time. Their unexpected moments of close contact when Selene lost her balance or stumbled only fueled his fascination with her. He found himself reaching out to steady her more often than he should.

Each night, he set up the campsite and built a fire while she prepared what came through the switch pouch for serving. It had been easy for them to fall into a routine. So far, everything had gone according to plan. Besides the rainstorm, their trek had been without dangers, until now.

The Padu.

Apprehension slithered down Sam's spine as faint strains of music, and the aroma of smoked meat drifted through the valley. His legs became heavy with dread.

"Is that a carnival or something?" Selene asked, pointing to the cluster of brightly colored tents ahead.

Sam calculated how much time they would lose if they took a different route. They couldn't go west; a large lake blocked their way. An eastern detour was possible, but it was swampy terrain. He inwardly cursed himself for not checking the Padu schedule when planning their route.

"Sam?"

He glanced down at her questioning face. "It's the Padu."

"Is it a town? Whatever's cooking up there smells amazing."

"It's the Padu traveling market," Sam said tightly. "Changes position every new moon."

"Wow, that sounds fun. What do they sell?"

He shrugged. "Market things."

Selene gave him a puzzled look, but he didn't elaborate. She didn't need to know the full extent of Padu's nature. There were many legitimate merchants at Padu—sellers of beautiful silks, rare jewels, and finely-crafted weaponry. But then there were other traders, ones that took advantage of Padu's transitory state to avoid scrutiny for their dark dealings.

Sam rubbed his thumb against the knives he kept strapped to his belt. He had thought he had only remembered flashes of color and noise from his time in Padu. A purple tent with black stripes. Shouting voices and jangling coins. Dust sticking to his bloodied feet. But the rhythmic drumming and smell of vinegar and garlic brought back many images and sensations he would prefer to forget.

Selene brushed back strands of hair from her face. "I'd kill for a hair tie. Or even a ribbon. Do you think we could pick up something like that there?"

Although Sam liked seeing the wind play with her loose hair, he knew she craved a way to restrain it. A few days ago, she had tried to twist the tawny-colored mass into a bun secured by a twig, but pieces kept sliding out.

"You can buy anything in Padu, but we're not stopping there," he said.

"Why not?"

"I don't want to."

"But... isn't it on our way?"

"We're taking a different route now. See that fork in the road ahead? We'll go east instead."

She seemed to consider this as they walked. After a moment, she asked, "Couldn't we just stop for a moment? Ten minutes tops."

Sam waited until a furry old Lycah pushing a jangling cart of pots passed them on the road before replying, "No. Put your Nereid cream on. We don't need everyone here knowing you're human."

She pulled out the jar from her pack and began to apply the fish scale cream to her face.

Their path had become more heavily trafficked as they approached the split in the road. As usual, Sam's size and appearance attracted many curious stares. Children stopped playing to watch him with wide eyes, while the adults either drew back in fear or tried to avoid eye contact.

The drumming grew louder and was now accompanied by off-key singing as they continued down the road. A Nereid male balancing a tray of seashells on his head splashed his face with a bottle of water as their paths crossed. When he noticed Selene's attention on him, he bowed. The tray didn't even jostle while drips of water streamed from his chin. Plucking a tiny cockleshell from his collection of goods, he presented it to Selene.

Sam shook his head. "No. We're not buying today."

The Nereid's silvery eyes twinkled. "A gift. No charge."

Selene accepted the shell, then gave a delighted smile to the Nereid. Sam felt a simmer of envy. *Witless fish creature.* He wanted to be the one causing that reaction.

After tucking the shell into her pocket, Selene said, "I've never seen anything like this."

Sam was about to repeat how they were not stopping, but her

expression made him pause. The yearning she had to explore the market was clear, and yet she did not voice it again. Something about that bothered him. He felt a pull—deep and instinctual. A sudden overwhelming need to indulge her. To please and satisfy. To be the male, the only male, that could give her what she desired. It was disturbing... but undeniable.

"Would Kevin P. Norton take you if he were here?" he asked.

"Kevin? Not a chance," she said with a laugh. "He'd say we don't need to buy any more junk, or he'd spend the whole time worrying he'd get his wallet stolen."

"Demons don't abide theft," Sam replied. "Fine. Let's go to Padu then. But we can't stay long."

"Yay!" she cried. Sam ducked his head to hide how his lips quirked at the joy he felt in seeing her excitement. Delighting her could prove addictive.

As the Padu came into focus, Sam tried to put aside his memories to see the market through Selene's eyes. It was vibrant, the air heated with life. Aurelians of all races were laughing, arguing, haggling, or shouting across the stalls. The aroma of sugar and butter eclipsed the smoked meat smell as they passed a cake stand. Jugglers walked up and down the aisles while artists offered to capture each passer-by's likeness on canvas. Sam worried some of the older merchants might recognize him, but they only viewed him as a potential buyer.

"Lady! Come touch! My silks are the best in Aurelia! Come see!" a Drago with heavily scaled eyelids called to Selene from her wooden cart.

Selene shook her head, but Sam led her over to the assortment of silk scarves. "You can look," he said.

He watched Selene run swathes of fabric between her fingers. The Drago leaned over to drape several scarves across Selene's shoulders, praising her fairness. She laughed off the compliment, and Sam wondered with a flash of anger who had taught her to deny her beauty.

On impulse, he decided he would buy her a gift. Anything she wanted. Perhaps she would look at him the way she did when that Nereid gave her a shell. It was a foolish notion, but he didn't care. Those in the market probably assumed he and Selene were mates, traveling together as they were. There was nothing unusual about a mate buying his treasured one something she desired.

The sky blue silk seemed to be the one she liked best, but when Sam offered to buy it, Selene refused, indicating she was ready to move on.

Next, they came upon a flower cart, bursting with fragrant blooms. He watched Selene linger over each blossom and briefly considered buying her a floral crown or garland. Yet he held back. He wanted his gift to be something more substantial.

He thought he had found such a gift when they approached a group of jewelers. It was crowded with Aurelians of wealth, judging by their clothes and grooming. Sam watched Selene's face while she looked over the bracelets, earrings, and rings. When she touched a pearled necklace, Sam asked, a little too eagerly, "Do you like that? Why don't you try it on?"

"Nah, it's a bit too elegant for me. I'd probably lose it or break it," Selene said.

Sam was about to protest that she deserved *only* the most elegant of adornments when something to their left caught her attention. "Oooo—soap!" she cried.

He followed Selene away from the jewelry toward a cart full of scented soaps. She held each bar to her nose.

"Mmm, this is nice—smells like leather and rose. What's this one?" She read the label on each basket. "This one smells like... coffee and old books. How do you bottle that?"

"My own recipe," the Malkina female behind the table murmured.

"They're beautiful. Oh, this one is like fresh pumpkin. And this one smells like tea with milk!" Selene closed her eyes to inhale. When she opened them to find Sam watching her, she asked, "Why are you looking at me like that?"

"I've never seen anyone so excited about soap." He took a step closer. "Tell me which ones you want. I'll buy them."

"No, I already have a big bar Hollen packed for me."

"I want to," Sam said in a voice that came out more husky than he intended. He held her gaze before she looked away.

"All right," she said. "Thank you."

"Pick out a bar for me too. I'm running low."

She continued to sniff bars, until Sam had to turn his head away to hide his amusement. *Most females covet jewels, but mine yearns for soap.* His smile quickly fell. *Stop this. She is not yours.*

"Okay," Selene tested each scent, until finally, she said, "Here. This one smells like you."

He took the green bar she offered and held it his nose. The pine scent was easily detected, but he also caught woodsmoke, along with a hint of elder bark and black ironwood. It was a very agreeable scent, but with a pleasing breath of darkness lurking below. The idea that he would be immersing himself in a scent that she preferred, one that she had chosen just for him, was intoxicating. Provocative.

"I'll take all of them," Sam said, gesturing to the nearly ten bars in the basket Selene had pulled from. "And as many as the lady would like too."

"Whoa, I don't need that many!" Selene protested. "I can't even decide which one is my favorite."

He was about to tell her to get one of each, then he paused. He became beset with the desire to choose for her. To know that she would be bathed in a scent that *he* preferred—one that would touch every inch of her skin. Perhaps it would make her think of him when she smelled it.

He held each bar to his nose. They all seemed cloyingly floral, until he sniffed a creamy dark pink one. It was a blend of vanilla, citrus and a berry scent that reminded him of her alluring pomegranate scent.

"This one," he said.

The soap maker only had three bars in stock, so he bought all of them too.

"Thank you, Sam," Selene said. The usual warmth that came from hearing his name on her lips spread throughout his body. His anxiety about being back at Padu became overshadowed by an enormous sense of satisfaction.

They walked up and down more stalls, stopping at the food row to buy a few things to complement their meals. When they stepped away from a tea vendor, Sam saw a stall selling elaborate hats, hair pieces, and combs.

"Look! Hair devices," he said to Selene.

Selene described what she was looking for to the merchant. As they talked, Sam noticed a young Lycah hovering by a nearby baker's stand. He was shabbily dressed with dark hollows under his eyes. His lupine face was pockmarked, and his shoes were too big for his feet. The boy looked around but did not notice Sam watching him. He approached a small table of bread loaves and quickly grabbed one to stuff under his ragged tunic.

Sam's entire body rippled as his instincts for vengeance roared to life.

Stealing!

Sam glanced at the baker to see if she had noticed the theft. Was she about to respond accordingly? If she did, his urges would cool, knowing that vengeance had been served. Yet her attention was turned toward the ovens.

Punish him, a voice whispered in his head. *He's getting away.*

No, Sam thought, he doesn't deserve it. He's only a sick boy.

Grab him, take all that he has.

Sam's breaths came quickly. His eyes bored into the back of the young man's head.

Chase him, catch him. Make him feel the betrayal and loss born of theft.

Another part of his mind pleaded, *no, not in front of Selene.* Sam wiped his sweaty palms against his tunic. The smell of fresh bread faded as he remembered the vinegary meat they were fed when the blood wagons stopped at Padu. The music and laughter of children running past turned into screams and pleas for mercy. His body became overwhelmed with the need to punish, even though his mind knew it was unwarranted.

Crush his bones, rip his skin, the voice said.

Breathe, focus, control, he chanted to himself, desperate for a reprieve. But his demonic instincts were too strong. He was sick with dread at the violence he knew was about to unfold.

All other thoughts fell, and he became consumed with need. With clenched fists, he closed his eyes, gathered his strength for attack. His powerful body tensed like the predator he was, and when he opened his eyes, his vision clouded with crimson. Heat flooded his body, readying him for combat. He focused in on the boy darting among the hundreds of Aurelians in the crowd.

Nothing else mattered at that moment. He had forgotten where he was or how he had gotten there. Time was irrelevant, and the atmosphere had become a void. All that existed was a demon and his prey.

Make him pay.

CHAPTER 13

Sam's body tensed to charge toward his target until a sound made him hesitate.

"Sam?"

He paused to listen again. The voice was hollow and seemed to come from far away.

"Sam, what's wrong?"

Someone was calling to him. He cocked his head, trying to determine its origin. Who would call to him, here in Aurelia? He was alone in this realm. He had always been. Who was here with him? Pushing past his urge to bolt toward the boy, he looked around.

Through his red haze of vengeance, he saw someone staring up at him, her brows knitted with concern. Her eyes were dazzling blue, her lips moist and pink. She was speaking, but he couldn't make out her words. She wasn't frightened of him and stood very close.

Why was she so near, Sam wondered. Females never came this close to him. Especially one so beautiful. Sam was about to tell her to run, to get away from him as quickly as she could and hide.

But then something cool touched his arm. She seemed to speak again. He felt the same sensation, but stronger, on the back of his hand. A delicious chill, like new snow. He leaned into the feeling, greedy for more. It bloomed gradually, creeping outwards from his arm into his chest, down to his stomach and legs. Its sharpness was crisp and clean.

He exhaled raggedly.

Lightness. The oppressive weight clawing at him suddenly lessened. The fury was cooling, the pull was easing, and the feelings of powerlessness, of being a slave to his nature dwindled.

It took him a moment before he remembered where he was. He was in Padu, but no crowds were watching him. No taunts or coins thrown at him. His feet were still planted where he stood, and he had not taken off through the market to inflict pain against his own will.

He had worked hard to control his impulses, but there were times when they simply spiraled beyond his control. And yet, for the first time in his life, he pulled himself back from the brink. He hadn't acted on his impulses at all, which meant there was no innocent blood on his hands.

A gentle breeze cooled the sweat dotting his forehead. He blinked as his vision returned to normal.

The beautiful female standing in front of him was Selene. Looking down, he saw her hand rested against his sleeve. Her other hand held his; her fingers curled gently around his tight fist. Skin to skin. With a rush of heat to his groin, he understood.

It was her. Like murk beetles scattering at a beam of light, Sam's need to hurt and punish had retreated. His mind cleared, and his will restored the moment Selene had touched him.

Sam's furious need for vengeance was abruptly replaced by desire. Hot, heavy, and urgent. Blood pulsed in his loins and desire clouded his thoughts. Boldly, he took Selene's hand and covered it with his, holding her in place. Savoring the feel of her bare flesh against his. Waiting until whatever calming effect she seemed to provide dissolved every last drop of his violent flare.

Closer.

He needed more. More of her touch. Her attention. The relief she brought.

He wanted to tear off his sleeve, shirt, and everything he wore, to have her run her soft hand over every inch of his body. He wanted to lift her onto the stall's surface so he could press more of himself against her. To grind his cock against her soft heat. He imagined laying her down in the forest, all barriers shed between them, to cover her body with his. To touch her and make her understand the effect she had on him. To see if he could bring *her* a fraction of the pleasure she had bestowed upon him.

They stood there silently for a moment, her small hand pressed between his large palms. She stared back with wide eyes, seeming to understand something significant had occurred but not knowing exactly what.

"Are you all right?" she whispered.

He nodded, unwilling to speak for fear that the lust coursing through him would show in the rumble of his voice. Despite his fantasies, reality was beginning to set in.

"What happened?" she asked.

Swallowing, he tried to think of a plausible explanation. He glanced at the nearby bread ovens. "The heat... I... "

"Good sir, can I help you with anything for your flowing locks?" the Goblyn hair device seller asked cheerfully while twining a ribbon around his spindly fingers.

Sam shot him a glower that made all color drain from the Goblyn's weathered face. Sam reluctantly released Selene's hand and said, "No."

"Are you sure you're okay?" Selene said. "You were so tense and seemed a bit woozy."

Sam straightened his posture. "Whatever 'woozy' is, I can assure you I do not suffer from it. Did you find what you needed?"

She held up a small bundle of thin leather ribbons. "Yep."

Sam paid for the items quickly, desperately wanting to leave Padu. The noise, the smell, the memories were all too much. He craved the quiet of the forest and the anonymity of darkness. He glanced up at the sky with unease. It was later than he anticipated. Sunset was imminent, and the vampires that frequented Padu were surely about to emerge.

"We need to leave this place," Sam said.

"Hmm? Oh yes. I'm finished. Thank you for letting us stop," she said. She seemed distracted after their strange interlude.

As he led her out of Padu, they ignored the vendors calling out offers of discounts and deals. The sky was growing darker, and Sam knew the switch pouch would expand soon with their dinner, but it would have to wait. He wanted more distance between Padu and their campsite.

They had nearly reached the last of Padu's stalls and were only steps away from the forest's embrace when their path was suddenly blocked. A petite figure in a red wool cloak stood in front of them, eerily motionless. Sam could tell by her bearing she was female, but a hood covered her face.

"Step aside," Sam said, but the obstacle didn't budge. He studied the stranger's slight build and the strands of black hair peeking out from beneath her hood. Then he caught a whiff of her perfume and froze. He knew that scent. The essence of violet water couldn't mask the odor of moldering flesh that hung in the air. The woman let out a creaky giggle.

Sam sighed. Had he really believed he could pass through Padu without anyone recognizing him?

"Margery," he said flatly.

The woman held up one finger, in a gesture that indicated *wait*. She remained motionless until the last sliver of sunlight was swallowed up by the horizon. Then, as if she were a stone statue gifted with life, she lifted her head to bare her face to the night.

Breathlessly she said, "Samael. You've come back."

~

Selene stood at Sam's side, wondering who or *what* this Margery person was. She was still reeling from the intense moment she and Sam had just shared at the hair stand, and having him stand so close wasn't helping her nerves. Selene squinted. Since they were in the darkest part of the market, she couldn't make out Margery's features. She could only see that she wore a lot of red—from the toe of her boots up to the hood of her cloak, like a demented Little Red Riding Hood.

"I haven't come back," Sam said. "We're leaving."

"So soon?" Margery made a disappointed sound, then gave Sam an appraising look. "You seem different. Less unhinged."

"And you haven't changed a bit."

"Naturally." She laughed, the sound as thin and sticky as a cobweb. "What brings you to Padu? Last I heard you were living like a beast in the forest."

"I have been serving the Malkina queen."

"The Malkina. Interesting choice."

"They have been good to me. Unlike others in this realm."

"You know it was all Julian's doing. I did what I had to just to survive," she said heatedly. "Come, let me show you my tent on the East row. People pay good money for my bite."

"Let us pass."

She sniffed the air, then focused on Selene. "Who's this?"

Unable to repress her Southern manners, Selene stretched out her hand to say, "Hi, it's nice to meet..." but the words faded as a nearby vendor lit a torch, fully illuminating the mysterious Margery.

At first glance, she was stunning. Glittering rubies dripped from her pale throat, perfectly matched to her cloak, dress, lipstick, and gloves. Her black hair was parted in the middle, with the ends brushing against a jeweled belt at her waist. Heavy eyeliner and thick eyelashes framed her eerie gray eyes. Yet the longer Selene looked at her, the more she realized there was something very wrong about her face. Something was wrong with everything.

Margery's cheekbones were bloated and misshapen, her lips

absurdly puffy. Her eyebrows were painted on at an unnaturally high angle, and the skin around her eyes was pulled tight across her skull. And that wealth of thick black hair? Clearly a wig.

Selene thought it might be a trick of the light, but when Margery turned her face, the effect was worse. She looked like a gothic plastic surgery nightmare. Normally, Selene felt pity when she saw the extreme lengths some people went to appear beautiful, but Margery was simply terrifying. She wasn't Little Red Riding Hood at all—this was the Big Bad Wolf.

"A Nereid girl. Isn't she lovely?" Margery crooned at Selene. "Oddly dressed though. Have you ever heard of *gowns*, darling? Or are you in disguise as some sort of pauper?"

"Don't speak to her," Sam warned Margery.

"I don't take orders from anyone but *me* now," Margery shot back. One of her odd eyebrows rose even higher when she looked back at Selene. "Oh, little minnow, you smell *delicious*. What's that scent you're wearing?"

Some instinctual drive was urging Selene to run, that she was being sized up as prey.

"It's soap you scent," Sam said quickly. "We visited a soap merchant,"

Margery smiled and the movement caused a crack to appear in the layers of pancake make-up she wore. A long, yellowed fang was revealed as Margery bit her lip hungrily, making Selene's body jerk.

Vampire.

This was it. She was real. A true predator and monster of legend, right in front of her. Except she didn't look anything like the glamorous lady vampires with porcelain skin and perfect bodies from the movies. The decay and corruption of Margery's flesh made it clear— she was one of the living dead.

Margery inhaled again. "There's something so familiar... you're sure it's just soap I scent?" she asked, her voice dropping.

Sam didn't respond to Margery's question with words. Instead, he took a step behind Selene and rested his warm palms on her shoulders. It was an undeniable gesture of possessiveness, a signal she was under his protection. Despite the terror of being ogled by a vampire, a rush of pleasure tingled through Selene at his touch.

"Don't worry, demon, I know I'm in your debt," Margery said irritably, flipping back her hair. "Though she certainly doesn't *smell* Nereid."

This made Selene uneasy. What would happen if she guessed she was human? But she reminded herself she was cloaked with a face full of glitter and had looked Nereid enough to have fooled the man who gave her a cockle shell. There was a beat of silence before Sam said, "I'm glad you're doing well for yourself."

Margery adjusted her velvet gloves. "Well, let's just say single life agrees with me. As does freedom, so thank you for that. There are more of us here from the wagons, did you know? Not only vampires—"

"I don't care." Sam interrupted. "Are you going to leave us now?"

Sighing, Margery said, "Yes, I suppose." Giving her cape a dramatic twirl, she turned to walk away. "Farewell Vengeance demon and... ," she looked pointedly at Selene. "You."

"Farewell, Margery," Sam said.

CHAPTER 14

The forest seemed unnaturally bright as residual light from Padu streamed through the trees. Selene walked quickly, with Sam close behind. She would have sprinted if her legs didn't feel so unsteady.

Keeping her voice low she said, "Margery is a vampire, isn't she?"

"Yes," Sam said.

"She was terrifying!"

"But harmless."

"I felt like she wanted to bite me or something," she said, shuddering.

"Perhaps, but I wouldn't have let her. No vampire will bother us as long we stay in the forest at night. They keep close to towns and villages to feed."

"Wait, that's why we always stop at sunset? I thought it was a camping thing."

"Traveling by daylight is preferred for visibility, yes."

"Well, obviously," Selene said, feeling stupid. "But you told me vampires were all old and harmless. She was old, but definitely did not seem harmless. How do you know her?"

"From long ago," he said evasively.

"When?"

"A time in my life before I came to Queen Thema's."

"What were you doing?"

His steps slowed. "I don't wish to say any more on the matter. Let's stop here and make camp."

Although Selene had known Sam for about a week, she had learned it was pointless to push when he didn't want to talk. She let the subject drop, vowing to grill him further another day. Selene shrugged off her backpack and sat on the ground. "Can we just rest for a minute? I'm a bit rattled."

"Certainly. Stay there and relax. I'll set up camp."

"I can help, I just need—"

"Rest," Sam said sternly. "Hand me your pack."

Selene complied. Sam pulled out her tent and set it to inflate, then he gathered firewood. He refilled their water jugs then set a pot to boil for tea. When the switch pouch expanded with a fish pie, Selene tried to set out their dishes, but Sam wouldn't hear of it. Instead, he made her a cup of mint tea, handed her one of his blankets, and told her not to get up again.

Normally, she felt guilty if she wasn't pitching in, but it was actually nice to just surrender. It wasn't as if he thought she was being lazy or selfish, he was simply giving her a break. She pulled off her boots and stretched her toes. The stress of meeting Margery dissolved as she watched the muscles of Sam's back shift while he strung up his hammock.

His size had been intimidating at first, but now she marveled at the way he carried himself. It was like he knew exactly what his strengths and weaknesses were and had trained his body to perform.

When he tied the hammock strap into knots, his face clouded with concentration. She sipped her tea, studying him. Although he wasn't traditionally handsome—wide jaw, deep-set eyes, and cheekbones too sharp to be human—she found his features appealing. Oh, and those horns. *Yum.*

Yet it wasn't only his looks she liked. He was so damn *capable*. There wasn't anything he didn't seem to know how to do. Not only could he tell time by the sun and make fire without a match, he could catch a fish, cook it, and do the dishes. All without complaining, needing help, or expecting showers of praise from her. Unlike someone else she knew...

She wasn't being unfair to Kevin, she told her herself. She was just noticing differences. Before the whole "let's press pause" thing happened, one of the things she liked about Kevin was there was no ambiguity with him. Unlike her parents' evolving expectations, she knew exactly what Kevin needed from her. The best way to show her love was by supporting what *he* loved—his music. It was exciting to date a musician, but before he went on tour, her to-do list for Kevin's career often felt like a part-time job. She was the brains of the Kevin P. Norton singer/songwriter brand, while he was the heart and soul. Yet now that she was in Aurelia, Selene found she quite liked spending time with a completely self-sufficient man—one who really didn't need her at all.

She wrapped Sam's blanket around her shoulders while he dished up their dinner. She studied his beefy forearms and wondered why she had never seen him without the leather bracers covering his wrists or asked him how he received the large scar that ran down his right eyebrow. Actually, she knew very little about him. After he passed her a full plate, Selene said, "May I ask you a personal question?"

Sam narrowed his eyes, suddenly feeling guarded. "You may."

"Why did you come to Aurelia from the Underworld?"

He blinked. "Queen Thema didn't tell you?"

"Was it to be special bodyguard for her?"

"No."

"Then why?"

Sam ran his palm over his face. Normally he hated talking about himself, especially details about his past. Years ago, one of the Queen's guards had tried to engage him by asking this same question and Sam had tossed him through a window. But unexpectedly, the question didn't bother him when it came from her.

"I was abducted from the Underworld," he said.

"Abducted!" she gasped, her hand covering her mouth. "Why?"

"I don't know. I was only a boy."

"What happened?"

Sam met her eyes. "You wish to know?"

"Yes, I mean, if you'd like to tell me."

Slowly, Sam began, "I had only seen eight winters—years, in human terms. I was sleeping in my bedroom, then woke abruptly. A creature had entered my room. I thought perhaps it was an imp come to play a trick, or one of my father's servants. But it was not."

Sam remembered the confusion he felt at the odor filling his room when Zaybris appeared. It wasn't a demonic scent. Nor was it the earthy aroma emitted by the dead when entering the Underworld. It was something else.

He continued, "Then I saw a man, a handsome human male with pale skin and long blonde hair standing over my bed. He wore a fine velvet jacket. I didn't understand how a human got past the royal guards. I-I sat up to cry out for my father but the man clamped a hand over my mouth. His face was anguished, his mouth... his mouth was red and pinched."

Sam's throat tightened as he remembered how he had also seen two yellow fangs within that red mouth. It was then that he understood the reason why the human smelled neither dead nor alive—he was a vampire. They couldn't enter the Underworld until fully dead, nor exist peacefully among the living.

"The human clamped a hand over my mouth then roughly pulled me onto his lap."

"You must have been so scared," she said softly.

Sam swallowed at the wave of emotion her words brought. It suddenly became difficult for him to speak as he thought back to the vampire's tone, his inflection. He remembered how his kidnapper's voice dripped with spite, *Well, well. Look at you, son of the great, captivating King Asmodeus. A little abomination. I am Zaybris. Have you heard my name before? I am loyal. Devoted. Steadfast.* Each word was bit out with malice.

Sam had struggled, but Zaybris only tightened his grip and said, *I have spent years searching for a way to enter the Underworld and now that I'm here, I find you!* The hatred and utter disgust that the stranger had for him was terrifying. Then Zaybris had twisted Sam's arm painfully before crying out, *Let her know the agony of loss as I have!* while pressing his thumb into the wire-wrapped stone hanging from a cord around his neck, lurching Sam into his new life.

Sam played those words over and over in his head thousands of times, desperate to make sense of them. *Let her know the agony of loss as I have.* Let who know? And why?

He met Selene's eyes over the fire. "Yes. I was scared," he admitted. "Then everything went dark. I was in great pain, and woke up in Aurelia."

"Do you know who it was that kidnapped you?"

"No," he lied. "He left me in this realm and I never saw him again."

"I'm very sorry. Who eventually found you?"

"A kindly couple who took care of me until I was grown," he said, only providing her with half of the story.

"And the queens can't take you back home?"

"No. It is a realm for the dead." He began removing his boots and set them near the fire. "What was it like for you when you came to Aurelia?"

Selene shuddered. "Very unpleasant. Queen Thema told me when she passes through her portals it feels as natural as blinking. But that is *not* how I felt. First, there was an odd smell. I remember that came first. Then it was as if the ground... it shook under me. Seemed to swallow me whole until I felt like I was falling. Or I had been pushed from a great height. But there was no relief of hitting the ground, I just kept dropping down further and further."

"I felt that too," Sam said. "Falling, but there was more to it. I was also being crushed. As though two great boulders were squeezing—"

"The squeezing!" Selene echoed emphatically. "As if all my bones were breaking."

"Yes." Sam picked up a nearby stick and poked it into the dirt. "For me, the squeezing and falling continued until all at once it stopped. Like a candle being blown out. Then I was thrown on my back against muddy ground. Blinded by a horrible yellow light and wheezing for breath."

Selene's eyebrows drew together. "A yellow light? I don't remember that."

"No, a human wouldn't have noticed it as remarkable," he said. "It was months before someone finally told me that harsh light was called the sun."

"Oh." She looked surprised then apologetic. "I guess coming to Aurelia was more of a shock for you than it was for me."

Sam didn't know how to respond so he just shrugged. They held each other's gaze for a beat until Sam looked away. A strange feeling welled up in his chest. Almost as if something had opened and shifted inside. He wanted more.

"Thank you for telling me your story." Selene yawned and handed the blanket back to Sam. "My feet are killing me so I'm going to turn in early tonight. Goodnight, Sam."

"Sleep well, Selene" he replied.

He watched Selene enter her tent then poured a jug of water over their fire. A nagging feeling that he was playing a dangerous game tugged at his gut. He was growing too fond of his beautiful human companion. Sharing parts of his life he hadn't told anyone ever, asking more than he should about hers. Queen Thema had assured him Selene would be better off in Aurelia, he knew that. And he had vowed to get Thema the information about her lost sister that she needed. He was doing the best thing for both of them; for all of Aurelia, really. The realm would lose a violent demon, but gain a peace-loving human. Perhaps even a lost queen.

But under the night sky with Selene's scent on his blanket and her boots sitting next to his, he wished things could be different.

CHAPTER 15

After two days of traveling along the road that would eventually take them into Harpy territory, Sam had them set up camp near the edge of Humbledew Lake. During their travels, Selene had told Sam more about her family and how she had learned to be adaptable from growing up in a state of constant unpredictability. Sam wondered if it was a normal human practice to mold one child to anticipate the needs of others, but he did not probe further. He understood what it was like to cope with inconstant circumstances.

Earlier that night, Sam told Selene about the time Queen Thema burned her mouth after mistaking a bud of heat-greens for a sweet cloudberry. Selene had laughed so heartily it made Sam feel as though he would burst with pride. Yet now, although Selene had gone to bed hours ago, Sam was troubled.

He swayed in his hammock, hoping the motion would lull him to sleep. He stared up at the moon, then closed his eyes. After directing his muscles to loosen, he commanded his mind to empty, or at least think of boring, innocuous things. Anything to keep his mind from weaving together a fantasy about something he could not have.

It was his own fault. He had trained his body to have certain expectations before falling asleep. To keep from reliving certain memories, he had learned to distract himself. Deep breathing and focusing on the present served him during the day, but at night he kept his mind occupied with elaborate fantasies, usually influenced by whatever erotic texts he had been reading.

Before drifting off, he would often imagine himself doing debauched, wicked things to an anonymous lover. One who reveled in his touch, desiring him so much she grew wet under his ministrations and moaned his name. He would satisfy her so thoroughly she would beg to reciprocate the pleasure she had received.

Formerly, his fantasy partner looked like a composite of the Aurelian features he found attractive—a generic female with emerald Malkina eyes, silvery Nereid skin, and the depraved hunger of a Lycah in season.

But as they traveled, he noticed his fantasy shifting. At first, he imagined a bedmate with glossy brown hair, the same shade as Selene's. Then he could picture delicate humanlike hands trailing over his body. One night, a familiar mouth with full lips smiled up at him, asking for a kiss. The next evening he ran his tongue over berry-scented skin.

It wasn't until last night when he saw himself staring into a pair of blue eyes that he knew. His fantasy wasn't faceless anymore. He had been imagining Selene. Kissing her, touching her, tasting her. His mind had at last found a face suitable for his perverse thoughts, and latched on for good.

His hammock creaked as he rolled over. He wondered what Selene wore to bed. Did she sleep in her clothes in case of attack as he did? Or did she change into nightwear? Did she languish in a shimmering swirl of lace like Malkina females favored? Or would she prefer something plain and discreet?

His shaft hardened as several possibilities progressed through his mind. It wasn't until he considered that she might not wear *anything* to bed that he had to suppress a groan. That thought led to a vision of Selene standing before him at their campsite, clad only in moon-light. She would look so beautiful, so ethereal, but her smile would be wicked. Wanton.

He imagined her beckoning him to come closer. And when he did, she would ask him to kiss and touch her. Take his scarred hands and place them on her body. He would knead her lush breasts until her head lolled back on her shoulder. Her moans would fill the forest as he caressed her hardened nipples, teasing and pinching the sensitive peaks just as he'd read about in his books.

Then he would take Selene's small hand and press it against the front of his breeches. Compel her to feel the way his cock strained toward her. Make her understand how able his body was to give her exactly what she needed so that she would ask him into the tent and beg him to pleasure her until sunrise.

The night air was brisk, but sweat dotted Sam's forehead. The imagined scenario made his erection pulse so hard against his pants he gasped. He kicked off his bedding and swung his legs out to plant his feet on the ground. *Stop this.* What started as a passing thought had turned into a carnal delusion—one that was making him crazed for relief.

At first, he decided to wade in the lake. Perhaps the cold water would quell the throbbing ache between his legs. He ran the heel of his hand down his erection and shuddered. No. The lake's chill wouldn't be enough. There was only one option.

Sam slipped away from the campsite. He headed toward the lake, hoping the sound of water would disguise what he was about to do. Making sure he wasn't so far out that he couldn't see Selene's tent, he dropped to his knees on a patch of dirt.

Tearing at the fly of his pants with a shaky hand, Sam winced as his heavy cock sprung free. With a practiced grip, he curled his fingers around himself. Stroked once, twice. And then before he could think, he was coming. His climax ripped through him so hard and fast he bit his lip to keep from crying out. Hot seed jetted out of him onto the ground as his big body trembled.

When it was over, he slumped back on his heels, panting. The metallic tang of blood filled his mouth, and he realized his teeth had sunk into his lip. Wiping the blood away with the back of his hand, he stumbled toward the lake to clean up.

Staring up at the stars, he let out a curse. His body was spent, but he felt no closer to relief. He hated this lust-mad part of himself. Loathed the way his body's urges could dominate his mind, turning him into a mindless beast who sought only pleasure. With practice, he had learned to negotiate his drive for vengeance. *Mostly.* But the desire he felt for Selene? Its intensity scared him and made him fear for her safety. He even pitied her for being unlucky enough to attract his attention.

He had seen the cruelty that unrestrained lust could inflict. On days when the worst of his memories flooded back, the scars encircling his wrists would ache as if he were still enchained and powerless to stop the violations that had occurred in the blood wagons every night. He had sworn never to be that sort of male—one who used force to satisfy his needs. He would rather die than cross that line.

And yet... if Selene ever did ask him to her bed, he wasn't certain he could be gentle. She would prefer a tender lover, surely. A practiced hand who could woo her, tease her, and build their passion softly. Slowly. Not an inexperienced, volatile demon who nearly came when she touched his hand.

He gritted his teeth, wondering how Kevin P. Norton might tend to her. Was he a masterful lover? Surely not, judging by the way she failed to pine for him. Yet he probably knew how to control his lusts. The sense of shame that pervaded the human race would hold the man back from acting out his most depraved desires. But demons were born with very little qualms and a fierce disregard for propriety in the bedroom. Sam feared he would frighten Selene with his debauched needs, or worse, become brutish in his quest to satisfy them.

He righted his pants and began to head back to their camp. It was foolish and pointless, this infatuation he had. Yet he couldn't deny his feelings for her went beyond lust.

Mate...

The word floated on the edges of his mind like a whispered secret. She could be his fated mate. That would explain his reaction, his obsession. He was undoubtedly attracted to her, but mates also had the ability to calm each other and bring perspective and peace. The concept had been hammered into him since birth, and he had seen his mother provide that to his father countless times in the Underworld.

But she was human. He was meant for a demon to complement his nature, not to restrain it. The only thing Selene was to him was a distraction.

His stomach contracted at the word. Distraction. That's exactly what she had become. There were times when he looked at her and felt as if Zaybris himself could walk right up and he wouldn't notice.

It was at that moment that he realized Thema's plan simply wasn't going to work. Things had gotten too complicated. His attraction to Selene had turned into a diversion he could not afford to indulge. Not when he needed to be at full capacity to return home.

They had to part ways.

Sam woke up tense and agitated the next morning. The pre-dawn sky was gray and overcast, mottled as a bruise. Dread writhed in him over the decision he needed to make. He hoped a solution would come easier after sleep, but he rose feeling even more conflicted. How to best separate himself from Selene?

He could leave right now. He could quietly pack his things and set off without a word. Selene was clever; she could find her way back to Thema's castle. He could leave the map, the switch pouch, and a note to explain how Thema's delusions about finding her sister had made her desperate. He would urge Selene to forgive the queen for her deception and make a life among the Malkina, where she would be protected.

Sam began to pace, considering Selene's panic, and the devastation she would feel when she woke to find him gone. He sighed as that idea fizzled out. Leaving Selene without a word would be cruel. And cowardly. There had to be another way.

"Is everything all right?"

Sam spun around to see Selene standing outside her tent, her hair tousled by sleep. She was dressed in a long white nightgown with a row of buttons down the front. It was held up by thick straps that exposed her arms, shoulders, and collarbone. *So that's what she wears to bed.* Seeing her in such an intimate state made blood rush to his groin.

"Everything's fine," he answered, a little too quickly. "Why do you ask?"

"I just woke up suddenly. I had a feeling something was wrong."

"Nothing is amiss."

A sudden wind blew a lock of hair across Selene's cheek, and she looked up at the sky. "Is there a storm coming?"

"No. Go back to sleep. It's not quite dawn. We'll leave in a few hours."

"Nah, I'm up now." She stretched her arms. "We can get an early start. Aren't we going through a town today?"

"It's more of a village, but yes, we travel through Iriswood."

"I'll get dressed."

After Selene ducked into her tent, a flash of movement on the ground to the left caught his eye. Something had expanded the switch pouch slightly. He reached inside and found a note.

Samael, I am planning contact with Zaybris soon to tempt him with our prize. When do you expect to reach him? My impatience to find my sister grows with each day. Please tell us how you fare — Thema

He crushed the note in his hand. Damn the queen's timing. He didn't know precisely when he would connect with Zaybris, especially not now when things had become so complicated.

As Sam moved to disassemble his hammock, an idea took form. Although he had never been there, Iriswood lay at the crossroads between Malkina lands and Harpy country. It was the gateway to Queen Aello's territory, with travelers coming through to rest and trade at the local inn. Many of them were also looking for work. Perhaps he could hire a guide in Iriswood to take Selene back to Queen Thema.

He considered the thought. Selene would not be abandoned and he could reach Zaybris in a few weeks. Plus, with the amount of gold he carried, he wouldn't even have to haggle a price, once he found a guide who seemed trustworthy. A fierce Harpy or a protective Lycah wouldn't be hard to find in Iriswood.

It would probably take most of the day to get there, and they could stay the night at the inn. Then he could get an early start that morning before Selene even knew he was gone.

It would be a relief to have the matter closed.

CHAPTER 16

It was late afternoon by the time they spotted the towering, spindly buildings of Iriswood peeking over the hillside. Lightning cracked overhead and Sam looked up to see swollen clouds churning over a yellow-green sky. It looked as if a storm were coming, but he didn't feel the ache in his knee that usually came before rain.

"It's getting dark early isn't it? Or is that just storm clouds?" Selene asked, her Nereid cream shimmering.

"Nightfall approaches. Iriswood can be a dangerous place at night. It would be best for us to stay at an inn so we don't have to camp so close."

"But I thought it was better to stay out of towns at night. You know, with vampires and all."

"Iriswood is different," Sam said, hating to lie so that she would agree to retire in a place where he could find a guide. Selene looked skeptical. "Wouldn't you like to sleep in a place with proper amenities? We'd get two rooms, of course," he added.

"Do they have bathtubs?"

"Yes."

"All right, if you think it's safe."

As they continued to walk toward Iriswood, the green of the forest gave way to rocks and thin trees. A stone archway and fence marking the village's entrance could be spotted up ahead. Birds, sacred animal of the Harpy race, filled the trees—some singing, others squawking. They peered down at Sam and Selene with curiosity.

"What's that smell?" Selene asked after a moment, her nose wrinkled.

The stench of rotting meat invaded Sam's senses. A gust of wind intensified the odor while something large and dark swooped over their heads. He looked up to see a winged creature with a female-shaped body circling over them like a vulture. Selene followed his gaze.

"What is it?"

"Just a Harpy." They watched her glide through the sky and dip once, twice, as if trying to get a good look at them. Then the Harpy sped toward them, emitting a high-pitched titter. Right before she made contact with the ground, she twisted to fly straight up again.

"You wish to enter Iriswood?" the Harpy squawked down at them. Her wings flapped slowly, silhouetted against the sky.

Sam's jaw clenched. He should have known there would be some sort of toll or challenge put up by the Harpies to enter their lands. With the exception of one Harpy he knew, they were mistrustful of males, and notorious for stealing what they wanted, especially food. He tightened his grip on his backpack. If this Harpy thought she would be stealing *anything* from him or Selene, she would regret it.

Apprehension grew as he watched the Harpy swoop erratically through the air. It was almost as though she wanted to soar higher, but a barrier prevented her from doing so. Sam squinted to get a better look, and saw sharp talons peeking out from under a tattered brown dress. Her spiky hair was tangled with debris, and streaks of dirt smeared her face.

Selene looked at Sam with alarm. He called out to the Harpy, "We only seek to pass through Iriswood."

"What queen do you serve?"

"Thema of the Malkina."

The Harpy drifted down to perch on top of the archway. She had a heavy brow, a pointed nose, and sickly blue skin that clashed with the red of her hair. Scarlet feathered wings extended from between her shoulder blades. Black and orange eyes peered down at them before the creature rolled her head and let out a caw. Selene stepped back, her body drawn tight with fear.

The Harpy looked at them and said, "Don't look Malkina."

"We serve Queen Thema, nonetheless," Sam replied. From the corner of his eye he saw Selene smooth her hair over her ears, no doubt taking care to hide their rounded tips.

"I serve Queen Aello," the Harpy said.

"Yes, I know," Sam said, his anger rising. He did not care for games or having his time wasted. "May we pass?"

The Harpy lifted her chin. Then she flew up and dove straight for Selene's backpack. Selene held up her arms and ducked, which left the Harpy's talons grasping at air. An angry shriek rang out, followed by a clap of thunder.

Next, the Harpy spiraled around to pluck Sam's pack from his shoulders. He swung out his arm defensively, which made the Harpy lose balance and crash to the ground. When she rose, Sam was surprised to see that she was nearly his height.

Her stench was so noxious it made his eyes water. Her talons looked razor sharp, capable of snatching supplies *and* tearing flesh. The Harpy spread her wings out menacingly and advanced.

"Queen Aello demands tribute!"

He glanced at Selene and saw beads of blood blooming from a scratch across her forearm. Sam's breath quickened as his instincts for vengeance roared to life.

Punish.

He motioned for Selene to stay back, while he moved toward the

Harpy. Once they stood eye-level with each other he growled, "You're not taking our food. Or anything else."

"Tribute!" the Harpy screeched.

Sam bared his teeth then said, "No. You can either step aside and let us pass or—"

"Or what?" the Harpy challenged. She shuffled her feet back and forth in the dirt, preparing to charge.

Wisps of shadow curled around Sam as his claws extended. "Or lose your wings."

The Harpy laughed—it was a nasal, unpleasant sound. Then she launched herself into the air. Sam pushed Selene back. "Go hide behind those trees," he commanded.

Seeing the fear in Selene's eyes made his rage grow. This creature thought to steal from them, prevent his entrance to Iriswood, and frighten Selene? No. Unlike the bread thief in Padu, he had no doubt about whether or not this Harpy deserved to be punished. It was time to take care of this situation.

Destroy her.

Vengeance.

Sam felt the weight of the twin knives strapped to his belt and began to strategize. A blade thrown just right could hit directly into the Harpy's heart or her eyes. And if that didn't stop her? He could do some real damage to those wings once she plummeted to the ground. Make the thing bleed, sob, and cry for mercy. She would truly regret the day she thought to thwart a demon.

The Harpy crowed above, taunting him. What was about to happen couldn't be helped—another obstacle between him and Zaybris had to be eliminated. More thunder rumbled and the sky turned dark when the Harpy released a piercing battle cry.

Sam looked into Selene's terrified face and said, "I'm sorry you have to see this." He cracked his knuckles, and with a deftness born from experience, pulled out the two knives from his belt.

"Wait!" Selene cried, sprinting out from behind the tree and holding up her hands. "Wait, both of you, please!"

Sam was startled by Selene's boldness. The Harpy dive-bombed toward them, but then landed silently in front of Selene. Cocking her rust-colored head to the side, she ignored Sam to fix her full attention on Selene.

Selene's voice was frantic as she asked, "What does Queen Aello require for tribute?" The Harpy tilted her head to the other side, her rough features lit with confusion. Sam stepped toward them, but Selene held up her hand. "No! We're just talking."

At the sound of her voice, the Harpy moved closer. Relaxing her posture, the winged female let out a soft coo. Selene swallowed and Sam could tell she was fighting the urge to run. He held his breath as Selene looked up to meet the Harpy's eyes. "M-my name is Selene. What's yours?"

The Harpy blinked, then murmured in a tinny voice, "Pydiana."

"That's a lovely name." The Harpy fluffed her feathers.

"Pydiana, you've been given an important duty to guard the entrance of Iriswood. Is that right?" Selene asked. Pydiana hooted her confirmation, then bent to sniff the top of Selene's head. "You're doing a wonderful job."

The Harpy rolled her neck, seeming to quiver with delight. There was a beat of silence as a few of the dark clouds overhead shifted. Sam tightened his grip on the twin knives. Selene saw the movement and gave him a small shake of her head.

In a dreamy tone, the Harpy implored, "Speak again, lady."

Selene bit her lip. "Pydiana, can you tell me what your Queen has asked you to collect?"

"Tribute."

"Yes. But what?"

When she didn't answer right away, Sam interjected, "Our food. Harpies steal food."

Pydiana made a hissing noise and shot him a look of contempt. Then she leaned closer toward Selene. With a conspiratorial air, she whispered, "A stolen offering."

Sam could smell the creature's putrid breath from where he

stood and couldn't imagine how Selene was enduring it. Her ability to remain so calm was unfathomable.

"What sort of offering?" Selene asked.

Pydiana showed a smile of chipped teeth, then shook her head.

"You won't tell us?"

The Harpy shook her head again. She began to giggle and started to twirl in a circle before Selene. Suddenly, she sang out, *"Lady Storm Swift feeds her brood by snatching a stranger's song or food!"*

The moment the words left her mouth, Pydiana gasped and stopped spinning. Her face was stricken.

Selene exchanged a look with Sam. "Song or food?"

"I shouldn't have told..." Pydiana said.

"We can give you a song as tribute?" Selene asked.

The Harpy shrugged. Then nodded. Shrugged again, then began to trace swirls into the ground with her talons. She nodded a second time.

Sam bristled. He should have known that a Harpy would covet a song. Especially a song from a stranger that she hadn't heard before. His patience was nearly at an end.

"Pydiana, what sort of song?" Selene asked.

The pupils inside Pydiana's orange irises widened. "One that speaks my name." She flicked her tail. "So that I may steal it. To sing for my queen."

Sam's unease grew. What song could a human know that speaks the name of Pydiana? Sam knew how powerful songs were to Harpies. They sang to heal, to sound an alarm, to share news, or even to call forth a storm. But they were also very particular about their songs. And quick to rage if they heard something they didn't like.

Certain that Selene was in over her head, Sam took a step closer. He was pleased at how well he was controlling his urges, but this game had to stop. He would show Selene how merciful he could be by giving Pydiana a quick death.

Selene's features shifted from worry to triumph, making him

pause. "Ah! I know just the song. Is there anything special I have to do besides sing it?"

Pydiana shook her head. Selene glanced at Sam and flashed him a grin that made him feel even more baffled than he already was. He didn't think humans possessed magic, but Selene clearly had a solution she believed in. Was she about to cast a spell? Murmur an incantation?

Selene drew a deep breath, then sang the words,

Happy birthday to you,
Happy birthday to you,
Happy birthday, dear Pydiana,
Happy birthday to you.

It was a short song with a simple melody. Sam was sure Pydiana would reject it. His palms began to sweat around the handles of his knives, yet the Harpy didn't shriek or attack. Her face shifted into an expression of wonder. Tears filled her big eyes, and she stretched her arms out to flap her wings joyfully. Pydiana sang the song back with Selene's encouragement. Despite her horrific screeching, the Harpy had a beautiful singing voice.

Sam's fingers uncurled from his knives. It seemed more like Selene was offering Pydiana a gift rather than having something stolen. Yet it appeared Pydiana's demands had been met. Her whole body seemed to uncoil with released tension, and even her skin tone morphed from dull blue to vibrant teal.

Crossing his arms over his chest, Sam felt utterly lost. How had Selene charmed such a detestable Harpy? After singing back Selene's song for a third time, Pydiana sighed with pleasure. With a soft hoot, she looked to Selene, then Sam. Her eyes glowed as her lips stretched into a disturbingly odd smile. Sam tensed with awareness that the whole song stealing story could be a diversion.

But Pydiana only dropped into a deep bow. Then she stepped aside to extend one wing out toward the village ahead. Her voice was strong as she said, "Lady. Companion of the Lady, I bid you welcome to Iriswood."

CHAPTER 17

The moment Selene swept past Pydiana, the Harpy let out a celebratory whoop. Selene looked back and saw her shooting up into a blue sky. The ominous clouds that had rumbled down at them were now gone.

Selene felt a mixture of happiness and relief. She couldn't hold back a smile as they passed under the stone archway that announced their official entry into Iriswood.

Mission accomplished.

Sam, on the other hand, didn't seem to feel so enthusiastic. He was looking at her like she was an alien.

Selene ignored him at first, but then asked, "What?"

"How did you do it?"

"Do what?"

"You just... " The corners of his mouth tightened as he trailed off.

They walked in silence for several moments until Sam said, "I asked you to follow my lead on this journey."

"And?"

"That was all I asked, and what did you do?"

"Got us into Iriswood," she quipped. She hadn't realized how many tricks she had picked up from breaking up fights between her parents—staying calm, practicing empathy, asking questions. Yet, instead of the fight ending in slammed doors or broken dishes, her efforts had actually diffused the situation this time. It felt quite satisfying.

Sam frowned. "That may be, but—"

"But what?"

"I thought humans didn't possess magic."

"What magic? It's called *talking*."

"No. You charmed her. Made her bend to your will. How?"

"It was no magic." The packed dirt of the trail was giving way to gravel. Selene kicked a large stone marring her path. "I figured not many people had been nice to her. So I tried talking to her like a person. It felt like that was what she needed."

"But that song. How did you create it?"

"I didn't! It was the birthday song!"

"And that is?"

Selene frowned. "Sorry, I guess you don't have that here. It's a song we sing in my world to celebrate the day a person was born."

"For what purpose?"

Craning her neck to watch the Harpies of Iriswood flit from one elevated building to the next, she said, "There's no purpose. It's just a custom to honor someone once a year. It was the first song I could think of with someone's name. We got lucky, I guess."

Sam was quiet, seeming to mull over the concept of birthdays and songs. Then said, "You did something to me too. Restrained me somehow."

"Now you're talking crazy."

"When my instincts to... to punish arise, it's difficult to stop them. But I felt different there. More calm. What did you do?"

"Nothing! I don't know what you mean."

"Hmm. Regardless, you didn't need to intervene back there. I was in full control of the situation. She could have easily killed you, stolen everything we had, then ripped off strips of your skin until—"

"You don't have to be so graphic."

"Look what she did to your arm!"

"It's nothing. See?" Selene held out her arm. The red scratch from Pydiana's talon had bled a little, but was already closed over.

Sam made a disgusted noise. When they entered into the main part of Iriswood, he commanded, "Pull up your hood. There could be vampires near, readying to emerge."

Selene obeyed, suddenly self-conscious, and fearful of rogue vampires. She tried to keep her head down as she watched the inhabitants of Iriswood go about their business.

Although Harpies seemed to be the dominant population, the village wasn't without other Aurelian races. Most of the buildings in Iriswood were built high on stilts or nestled into tree branches. She watched a Drago emerge from an elevated red house and use the small claws of his toes to climb down a rope. A Nereid splashed her feet in a puddle. Two Lycahs circled each other like wolves, before embracing in a hug.

They seemed harmless enough, but Selene could tell from the way Sam kept rubbing the back of his neck he was growing nervous. When they reached the end of the main road, Selene spotted the only building in Iriswood built at ground level. It was a narrow brick structure with a faded sign that read *The Golden Gust.* Underneath the letters were a painted mug of beer and a crudely drawn bed. She pointed to it. "Look, is that the inn?"

Tension branched from Sam's eyes as he looked down at her, then the inn. "Yes. But... " He tugged at one of the leather bracers encircling his forearm.

Selene's eyes narrowed. "What's wrong?"

"Nothing."

"Really?"

"My... feelings have changed," Sam spoke hesitantly before his words came out in a rush. "Perhaps we should just pass through Iriswood and keep going. Not stay here tonight."

"I thought you said we needed to stay at the inn."

"The woods will be safe. I think."

"You *think*?" Selene asked. "Oh. I was so looking forward to a real bath. In a tub. Why the sudden change of heart?"

Sam shrugged.

"Is it too expensive?" she asked. "I'm sorry I didn't think about that."

"I am not lacking for gold!" he thundered as a rowdy-looking group of Lycah men pushed past them to enter the tavern, followed by a Harpy with glossy emerald wings.

"Well, if you don't think it's safe, then let's not stop."

Sam stood silent for so long Selene feared he hadn't heard her. But then he muttered, "Very well. We'll stay the night."

The Golden Gust was larger than it appeared from the outside, but the myriad of junk tacked to the walls made the space feel cramped. Corroded horseshoes, faded paintings, rusted utensils, and taxidermic creatures occupied every inch of vertical space. Even the wooden beams running across the ceiling had things tacked to them. Most patrons were hunched over their drinks at small wooden tables, but others played cards or talked with animated gestures.

Selene could tell from Sam's concentrated expression that he was scanning the room for threats as they entered. He seemed to be sizing up every person in the tavern, but no one paid them any notice. When he placed his hand on her lower back to guide her toward a stool at the end of the bar, Selene slowed her steps to make the contact last.

The tavern was warm from the large fire crackling in the back. The green-winged Harpy they had seen outside stood in front of it, and began to sing.

Selene took in the small jarred candles burning at each table and the mostly elderly clientele. It was a cozy little place. Sam's forehead was creased, but she didn't see any reason for alarm.

"Do you want a drink?" he asked.

"Sure."

"Ale?"

"I'm not a huge fan of beer, or ale... whatever. Do they have wine? Preferably red?"

"We only have rose thorn wine, my lady," a deep voice intoned from her right.

Selene turned to see a huge creature covered in brown fur emerging from a doorway behind the bar. He gave her a shy smile with big, crooked teeth and wiped his hands across a green apron.

Selene's scalp tingled as she realized she was looking at Bigfoot. No, a Sasquatch. No... that wasn't right. What were they called here? The Vowa! Her first sighting of a Vowa in the flesh! Most Aurelians looked vaguely humanlike to her, apart from the animalistic features indicative of their race. But this guy looked like he had come straight from a cryptozoology book, maybe with a bit less fur.

"Rose thorn wine sounds good," she said, trying not to stare. Or let on that she had no idea what rose thorn wine tasted like.

"And I'll have an ale," Sam said. "Do you have any rooms?"

"We have two available."

"With bathtubs?" Selene asked, hopefully.

"I'm sorry, no. They share a bathing chamber with the other rooms on the second floor."

Sam's face clouded into a scowl. "Unacceptable. The lady wants a private bath—"

"It's fine," Selene interrupted.

"If it's a bath you want, then you shall have it."

The bartender looked nervously at Sam. "The other rooms are occupied. We can bring a tub and buckets of hot water to the room if you like—"

"That would be perfect," Selene said quickly. "Thank you so much."

The bartender nodded, then tilted his big head toward Sam

before taking a step back. His voice quavered as he said, "I know who you are. You're that demon—"

Sam slammed a fist down on the bar so hard a crack formed in the wood. "We're still waiting on our drinks."

The bartender gulped, then rushed to pull two glasses hanging from the ceiling with shaking hands.

Selene turned to Sam. "Are you all right?"

"Fine," he snapped.

"You're being rude."

"Yes."

The Vowa placed both drinks before them and quickly headed for the other side of the bar. He retrieved two keys from a row of hooks, then slid them down into Sam's waiting palm.

Selene took a sip of the pink liquid and was surprised by how sweet it tasted. Minty, floral, and fresh—almost like drinking liquid springtime. Sam was not one to savor his drink, apparently. He tipped back his mug to swallow the entire contents. Then his eyes continued to dart back and forth throughout the room.

"I... I need to excuse myself for a moment," he said. "Keep your head down and don't talk to anyone."

Selene nodded and watched as Sam traveled through the room, seeming to size up every Aurelian he passed before disappearing through a doorway at the back. He was thrumming with tension, and Selene wondered if the Harpy incident had bothered him more than he let on.

She still couldn't believe the birthday song had saved her. She mentally proposed a toast to herself and took a sip of wine. Already her limbs felt pleasantly warm, and the knot between her shoulders was loosening.

It was nice to have a moment to herself. There was no buzzing phone in her pocket, no emails to check, no deadlines looming. Being in another dimension wasn't exactly a vacation, but it did have its perks. She could just *be* in Aurelia.

Gazing across the bar, Selene caught a reflection of herself in a mirror tacked to the wall and lifted her chin to examine her profile. Not bad for no make-up and a one-step cleansing routine. It was dark in the tavern, but the woman staring back wasn't what she expected. The Nereid disguise made her skin glitter, but there was something more. This version of her looked confident and capable. Mysterious and interesting. Almost like a secret agent.

Dressed in black, with a hood that cast mysterious shadows on her face, she didn't stick out nearly as much as she expected. Honestly, she looked quite comfortable in The Golden Gust. And then a thought came to her: *I can be whoever I want to be here.*

Tilting her face, she looked into the mirror again, and a smile appeared on her lips. No one knew her in Aurelia or had any expectations of who she was supposed to be. She was free. She didn't have to play Simpering Selene to suit her insecure boss, Therapist Selene for her friends, Manager Selene for Kevin, or Peacekeeper Selene with her family.

After swallowing another gulp of wine, her mind raced with possibilities. She scowled menacingly at her reflection to become Secret Agent Selene. The one who travels through strange towns unnoticed and unseen.

Fluttered her eyelashes to be Charming Selene. The one who ingratiates herself to queens and Harpies.

Lifted her chin to be Badass Selene. The one who faces her fears and overcomes all obstacles.

Puckered her lips to be Temptress Selene. The one who propositions her sexy demon lover.

Wait...what?

Abruptly, her game turned sour, and she dropped her gaze from the mirror. It was a stupid idea. Ridiculous even. He was a *demon.* They wouldn't work on so many levels.

But then she paused to reconsider. What was the harm in a little fantasy? It wasn't a crime to wonder what being with Sam would be like. This was the new and improved Aurelian Selene. His deep voice skimmed over her nerves like a caress, but what would it be like to run her fingers through his inky black hair? Or snuggle her cheek against his broad chest? Lose herself as he kissed her senseless?

She rubbed her temples. It was official—she was attracted to him. Big time. It wasn't a schoolgirl crush, Stockholm syndrome, or even a weird fetish for horns. This was legit. A grown-up, big-girl attraction to the ultimate bad boy. Except he wasn't that bad. Sure, he could be grumpy and gruff, but not all the time. Underlying that bluster was a tenderness she found irresistible.

The large group of Lycahs playing darts began to howl like jubilant wolves. Selene looked over her shoulder, worried Sam might come back before she got a handle on herself. She traced her fingertip over the crack in the wood that Sam had made with his fist. Yes, he had a soft side, but he could be volatile too. How would that work in bed?

He was all muscle and menace. Would he be violent? No. She didn't think so. Passionate? *Yes.* Wild. Maybe a bit rough, but not from aggression. He would take care with his size and temper his strength. And what he might lack in finesse, she imagined he would make up for in enthusiasm. The man would be thorough, of that she was sure. His smoldering gaze seemed to promise it.

She shifted her position on the barstool, trying to ignore the ache growing deep in her belly. The phrase *demon in the sack* had to come from somewhere, didn't it? The thought made her shiver.

Oh God, I don't just want to kiss him—I want him to fuck my brains out.

Wet heat flared between her thighs, and she quickly took another drink of wine, scandalized by her thoughts. The tavern suddenly seemed unbearably hot, and she fanned herself, bracing for a wave of guilt for the thought of cheating on Kevin.

But hang on, was it cheating? When Kevin told her he wanted a break, he had certainly made it clear that *he* was free to see other people. Wasn't she free to do the same?

As she pondered this, it surprised her to realize that there was nothing about Kevin she missed. Since coming to Aurelia, he had barely crossed her mind outside of the times Sam had mentioned him. She felt a little guilty at first, then angry. It was time to face facts. Kevin wanted to "press pause" so he could sleep with anyone he wanted on tour. She had always known that, deep down, but the reality was too painful to face.

She sighed, thinking about all the other times Kevin had hurt her, and she had brushed it aside. All the texts and calls he ignored, the little insults he made "as a joke," the way his attention drifted when she spoke, Selene had grown used to it, really. He was the complete opposite of Sam, who looked at her like she was some rare, exotic flower and listened to her as though nothing else mattered but what she was about to say. Traveling with someone as capable as Sam had also made her realize how much she did for Kevin, yet what did he do for her? She thought hard and could only come up with that time he'd brought flowers on her birthday.

Enough was enough. It was settled. Once she got back home, she was ending it with Kevin for good. He would be free to "explore" in every sense of the word, and so would she.

She felt strangely liberated by this decision but also troubled. Now one of her main objections to being with Sam was gone. The thought of being in his big, strong demonic arms felt very *right*, disturbingly so. And it wasn't just because she suspected he would be scorchingly good in bed. It was because of who he would allow her to be. How he would want her to be.

Unrestrained.

Selene closed her eyes as desire pounded through her. Absorbing the full implications of the thought made her insides scramble.

In her experience, most men talked a big game about wanting a sexually liberated woman—a partner who didn't hold back, one that was willing to explore and knew what she wanted. But when they actually got one?

It intimidated the hell out of them.

Selene had learned that quickly with her college boyfriend. After they had sex, the first time for them both, she felt like she had found a missing piece of herself. It wasn't spectacular, but she loved the sensations, the connection, and the release it brought. She didn't have a lot of baggage or guilt around sex—as long as it took place between consenting adults. And so, being the curious but committed girlfriend that she was, she had dived into this new side of herself with gusto. She checked out the Kama Sutra from the campus library, picked out lingerie at the mall, and even bought some basic sex toys online.

And what had it gotten her? A happy boyfriend and a flourishing sex life? Nope. Dumped, that was what it got her. And called a nympho.

So she had toned it down with her next boyfriend. She waited for him to make all the moves, and responded as she thought a nice, normal girl would. Never made any demands, never asked for anything she wanted. But she was so bored. When a magazine advised leaving out a bookmarked manual of sex positions to spice things up, she had tried it. He hadn't even bothered to crack the book open.

And then there was Kevin. Once when she had tried to initiate sex twice in one week, he joked that she was "insatiable." It had hurt, and she wasn't sure why she had even bothered. The waterproof vibrator she kept hidden in the bathroom gave her more satisfying experiences than he did.

Being with someone as fierce as Sam could be... interesting. Definitely illuminating. Was she bold enough to make the first move? She knew if he were going to initiate anything, he would have done so by now. He seemed far too honorable to ever to give her cause to mistrust him. So it was up to her. She twirled a lock of hair around her finger and looked up to meet her reflection.

What would the newly single *Aurelian* Selene do? It was almost as if they had just met, so she wasn't sure. Instead, she thought of the women she had met in Aurelia and what advice they would give.

Queen Thema would tell her that the Malkina took pleasure wherever they could find it, so she should do the same. Hollen's advice would be to tell Sam, point-blank, that they were going to sleep together. And Arkaya? She would scold her for being so indecisive and question why she would want to speak of anything but her own truth.

Selene swallowed. What was her truth? When she cut away all of the noise of propriety and obligations and what she *should* want, what remained?

Only desire. For Sam.

And so it was decided—no more overthinking. No more asking for permission. This was happening. It didn't have to be forever, and it didn't have to make sense.

She was going to tell Sam they needed just one room.

CHAPTER 18

When Sam made his way back to Selene through the tavern, he noticed she was sitting unusually straight. He motioned for another ale, then sat down. He could tell something was off with her; she seemed nervous.

She turned to face him. "Sam. I-I have something to say."

There was a quality about her posture, or maybe it was a subtle shift in her scent that made everything male in him suddenly alert.

She paused to fan her face. "Wow, is it really hot in here? Do you think it's okay if I take off my hoodie? I'm taking it off." She tugged off her black jacket, then began rubbing her palms up and down her thighs. "I... I want... I think we should... " she said, then trailed off.

"Yes?" he probed.

She pulled her shoulders back, then took a deep breath. Opened her mouth, closed it. Dropping her eyes, she bit her lip then blurted out, "I'll tell you in a minute. I have to go to the bathroom!"

Sam nodded, though she wasn't asking for his permission. Scrambling down from her stool, she rushed toward the back of the tavern where the passages of relief were located. He rubbed a hand over his chin. *Odd human.* Changeability must be a quirk of her race.

Another thing about her he had yet to understand. When he turned back toward the bar, something soft brushed his foot. Glancing down, he saw that Selene's jacket had fallen to the floor.

He bent to pick it up, then held the fabric to his nose. It smelled of the berry soap he had picked for her in Padu. A deep feeling of possessiveness coursed through him, making him even more certain of the decision he had come to moments before.

I'm keeping her.

Selene would not be traveling back to Queen Thema's castle that day or any day soon. Not until this mission was over.

It was a decision based purely on logic, arrived at with rational deliberation, or so he told himself. First off, there were no suitable guides in The Golden Gust. The tavern was full of doddering elders, impulsive Harpies, and a group of obnoxious Lycahs. There were no warriors, capable *female* warriors like he had imagined to shepherd Selene back to Queen Thema.

Secondly, as much as the idea discomforted him, Selene could be used as leverage with Zaybris. When the stakes were this high, could he forfeit such an advantage? Of course, he wouldn't let her come to any harm. Zaybris wouldn't touch one hair on her head. But he would be a fool to let such a treasure go, despite the complications she brought.

The bartender delivered Sam his drink. The singing Harpy took a bow after finishing her performance, and the tavern erupted into applause. The quartet of Lycahs demanded an encore by whistling and pounding their fists on the table. Sam rolled his eyes at their drunken antics and took a drink. One of the Lycahs slowed his cheering to focus on something across the room, then nudged his companions to do the same. He let out a low whistle that revealed his sharp lower teeth. Sam followed their gaze to see Selene moving through the crowd, making her way back toward the bar.

Her shoulders were pushed back, and her hips swayed with every step. There was a determined set to her jaw, and the firelight cast a soft light on her face. A draft from the front door blew her hair back, and Sam became very aware of how it was not only the Lycahs, but every creature in the room watching her. He knew this should concern him because a vampire could have snuck in unseen, yet he felt bespelled by her as well.

Sam had seen Malkina women enter a room as if they were acting on a stage, each movement deliberate and coy. They could command notice as they saw fit, wielding it like a weapon or a scepter. But Selene was oblivious to the attention she attracted. *And she passes by every male here to be at my side.*

Sam tried not to sigh like a besotted fool. Her long legs encased in those blue human breeches she preferred ate up the distance between them.

Just as Selene was about to reach him, one of the Lycahs shot out a clawed hand toward her. The sound of his palm slapping her backside made a *whap* that reverberated through the room. Selene turned back with an outraged "Hey!" but the Lycah pulled her into his lap. Then he pressed his lips against her neck as Selene struggled to stand.

His companions looked on, howling and laughing raucously. Until suddenly, they weren't laughing at all. They were screaming.

Sam didn't remember much about what happened next. Only the cold chill of shadows as they chased around him. The feel of his horns sharpening, and his claws extending. The sound of wood cracking and the shatter of glass. The warm rush of liquid against his palms as his fingers wrapped around something hollow and soft.

And then the smell of blood.

Selene fell to the ground with a thud. Her palms scraped against the rough floor, and pain radiated through her knees at the impact. Pushing back her disheveled hair, she tried to reorient herself. What had just happened? One minute she had been trying to escape that nasty wolfman's grip, and the next minute, she had awkwardly fallen to the ground. So much for her new identity as a strong, assertive Aurelian woman.

She sat back on her heels and looked down to see small beads of blood rising on her palms. The burning sensation in her arm let her know Pydiana's scratch had opened up again too. She frowned at the red slash, then grabbed a cleanish-looking cloth napkin from a nearby table to dab at her injuries. When that was done, awareness set in that the room had gone silent. Everyone was looking at something, but not her.

Then she heard a voice that was so deadly, it made her blood turn cold.

"You dare to touch my female?"

It was Sam's voice, but the tone was unlike anything she had ever heard. Her heart pounded once she saw him. He was standing by the fireplace with his right hand wrapped around the throat of the Lycah that had grabbed her, pinning him high against the wall. Every muscle in his powerful body was clenched tight, and he seemed to stand nearly seven feet tall. His skin had flushed from its usual pearlescent copper to deep red. Sweat ran down his temple while wisps of black vapor swirled around him. His horns were huge now, gleaming in the firelight.

She replayed Sam's words in her mind. When understanding dawned, she went dizzy. *Oh God, I'm the female. He's talking about me.*

Blood was dripping from the back of the Lycah's shaggy head as if he had been slammed into the brick. Sam gave the creature a shake that made him whimper. Then in that same savage voice, he said, "I asked you a question!"

To Selene, Lycahs looked like a cross between a werewolf and a lumberjack, and this one was no different. He was strong, but although he clawed and kicked at Sam with all his strength, Sam didn't budge. Selene wasn't certain he even felt the Lycah's blows until Sam reached up to close his fingers around the Lycah's muscled arm. Then with a *snap*, he broke his forearm like a twig.

Selene jumped at the sound. She looked away when Sam did the same with the other flailing arm. The sound of two more, louder cracks made her drop her head and cover her ears. When she dared to look back up again, the Lycah's lips were turning blue within his beard.

"Oh no, you're not leaving us yet," Sam said as he loosened his grip. "Breathe deep," he commanded, and the Lycah complied, his broken limbs dangling uselessly with each inhale.

Selene gulped and looked around frantically. Why wasn't someone stepping in? Didn't they have some sort of bouncer or security guard to intervene? The Lycah's companions were clutching each other and shaking. An old Drago shook his green head with disgust while a pair of white-haired Goblyn men sat frozen in the middle of their card game. There were a few other patrons hidden in dark corners, but none stepped forward to help.

She looked for the Bigfoot bartender. Surely he was used to diffusing situations like this. Bar fights were probably a regular occurrence at The Golden Gust. Because that's all this was, she told herself. An ordinary bar fight. She was just watching a misunderstanding unfold, like Sam had earlier with Pydiana. And that had turned out fine.

Because of me.

Selene's breath caught. It was because of her that Sam hadn't completely ripped Pydiana apart. And because of her, Pydiana hadn't stolen all their belongings or done whatever ruthless things a pissed off Harpy did. It was her well-practiced mediator skills that had averted disaster, not any special fighting moves or magic spell.

No one had ever come to her rescue in her old life, and there was no one coming to the rescue here.

She stood. "Sam?" she tried to call, but only a squeak came out. Sam turned from the Lycah to look around the room. When his red eyes landed on Selene, he looked so fierce, so *demonic*, she began to tremble.

"Are you all right?" Sam asked. His eyes darted down to the

napkin she was still pressing against her the cut on her arm, and he snarled.

She quickly let the cloth fall to the floor to show she wasn't injured. "I-I'm fine. It was just the scratch from before."

Sam snarled again and gave the Lycah a small jostle. "How would you like me to kill him?"

Selene didn't think her heart could beat any faster, but his question made it feel like her sternum might split. She tried to protest but could only shake her head. The Lycah began to thrash weakly, then stopped when Sam lunged at his face, just shy of contact.

"No," was all she could manage.

"No? He grabbed you. He *touched* you," Sam seethed.

"Please don't do this."

"I don't tolerate his sort of behavior. He must be punished."

"No."

Sam's roar of protest echoed through the room so loudly, it made her ears ring. Sam raised his left fist to swiftly punch the wall next to the Lycah's head in frustration, creating a crumpled hole in the brick.

Holding up her palms, Selene said, "Sam, please. That's enough, let him go."

He didn't react. Black shadows swirled around them, seeming to pulse with the hatred and anger radiating off him. Part of her felt like running out the door screaming, but something was pulling her toward him. Selene took a step closer. Sam didn't seem to notice. She looked up at his horns and thought about how easily he could gore the Lycah with them or anyone in the room. She took another step. Only the crackle of the fire and the drip of blood on the floor could be heard.

Tentatively, she reached out her hand. Sam snapped his teeth, warning her to pull back. She continued to reach out until her hand rested against the clenched fist at his side--just as she had done in Padu.

"Sam?" she whispered.

He groaned when her fingers met his skin, and his big body shuddered. "No. Don't touch me."

She coaxed his fingers open so she could fully clasp his hand. When his hand relaxed a fraction, she slipped her fingers across his palm and squeezed.

"Please let him go. You've punished him enough." Her voice was coming steadier now. He looked at her again, and she saw his red eyes flicker to brown. "Sam, I want you to leave him alone. I'm fine."

"I want to give you vengeance," he said. "Let me do this for you. Please."

"You have. And I... I appreciate it," Selene winced at the falseness of her words. "Thank you for the... vengeance. Now I want you to let him go."

"But—"

"Stop this."

Sam looked from Selene's face to the Lycah's, and back again. With a roar, he dropped the Lycah to the ground, then tore his hand from her grip.

Selene took two steps backward. "Thank you."

Sam stood over the creature as it moaned in pain. Though Sam had complied with Selene's request, he was practically vibrating with rage.

"Sam, please get away from him. Go... go stand somewhere else," Selene said, unsure of why she thought he would follow orders. Yet he complied.

Selene looked around the room and called out, "Is anyone a doctor here? Or a... a healer?"

After an agonizing beat of silence, an old Drago in a blue vest shuffled toward her. "Step aside. I'll take a look at him." Bending down to take a closer look, his reptilian scales rippled while taking the Lycah's pulse.

"He'll be fine," he said, more to the Lycah's companions than Selene. "Just needs to drink a pot of horsetail tea in a room with two purring cats. He'll be good as new soon." Before Selene could puzzle over his strange prescription, the Drago added with a chuckle, "And he should think twice before troubling a demon's mate again, eh?"

Selene bristled, resenting his inference that she was mated to a creature who snapped bones for fun. "Thank you."

She could feel the eyes of the entire tavern on her and was uncertain of what to do next. Keeping her head down, she pretended to busy herself looking through her backpack then pulled on her hoodie. When the adrenaline coursing through her finally began to ebb, she saw the Vowa had reappeared.

Forcing herself to smile at him, she said, "Hi. I... uh... sorry about that. Can we go to our rooms now? Two rooms. Definitely two rooms, please."

The Vowa shook his head. "No. We don't tolerate violence here. You both need to leave."

Sam stalked toward them; his expression was murderous. Selene's breath started to come in pants. There was no way she could break up a fight between a demon and Bigfoot! But Sam simply picked up his backpack and walked toward the tavern door.

"Come," he said in a rough voice.

I can't go with him. He's a monster!

She turned from Sam to look around The Golden Gust for a friendly face. Someone sensible like Arkaya or Hollen to rescue her, then translate for her tiny human brain what the hell had just happened. But there was no one to help her. The Lycahs were crowded around their wounded comrade, the Harpies ignored her, and the Drago man had started a game of darts with the Goblyns.

Quick movements to her right made her turn. She watched a pale figure in a gray cloak swoop toward the fallen Lycah, then drop to his knees. The stranger leaned down to press his head close to the Lycah's pointed ear, causing his friends to draw back. Selene felt relieved—he must be another Drago coming to provide medical care.

But then came an odd sound, like a dog slurping at a water bowl. She stumbled backwards. She wasn't watching a Drago, and this guy certainly wasn't providing first aid. The gray-cloaked creature's hood slipped back, revealing a patchy brown scalp and a wet, red mouth.

Vampire.

He was lapping the Lycah's blood from the floor, and clutching the napkin Selene had dropped with his gnarled fingers.

Selene quickly turned from the gruesome sight. Her legs felt so shaky she slumped down onto a stool. My God, she was homesick. What an idiot she had been. Convincing herself that Aurelia was some enchanted paradise—the best parts of places like Wonderland, Oz, and Hogwarts, without the villains. Without the darkness or the consequences.

She could see Sam waiting by the door with his head bent. He was still angry, so angry, but he no longer looked like a bomb about to blow. Tears were trying to bubble up, so Selene closed her eyes. Caught between a vampire and a demon.

What choice do I have?

Opening her eyes, she stumbled toward Sam with heavy feet. He opened The Golden Gust's door, and they went out into the night. Together.

CHAPTER 19

S lumping into the throne formerly belonging to Queen Lilith, Zaybris frowned. He picked at the seat's crumbling leather lining and swung his legs over the armrest. A handful of servants, both Goblyn and vampire, rushed in, but Zaybris waved them away. Tonight was an evening for contemplation.

His black boots gleamed under the candlelit chandeliers. He held one leg up, pleased to see that his calves filled out the boot again. His linen pants fit better too, no longer bunched at the knee. His flesh was slowly regenerating, thanks to more frequent visits to the human world. Since his experience with the last human he had presumptuously named Adam, his trips were now focused strictly on feeding. Zaybris was no longer certain that bringing a human to Aurelia was God's will.

He absently ran his fingers over the traveler's stone suspended from a chain around his neck. What *was* God's plan for him now? He held the stone up to the light, marveling at how innocuous it seemed, yet its ability to take its keeper to any dimension was astounding. There was nothing like it, not even in the Faerie Realm, where he had mistakenly spent the past twenty years. His grip tightened around the stone, angry about how foolish he had been, but he released it abruptly. It was dangerous to touch it while dreaming of other lands.

Yes, the legends were true, a minute spent in the Faerie realm did equate to the passing of twenty years in other lands. But how was he to have known? He had been so distraught from his disastrous trip to the Underworld. After disposing of that vile little demon spawn in Aurelia, he transported himself to the first realm that had crossed his mind.

He slammed a fist down on his knee. So much time wasted! And what had it gotten him? Only pain. Not redemption, not revenge. Not even recognition.

A crackle, then a soft thump drew his attention to the left. Another chunk of the brick had fallen from the throne room's ceiling, exposing a sliver of the night sky. He groaned, hating that yet another repair must be added to his list.

Was he being tested? Zaybris had always known his fate was greater than that of a barber's son. It was confirmed the day he was reborn. One moment he had been sipping champagne at a party, celebrating the close of the nineteenth century. The next, a band of caped creatures had swarmed the room. He had watched in horror as everyone at the party was attacked and drained, his friends' bodies lying bloodless and still on the floor.

Zaybris knew the myth of vampires, yet had never dreamed they were real. There was no denying the truth, though, once he felt a cold hand at his throat and fangs sink into his skin. He had struggled, but his efforts were useless. The only thing he could do as his life force flowed out of him was pray. He had prayed for strength and courage for the next part of his journey, and forgiveness for all the pain he had caused others in life.

He remembered how, when his eyes slid shut, a white light appeared—warm and welcoming. But as he moved toward the light, it abruptly winked out, leaving him lost in an abyss of darkness.

When he woke, he had been surprised to find himself not within that warm light, but in the same room where he had taken his last breath. He looked around, feeling no emotion at the multitude of dead bodies surrounding him. A great hunger had replaced the pain he felt, and his teeth throbbed sweetly. His mouth was dry, yet it wasn't water he craved. When he saw blood trickle from the mouth of a dead woman beside him, desire as he had never known stirred.

That day he knew he was no longer a vessel of flesh, but a being of spiritual glory. He had been chosen to serve as one of God's favored children—the vampire. While other survivors in the room, like his colleague Waldron, grieved their change, Zaybris had rejoiced. For he knew the Creator had selected only those most worthy to walk eternally upon His creation.

Running his tongue over his fangs, Zaybris thought back to how proud he felt when his brother, Julian, had begged him to make him immortal. It wasn't up to him, Zaybris had warned before sinking his fangs into his brother's flesh, it was fate that decided who rose again. Fortunately, Julian did not succumb to death, and the brothers joined with other vampires in Newark to feed on lesser beings.

Zaybris had never felt so invigorated. At last, he belonged. He finally understood his purpose in life after decades of feeling like an outcast—until he realized that being highly favored had consequences.

Astrologers and mediums spoke of how his kind violated the order of life and death. Fringe newspapers had called for the eradication of his race, and books imagined them not as higher beings, but ancient villains. Then when some jealous, unworthy mortals on the edge of society began slaughtering vampires with stakes and sunlight, God had sent not an angel, but a divine protector—a shining queen who would lead their exodus into the land of Aurelia.

Lilith...

He would never forget the first time he saw her. She appeared as a winged creature on the Gaia plane with a long neck, clawed feet, and tail. He had been frightened when she descended upon his horde, for she embodied the local legend of the Leeds Devil.

However, he quickly became enamored with her gentle voice and promises to care for his people in her lands.

The less violent vampires among them accepted her offer of sanctuary immediately. They were eager to live a respectable life despite their new hungers. Julian and his lover Margery were less inclined to join but relented when Lilith explained that they could accompany her into Aurelia or meet their true death at the end of a stake.

Zaybris did not need convincing. Lurking in the shadows and preying on the weak had suited him, but Lilith's brown eyes were compelling. He was even more certain of his decision once they arrived in Aurelia and he saw her regain her true form. The Goblyn queen looked more like an angel than a devil or monster. She was tall with long, auburn hair, skin as prismatic as an opal, and gracefully pointed ears. Her majestic wings swayed when she was calm and quivered when she was angry. Zaybris was in awe of his queen. Immediately he volunteered to help her acclimatize vampires to their new world, and she accepted.

The Aurelian queens did not condone the killing of innocents so gone were the days of tearing flesh and violence. Vampires in Aurelia were nourished by blood donated by Aurelian citizens and sipped from crystal goblets.

Time moved strangely in Aurelia, so Zaybris was not sure when the changes to their bodies occurred, but they came slowly. First, he noticed a childhood injury to his shoulder had begun to ache again. Others complained of arthritis flares and diminished energy. Zaybris's hair was losing its shine, and his feet hurt when strolling through Queen Lilith's night-blooming gardens.

Zaybris had begged the queen to explore other ways to stop the decay of their bodies, perhaps with live feedings from the vein, but she dismissed him. Growing older was natural, Lilith had said. Plus, she did not trust vampires to limit themselves to "just a sip."

Julian had grown particularly angry about her inaction and left Goblyn lands in search of better nourishment. Zaybris had worried about him, but soon after, their lands were left without a ruler. Then there were more pressing concerns for him to attend to.

Yet, I still failed.

He used his sleeve to dash the tears pricking his eyes. Foolishness. There was no time for sentimentality or pining. Lilith was gone, but now he would rule in her stead. He would unite the vampires to seize their destiny as the dominant race of Aurelia. But first, he must heal their decomposing bodies.

"You seem troubled," said a baritone voice from his right. Zaybris turned to see Waldron studying him from the doorway, dressed in a brown tweed suit with a red bow tie. "Finding it difficult to be back in Aurelia, my friend?"

Anger rippled through Zaybris at the casualness of Waldron's tone. He bared his teeth at the other vampire and shouted, "You will address me as your king!"

Waldron didn't react. One hand rested over his rounded belly, while the other stroked what was left of his formerly grand mustache. Zaybris studied him from the bottom of his polished loafers to the top of his bushy gray head. His eyes looked tired, his skin sallow.

Unlike Zaybris, who dressed with an elegance bordering on extravagance, Waldron preferred the simple tailoring of brushed cotton sack suits, waistcoats, silk cravats, and well-tailored vests that had been fashionable in the 1890s. His ability to stay calm in the face of strong emotions hadn't changed either. It had been an admirable trait when they practiced law together, but now it only irritated Zaybris.

Deciding to let Waldron's impertinence slide, Zaybris said, "Yes, your king is troubled, and frankly, I cannot understand why you are not. Don't you yearn for true nourishment? Something to turn your hair from silver to ginger again?"

Waldron's face showed pure disappointment. "Not this again, Lawrence..."

Rage. Sheer, blind rage rushed through Zaybris, overwhelming him. He leaped from his throne to grab Waldron by the throat before throwing him to the ground. Crouching over him, he seethed, "I told you never to call me that! Lawrence is dead!" Waldron's eyes widened as Zaybris's fingernails squeezed into his jowls.

"I... apologize... " Waldron wheezed.

"To whom? You apologize to whom?"

"I apologize, King Zaybris... Your... Your majesty."

Releasing his grip, Zaybris smoothed his hands down the other man's vest. It took a moment for every last drop of fury to leave his body. Quietly he explained, "I relinquished that name, along with all the failures associated with it, the day I became an immortal. Do you not remember?"

Waldron coughed several times before answering, "I do. Forgive me."

Zaybris walked back to the throne, which creaked as he fell into it. He rubbed his temples then motioned for Waldron to approach. "Ah, I forgive you. Come. Sit at my feet while I unburden myself."

Waldron lowered himself to the steps leading up to the throne, the effort of the movement obvious in his face. "My king, something arrived—"

"Am I such a villain to desire what's best for our people?" Zaybris interrupted. He stared up at the castle's vaulted ceiling. "I want our people to thrive here, not simply survive on inferior blood. Is that so wrong? We were meant to rule this land at our full strength. Are you not tired of living in a body as battered as this castle? Do you not wish to be renewed?"

Waldron averted his eyes.

"Answer me," Zaybris said.

"There are many vampires that support your work. But me? I crave my end. My wife craves her end. We're content with letting nature take its course."

Zaybris waved his hand. "Trapped in those bodies, how could you not wish for release? But you'll soon change your mind."

"I'm afraid I won't," he said. "We aren't immortal. We believed ourselves to be, but it's not true."

"What do you mean?"

"We are starting to die naturally—the older ones of us, especially. My neighbor passed last week. He laid down before dawn and never woke again. The same happened to a vampire in Drago lands a month before. Her daughter followed soon after."

Zaybris was suddenly deeply uncomfortable. "Hogwash."

"It's not. We have a lifespan, it seems." Waldron motioned to the spots of decomposition on his formerly ruddy face. "As our outer body decays, so do our organs. It's only a matter of time."

Zaybris tapped his boot on the floor anxiously. He was about to probe Waldron further about these deaths when his friend extended his hand. A shard of crystal lay across his palm.

"I came to show you this, my king. A courier brought it from the Malkina lands. It's for you," Waldron said.

Zaybris looked down at the white crystal with suspicion. It was about the size of a cigar, jagged at both ends with one side polished flat. "What am I to do with it?"

"The courier said it would reveal a message for the recipient."

"Do you think it's enchanted? How do I know it's not poison?"

"I can't say, but it hasn't harmed me so far."

Curiosity outweighed caution, and Zaybris withdrew the shard from Waldron's hand. Nothing happened at first until he held it up to the light. The image of a face glowed within.

"It's Queen Thema of the Malkina," Zaybris said.

"Do you want to receive the message in private?" Waldron asked.

"No, you may—" His words were cut off when the queen's voice began to resonate from within the crystal.

"Dearest Zaybris, King Zaybris, welcome home," the queen purred in her sultry voice. *"My sisters and I are so pleased to have a strong leader like you return to our realm."*

The queen smiled demurely, and pride rushed through Zaybris at the compliment. "Greetings," he said, then realized she could not see or hear him. The message was embedded in the crystal.

"We hate seeing what's become of your people and want to help. So, to welcome you as the new ruler of the vampire and Goblyn race, I would like to offer you a gift. Consider it a peace offering to Aurelia's new king."

Zaybris's lips parted. A gift? For him? How delightful. And appropriate. Actually, why hadn't he received more gifts since he took reign? He had always found Thema to be Lilith's orneriest of sisters, but perhaps she had softened with time. He leaned closer as the message continued.

"King Zaybris, I want to offer you a human. A living human, here in Aurelia. She is beautiful, healthy, and robust with life. She came to us by chance, but I give her to you by choice."

Zaybris's body began to tremble. Could this be true?

"She will be delivered to you at your castle in the coming weeks. I hope you will make her feel... welcome. There are others who would do anything to possess her. So I ask of you, King Zaybris, when my servant arrives, please receive him and the human alone. Put an old queen's mind at ease that this precious gift will go directly into your care."

Zaybris knew Queen Thema could not see him, but he nodded furiously all the same. He turned to see if Waldron was as thrilled as he was, but his expression was serious.

A coquettish smile lit the queen's face, and her golden eyes twinkled. *"Very well then, King Zaybris. I bid you good night. I look forward to the boons of our new friendship."*

The image faded, and the crystal turned clear again.

It was several minutes before Zaybris felt he could speak. When sound finally rose from his throat, it wasn't speech. It was laughter, so joyful and fervent that it made Waldron lean back.

His prayers had been answered. A true miracle! The reason why all of his missions had failed dawned on him. Greater mysteries had been at work this entire time.

He turned to Waldron. Clasping the other vampire's hands, he said, "At last, our salvation has come!"

"Eh, this seems very strange, my king... " Waldron said.

"It's not strange. It's good fortune! At last." Zaybris did a little dance around Waldron then clapped him on the back. "However, if it will take weeks for her to arrive, I don't know if I can wait until then. If vampires are dying, as you say, lives are at stake. I want the human now. And a king always gets what he wants."

Placing his hands on his hips, Zaybris roared for his servants. After they came skittering in, he declared, "Send word to every vampire—there is a human in Aurelia! He who finds her and brings her to me untouched will receive a great reward. They will be appointed to my counsel of advisors, receive ten bags of gold, and... they will be among the first of my subjects to receive a vial of her blood. After I take my share, of course."

The servants looked confused and failed to leap into action, which enraged Zaybris. "YOUR KING HAS SPOKEN!" he shouted, and each of the servants began to run in different directions. He stuffed the crystal into the breast pocket of Waldron's jacket, instructing him to keep it safe.

Zaybris adjusted the ruffles that ringed his shirt cuffs. Everything was coming together beautifully.

Soon Lilith will see how worthy I am of her.

CHAPTER 20

When Selene woke the next morning, she wanted nothing more than to hide in her sleeping bag. The light coming through the tent meant the sun had risen, but the air was damp and cold. She had slept terribly, plagued by dreams of bloody Lycahs and vampiric smiles. Rubbing at her gritty eyes, she rolled to her side.

Her limbs felt heavy, and her stomach knotted with regret. She had been a fool. An idiot whose hormones told her sleeping with a demon was a good idea. What was wrong with her? She was romanticizing a creature known for evil, mainly because he was hot and smelled good.

As both a demon and a royal guard to Queen Thema, Selene knew Sam wouldn't be a stranger to violence, but she hadn't imagined him capable of such brutality. The gleam of viciousness in his eyes, the unholy strength of his body—it was a sight she wouldn't forget.

She stretched her arms up above her head, then quickly pulled them back, remembering the *snap* of Sam breaking the Lycah's bones. A bout of nausea welled up in her throat, but she held it back.

She suddenly felt grateful that despite all the drama in her house growing up, there was never physical violence. There was yelling, door slamming, and the occasional silent treatment, but her parents had never hurt each other. Their faces swam in her mind, filling her with a deep sense of homesickness. Her nose began to burn with the prick of tears, but she wouldn't allow them.

Focus on the positive. She was alive. Whole and unhurt. No one had actually died. She had seen a disturbing new facet of Sam, but nothing had changed in her mission. They had made a lot of progress on the road, and she was proud of the way she had adapted to her strange circumstances. Her physical stamina had increased, and she couldn't let her mental fortitude slip now. It wouldn't be long until she could file away this whole experience as a bad dream.

She rubbed her forehead. Enough stewing. She would only work herself into more of a fizz if she stayed in bed. It was time to pull herself together and get dressed.

When she stepped out of her tent, Sam was still in his hammock, snoring softly. The sight was so unusual it made her pause. She had always been the first to go to bed, and the last to get up. And when they were awake, Sam was always busy—fixing this, adjusting that—she had rarely seen him still.

His hair was disheveled around his horns, and black eyelashes cast spiky shadows against his cheeks. He still wore his regular trousers but had shed his leather vest and black tunic, leaving his top half covered by a thin white shirt. One muscled arm dangled out of the hammock, while the other rested on his chest. Selene was surprised to see a web of light-colored scars hatch-marked up and down his skin. They were old injuries, long healed. But they made her very curious, especially the jagged marks around his wrists.

In the morning light, he looked more like a huge, dark angel than a murderous demon. He seemed so peaceful it made her feel a flicker of resentment that he should sleep so soundly when she had tossed all night.

Tearing her eyes from him, she began to pack up for the day. A renewed sense of determination burned within her. She was on this trip to get home—back to worrying only about wonderfully boring things like paying bills, doing laundry, and keeping her phone charged. She wasn't in Aurelia to sightsee, mix with the locals, or have a vacation fling. It was time to stop acting like a clueless tourist and get on with it. After gathering her things, she set her tent to deflate. The noise roused Sam.

"What time is it?" he said. Those were the first words spoken between them since leaving Iriswood. He scrubbed a hand over his face and peered up at the sky. "I must have overslept."

"No, I just got up early," Selene said, shoving last night's dirty clothes into her backpack. "I couldn't sleep."

When their eyes met, she was surprised to see him look away. Reaching down for his blanket, he pulled it up around his shoulders, seeming to shrink under her gaze. The serenity sleep had brought to his face was gone, replaced with a deep weariness. It showed in the dark circles under his eyes and the way he clenched his jaw. He was obviously uncomfortable, but Selene wasn't sure if it was due to her being awake before him, or regret about last night.

With hands on hips, she asked, "So what's the plan for today?"

"Plan?"

"Where are we going? When will we get there? How long before we reach Zaybris?"

Sam responded by pulling a map from his pack and thrusting it toward her. She took it, stupidly realizing it was the first time she had actually looked at it. It was a hand-drawn map, but well detailed. Pointing at a small dot on the rough parchment, he said, "This is where we were in Iriswood. We continue north until we enter the town of Snowmelt, where we will stay for one or two nights. After that, we should be able to reach Zaybris in about a week."

"A week? Can't we get there any sooner?" Selene asked. The question came out as a whine, but she refused to care.

"Doubtful."

"That town, Snowmelt—can't we just pass through and camp in the woods?" The thought of spending time in another town, with more people, made her stomach churn.

He pulled the blanket tighter to his body. "No. I have two friends there I must see. I've sent word that we are coming, and they invited us to stay at their home."

Selene stiffened. What kind of *friends* did demons keep? Krampus and the Grim Reaper? The prospect of staying with two unknown entities made her feel very vulnerable. "What are your friends like?"

"Trustworthy."

"Okaaay." When he didn't expand his answer, she said, "Anything else?"

"They are honorable."

"Any other details you'd like to share? How do you know them? Are they Malkina? Dragos? Vowa? What is their home like?"

He pulled on his tunic with clipped movements. "None of that matters."

Selene slipped the map back into Sam's pack without comment. It was another classic Sam non-answer, but she was tired of begging for scraps of information. She resolved if she didn't like Sam's "trustworthy and honorable" friends, she didn't have to keep traveling with him. She could take the map and set out on her own to find Zaybris. Theoretically.

Wringing her hands, she considered the idea further. Sam was only with her because Queen Thema had ordered him to do so. What if she told him he was free to go so she could carry on alone? He would probably relish the chance to return to his normal life, instead of playing babysitter.

Sam asked, "Do you want me to start a fire for breakfast? Or did you already eat?"

"I'm not hungry."

His features grew apprehensive as he watched her twirl her hair into a bun. "We have a long day ahead," he said.

Selene shrugged.

"You need sustenance. At least a cup of tea and some fruit." He took a step forward to loom over her.

Involuntarily, she cowered. "I said I'm not hungry!"

Sam blinked at the heat in her voice, then his shoulders slumped. He withdrew from her and began to disassemble his hammock. Selene kneeled to roll up her tent. A cold drizzle of rain began to fall. She wiped droplets of water from her face and pulled out the thick cloak Hollen had placed in her pack. As she stood to shake it out, Sam's voice rang through the quiet of the forest. The tone was sad, almost defeated.

"I've frightened you."

The words felt as though they came from far away, though he stood across from her. She looked over to see him staring at his feet, an expression of mute anguish on his face. A cold breeze blew tendrils of his long hair against his cheek.

"Yes," she admitted.

Sam gave her a searing look. The vulnerability in his dark eyes was so stark it made her throat tighten.

"I am sorry," he said.

Selene opened her mouth, then paused. She pressed her lips together, struggling for a response. Normally when someone apologized, her automatic reply was a cheerful "That's okay!" as she charged ahead like nothing had happened. Someone could interrupt her during a meeting, step on her foot at the movies, or even rear-end her car, and she would act as if everything was fine. But this time, she would not say that. Because it was not okay.

"Why did you do it?" she asked. "Attack that Lycah like that."

"He *touched* you," Sam said as if that were explanation enough.

"He didn't hurt me."

"But he grabbed you. Without your permission."

"I know, but—"

"Is it acceptable for males of your world to grope unwilling females?" he asked.

"Well, no, but... stuff like that happens all the time."

"I can't let behavior like that go unpunished when I see it. Especially toward you," he said in a tone edged with menace. And possessiveness. Selene remembered how he had referred to her as "my female" yesterday. What did that mean? She was a female under his protection? Or something more? She filed away the thought for later.

"What do you mean by unpunished?" she asked.

A muscle ticked in his jaw. She could tell he was fighting some internal battle in the way he struggled to find his words. "I'm a Vengeance demon," he said.

When he failed to elaborate, Selene asked, "Am I supposed to know what that is?"

"No, of course not. A human wouldn't know," he said. "I was born to live among the souls of the dead and exact vengeance upon those that deserve it. Punish cruelties."

He picked at a twig on a nearby tree. "Sometimes it... it can be hard for me to judge the actions of the living. If I focus very hard, I can see into their pasts and seek vengeance for those they have wronged. But it isn't fair to judge those who may still atone. So I try very hard to not punish them without just cause. Do you understand?"

"Not really, but go on."

"My father would have taught me more about my Vengeance instincts when I turned thirteen, but since I was taken before that, I never learned to properly control them. In Aurelia, I was taught to manage my drives based on the rules of this land. I was taught to practice compassion and forgiveness. But there are times when I cannot suppress my nature. Last night was one of them."

"So that's happened before? You 'punishing' someone?"

He tilted his head back. There seemed to be so much going on within him. "Yes."

"Would you have killed him? If I hadn't stopped you?" she asked, even though she wasn't sure she wanted to hear the answer.

"Demons aren't supposed to kill, but if you had wanted me to, I would have. For your vengeance."

She swallowed. "Have you ever killed anyone?"

It was as if her question had scalded him. Claws shot out of his fingertips before quickly retracting.

Raising his chin, he said defiantly, "As a guard for Queen Thema, I have not."

Selene narrowed her eyes. "That wasn't what I asked."

Sam let out a small growl, then quickly silenced it. "Before I met the queen, I was put in situations—against my will—where... sometimes death was the outcome." Then he gave her a pleading look. "But please understand I would never hurt you. Ever."

Death was the outcome.

Selene stared down at the cloak bunched in her arms as she absorbed his words. She noticed that water beaded on the surface instead of soaking into the fabric. The droplets were small, like hundreds of tiny shimmering diamonds. She smoothed her palm against the moisture, feeling the cold wetness seep into her skin. The falling raindrops patted softly against the tree leaves around them.

"Selene, please say something," he begged after a moment.

The racing pulse in her ears made her voice sound tinny as she said, "Watching you back there, what you did, it was... it was horrible."

"I know. I'm sorry."

"Maybe it would be best if I continue on alone."

"What do you mean?"

"I mean, maybe our time together should end."

His chest began to rise and fall rapidly. "Why? You don't fear I would attack you like that, do you?"

"Well, it did cross my mind."

"I wouldn't! You must understand that my feelings for you are... different. Maybe its because you're human, but being with you brings me—" He paused, regret and pain evident on his face. Then he released a ragged breath. "I hate seeing fear in your eyes. It *shatters* me. Please don't be afraid of me. I won't lose control like that again.

Just let me stay at your side until we get to Zaybris. I won't do anything violent again. I'll only protect you."

A terrible urge to go hug him rose, but she pushed it back. She couldn't get caught up in *feelings*. She had to be practical about this. He certainly seemed sincere. And repentant. But wasn't that how all violent men acted after an episode? She wasn't about to be one of those people that swept behaviors like that under the rug.

Selene hugged the bundle of fabric to her chest. What were the facts? She was stuck in a strange dimension. The only way to get home was by asking a vampire. This demon knew where that vampire lived and how to get there. She didn't. Even if she took the map and set out on her own, she was vulnerable—both physically and intellectually. She didn't know the rules and customs of this world. Sam did.

He had behaved horribly. Carried out violence like she had never seen, but she didn't believe he was innately cruel. He thought he was protecting her. Giving her "vengeance," as he had said, like it was a gift. His mention of losing control was a surprise, almost as if he had acted outside of his own volition. And he was obviously deeply regretful. Deep down, she didn't believe he would hurt her.

Selene swung the cloak out around her shoulders and snapped it shut. Yes, things had gotten more complicated. But at the end of the day, Sam was still the best chance she had to get home. More time spent pondering or planning was a waste of energy.

"All right," she said. "Let's go to Snowmelt."

CHAPTER 21

I t took Sam and Selene almost a week to reach Snowmelt. At first, they spoke only when necessary, usually on the topics of meals and campsite selections. Initially, this had irritated Selene—another example of Sam's problematic mood swings. But it wasn't until she noticed how he used any little remark she made to start a conversation that she understood. He wasn't being quiet out of spite. He was giving her space.

She was determined to embrace Aurelian Selene by kicking her old habit of faking a cheerful attitude, even when she didn't feel it. Surprisingly, Sam let her do so. He never whined or said things like, "You're not still mad, are you?" or "Stop being so dramatic." He never sulked because she wasn't paying him enough attention or tried to draw her out when she was feeling introspective. It was a new experience—being allowed to *act* how she felt. It made it easy to soften towards him and admit there was more to this demon than the ruthless creature she saw in Iriswood.

Yet the closer they came to Snowmelt, the more her anxiety about meeting his friends grew. Queen Thema had assured her she could trust Sam, but she had never vouched for his friends. What if they were violent too? It was common advice that if you wanted to know the true quality of a man, look at his friends. Would his friends present another red flag about Sam's character? Why did she care so much when she was going home soon?

Selene's aching back was making her grumpy when Sam stopped to point out Snowmelt in the distance. Her mood lifted as she peered over the cliffside to the little village nestled among acres of farmland below. Sam explained that Snowmelt's name originated because of its location between below a range of mountains. The run-off of melted snow created lush farmlands and filled the river running through the center of town. From their vantage point, Selene could see rows of thatched-roof buildings, each with late-season flowers bursting from window boxes. Cobblestone streets ran through the town, while a stone bridge arched over the river. It was the type of scene that would be at home on a jigsaw puzzle.

After trekking down the cliffside, they found the streets of Snowmelt quiet, but not deserted. A large stone fountain bubbled in the town square, surrounded by shops selling cozy things like books, tea, knitted goods, and honey tarts. A Lycah couple dressed in matching red coats flashed them a big smile as they passed, almost as if they expected to see two strangers in their village. A Malkina man tipped his felt hat and wished them a good evening, while a Nereid woman slipped into the fountain, fully clothed, as if it were a warm bath.

Selene glanced at Sam. He still had that same vigilant look he got when they traveled, but he seemed less anxious. He was more at ease than Selene had ever seen him.

"Do your friends live here in town?" she asked.

"They live on a farm outside the village," Sam said. "We'll be there soon. Are you warm enough?"

"Yes, I'm fine," she said, pulling her cloak closer around her shoulders. "Wait, I forgot to put on my Nereid cream—"

Sam stopped in the middle of the road, sniffing the air. A noise like a battle cry sounded from behind them. Footsteps approached, and she whipped around to see an elderly Goblyn man fly through the air and land on the top of Sam's backpack. His bat-like wings fluttered as he wrapped his small legs around the back of Sam's neck, gripping his horns with his hands. A green, Robin Hood-style hat was perched on his head.

Selene drew back, fearing she was about to see Sam destroy his attacker, but Sam said, "Is this how you greet all your guests?"

"Only the ones who think they can beat me at wrestling," the Goblyn cried, beating his heels against Sam's shoulders.

"I surrender," Sam said, holding up his palms.

Was that actual *amusement* Selene heard tinging his voice?

The Goblyn lifted off Sam's back to hover in the air. Sam turned, and they embraced. Right there in the road, a tiny Goblyn and a huge demon, hugging as if it were the most normal thing in the world. After a moment, the Goblyn dropped to the ground.

Sam turned to Selene. "This is my friend Eldridge. He and his mate Brunie will be hosting us tonight."

Eldridge pulled off his hat to reveal a shiny head dusted with wisps of white hair. "Selene, it's a pleasure to meet you. Sam has told us all about you in his letters."

"He has? It's nice to meet you too," she said. Eldridge's violet eyes twinkled. There was a roguish quality about him, like a friendly pirate. She liked him immediately.

"I know your kind greet by clasping hands, but may I welcome you with a hug?"

"Sure." She had to bend to meet the Goblyn's embrace since he only came up to her shoulder. He had a surprisingly strong grip and smelled of peppermint and tobacco. The white sideburns hugging his face were soft as they brushed against her neck, and his smile was warm as they pulled apart. He had pearlescent skin similar to Sam's, but with greenish undertones. Long pointed ears stuck out on either side of his head.

"You didn't have to meet us in town," Sam said. "We were planning to come out to the farm."

"Nonsense," Eldridge said. Brunie would have come too if she weren't busy cooking." He motioned for them to follow him toward a horse-drawn carriage parked nearby. It was black with a raised driver's seat at the front, and a padded bench in the back. The brown horse attached to it stamped the ground impatiently.

"Who wants to sit up front?" Eldridge asked.

"I will," Sam volunteered. "The back will be more comfortable for Selene."

After tossing in their packs, Sam held out a hand to help Selene onto the carriage step. She took it, and when their fingers met, heat licked up her arm. It surged through her veins to settle with a distracting dip of pleasure between her legs. She tried keeping her eyes downcast, so that he couldn't see the effect of his touch, but he caught her gaze. His eyes burned with intensity.

It wasn't until Eldridge cleared his throat that Sam finally let her go of her hand. "Come now, we can't keep Brunie waiting, can we?" Eldridge said from the driver's seat. Sam climbed aboard, and they set off.

During the carriage ride from Snowmelt to the cottage, Eldridge chatted animatedly with Sam, and Selene luxuriated in being chauffeured to her next destination. Eventually, after passing by countless rolling hills, the carriage slowed.

"Welcome to Azuresong Pastures!" Eldridge called back to Selene.

The carriage stopped in front of a blue and white cottage tucked between two soaring trees. A chimney of mismatched stone puffed smoke out over a straw-thatched roof. Ivy chased up the north side of the house, while boxes of bright yellow flowers hung below each leaded window. A large blue barn sat behind the house.

Selene heard the sound of a door slam, followed by a high-pitched squeal. She sucked in a breath at the sight of a six-foot-tall Harpy in a turquoise dress half-running, half-flying down the stone path to meet them. Her taloned feet made scraping sounds against the ground until she launched herself up to wrap her thick arms around Sam.

The Harpy made little cooing sounds as she squeezed, and Sam awkwardly patted above her light blue feathered wings.

"Hello, Brunie," he said fondly.

The Harpy looked into his face. "We've missed you. How have you been?" Then she hugged him again and murmured, "You seem a bit thinner. Don't those Malkina feed you?"

"They do."

"Fish and mice, I bet! Or are they too busy chasing balls of string?"

"No one cooks as well as you," Sam said, then smiled.

It was a full smile, not the usual small tug at the corner of his mouth. The dimples Selene had seen hints of made a full appearance, while the lines of tension usually found around his eyes disappeared. The expression transformed his normally scowling face so completely, so *gorgeously*, that when Selene stood to get down from the carriage, her knees wobbled.

Eldridge seemed to notice her unsteadiness and came to help her. Then he called out, "Brunie, let the boy go! You're neglecting our guest."

Brunie squawked then used her wings to drop toward the ground. Turning toward Selene, she said, "Forgive me, dearest! I'm Brunie. Sam tells us you're on a quest to find a way home. We're so honored to meet you."

Brunie had bright amber-colored eyes, round and alert as an owl. Her gaze was bold but kind. Almost as if she were welcoming Selene to study the unusual planes of her face, knowing she would be helpless not to.

Selene's eyes traveled from the left side of Brunie's face, where the skin was smooth and pale, gently lined with age. The right side, however, was puckered and warped with scar tissue. It stretched from her hairline down to where her short neck disappeared under her collar, making her eye droop slightly and the corner of her mouth sag. It was clear Brunie must have suffered a terrible burn at some point.

"Thank you. It's nice to meet you too. You have a beautiful home," Selene said, gesturing toward the house.

Brunie gave a delighted hoot. "You must be hungry. Craving a hot bath after all this travel, I'd say."

"That would be wonderful."

"Come in. Supper will be ready soon."

Once inside, Selene was whisked past the wood-paneled living room and taken up a log staircase. Brunie led her into a small, neat room with a wrought-iron bed covered in quilts. After Brunie pointed out the bathroom down the hall, she called for Sam to take his "usual room" in the attic. This made Selene curious; how often had he come to visit this odd pair?

Once she was sure Selene was comfortable, Brunie bustled back into the kitchen. After unpacking a few things, Selene had enough time to brush her hair and wash her face before Brunie announced, "Supper's ready!"

As soon as Selene entered the main room, she gaped at the spread laid out for them. An enormous roast of some sort sat in the middle, along with a huge basket of rolls. There was also a plate of fish, a tray of sliced fruit, a teapot, and at least eight large bowls of sides.

"Now Selene, I've done a lot of reading and made all the food humans prefer," Brunie said with pride, pointing at each of the bowls, "We have porridge here, gingerbread, and that's plum pudding. Over there are peas, poison-free apples, beans taken straight from the stalk, and radishes."

"And the cakes, love. Tell her about the cakes!" Eldridge said, taking a seat across from Selene.

"And cakes! We know how your kind love cakes, so I made twelve."

"T-twelve?" Selene sputtered.

A concerned look crossed Brunie's face. "Should I have made more?"

"Oh no, I... "

Sam seemed to sense Selene's reluctance and jumped in, "Humans don't eat as much as the legends say. But I'll finish off anything she can't."

Brunie made a sound like a goose honk, which Selene realized was a laugh. "Of course, you will! You always finished your plate, didn't you? Now let's sit down."

"Dearest, if there's anything left over, we can bring it to the Founder's Day party," Eldridge said. He looked to Sam, hopefully, "You are staying for that, aren't you? Tomorrow night? I'm singing and Brunie's baking."

Eldridge turned his attention across the table to Selene. His eyes shone as he asked, "Do you like dancing?"

"I love it," she said. "Although I haven't done it in a long time."

Sam turned to her. "Do you mind staying two nights?"

Now that she knew Sam's friends were more like Aurelia's cutest grandparents than a pair of bogeymen, the decision was easy. "Sure. I wouldn't mind another night to rest. If that's all right with—"

"We'll stay," Sam said quickly. Eldridge clapped, and Brunie beamed.

After Brunie carved up the roast and filled everyone's plate, Selene took small portions of each dish as it was passed around. Although random, everything was delicious.

"How did you research these foods, Brunie?" Selene asked.

"From stories about your kind that the Queens have brought back. Books and songs sacred to your people."

"What stories?"

"Oh, there's one about a little girl and some bears, one about a lass with very long hair, another about some lost children and a house made of sweets."

Selene suppressed a giggle, as the assortment suddenly made

sense. She supposed she should be grateful Brunie hadn't served her four and twenty blackbirds baked in a pie.

Eldridge wiped his mouth with a napkin and said, "So, tell us all about what sort of adventures you two have had on your journey."

Selene's amusement disappeared as she recalled their most recent "adventure" in Iriswood. Sam shifted in his seat. Their mutual silence made the air taut.

Eldridge's face clouded. "What happened?"

Sam set down his fork. "Overall, we have had fine weather and good fortune on this journey. After leaving Queen Thema's, we journeyed through forests and meadows, passing through one of the Padu's stops and then Iriswood. Selene outwitted a Harpy outside of Iriswood who tried to steal from us."

Brunie stopped chewing, "Pydiana?"

"Yes," Sam said. "Selene sang her a song and she flew away to let us pass."

Brunie looked at Selene. "You freed Pydiana?"

Fear gripped Selene. "Is that bad?"

"Not at all," Brunie clucked. "The poor creature was being punished by Queen Aello, for trying to sneak into your world and cause a ruckus. If she let you pass and flew away, then she's free!"

"Well done, Selene," Eldridge cried. "You'll be favored among the Harpies, that's for sure."

Selene shrugged, feeling slightly embarrassed.

"Oh, this is so exciting. Tell us more about your journey," Brunie urged.

Sam cleared his throat. "It wasn't all favorable. Several nights ago, I made a mistake and attacked a Lycah who was harassing Selene in a tavern."

Selene nearly choked on her bite of bread. She hadn't dreamed of bringing that up in front of Brunie and Eldridge, and was floored that he would do so.

"Oh, Samael, you didn't," Brunie said.

"What happened?" Eldridge asked.

"A Lycah grabbed at Selene. So I strangled him, then broke both his arms and legs. I may have injured his head as well," Sam said.

"Samael! You must have scared Selene terribly," Brunie said.

Eldridge made a grunt of disappointment. Selene was surprised that they both seemed very familiar with Sam's temper.

"Have you been practicing your breathing, lad?" Eldridge asked.

"Yes, but on this occasion, it wasn't enough."

"Selene, were you hurt by the Lycah?" Brunie asked.

"No, just... startled," she mumbled.

Sam's voice was tight as he said, "The Lycah *struck* her, then pulled her into his lap. I couldn't have stood by and done nothing."

"That may be, but was violence truly called for?" Eldridge asked. "How else do you think you could have responded?"

A crease appeared between Sam's brows.

Counting off on his long fingers, Eldridge said, "One—you could have pulled Selene to safety, then asked the Lycah to leave the tavern. Two—you could have just frightened him. Never touched him at all, but used your size and demonic presence to stop his behavior. Three—you could have called upon the tavern owners to deal with the situation. Surely they have a process in place for when guests become rowdy—"

"Or if none of those worked, you could have broken only one bone," Brunie interrupted. "Four is excessive."

Sam looked thoughtful. It was almost as though Selene could see the gears turning in his mind.

"What stopped you from killing the brute?" Brunie asked.

"Selene did," Sam said. "She approached and was able to calm me. Just as she did when I felt unsteady in Padu. She has many gifts, but her ability to soothe others is the one that I... I admire deeply."

Selene blinked. *Wait—was that what was going on with him in Padu?* She had suspected something intense was happening, but knowing the extent of how it could have escalated was a surprise.

Brunie puffed with indignation. "It's not Selene's responsibility to manage your instincts! Don't put that on her."

"I didn't do anything special," Selene protested.

Sam plucked at the edge of the tablecloth "I won't make any excuses for how I behaved, but I wanted you both to know. And for Selene to hear again that I am sorry."

The room was silent until Eldridge spoke. "Well, I'm sorry to hear it happened, but you did well to stop before it was too late." He patted Sam on the back.

"Thank you for the advice on how I could have handled it differently," Sam said.

Brunie stood, then gave Sam a quick kiss on the forehead. "You're a good boy for always trying to do better. Now, let's speak of more pleasant things. Who's ready for cake?"

The room filled with the sounds of Sam and Eldridge cleaning their plates as Brunie disappeared into the kitchen. Selene finished her last bite of porridge and snuck a glance at Sam across the table.

Who knew that a man admitting to his mistakes could be so attractive? Although Sam's slip-ups were a far cry from the time Kevin lied about denting her car, his confession impressed her. He hadn't minimized what happened or made her feel like she was overreacting. He obviously placed great stock in Brunie and Eldridge's advice, and in turn, they wanted what was best for him. Seeing how much these gentle creatures cared for Sam brought up all sorts of feelings within her. Mainly warm and squishy ones.

He wasn't a monster. He had issues, that was certain, but he was working on them. Both Aurelian Selene and Ordinary Selene could appreciate that.

CHAPTER 22

After dinner, Sam had Eldridge show him what work needed to be done around the farm. Although the Goblyn was strong for his size, Sam knew he tired easily. Sam began working in the barn, moving a tower of hay bales up into the loft. The work was slow, but the burn of strain in his arms and legs felt welcome.

Sam had always enjoyed helping with any projects the couple needed during his visits. This time he was especially anxious to do as much as he could—because unbeknownst to Brunie and Eldridge, this was goodbye. Since he was planning to take the stone from Zaybris soon, this trip would mark the last time Sam would ever see them, until their souls descended to the Underworld.

He dropped a hay bale on the loft floor, trying not to dwell on how they would react if they knew what he was planning to do. That morning, Sam had received a letter from Queen Thema in the switch pouch confirming how she had sent word to Zaybris that a gift was forthcoming. A hot, prickly feeling of guilt crept across the back of Sam's neck, but he shook it off.

Glancing down to the floor below, he saw Eldridge humming as he ran a brush over his sturdy brown horse, Rainsilver. The Goblyn called to Sam. "It's getting late, lad. We can do the rest tomorrow."

"It's fine. I want to finish."

"Then stop for a break. Have a whiskey with me before I turn in."

"All right."

Sam descended the stairs and heard the clang of glasses on the small table that stood near the horse stall. The lower level was colder than the loft, and the night air felt invigorating.

Sam sat at the bench in front of the table, noticing how it wiggled more than he cared to see. Another chore to add to his list. Eldridge eased himself onto the bench opposite Sam, and they tapped their cups in an informal toast. The Goblyn took a sip, then fixed his sharp eyes on Sam.

"So, my lad," he began without preamble. "Were you in love with Selene before leaving to take her north? Or did it develop along the way?"

Sam's back went ramrod straight. His claws shot out, and shadows darted from the dark corners of the barn to swirl around him. The question was so unexpected, the ceramic cup he held was crushed to powder in his grip.

Eldridge smiled wryly. "There's no point in denying it. I knew from the moment I saw you help her into the carriage."

"You don't know anything," Sam snarled. His left leg jogged as he struggled to find his next words. Words to somehow make him feel less exposed and convince Eldridge how in control he was of the situation. He had to convince himself, too.

"Human women are known for their beauty. Is it wrong if I find her... pleasing?" Sam asked.

"Pleasing?" Eldridge snorted. "Tell me this, you've been in Aurelia for more than twenty years. You've encountered many females in that time, correct? Malkina, Nereid, Harpies, Dragos. Many of them quite beautiful. You've found some of them *pleasing*, haven't you?"

"Yes."

"Of course, but I have never seen you look at another as you do Selene. You're smitten," he chuckled.

"I am not... "

The way Eldridge raised one bushy eyebrow made Sam ground his teeth. Were his feelings for her that obvious? A deep growl rumbled in Sam's chest. The sound climbed in his throat, then burst out past his lips as a sharp roar. It echoed through the barn, reverberating off the wooden walls and beams. Rainsilver flicked her ears.

Then all demonic bluster fled as Sam dropped his head in his hands. Slumping forward, he mumbled, "It's just a foolish infatuation."

Eldridge let the words hang in the air, as though to allow space for Sam to offer more. When met with silence, he said, "What is it about her that you like?"

Sam pulled his hands out of his hair and looked up at Eldridge. "I don't know. She's brave and clever. Beautiful. But there's something about her scent. It's like it... calls to me."

"How do you mean?"

"Her scent is like pomegranate. It's a berry that grows only in Gaia and the Underworld. I hadn't smelled that since I left home. It woke me up in the morning when she came through the portal before I even saw her. It affected me all day."

"Interesting. And as you have traveled? Did your feelings wane or—"

"They grow. Every day."

"I see." Eldridge stroked his chin. "Why are you trying so hard to fight this attraction?"

"Isn't it obvious? She's human."

"So? Brunie's people disapprove of her being with a male and a Goblyn, yet here we are."

Sam began to pace the barn floor. "That's different. Selene only wants to go home. It doesn't matter what my feelings for her are. We are soon going to part ways."

"But what if she had a reason to stay in Aurelia?"

"She's attached to another."

"Attachments can be broken," Eldridge said. "You don't think she might share your feelings?"

"No," Sam responded flatly.

"Why?"

"I probably disgust her as I do everyone of this realm." He gestured around his head and body. "My scars... my horns. She abhors violence. A few days ago, she asked me if I had ever killed anyone."

"Ah," Eldridge said. "But surely you've told her how we all met. Or she heard about it while at Thema's castle?"

Sam tugged at the laces of his right arm bracer. "No. She doesn't know, and I want it to stay that way."

"Samael, be reasonable—"

"I don't want her to see or hear about more violence from me," Sam interrupted. "Not after Iriswood."

"That's why you think she couldn't care for you?" Eldridge appeared thoughtful as he tapped the bottom of his cup against the table. "She may have gotten a fright at the time, but she's not afraid of you now. In fact, I'd venture to guess she's a bit fond of you."

"Don't mock me."

"I wouldn't dream of it," Eldridge said. Folding his hands across his belly, he explained, "It's all in the way she leans her body toward you when you're near. Twirls her hair when you speak. Moistens her lips. That's not how females act when disgusted. Females of any race." He waggled his eyebrows.

A bud of pleasure unfurled inside of Sam at Eldridge's assessment, but he quickly stomped it out. He turned to walk toward the horse stall. "Goblyn nonsense."

"I don't deal in nonsense," Eldridge said. The joking tone dropped from his voice as he asked, "Samael, if all barriers were gone, what is it that you would want with her?"

Sam moved toward Rainsilver and began to stroke the horse's

mane. "I want you to tell me how to fight this. How can I stop feeling this way?"

"You're lying," Eldridge said sharply. He rose to stand in front of Sam, gently pushing away Rainsilver when she bent to nibble his ear. "What do you want? Do you just want to bed her once? Become her lover? Or more?"

Sam was about to claim he only wanted to be her lover, but paused, realizing that was only partially true. There was more to it. She was the bait he needed to escape Aurelia, but the idea of leaving her behind was becoming more and more troublesome. He hated to hear the desperation in his voice when he said, "I want to *keep* her. I don't want to ever leave her side."

Eldridge's face cracked into a grin. He started to beat his small wings, hovering up and down with excitement. "I knew it! I knew it!"

Sam watched the bobbing Goblyn. "What?" When Eldridge began to laugh, Sam grew angry. "You think this is amusing?"

"She's your mate! She's your mate, lad!"

"My mate? Country life has turned your wits dull. She's a human," Sam said dismissively, though his heart started to race. He didn't want to admit he had already mistaken Selene for his mate in the ballroom. The disappointment at finding her human had been crushing.

"Hear me out. You were probably too small for your parents to have explained it to you, but I've read up on this. Demons don't always have the same ideas about fidelity as others, but they believe in fated mates. It's said that each demon is destined to find a consort, one to be held up above all others."

"I know of the legends," Sam snapped. "But if I had a fated mate, wouldn't she be in the Underworld?"

"Not necessarily. From what I've read, when a demon male encounters his mate, he will know her by scent. That scent will call him to protect and cherish her."

"This is just another story like the ones you used to tell me in the wagons," Sam retorted.

"Imagine it's true. What then?"

Sam fidgeted with Rainsilver's bridle hanging from a nearby hook. Damn that Goblyn! Always pushing with his *breathe, focus, control* nonsense. Pushing him to deny his baser urges, pushing him to master his instincts, pushing him to believe in delusions.

An image of Sam's mother giggling while his father whispered in her ear came to mind. He thought about how the demon king would gaze at his mate with utter devotion and seek her advice on royal matters. He had been too young to know the intricacies of the Underworld court, but he had always known his mother did not carry royal blood. Her wings were gray as a Goblyn's instead of coal black as other female demons, and her nature was not as ruthless. Yet she was considered queen—the one his father adored above all others. Could Selene be that for him?

If so, it could change everything.

"Fine. Let's say it's true. It's all true, and by fate or some act of great magic, she wants to be with me. What if... " he swallowed thickly. "What if I can't control my instincts? What if... when we are intimate... I lose control and hurt her? I can't hurt her. It would destroy me."

"You have to trust yourself. Ask her to tell you if she senses a change in you, or you become too rough. Go slow."

"But how would I even court her? I know nothing of females and what they want."

"It's not so hard. Offer her compliments, bring her gifts. Be kind. Listen to her. Respect her. Show her there's no one able to protect or love her better than you can."

When Sam didn't respond, Eldridge left his side to stack the drinkware on a tray. When that was done, he pulled the barn door open. A blast of cool air blew Sam's hair back.

Eldridge's voice was gentle. "You have to see where this might go, my boy. If fate is offering you a chance at happiness, you mustn't spurn it. Goodnight."

CHAPTER 23

S elene traced her finger across a seam of the quilt on her bed
and frowned. She counted her breaths for a full minute. Then
another minute. And another before she punched her pillow
in frustration. It must be well past midnight, and she still hadn't
been able to fall asleep.

When she let out a huff of annoyance, the sound scratched her
throat, making her realize she was thirsty. That must be it. She was
restless and agitated because she was thirsty. Definitely not because
she couldn't stop thinking about Sam.

She wondered how he was sleeping tonight. For her, it felt posi-
tively luxurious to have a room to herself. And yet, after many nights
of sleeping within a few feet of each other, it felt strange to be
separated.

I miss him.

She pinched the bridge of her nose, wishing it wasn't so easy to
lose herself in daydreams of Sam. All night she had been stifling
fantasies about how his muscles would feel flexing under her hands
or how his lips would taste.

Get a grip. She was playing a dangerous game, especially now that she had seen his darker side. Selene flung back the covers. Maybe if she got up to grab a quick glass of water, she'd doze off soon after.

The house was peaceful as she crept out, but the wooden stairs squeaked as she descended. She waited to see if the sound had disturbed anyone, but all she could hear was Eldridge snoring. Or was that Brunie? She glanced back at the door leading to Sam's attic room and saw it was closed.

Selene was not surprised to find the kitchen as snug and tidy as the rest of the house. It even smelled clean, like lemon and sugar. Cool light from a full moon streamed in through the wide bank of windows that ran above the sink and counter. Bundles of herbs hung from the ceiling beams along with a variety of pots and pans.

When she approached the sink, she caught a glimpse of the brilliant moon through the window. It was too high to see from where she stood, so impulsively, she hoisted herself up to sit on the wooden countertop. She pressed her face closer to the glass.

The silver orb was like a luminous pearl. Its light bathed the trees and plants outside the cottage with a dreamy glow. Selene sighed. Was it a full moon back home too? She tucked her bare feet up under her nightgown and leaned her head against the window frame.

No matter how strange Aurelia was, no matter how many monsters, legends, and strange beasts it held, it was nice to imagine that they all looked up at the same moon. Cass and Evan could be looking up at that moon right then too. The familiar wave of worry and guilt surfaced when she thought about how concerned everyone must be about her. Would she ever see them again? Would they ever know what happened to her?

A blast of cold air and the sound of a door shutting made her jump. She looked toward the side door with alarm, trying not to pitch herself over into the sink. It was only Sam.

"What's wrong?" he asked sharply. "Why are you down here?" His thick hair was disheveled, and his boots were dirty. The darkness of the hallway made his chiseled cheekbones more pronounced, and his horns gleamed. He looked wild, brooding, and a bit dangerous.

"Nothing. I came down for a glass of water," she said. Her fingers curled around the edge of the counter while her feet dangled.

"Why are you sitting up there?" His movements were agitated as he took off his coat.

"Oh, I... I wanted to see the moon. It's so pretty tonight," she gestured to the window, realizing how silly she must sound. "What were you doing outside?"

"I was helping Eldridge in the barn. He grew tired, but I stayed to finish a few things."

"That's sweet of you."

He frowned before bending to remove his boots, making her wonder if it would actually kill him to accept a compliment. The muscles in his arms flexed through his tunic while powerful hands pulled at the laces of his boots. His hands were surprisingly nimble for their size. She had seen him crush bones with those hands but also tenderly scratch a kitten behind its ears. Her face grew hot as she wondered if he could be that deliberate with her. What his rough palms would feel like on her skin.

He met her eyes, almost as if he could sense what she was thinking. His gaze flickered to her mouth, her breasts, the junction of her thighs, then down to her bare feet before traveling back up again. Her cotton nightgown felt very thin and insubstantial. She began to twirl a lock of hair between her fingers, and his eyes locked on the action.

Tentatively he said, "The moonlight. It makes you look... nice."

Her eyebrows lifted. "Thank you."

He began patting dirt and dust away from his clothes while Selene wondered why she was still hanging around the kitchen. A sensible person would have hopped off the counter and run up to bed by now. Yet the ache in her belly seemed to anchor her to where she sat.

Sam cleared his throat. "Did you get your water? I don't see a glass."

Selene felt like an idiot. "Oh, no, I got distracted by the moon. Do you know where Brunie keeps the glasses?"

Sam came toward her with slow, measured steps. Blood throbbed in her veins at the way he was moving, almost like a predator. The top of his tunic was open, revealing a patch of pearlescent skin. Selene swallowed, suddenly very clear on what other women meant when they used the word "mouthwatering" to describe certain men. She reached up to rub her shoulder, hoping the gesture would hide the way her nipples tightened.

Wordlessly, he pulled out a glass from a nearby cupboard and began filling it. The movement caused the side of his body to bump into her knees, and he drew back, almost as if the contact burned. Then he paused before deliberately brushing his hip against her knees and leaning into the touch. She didn't pull away. Delicious warmth radiated from him, and she caught a hint of the woodsy soap she had picked for him in Padu mixing with the scent of hay. He handed her the glass.

"Thank you," she said. Her fingers brushed against his, causing little fireworks of pleasure throughout her body. She had intended to sip the water but found herself gulping it.

She expected Sam to huff out of the kitchen at any moment, but he stayed, watching her with hooded eyes. He was unabashedly staring at her mouth as a drop of water clung to her bottom lip. She wiped it away with her tongue and could have sworn she saw him sway on his feet.

She set the glass down. Her head was beginning to swim as if she were buzzed from too much wine. The feel of him pressed against her legs was distracting. What if she changed position and spread her knees apart? Would he come closer? Wedge his body between her thighs and pull her against him?

Shut up, stop this.

The tension of the moment was getting to be unbearable, and

she couldn't seem to stop herself from breaking it.

"So, uh... did you see the moon when you were outside? You might not be able to see it from where you're standing. That's why I climbed up here. I was thinking how funny it is how everyone looks up at the same moon. Not funny, 'ha ha,' but funny odd. The moon I grew up seeing is the same one everyone in Aurelia looks at. I guess it's the same in the other worlds too. Same with the sun. Reassuring in a way, isn't it? Same moon. Everybody sees it. But not in the Underworld, right?" Nervously, she brushed an errant strand of hair from her eyes.

Sam leaned forward to look out the window.

"No. Its light does not reach the Underworld. I'm glad it gives you comfort."

She looked at her knees, hoping he didn't notice the goosebumps scattered across her bare arms. Being at eye level with his body next to hers was... disconcerting. His sheer maleness felt overwhelming. So much power, brutality, and strength, and yet his eyes were haunted. His scarred hands were at his sides, opening and closing as if he were trying to resist touching something. Possibly her.

In a strained voice, he asked, "Do you want more water?"

"No, I'm fine. I should get back to bed," she said, halfway hoping he would ask her to stay. "It's late. I couldn't sleep, but I guess I'm pretty tired now. Oh look, you've got a bit of hay in your hair."

Without thinking, she reached up to touch the errant piece of hay tangled in the hair at the top of his head. As her fingers threaded through the soft thickness, one of his hands gripped the edge of the sink, his knuckles gone white.

As she drew out the hay, her fingers brushed against one of his horns, and he sucked in a breath. His eyes squeezed shut, as if in pain, and quickly, she pulled her hand back into her lap.

"Oh, gosh, I'm sorry. I shouldn't have... Are you okay?" His chest heaved causing Selene to feel mortified by her bold gesture. Touching a demon's horns must be very taboo, or maybe very painful? "I'm so sorry. Does it... does it hurt to have them touched?"

He opened his eyes. Bright red irises met hers, but they weren't looking at her with murderous rage like when he attacked that Lycah. Searing desire burned in his gaze, along with a yearning so stark it made her gasp. Before her brain could decide if she should be afraid or aroused, he spoke.

"Do it again."

It felt like all the air had gone out of the room. Their eyes locked, and liquid fire pooled in her abdomen. He wanted more. More of her touch. More of her. She was helpless to deny him.

Hesitantly, she traced her fingers around his horn, slowly stroking it from the base, up the S-shaped curve to the sharp tip. It was surprisingly warm, unyielding as steel and so foreign to anything she had ever touched before.

He let out a soft moan and closed his eyes. Taking it as a sound of encouragement, she continued to caress his horn before lacing her fingers into his hair. As she did, his hand tightened on the edge of the sink while the other shot out to grip the counter opposite her knees. He stood perfectly still as she continued to touch him, twining her fingers through the dark strands and admiring how shiny they looked in the moonlight. Her heart hammered in her chest so loudly she wondered if he could hear it.

As she continued to revel in the feel of him, the back of her fingers brushed against his temple. His big body jerked in response. She waited to see if he would tell her to stop, yet he continued to stand still. A silent plea for more. Experimentally, she drew her fingers down his face and watched a look of rapture transform his features. When her hand met his jawline, Sam's hand flew up to capture her arm.

With an agonized groan, he pressed his lips to the inside of her wrist. The searing kiss sent out jolts of heat that settled between her legs. The delicate skin of her wrist was like a conductor of erotic pleasure to the rest of her body, his mouth calling awake parts of her that she had long denied.

Her head tipped back. The pleasure of his touch, his heady

187

fragrance, and the warmth of his body so close to hers became so overwhelming, she couldn't suppress a moan.

His eyes flew open at the sound, and he abruptly dropped her wrist. He took a step back. "Forgive me, forgive me... my control... I... "

He had mistaken her sound of pleasure as a protest. Selene could see him gearing up to storm off in a brooding tornado of self-loathing. But she couldn't let that happen. He needed to know he wasn't the only one who felt the pull they had to each other or this feeling of connection, of desire that she couldn't seem to shake. He wasn't going to leave her alone with those feelings, not tonight.

"Wait!" She grabbed both of his shoulders to hold him in place. And then, without thinking, weighing the pros and cons, or dissecting her decision, she kissed him fully on the mouth.

When he froze, Selene felt a stab of panic that her advances were unwelcome. But then he took a clumsy step closer and seemed to melt into her. His arms shot around her back and waist to squeeze her to him. Emboldened, Selene spread her knees, inviting him closer and offering more access to her body. He greedily accepted.

Grabbing her hips, he jerked her body toward him, and she gasped at the feel of his massive erection pressing right where she needed it most. The tips of his claws bit into her as he clasped her to him. His mouth was hot and insistent on hers. When his lips parted slightly, Selene seized the opportunity to sweep her tongue inside. He responded instantly, rolling and thrusting his tongue against hers. His taste was addictive, dark but with an edge of smoky sweetness, like good whiskey. All she wanted was more. Her head angled to the side to deepen the kiss, and she felt him shudder.

It was a kiss that spoke of hunger and desperation. A kiss of unleashed passion and barely restrained control. A kiss that burned like fire but quenched a biting ache inside her.

Her hands roved up and down his back before he traced his lips across her jaw and down her neck. The way his muscles twitched and jerked under her fingers was thrilling. A demon—a huge, fearsome creature straight from the Underworld—was trembling under her touch. Holding her body against his as if he would die without it.

One of Sam's hands tangled in her hair, pulling her head back to expose her throat. The light kisses on her neck turned to swirling licks of his tongue and not-so-gentle nips of teeth before his tongue danced around the V-neck of her nightgown. His touch was becoming rougher, more urgent, and she pressed closer to him. She wanted to drown in his passion. Bury herself in his strength and fully embrace the wild abandon she felt.

Smoothing his hands to her shoulders, he gathered handfuls of her nightgown, as though he were about to rip the fabric straight from her body. A tiny, practical part of her brain cried out that he was about to destroy the gorgeous nightgown Arkaya had made for her, and she stiffened.

The buttons! Use the buttons!

He seemed to notice her tension in her and growled. The sound was menacing—a wordless warning that said, *don't deny me*. His fists tightened on her nightgown, and all she could gasp out was a weak, "No!"

He abruptly dropped his hands and stumbled back, his chest heaving.

Selene's lust-addled brain wasn't working right, so she just stared at him. When she regained the slightest composure, she opened her mouth to tell him what she meant. That she didn't mean for him to stop completely, but he cut her off. "Don't say a word. My control is not... This was a mistake."

"But Sam, I—"

"Don't!"

Her mouth snapped shut at the threat in his voice. His jaw clenched, and he looked up at the ceiling, seeming to fight for control. He ran a shaky hand over his face and then looked at her, his red eyes skimming over her bare skin before a mask of cold indifference shuttered his features. He snarled, "This cannot happen again," then stomped out of the kitchen.

CHAPTER 24

Selene stayed in the kitchen for several minutes after Sam stormed off, waiting for her heart to steady. Part of her hoped he might come back, but that didn't seem likely. Once her nerves had settled, she crept back to her room. The cold floor on her bare feet was shocking, but each step grounded her. It was clearing the fog in her head, and pulling her down to reality.

Sam's red eyes burned in her mind when she climbed back under the covers. His words had stung, but maybe he was right. Maybe it shouldn't happen again. Who was she fooling? Mindlessly kissing and rubbing up against someone like that. Fantasizing about having a fling, taking a lover. Letting that lover do whatever he had wanted to her right there in the kitchen. On the counter. With their hosts sleeping in the next room.

Good grief. That wasn't like her at all.

Or was it? Damn it; she had been enjoying that kiss. And not opposed to what would happen next. For a moment, she thought about bursting into the attic to finish what they had started. Take him by the horns, so to speak, and scratch this itch so she could stop obsessing about it. But she put the idea aside.

Selene stared up at the ceiling, marveling at how much could change in just a moment. Now that their attraction to each other was out in the open, what would happen next?

When Selene came downstairs the next morning, Brunie had another full spread on the table. Instead of a roast, a tower of fried meat dominated the table. Softball-sized muffins replaced the bread rolls, with sides that looked like Aurelian versions of fried potatoes, scrambled eggs, and toast. Selene's mouth watered.

"There she is, our lovely Selene. Good morning!" Eldridge gestured for her to pull up a chair. Sam was nowhere in sight. "Would you like some tea?"

Selene heard the sharp click of Brunie's talons behind her and sat down. A platter of sausages was placed near her elbow, followed by a massive fruit salad.

"Eat up, dear," Brunie said, patting Selene's shoulder. Selene began to fill her plate and smiled. Although she had only known them for a day, Brunie and Eldridge made her feel like family. It was easy being with them. She could relax instead of being hyper-vigilant to avoid a fight or shrink in her chair so she wouldn't be criticized.

"So... where's Sam?" Selene asked, trying to sound casual. She tapped her fork against her plate. "He's missing out."

"He's outside, building me a new workbench. Go call him in, Brunie," Eldridge said.

Brunie pulled open the side door to yell, "Samael! Breakfast!" When she got no reply, she marched outside. Soon the sound of raised voices drifted in. Although the words were muffled, it was clear that Sam was refusing to come in. Brunie did not accept that answer. They argued back and forth until Brunie sailed back in the house triumphantly, with Sam glowering behind her.

"Good morning, Samael," Eldridge chirped. Sam mumbled a greeting and slumped into his chair, glancing over at Selene before plowing a hand through his hair. Brunie began to fill his plate with eggs. His sullen attitude made Selene feel like she needed to fill the silence with something pleasant.

"Brunie, I meant to ask last night, how did you all meet? Have you both spent time at Queen Thema's castle?"

Brunie's eyes lit up. "Samael didn't tell you?"

"No," Selene said. "But I'd love to hear about it."

Brunie leaned back as though she were about launch into a sweeping epic, but the sound of a growl made them all turn.

"No," Sam said. "We don't need to discuss that."

"Pardon?" Brunie said.

"We're not discussing it."

"Why?" Brunie asked.

"Because I forbid it," Sam replied.

"Ha! You think you can tell me what I can and can't say in my own home?" Brunie said.

Eldridge cut in, "Eh... Selene, we know Samael from long ago—a time that's not worth mentioning. Isn't that right, Brunie? Not worth mentioning."

Brunie's tail-feathers pulsed. She and Sam glared at each other until he said, "Selene, I appreciate your interest, but I don't wish to reminisce today."

Selene bit her lip. "I'm sorry, I was only curious about how everyone knew each other."

Brunie leaned forward to meet Selene's eye. Then a string of words tumbled out of her mouth in one continuous sentence, "We were all held prisoner by vampires who did terrible things until Samael killed them all and burned everything!" When she finished, she sat back in her chair with a satisfied smile.

Sam's eyes turned from soft brown to a cold red. Then he stood up so fast his chair fell to the ground with a *bang* that made everyone jump and stormed out of the house.

Eldridge sighed. "Brunie, my love... "

"What? Selene asked me a question, and you know I can't keep a secret."

"I think he wanted to tell her in his own time."

"It's my story too!" Brunie said.

Selene wished there was a nearby hole she could crawl into. "I'm sorry. I didn't mean to cause any trouble."

Eldridge's eyes were gentle. "You didn't. Samael is just a bit... sensitive about his past. I'm sure he wanted to tell you, but... " He stroked his chin thoughtfully. "Now that's it's out in the open, I suppose it would be better that you hear it from us. He would only give you half the story."

"That's right," Brunie said. She ran her knuckles over the scarred side of her face. "It was the greatest day of my life when I received these scars, but you'd think it was the worst to hear it from him. Would you like a muffin?"

Selene shook her head, her appetite suddenly gone.

Eldridge crossed his arms. "Brunie and I met Samael when he was a boy. You know he was kidnapped from the Underworld and brought here, don't you?"

"Yes."

"Right. Well, he was left in the care of a cruel, terrible vampire named Julian. There are a few things you need to know about Julian. First is, he enjoyed gambling, he did. And gold. But many of the queens don't approve of gambling and have banned it from their lands."

"Queen Aello of the Harpies is one of them," Brunie said with pride. "As is Queen Kebee, Queen Yerena, Queen Cebna—"

"Many of the queens," Eldridge interrupted. "The second thing you need to know about Julian is that he had some... odd notions."

"About blood," Brunie said.

"Yes. And the superiority of different races, but mainly about blood. Julian believed Aurelian blood was inferior, but could be made more potent, more nourishing if the heart beat faster before drinking. If the victim was quite frightened."

"Or tortured. Or in pain," Brunie added.

The eggs and toast in Selene's stomach turned sour.

Eldridge continued, "Julian was a charming sort and convinced a lot of vampires to believe in the power of tormented blood, just as he did. So he found a way to combine all the things he loved—gambling, gold, and torture—and called it sport.

Selene listened as Eldridge explained how Julian held fighting matches where the losers would be drained to death by the highest vampire bidder. He traveled by wagon so he could sleep during the day, and added more wagons to his operation as he recruited young males to fight.

"You look a bit pale, dear. Do you want us to stop telling this story?" Brunie asked.

"I'm all right," Selene lied. Mounting dread as to how the three of them fit into all of this was making her nauseated. "Please continue."

Eldridge's ears twitched. "Julian had a team of fighters that were making him a lot of money and a lot of tormented blood. But they were frequently injured, and it was expensive to keep buying meals from taverns. So he went in search of staff."

"He found me first," Brunie said as she stood to take Selene's plate. "I was cooking at an inn called The Whiskered Fish until he came along. People used to come from all over for my pies," Her voice trailed off and pain clouded her features. "Snatched me up while I was taking out the rubbish bin. Clipped my wings, and that was that. They're fine now, but it was very painful."

Eldridge reached out to take her hand, but Brunie waved him away to go into the kitchen. His eyes were sad as he looked at Selene. "Then he found me living in a town called Redfalls. I used to handle transactions for the local merchants until Julian walked in one day and plucked me from my desk. He tossed me into a wagon and told me I would be managing his gold."

Brunie came back into the room. "It was just a few weeks before little Samael arrived."

"But by that time, Julian had gotten himself into trouble with debts. He couldn't afford to buy another wagon, so he put Samael in my cell with me," Eldridge said.

Brunie put her hand over her heart. "The only bit of good fortune the boy had at the time."

"He was so frightened," Eldridge said. "Didn't understand what had happened to him and cried for his mother for months, he did. I did my best to comfort him, as did Brunie. None of us knew much about demons, but we noticed the lad had a temper. He would get very angry, very fast if someone did something he didn't like. Vengeance, he used to say over and over. Vengeance. And he had a preoccupation with rules. Always wanting to know what was allowed, what was forbidden. Each night, we talked about what was right and wrong in Aurelia. Then Julian found a use for his demon prisoner."

"How?" Selene asked.

"Tormented blood. He began using the boy to get it. It started with Julian making Samael growl and intimidate his fighters to get their fear flowing. Even as a young demon, he could be very frightening. Then when Julian grew bored of that, he began to place petty criminals before Samael and encouraged him to respond with violence."

"Which he did. To the delight of the crowds," Brunie added. "Soon, Samael's part of the show began to eclipse the fights themselves."

"Oh God," Selene murmured.

"As he grew, he became quite gifted at combat. He had to learn quickly, as many of Julian's victims fought hard for their own survival. Julian didn't like for Samael to kill within the tent—it was tormented, living blood he was after. But sometimes... " Eldridge paused. "Sometimes, the lad didn't always know how to temper his strength. When the rage would overtake him, his body became even more demonlike. In those moments, he possessed the least amount of control and would often do the most damage."

Selene remembered how haunted Sam's face had looked when she asked if he had ever killed anyone. "I see," she murmured.

"He cried for weeks every time he took a life," Eldridge said. "We thought it was strange at first, a demon with remorse? But we bought a book on demons from a traveling merchant and learned it was forbidden for his kind to kill. It interfered with the order of things, you see. Demons have a strong belief in fate and don't like to see souls come to the Underworld by the hand of their own. And we knew how fixated with rules Samael was. So, we tried to teach him how to control his rage and focus his mind. The calmer Samael was, the less Julian used him."

The room was quiet until Eldridge exhaled. "Samael and I continued to share a cell, even when he grew very large. I taught him how to read, and every day we worked on the difference between right and wrong. He learned how to control his instincts, and Brunie and I fell in love, despite the terrible circumstances. We did our best to protect Samael, and he protected us. We protected each other from the misery that was our life."

"We survived," Brunie said.

The atmosphere was heavy until Selene asked, "How did you escape?"

Her question seemed to drop the veil of sadness from Brunie's face, replacing it with a ruthless grin. "With fire. And vengeance!"

Eldridge chuckled. "Yes, that's a good way to describe it. I believe it started with Julian beating his woman in the Padu. Is that right, dear?"

"Yes, he was abusing Margery. She had failed to lure enough bettors to the tent that night. We had been traveling with the Padu market at that time."

Selene's pulse picked up at the familiar name.

"Normally, Julian kept Samael in shackles until just before a show and then cuffed him immediately after. But that night the crowds were sparse and Julian was angry. After he had unshackled Samael, he turned to pull Margery by the hair. The crowd began to cheer—they were a cruel, savage group—so Julian continued to abuse her."

"That's awful," Selene said. Her thoughts went back to the gruesome scars she had seen around Sam's wrists and the leather bracers he wore to hide them.

"I don't know if it was too much for Samael to bear or if he knew there wouldn't be another opportunity without the chains, but he took his chance. We all watched as he reached out and grasped Julian's head—"

"Twisted it right off his body," Brunie exclaimed.

"Clean off," Eldridge said. "I've never seen anything like it. The audience started screaming. I watched as Samael gave fully into his demonic instincts. He began plucking the heads from any vampire he could reach. And when they started to flee the tent?"

"Fire!" Brunie cried. "The fire he set grew until vampires came running out screaming—it was a glorious sight! But I was locked in my wagon, you see, and eventually, the flames spread."

"Once Samael realized, he ran to pull the doors off each wagon. But for some, it was too late," Eldridge said sadly. "He got to Brunie's tent a bit later than he would have liked."

Brunie gestured to the burned side of her face. "I welcomed the pain. I would have endured burns throughout my entire body to see Julian die!"

Eldridge shrugged. "And die, he did. Without a head, well, there's no coming back from that. And as for the rest of the vampires that were burned but not beheaded? The morning sun took care of them."

"He spared Margery, though. And anyone else who was innocent or had been kind to him. He freed us all," Brunie said, her eyes misting with tears.

"A true hero," Eldridge said.

Selene felt spellbound. She was in awe of everything Sam had been through as well as the resilience of Brunie and Eldridge. How did they have the fortitude to survive such an ordeal, let alone take a little demon under their wing?

"After that we came here." Eldridge gestured around the room. "Built this house. Tried to forget."

"We had begged Samael to come with us, but he refused," Brunie said. "He wanted to live alone, he had said, and fled into the forest. Of course, we were sick with worry for him."

Selene nodded, remembering Queen Thema's story of how Sam rescued her in the forest.

Eldridge smiled. "But then one day, years later, we received a letter from Samael telling us how he was working as a guard at Queen Thema's castle. A few months later, he came to visit. It was a glorious day. He built much of our furniture, and continues to visit us every so often. We've asked him to stay on many times, but he's always refused."

"What's so wonderful about the Malkina that keeps him there?" Brunie grumbled. "They're haughty and vain. Terrible cooks too, from what I hear."

"Dearest, I think he believes himself to be bad luck for us."

"Rubbish."

"It's his choice, Brunie. I've always said he's as clever as a Goblyn. Seems he's stubborn as a Harpy too."

Brunie swatted him on the arm and got up to go back in the kitchen, leaving Selene alone with Eldridge. The strain of reliving such painful memories was evident in his face. Leaning toward her, the Goblyn met her eyes.

"Selene, you must understand that although many terrible things have happened to Samael, he's never given into true evil. He tries very hard to do his best and control his instincts. He believes in justice and is driven to uphold it."

"I understand."

"Sometimes, he just needs a bit of patience. And *permission*. His experience with females is... limited. He doesn't always understand the unspoken, and he fears making a mistake. Fears losing control. If someone were to want something from Samael, well... "

He paused and gave her a meaningful look. "She should be bold in asking for it."

CHAPTER 25

After obsessing all day about what Selene had thought about his time in the blood wagons, the last way Sam wanted to spend his evening was at a boisterous party to celebrate the founding of Snowmelt. Though as Eldridge nudged him toward the waiting carriage, it seemed he didn't have a choice. Selene and Brunie were already seated in the back, their laps stacked with the pies they had spent the day baking.

Without even bothering to brush the sawdust from his tunic, Sam stole a glance at Selene before climbing up into the front seat. He had kept his distance from her all day and was surprised to see that she wore a formal dress. It was pink with delicate straps skimming over her Nereid-creamed shoulders, with a skirt made of voluminous netting. The brief glimpse had made his pulse pound, yet he declined to comment as Rainsilver set off for the town hall.

While they rode, Brunie jabbered away, pointing out local landmarks. Sam could tell from Eldridge's posture he wanted to talk, but Sam didn't initiate conversation. They had conversed enough for the day.

Eldridge had found him in the barn about an hour after he had stormed out at breakfast. Not only did the Goblyn chastise him for leaving the table so rudely, he quietly explained that they had told Selene everything about their past together. Sam had felt sick, but he should have known that a Harpy can't resist answering a question posed to her. He had wanted Selene to see him as a self-commanded male who valued justice and reason—steadfast, controlled, and merciful. Not a sadistic killer who had taken the lives of innocents. Or someone who was easily manipulated and unable to escape his own confinement for many years.

Yet Eldridge had assured him Selene wasn't upset by the news. She was sympathetic, he had said. She was horrified by what Julian had done, but not by Sam's violence. Sam refused to believe him. It was too much, too confusing for him to take in, especially after how he had lost control in the kitchen the night before.

So he had spent the day avoiding everyone, fixing any little thing he could find around the farm, and telling himself he wasn't affected at all by what a human thought of him. He reminded himself that he was using her to get to Zaybris, nothing more. It had worked, almost —until he saw Selene in that dress.

After they arrived at the community hall, Sam lingered outside as the others went in. Using the excuse of tying up the horse, he performed a thorough inspection of every spring, strap, axle, and spoke of the carriage. When he was certain everything was in working order, and he had no more excuses to stay outside, he entered the hall.

A wall of sound hit him when he passed through doors—music, singing, and laughter. The hall's design was humble but appropriate for the needs of Snowmelt. It was in the shape of a rectangle, with hardwood floors gleaming under lamps hung from the ceiling. Homespun quilts decorated the brick walls, while two massive port-hole windows were set high up near the ceiling on either side of the building. The twin surfaces were foggy with the heat of so many bodies, but stars could be seen glinting through the glass.

Brunie caught his eye from her post behind a table serving pie.

She pointed to the stage. Eldridge stood singing in front of a handful of musicians while a small crowd of Harpies cheered for him from the floor. The tune was fast and upbeat, and Sam's mouth tugged up at the sight of Eldridge's enthusiasm.

The sound of Eldridge's voice and the scent of Brunie's pies made Sam feel gratified. It was good to see them both so happy. If he did nothing else honorable, at least he would know that the two he loved best in this realm had found peace.

Sam made his way toward the drink table. Snowmelt was mostly a town of farmers, and it was obvious that the presence of a demon flustered them. After receiving a generous pour of ale, he found a quiet corner to disappear into.

He hadn't called the shadows, but they seemed to know when he was in turmoil and came swirling. Slumping onto a tiny stool, he stared down into the ale's foamy surface. A familiar laugh jerked his attention up.

It was Selene. Far across the room, giggling and stepping from one male's embrace to the next in a line dance. It seemed to be a well-practiced routine from the movements of the other partici-pants, but Selene did not appear embarrassed about her inability to keep up. On the contrary, she seemed to find it delightful. Other males took advantage of her ignorance with hands-on corrections, extra touches, twirls, and dips.

Sam watched them with narrowed eyes. Did she relish being pawed at by so many strange hands? Where was her sense of prudence? He began to fantasize about elaborate ways to torture each male she touched. He wondered what the Underworld's Master of Pain would recommend. Skin flaying? Acid? Impalement? The possibilities were as endless as they were intriguing.

The musicians ended their up-tempo song and started a slower-paced tune. More couples strolled out to the dance floor, and Selene became surrounded by males trying to press a drink into her hand. Most of them held mugs of ale, which made Sam snort. *She loathes ale, you fools.* It was the Nereid with the wineglass who gained her favor. When Selene took a sip, a tremor ran through him. It was her desire for a glass of water that had brought on the events of last night.

He still wasn't convinced he hadn't imagined the whole thing. The feel of her in his arms, so pliant and lush, was like a dream. He couldn't get enough—her touch, her taste, her scent. To have her warm skin under his tongue and her hands on his body had made him crazed. Desperate and greedy for more.

Why had she kissed him? The movement had been so unexpected he froze—he was sure she hadn't meant to kiss him fully on the mouth. But she didn't pull away. She had parted her thighs as if in welcome and arched her back towards him. She had made him feel as if she wanted his mouth, his hands on her. Suddenly Eldridge's idea that she was a little bit fond of him didn't seem so outlandish.

It was her hair that smelled of honey, he had realized. Her skin was like red berries, but the honey scent came from her hair. Exquisite. Addicting. And the sounds she made? He could have come just from hearing her little gasps and moans.

But then his control... faltered. He had become mindless. Selfishly dragging his mouth all over her tender flesh, ready to tear her clothes off and slake his desire any way he could. A slave to sensation, no better than a filthy vampire.

He watched the Nereid male across the room whisper in Selene's ear and her head tip back with laughter. Familiar urges to punish rose. Dark possessiveness shot through Sam as his mind fogged with one word—*mine.*

It flashed across his consciousness for only a second, but the effect was powerful. *Mine.* That was how he was starting to place her. He rubbed his forehead, startled by the way his mind was now beginning to keep pace with his body's absurd delusions of matehood. The pair spun around, and he stared at the skin of Selene's exposed back. Wingless. Very human shoulder blades and nothing more.

The hall felt too hot, and the air seemed stale. He needed to leave. Now.

After slipping out the front doors, he relished the brisk night air. The hall had been built on a wooded area near the river, and the water's sound was soothing.

Mine. What was wrong with him? One kiss from a beautiful human, and he was certain she was his mate? Absurd. He tried not to relive each moment of their encounter in the kitchen, but he couldn't stop. He wished he had gone slower, taken the time to savor every second, every moment until he had started to lose control.

The sound of footsteps crunching along the ground made Sam turn, then mutter a curse. Of all the people who could have come out at that moment, it had to be Selene. She sank onto a wooden bench overlooking the water. Her breathing was still choppy from dancing as she slumped back and sighed.

"Grown tired of cavorting with simpletons, have you?" Sam asked, unable to keep the bitterness from his voice.

Selene jerked upright. "Where are you?"

Sam moved from behind the tree to stand in front of her.

"You nearly gave me a heart attack," Selene said. Her relieved expression changed to one of indignation. "Did you just say 'cavorting?'"

"That's one word to describe your wanton display."

"Really? Cavorting? What am I, a nymph?"

"I imagine nymphs would have more discretion," he said coldly. "Where did you get that dress?"

She gaped at him. "Hollen packed it for me. But hold on, are you slut-shaming me right now? Seriously?"

"I don't know what that means, but it's obvious that you enjoyed having many, many dance partners tonight."

She pressed her lips together. "I like dancing, okay? And men who don't go out of their way to avoid me."

"Enjoy talk of crop diseases and hay mowing, do you?"

Selene scowled up at him. "If you wanted a dance, all you had to do was ask."

"I do not dance!" he thundered.

He instantly regretted his tone when she shrank back on the bench. After they regarded each other in silence, she said, "Why are you so angry with me?"

He shrugged.

"This is about more than me dancing," she said.

He shrugged again.

"Is this about what Brunie and Eldridge told me? Whatever happened in your past, I don't care," she said. "To be honest, I'm in awe of how you came through it."

He touched a cluster of green berries sprouting from a bush. "I don't need your pity."

"It's not pity."

"Now that you know what happened I don't want to ever talk about it again. Do you understand?" he said.

"I understand. But I want to say that I think you're very brave. And resilient. That's all."

He frowned. Her words were gratifying, but he was unsure of how to respond. He was also tired of thinking, talking, obsessing about his past. If she were agreeable to letting it go, he would be as well. To change the subject, he asked the question that had been plaguing him all day.

"Last night, in the kitchen... why did you do it?"

"What?"

He scowled, reluctant to actually say the word *kiss*. It seemed too subdued, too chaste for what they had shared. "What do you think?"

She returned the same ambiguous shrug he had given her a moment before.

His shoulders tightened. Why was she being so difficult? He took a step closer and dropped his voice, hoping to intimidate her into being truthful. "If you are playing a game, take care. Do not mistake me for one of your human men or even an Aurelian. You don't understand the drives you invoke when tempting a demon. Now tell me why you did it."

She twirled a lock of hair around her finger. "I did it because I... I've wondered for so long what it would be like to kiss you. So when the opportunity came—"

"You've thought about kissing me? Before last night?"

"Yes."

Pleasure rushed through him. Wondered for so long, she had said. *How long? And how detailed had those wonderings been?* But the feeling was short-lived. "Last night was a mistake. My control slipped, and I... " He glanced at the skin of her collarbone and chest, surprised there were no bruises there. "I did things I regret."

A look he couldn't recognize passed across her face. "I don't have any regrets," she said. "Maybe that it ended too soon." Her cheeks flushed.

Maddening human! Sam scanned her face suspiciously, looking for any signs of jest or duplicity, yet she seemed sincere.

He began to pace in front of her. She made him feel so off-balance, so uncertain of everything he knew to be true. Combat against an enemy he understood. He was gifted at doling out punishment. Masterful at upholding justice. But interpreting females? He had never felt so adrift. All of his conflicted feelings bubbled up into one emotion that he was very familiar with—anger.

"How can you say it ended too soon when you told me to stop?" he seethed, pointing an accusatory finger.

"I never asked you to stop."

"You said 'no,' and I stopped."

"Yes, but you didn't let me finish!"

"What could come after that? I did as you asked!" His voice continued to rise. "Are all humans this contrary, or is it just you?"

Selene raised her chin. Her face contorted from irritation into a look that could only be described as severe. She stood and walked toward him. He felt himself sway like her body held a pulling force that he was helpless to resist. Standing toe to toe, she looked up into his eyes. She wetted her lips, and he instantly went rock hard. Was she going to kiss him again? Ask him to kiss her? His breath quickened in anticipation. All his anger evaporated, and his hands reached for her waist.

In a voice like sugared venom, she whispered, "I said 'no' because I thought you were about to tear off my nightgown. If you had let me *speak*, I would have told you to unbutton it."

Then without waiting for him to respond, she turned on her heel and marched back into the hall. The doors slammed, and the sound echoed throughout the valley, causing birds to bolt out of the trees. Sam stood speechless in the dark for several moments, just staring at the bench where she had sat.

When the full effect of her words hit, the surge of lust nearly sent him to his knees. He resumed his pacing.

She had enjoyed their kiss. Didn't want him to stop. He had not hurt her or gotten too rough. Instead, he had abandoned her and left her wanting. Alone in her need and returning to a cold bed. Unfulfilled. He had been so lost to his own pleasure, he had failed to tend to her properly.

Shame at his ineptitude washed over him, and he let out a howl of rage. If she had felt anything close to the deprived ache he felt that night...

And now she was in the arms of other males. Possibly seeking from them that which he denied her. Reveling in the attention of those more skilled at flattery and seduction than he was. Allowing the invasion of their filthy hands, pressing bodies, and whispers of promised delights.

A red haze clouded his vision, and his body strained. Power, strength, and the rush of determined focus flooded his veins. The shadows flocked to pulsate around him, and his claws extended. Horns flaring, he knew what needed to be done.

Nothing would keep him from her this time.

CHAPTER 26

S elene hadn't meant to slam the doors so hard behind her, but damn, the noise was satisfying. The musicians were playing something like a polka when she came in, and several of her dance partners swarmed. They were obviously anxious for her return, and she offered a smile to each of them.

I'll show him cavorting!

Grasping the first hand that was extended to her, Selene was swept into an embrace by one of the reptilian Drago men. He introduced himself as Levi then began to twirl her across the dance floor. The air rushing over her skin felt heavenly, almost cooling some of the righteous anger that heated her face.

Stupid demon.

Sure, Sam looked good in a pair of horns, but his moods gave her whiplash. And so sulky! The way he had avoided her today had stung, especially when all she could think about was kissing him again. Even though apparently he regretted it—that was a treat to hear. Had she been too forward last night? A familiar rush of shame made her throat tighten as they danced.

No. You're not going there.

207

Her posture straightened as she stopped the speeding train of self-doubt in its tracks. For years she had blamed herself for her dismal sex life—wondering if she was too needy, too demanding, too idealistic, or maybe she simply wasn't attractive enough to have the passion she craved. It had never occurred to her that maybe *she* wasn't the one broken. But Aurelian Selene didn't put up with any of that. She was done catering to the sexual hang-ups of men. She refused to feel bad about what happened last night, or about what she had said about the buttons. And she sure as hell wasn't going to stop dancing just because Sam didn't approve.

She had spent her life whittling herself down to be the person others wanted her to be. It was as exhausting as it was useless. *Never again.*

When the band changed tempo to a slower song Levi waltzed her to the back of the hall near a cluster of benches. But the last thing Selene wanted was to sit and chat, especially with a man whose forked tongue peeked out with each syllable. Peering over his shoulder, she scanned the crowd for a new dance partner. Feeling reckless, she decided to walk on the wild side and invite one of the burly Lycah to dance.

But as she moved to slip out of Levi's arms, she felt a crackle in the air, like the charge that comes before a lightning strike. A rush of cold air blew through the hall followed by the sound of wood banging against brick. Someone cried out indignantly. She looked across the room and gasped when she saw Sam, huge and terrifying, cutting a path across the floor.

Pulsing black mist surrounded him as he moved. His horns seemed bigger, the tips curved out as if ready for attack. The fabric of his clothes was pulled taut around his muscles, while his height pushed seven feet. His brows were drawn together, and his mouth was set in a grim line.

Blazing red eyes.

Locked squarely on her.

Her stomach flipped. He was coming for her. To do what, she

didn't know, but he looked absolutely terrifying. "Shit!" she cried as her heart began to jackhammer. What had Aurelian Selene unleashed?

People were moving out of Sam's path and Selene stiffened as he came close, causing Levi to follow her gaze. "Who is--"

The words died on his lips when Sam stopped in front of them. Levi released Selene and stumbled back. The demon's frame was vibrating with tension. Vaporous black shapes churned around them like hungry wraiths until Sam murmured a command and they dissolved.

With an inscrutable expression, Sam slowly raised his hand. Selene flinched, certain that he was about to grab Levi and tear him apart. Him and every other guy she had danced with, just as he did to the Lycah in Iriswood. Frantically, she looked around for Eldridge or someone to intervene.

But Sam didn't attack; he seemed oblivious to Levi's presence. He locked eyes with Selene and turned his palm up, extending it to her. His breaths were choppy as he gazed down at her.

"Will you dance?"

Selene looked down at his outstretched hand, then up to his face. Gradually she realized his eyelids weren't hooded with savage rage —they were dark with desire. Single-minded, unrelenting hunger.

For her.

Wordlessly, she slipped her hand into his. Roughly, he pulled her close until her breasts were crushed against his front. One large palm pressed into her lower back while the other threaded his fingers through hers. He tucked their entwined hands against his chest before she rested her other hand on his shoulder.

They stayed that way for a moment—staring into each other's eyes while couples danced around them. She felt him exhale as if a great pressure within him had lightened. His breath trailed down her neck like a caress.

Then awkwardly, he took a step to the side. And a step backward. Mimicking the other couples on the floor. He was obviously uncomfortable and very uncoordinated. Yet the earnestness of his effort made Selene's heart feel like it might burst. He was trying. Really trying. For her.

Suddenly she was overwhelmed with the need to kiss him. Just to make sure this... whatever *this* was between them wasn't only in her imagination. But just as she curled her fingers into the nape of his neck, they heard a crash, followed by screams. Blood-curdling shrieks came from the other side of the hall, followed by the sound of furniture breaking. The music stopped without warning.

Eldridge suddenly appeared to tug at Sam's arm. "Vampires have come!"

The panic in Eldridge's voice made Sam seethe. He let go of Selene and whirled around to see a swarm of figures in black capes streaming into the hall. Vampires in Snowmelt weren't unheard of, but the sheer number of them descending at once was alarming. He nudged Selene until her back hit the wall so he could shield her.

"What do they want?" she asked.

"I don't know," said Eldridge. He began breaking apart a nearby chair and stuffing pieces of wood into his pockets.

They watched the figures move through the crowd. One grabbed a Nereid and examined her face and ears. When she responded with a quick head-butt, he threw her to the ground. Other vampires did the same—examining each person's face and ears, then tossing them aside. Some were biting, then spitting the blood onto the floor, as if in disgust. Many Aurelians were fighting back, but most were trying to flee. Sam tensed when he realized they were looking for someone.

Selene.

"We need to get everyone out—" Eldridge's words were cut short as a vampire lunged for him with fangs bared. Quickly, the Goblyn sunk a shard of wood into the creature's chest, causing it to fall with a gurgle of disbelief. "I have to find Brunie!" he said, and began running toward the crowd of those trying to escape.

Sam was grateful that both Eldridge and Brunie knew how to handle themselves in an attack like this. More vampires were rushing in, blocking the door. Now they were simply assaulting and biting anyone they encountered.

"What's happening?" Selene whispered frantically.

"Stay quiet," Sam growled over his shoulder. He quickly commanded the shadows to bathe Selene in darkness until he could think of a way to get her out. When the dark shapes made her flinch, Sam said, "They won't hurt you. I just need to keep you hidden."

A pained moan drew his attention to the right. A vampire was gulping blood from a Drago's throat. Realizing it was the male that had been dancing with Selene, Sam moved to block her view, but it was too late. She made an involuntary noise, and the vampire paused. He looked at Sam curiously, as though he had just noticed there was a demon in their midst, protecting something.

The vampire dropped his kill to creep closer, but then another one sprung out from the left. It extended a bony arm to grasp at Selene, which Sam quickly snapped in two, causing the vampire to fall back in pain.

The vampire that had been stalking them neared, craning his neck to see behind Sam. His grin fell when Sam grasped his head and twisted it off. His corpse thumped to the ground near Selene's feet and Sam tossed the head away. He hated that Selene had to see him perform such a gruesome act, but he was also grateful she had not screamed.

More vampires swarmed, making Sam's anger intensify. He took a step backward, further enclosing Selene between his body and the wall. Her breath was coming fast and his insides plummeted, realizing they were trapped. The only exit was the front door, which now teemed with vampires.

The caped figures approached them with fangs dripping. Some with saliva, others with blood. The smell was revolting. The combination of being cornered, the threat to Selene, and his hatred of vampires was making him frenzied. He glanced back to see that Selene's face was pale with fright through the shadows. He reached his hand behind him and she took it.

He needed to strike. To stake, behead, and attack. But to do so would leave Selene exposed, and that was a risk he would not take.

Protect.

Perhaps if he offered himself to the vampires, Selene could slip away. He was immune to disease and age, but he could still be killed. A draining might not kill him completely, but the pain would be excruciating. Especially if the vampires ripped and tore at his flesh as they were doing to the Aurelians.

But as he was about to step forward to sacrifice himself, a gust of wind hit them from above, followed by a horrendous chorus of screeching. He looked up to see Brunie and every other Harpy in Snowmelt hovering above them, nearly twenty in total. Batting their great wings, they stretched out their feet to furiously claw at the vampires surrounding him and Selene.

The undead horde drew back. Some fell to the ground, others cried out as sharp talons tore through their eyes and gored their decayed faces.

"Kill them all!" Brunie shrieked. And then to Sam she shouted, "We've got Selene!"

Sam gave her a salute as a deadly smile crossed his lips. Brunie and the Harpies would allow no harm to come to Selene. And now that she was taken care of, he would eliminate the threat.

Punish them.

Sam turned and lifted Selene's hand. He pressed his lips to her knuckles. "Selene, I'm going to have to use... violence."

She nodded quickly. "Yes, I know."

"Go with Brunie. I'll come to you soon," he said roughly. The desperate way she looked back at him made him feel crazed. His drive to vanquish her enemies warred with a deep need to soothe her. He quickly dropped her hand before he lost focus.

His body quaked as he stepped forward. Inhaling deeply, he called the shadows back to him as his demonic urges took hold. *Kill them all. Protect my mate.* His horns grew, his vision turned red. Power and strength flooded his limbs as his mind focused on one thing —vengeance.

CHAPTER 27

S elene felt lost as Sam charged into the fray. *Don't leave me!* But she was alone only for a second before Brunie swooped in front of her. Before they could speak, a wooden table came skidding toward them. Another Harpy with black wings appeared and tugged Selene to the floor. Pointing to the table, she shouted, "Get under there. Now!"

Selene dropped to her knees and crawled under, gripping the thick table legs. She then watched as Brunie grabbed one of the hall's heavy wooden chairs and shot toward the ceiling with it. She swung the chair over her head to bang against one of the enormous port-hole windows set into the brick. A second Harpy grabbed another chair to help. It took them four tries before a shower of glass rained down from above. Although Selene was safe under the table, the shards of glass pebbling the floor around her made her cover her head defensively.

Seconds later, Brunie was in front of Selene, pulling her out to stand. "Watch your step! Are you afraid of heights, dear?" she asked. Before Selene could answer, a vampire lunged at Brunie on the right.

Selene scrambled back, muffling her scream when the vampire came so close, she could see blood dripping from his fangs.

"Hello again," the vampire snarled as one hand reached for her, his other hand clenched around a white scrap of fabric.

Selene stumbled, certain this was it—she was about to die. But Brunie was too quick. Using her powerful wings, she launched herself into the air, and with an ear-piercing shriek, clawed through the vampire's gut. Rotted organs tumbled to the ground, the smell making Selene gag. The vampire dropped to his knees, then lifted the white fabric to his nose, huffing it like a drug. He met Selene's eyes and she blinked in recognition. It was the vampire that had lapped up the Lycah's blood in Iriswood. When she realized what he held in his hand, horror rose. It looked just like the napkin she had used to wipe blood from her hands at the tavern.

Brunie tugged Selene's shoulder, pulling her attention away from the vampire as it writhed in the throes of death. Extending her arms out into the shape of a T, Brunie said, "Hold your arms out like this, and we'll be off. Quick now."

Selene was too numb to ask why, so she did. Brunie hovered above her, then something sharp and strong curled under Selene's arms before her feet lifted off the ground. The feeling made her stomach bottom out, and instinctively, she reached up to grab something stable. Her fingers wrapped around Brunie's ankles, still sticky with vampire blood.

"I've got you!" Brunie called, her talons tightening around Selene's arms. As they continued to rise, another Harpy flew alongside them.

Selene tried to be grateful for her rescue instead of dwelling on how she dangled mid-air. One of the white slippers Hollen packed slipped off her foot, and as she watched it fall, she took in the battle below. Eldridge was sparring near the stage, a pile of dead vampires littering the ground near him. Other Harpies continued to use their talons to maim their attackers. A Malkina man was smashing furniture, tossing stakes to anyone nearby, and a group of Lycah was circling a trio of vampires.

In the middle of the room, she saw Sam. He looked different, larger and scarier than she had ever seen him before. More like a storybook demon with massive S-shaped horns, deep red skin, and an incredibly powerful build. He towered over everyone else in the room. Figures surrounded him, but he fought quickly and efficiently —beheading or staking every vampire that came near. His strength was staggering, and the grace he exuded when eliminating each threat was oddly beautiful.

Frightened as she was, a strange feeling rose inside her. It wasn't terror or panic. It was awe. Admiration. There was something deeply satisfying about watching him move. Seeing him ruthlessly defeat every enemy he encountered. Punishing those who wished to hurt her and others. Exacting vengeance, just as he was born to do.

Powerful. Mythic. Glorious.

My demon.

Selene's attention was pulled away by a blast of cold air. She looked up to see the smashed porthole window, and Brunie's destination became clear. The edges were jagged with broken glass, but the window was big enough to accommodate them both. With a puff of effort, Brunie propelled them forward. Selene's body swayed mid-air as they flew through the window, while the black-winged Harpy followed behind.

Selene's eyes watered against the rushing wind. The sounds of battle faded as they flew, replaced by the steady *whap* and *whoosh* of Harpy wings. She tightened her grip on Brunie's ankles, feeling like a mouse carried by a friendly hawk. She was not afraid of heights, but this experience was far different from the hot air balloon ride she had taken once at the fair.

They passed over the lights of Snowmelt, then a handful of farms and meadows. The Harpy flying behind them darted in front, her gray hair streaming out behind her. "Almost home!"

Relief flooded her when she saw the familiar blue barn and

cottage of Brunie and Eldridge's farm below. As they neared the ground, Brunie's wings slowed. She hovered in the air until Selene's feet touched the grass. When Brunie released her talons, Selene fell to her knees. The Harpy with the black wings was at her side, helping her to stand.

"You did well, girl!" she boomed, clapping her on the back. "Not many can endure a Harpy's flight, but you seemed to enjoy it! Care for another go in the daylight?"

"Definitely not," Selene muttered.

Brunie embraced her fiercely. "Selene, I'm proud of you. Now, go inside into the attic. Shut the door and stay quiet."

Selene spoke against Brunie's shoulder, "You're leaving me here? Alone?" The farm was eerily calm.

"Yes," Brunie said. "We're going back to finish off anything Samael and the others haven't."

"But... what if—"

"They won't find you here. Eldridge hired an enchantress to make the attic a safe room when he built this house," Brunie said. "Samael has probably killed all the vampires by now anyway."

Selene's chin began to tremble. *Don't cry, don't cry.* "I'm so scared for him. Do you think he's all right?"

Brunie laughed. "Oh, yes. Worried for you, I'd imagine, but not in any danger. You couldn't have a more devoted protector. Now run along."

"Yes. All right."

"Don't be frightened," Brunie said. "Go on."

The other Harpy stopped rearranging her feathers to give Selene an appraising look. "Where is your anger, girl?"

Selene didn't respond, not sure if she was asking a trick question.

The Harpy placed her hands on her hips. "Vampires were just trying to drain you! They wished to steal your blood and defile your flesh. You should be outraged, not fearful!"

"Be kind, Deryn," Brunie urged.

"I-I thought I was going to die," Selene answered.

"So?" Deryn thumped a fist to her own chest, then tossed her head back to let out a screech that caused lightning to flash in the sky. "Remember your anger, sweet one! There is nothing more powerful than a female's fury. Feel it, use it!"

Brunie shook her wings impatiently. "Yes, yes, our anger is as commanding as it is infinite. Now let the girl be." She nudged Selene's shoulder. "Give us a wave from the window, and we'll be off."

"Ah, I love a battle!" Deryn said jovially. "Let's call a storm once it's over!"

"Wonderful idea! Once you hear our thunder, Selene, you'll know everything's fine," Brunie said.

Selene rushed into the house. Her joints ached when she rushed up the stairs, and it took most of her strength to open the attic's big metal door. Once inside, Selene crossed the wooden floor to one of the windows. She waved down to the Harpies, and they waved back before launching themselves in the air, singing a melody that sounded like a battle march.

She watched until they were out of sight then looked around the room. It was clear why Sam stayed in the attic during visits. The space was huge. An enormous bed dominated the space, while shelves of cooking equipment lined the walls. A small sink stood in the corner.

Like a zombie, she began to wash her hands. With a nearby washcloth, she scrubbed off the Nereid cream and vampire blood splattering her skin. She tried not to think about all the dead bodies she had just seen. Why would vampires come to a little place like Snowmelt?

Yet again, she was reminded that there was so much of Aurelia she didn't understand. But for the first time since she arrived, the thought of escaping its strangeness wasn't a comfort. Because going home meant leaving Sam.

CHAPTER 28

Thunder cracked overhead. Sam pulled Rainsilver's reins to stop the carriage outside Brunie and Eldridge's cottage and shouted, "Selene!"

He knew she probably couldn't hear him, but he couldn't hold back as he leapt to the ground and sprinted past Rainsilver. Pulling the front door open, Sam burst into the house and thundered up to the attic. "Selene, it's me! Open the door!"

When she did not respond, a barrage of worries flooded him. What if one of the vampires had spotted Brunie and followed them? Selene could be miles away, being drained at that very moment. Or what if she had been injured? Perhaps Selene was lying on the attic floor right now, bleeding out.

He jiggled the handle, about to tear the door from its hinges. Finally, he heard the click of locks being undone, and the door cracked open. Selene appeared, barefoot and looking up at him with huge, frightened eyes.

Sam stepped inside. He barely had the chance to shut the door when Selene wrapped her arms around his torso. He enveloped her in his embrace.

She was alive.

She was whole.

He had kept her safe.

He squeezed her tighter against his chest, not ever wanting to let go. Dropping his cheek to her hair, he whispered, "Are you all right?"

"Yes. Are you? And Brunie and Eldridge?"

"All fine. They're back at the hall. Cleaning up." He stroked her hair, hoping the dampness of his clothes didn't bother her.

When the last of the vampires were dead, he had dived straight into the river. Fetid, gelatinous blood had coated his hands and splattered his face and horns, making him nauseous. After he had scrubbed himself clean, Eldridge appeared at the riverbank to say, "Take the carriage, go see to your mate. Brunie can fly me home."

Sam didn't quibble over the "mate" remark, just leapt onto the carriage, and took off. As the Rainsilver ran, Sam considered all of the ways Selene might be reacting to what she had seen. She was undoubtedly frightened, but how would she respond to *him?* She had seen the worst of his nature now. There was no coming back from this—yet now she had rushed into his arms.

"How many people were killed?" she asked.

"Not many," he lied. They continued to hold each other, while moonlight poured through the attic windows. He was uncertain of the correct protocol for comforting a female, but he was trying his best. "You're safe now."

After a moment, he pulled back to look at her, but his gaze fell to her dress. Red and brown stains were splashed across the bodice while bits of viscera were tangled in the skirt. "Your dress... "

She looked at the ruined garment. "I was going to change but I didn't want to leave the attic."

"Brunie might have something you can wear. Come." He let go of Selene to open a wooden chest in the corner. After some digging, he pulled out a midnight blue robe. "There are wing slits in the back, but this might do."

Running the silky fabric between her fingers she said, "Perfect."

"I'll... I'll just step out of the room while you change," he mumbled, then tossed the robe on the bed.

"Don't leave," she said quickly.

He nodded, then turned his back to her. The sound of fabric rustling filled the attic while he poured all his concentration into a protruding nail in the wall. After a few moments, Selene said, "The zipper's stuck. Can you try?" She came toward him and pointed to the back fastening.

"You want me to... ?"

"Unzip it. Or tear it off, I don't care. I don't ever want to see this thing again."

His fingers made contact with her back, and he paused. How often had he fantasized about disrobing her? Just last night he had nearly torn off her nightgown, but this was different. He silently cursed fate for giving him what he had wanted, but under the worst of circumstances.

Gently, he tugged the zipper, but it wouldn't budge. He tried again, but it was completely locked up. "I'm going to have to tear it."

"That's fine."

The fabric gave easily at his tug. The curve of her back was exposed as he pulled the rest of the fabric apart. Quickly, he grabbed the robe from the bed and draped it over her. She pulled the robe closed.

Sam tossed the soiled dress into the cold fireplace while she sat on the bed. Knowing she wore very little under that robe was making him nervous, and he wasn't sure how else to bring her comfort.

"Do you want to sleep?" he asked. He estimated it was several hours before the safety of sunrise. "I'll stand guard."

"No. I don't think I could."

"Would you like something to drink?"

"I'm fine." Then after a moment she pinched her forehead. "No, that's not true. I'm not fine. That was horrible."

He sat down to take her hand. Seeing her in so much pain was unbearable, and he hated feeling so inept. Squeezing her hand, he said, "Selene, I want very much to comfort you, but I don't know how. Tell me how."

She looked up at him. "Tell you?"

"What can I do to ease your pain? What do you need?"

She went quiet. "No one has ever asked me that before."

"Anything."

"I have so many questions, but... " She stared down at her lap. "I just want to forget for a moment."

"How can I give you that?"

Sam thought he saw uncertainty, followed by determination play across her face.

When she raised her eyes to his, what he saw took his breath away. It was desire. Heat. *Need*. Her eyes were hooded, her cheeks pink. Nothing had ever aroused him so much as that look. His heart began to thunder against his chest as his cock went hard in an instant. Not even in his most fevered fantasies had he imagined her looking at him like this.

Moving closer to him on the bed, she reached up to cup his jaw. Gently pulling his head down to meet hers, she paused right before their lips met. Her voice was husky and a bit pleading as she whispered, "Distract me."

CHAPTER 29

S am's every muscle tensed with uncertainty. Distract her? Surely she couldn't mean... she couldn't actually want to... He closed his eyes. Her scent and proximity were making him doubt his ability to understand her intentions.

"Sam?" she said softly. Her hand was still on his jaw. "Is this okay? If I kiss you?"

Swallowing thickly, he asked, "This is what you want?"

"Yes, I mean, not... all the way. Just messing around. Kissing and stuff," She bit her lip and leaned back. "Unless you don't want to—"

"I want to," he interrupted, suddenly panicked that his hesitation could change her mind. He brought his mouth down to kiss her. Hard.

Sensation spread through his body, making him feel drunk with desire. Her lips were so giving against his. Soon he found himself stroking his tongue over her bottom lip.

Her mouth opened, and he swept his tongue inside then angled his head to deepen their kiss. She moaned, and this time he recognized the sound as one of pleasure. The way she teased and licked at him was maddening, but he needed more contact. Encircling her waist with his hands, he dragged her to sit sideways across his lap.

When she looped her arms around his neck, the hard points of her nipples rubbed against his chest through the robe, making tension coil even tighter within him. Her fingertips danced over his chest, making him consider tearing off his shirt. But that would mean he'd have to let go of her for a moment, which was unthinkable. Not when he desperately wanted to touch her more. He wanted to cup her breasts, to tease her nipples, then slip his hand between her thighs. To feel how soft she was there, how well she could receive him if he were to take her now. He could scent her arousal, but to *feel* her become wet for him was unbearably tempting.

Yet he held back. Merely kissing and holding her was so arousing, he wasn't certain he could handle any more. She began to writhe on his lap, causing dark urges to claw at his mind. His horns, deeply connected with his emotions, began to pulse.

Need more.

He needed to claim her. To take her body, hard and fast, right now. He imagined himself pushing her back on the bed. Immobilizing her so she couldn't rub against him in that intoxicating way, then tearing off everything she wore. He would pin her wrists above her head so he could lick every part of her, possess every inch. Cover her body with his and drive into her, deep and hard. Then pound against her until she clawed at his back and cried out his name.

No. Gentle.

He needed to slow down before he lost control. She had asked for distraction—more precisely, a kiss. Not to be rutted over by a lust-drunk demon. He broke away from her mouth to brush his lips down her neck. Lightly. Softly. To settle him and cool his ardor.

She could undoubtedly feel his erection throbbing against her, and at first, he relished it. But when her fingers skimmed the top of his trousers, he pushed her hand away. She made a sound of frustration, but he didn't care. There was only so much he could take. He noticed that she was wriggling out of his lap, and anger flared that she was trying to escape him.

"What is it?" he demanded. She wore an expression of building ecstasy, but perhaps he had gotten too rough.

"Sam... I... I need you to... " her voice was breathy as she kneeled on the bed.

"Tell me."

"Don't hold back. Touch me."

His entire body shuddered. To be *asked* to perform his deepest desire? He had never imagined such sweet torture. "Where?" he demanded.

"Everywhere."

He tried not to lunge for her. She wanted more? He could give her more. He could give her everything she needed.

"Lie back," he commanded, drawing from the deepest depths of his self-discipline. He needed to exercise some measure of control. To put limits on their encounter and remind himself that he was in charge of his own drives.

She did as he asked, and he stretched out beside her. This was his fantasy come to life. She was here—in a bed, willing and needful. And yet, he had become paralyzed with fear of making a mistake or spiraling out of control.

Propping himself up on an elbow, he couldn't resist grinding his cock against her hip. She stretched her arms out, but he pushed her hands away.

"No. I need you to not touch me," he said gruffly. When her face fell, he shook his head, hating that she thought this was a rejection.

"It's too much," he explained. "My control is... tenuous right now. I just need less pleasure. Will you help me in this way?"

She didn't look convinced, yet she agreed. He gathered her wrists in one hand and lifted her arms to rest above her head on the bed. He brushed a stray hair from her face before saying, "Stay like this. Please?"

"Yes."

When he had raised her arms, the motion pulled the robe apart, revealing a sliver of flesh. His eyes locked on the bare skin that stretched from her neck to her waist. Where should he start? What would she expect? He wished that instead of asking "where" she wanted to be touched, he had asked, "how."

Slow build.

The term came to him suddenly. It was one of the tenets he remembered from his many explicit books. Females like a slow build. They like to be teased and tantalized, not pounced upon, and clumsily groped. So even though she was laid out for him like a banquet, straining for his touch, he would go slow. To make it good for her. To make her forget everything she had seen that night.

Softly, he touched her collarbone, careful to keep his claws sheathed. Then he traced his fingertips down the exposed flesh between the lapels of her robe. He caressed her from the hollow at her throat, across the valley between her breasts, to her quivering stomach. And when he reached her navel, he circled back to do it again. Back and forth, slowly. Gently.

She rocked her hips, seeming impatient. Tentatively, he became bolder with his strokes and skimmed his hand over the silk covering her breast. She arched up into his touch, so he did it again. When his hand fully closed around her fullness, his cock jerked. When she whispered, "Yes," he couldn't hold back his groan.

He swiped his thumb over the fabric straining around her nipple, fascinated by how tight it had become. This motion made her gasp, so he continued, growing more bold with his touch. Pinching and tweaking her flesh until she cried, "Ah! Too hard."

He jerked his hand back. He knew he was going to ruin the moment somehow. His inexperience and questionable restraint could only be hidden for so long. "Sorry," he mumbled.

She pulled his hand back to her. "Don't look so stricken," she said, smiling. "Just do it a bit lighter."

He studied her. She wasn't upset or angry; she was expecting him to continue. A slow smile spread across his face. *She's teaching me how to touch her.* He suddenly became filled by a rush of appreciation—for her patience, understanding, and the serene way she carried herself. Even in intimacy, she eased his qualms. Heartened by her instructions, he took more care as he lavished attention on the other breast.

Just as he was debating what to do next, she shifted her hips again. The motion dislodged the robe, exposing her body fully to his gaze.

He sucked in his breath, staggered by the sight. Queen Thema's library had an extensive collection of nude depictions, but Sam was certain that none of them rivaled Selene. The breasts that he had been fondling were full and lush, with pink-tipped nipples that made his mouth water. Her stomach was sweetly rounded, the waist nipped in before her hips gracefully curved out. Her legs were long and shapely, but it was the triangle of dark hair visible through the cotton she wore that drove him close to the edge.

Tear it away. Bare all of her.

"Sam?" she whispered, making him realize that he had been staring for several moments.

"Beautiful," he murmured. He would *not* tear off her underlinen. Not unless she asked him to. He would enjoy this moment as it unfolded.

He traced light circles around her breast with his finger. "May I kiss you here?" he asked.

"God, yes."

Their eyes met before he leaned down to run his tongue over her nipple then drew it into his mouth. Selene moaned and forgetting his instructions, tangled her hands in his hair. He didn't correct her. The idea that she wanted to hold him in place while he did this was too exciting.

He flicked his tongue, then sucked wetly, surrounding the pearled bud with heat. At first, he wondered if he was being too greedy, but when she arched against him, he realized she was enjoying this as much as he was.

As he moved to kiss her other breast, his free hand roved over her body. He was growing fevered, dancing on the edge of pain, but he didn't want it to end. Nothing had ever been as good as this.

He drew his hand down the full length of her body, and she moaned when his hand brushed against the mound between her legs. He brought it back up to cup her core and found it wet. She was wet *for him*. She spread her thighs wider so that the heel of his hand pushed into the top of her sex.

"Oh! Like that!" she cried. "Just like that. Again!"

Her instructions made him nearly come. Right there, in his trousers. But he didn't release his control. He couldn't, not when she was so clearly enjoying what he was doing.

Sam did as she asked, pressing down, then moving his hand in a slow circle. He wanted to touch more of her, to dive past the fabric barrier to stroke her slick folds. But she hadn't asked him for that. She had asked him to keep touching her just as he was doing now.

She began to pant, and her head thrashed from side to side. He knew what it meant, and the sight made him surge with satisfaction.

When he was young, and Eldridge had talked to him about the act of mating, the Goblyn had stressed that the female should always find release first. *If you take care of her, she'll take great care of you*, he had said. But the stories Sam had read of pleasuring females made it seem difficult, as though only a very experienced lover with honed techniques would do.

It was not so with Selene. She made it easy. All her little moans and gasps were like signals to him. Guideposts on how to delight her. All he had to do was pay attention. And when that failed? She simply gave him instructions. A revelation. He rubbed his erection against her, feeling as desperate to come as she was.

"Keep going," she murmured, as if anything could make him stop.

This was real. It wasn't a dream or a fantasy. This beautiful, passionate creature was nearly naked and asking for more of his touch. He hovered above her lips, overwhelmed by a deep need to kiss her. But then the sound of a loud bang coming from outside the cottage made them both freeze.

"What was that?" Selene whispered; her voice panicked.

"Probably just Brunie and Eldridge coming back," he said, turning his head to listen.

The sound happened again, followed by a shout.

Selene sat up on her elbows. "Someone's outside."

That someone was about to die. Using a power of will he didn't know he possessed, he pulled away from her to stand.

Sam's senses for danger tingled. More vampires could be lurking. Some could have strayed from the hall, or seen the Harpies carry off Selene. Cautiously, he peered out the window. The yard was empty and dark. "I don't see anything, but I'll go down and check. Stay here."

Selene sat up fully. He watched with regret as she belted the robe closed. "Be careful."

Sam crept down the stairs. The house was still dark, but there was movement outside. He went to the window and pulled back the curtain a fraction.

It was Brunie and Eldridge. Each filling buckets of water from the pump at the side of the house then pouring the contents over each other. Eldridge spotted him in the window and beckoned. Sam trudged out, right as Brunie poured another bucket of water on Eldridge.

"C-c-cold!" Eldridge cried.

"You're not tracking vampire blood inside!" Brunie scolded. She turned to Sam. "Are you all right? How is Selene?"

"She's fine. My thanks to you and the Harpies for rescuing her. All is well back at the hall?"

"Fine, fine," Eldridge said. He gestured to the sky where Sam could see a tower of smoke rising. "We had to set fire to everything, but the threat is gone."

Eldridge shook water from his ear. "There were more than a few vampires who cried out for Zaybris before their final end. One even asked me to tell his king that he never wanted the gold, only his gratitude. Why would they say that?"

Sam shifted his weight uneasily. Queen Thema must have sent word to Zaybris that a human gift was forthcoming. And naturally, being the greedy parasite Zaybris was, he didn't want to wait. Sam cursed Queen Thema's recklessness. Her obsession with finding her lost sister was endangering more than just Selene. It was putting Aurelians in jeopardy too.

"I'm not certain," Sam said.

"Selene should give up her quest to go home and build a life in Aurelia," Brunie said. "Perhaps with you, dearest. There's a darling little cottage for sale just past the mill--"

"I don't want to discuss this," Sam said. "Selene and I will leave as soon as the sun rises."

"It's late, and we're all tired," Eldridge said. "Let's all get some sleep. There'll be no more violence tonight."

Sam had not forgotten he had left Selene unfulfilled, and when he climbed the stairs he imagined her fully naked, arms outstretched waiting for him. However, when he crept into the room, she was tucked under the covers, sleeping peacefully. Her hair fanned out over his pillow, while her chest rose and fell softly.

Looking down at her, his throat choked with emotion. He had nearly lost her tonight. If the Harpies hadn't intervened, he was certain she would have been taken from him. She would have been drained on the spot or turned into a blood slave for Zaybris's pleasure. This human, who had been ripped from everything she knew and brought to a strange realm just as he was.

My mate.

Was it possible that she was truly his fated mate? His feelings were deeper than an infatuation, more fervent than an obsession. She was calm when he was volatile, gentle as he was fierce. He was full of secrets and shadows while she brought light to all darkness. There was no one he could imagine more perfectly matched for him. He could no longer deny the pull that drew him to her.

In that moment, he made a decision. They would continue their journey north to Queen Lilith's castle. He would keep up the ruse, and use Selene as bait to gain an audience with Zaybris. However, when they met, Sam would kill the vampire quickly. A true act of mercy when he deserved nothing but an eternity of pain. And then once the traveler's stone was in Sam's possession, he would scry for Thema's lost sister, as he promised, before using the stone to transport himself home.

But he would not be leaving Selene behind in Aurelia.

He was taking her to the Underworld with him.

CHAPTER 30

Selene woke to a sharp rap at the door. How did she end up in such a huge bed? And why was everything so bright? She squinted against the rays of sun pouring through the windows and remembered she was in Brunie and Eldridge's attic. In Sam's bed. Alone. And it was morning. Sunlight meant safety. They were free from the vampire threat, at least until nightfall.

The knock sounded again, more forceful this time.

"Selene?" came Sam's urgent voice.

"I'm awake! Just a minute," she called back. Scrambling out of bed, she cinched her robe before opening the attic door. Sam stood in the doorway.

"Good morning," she drawled, leaning a hip against the doorframe.

His expression was tense, but when his gaze flickered down over her body, it softened. "Good morning," he murmured. Then he leaned forward, as if he were about to kiss her, then abruptly straightened, seeming to think better of it. "We need to leave to take advantage of the sunlight. There could still be vampires around."

Selene smoothed her hair. "Yes, of course. Do I have time to wash up?"

"If you do so quickly. We'll be outside."

"Okay. I'll be down soon."

He nodded and walked away without another word, leaving Selene a little unnerved by his sudden businesslike tone. As she hurried to the bathroom, she wondered why he hadn't rejoined her in bed last night. Were Brunie and Eldridge all right, or had something gone wrong? After what they had shared last night, she wished he would have just come in to wake her, preferably with a kiss...

Her body flushed, remembering the feel of his hands on her body and the heat of his mouth on her skin. Last night had been more intense than their kiss in the kitchen, even though she was certain he had been holding back. Did he regret what they had done? Or worse, was there something about her that had put him off? Her mother's voice rang in her ear as she pulled on her jeans, asking if she was exfoliating regularly or doing enough cardio. She pushed it aside.

She was not going to fall back into old habits. That was old Ordinary Selene territory, she chided herself. Aurelian Selene took her joy where she found it. She didn't tie herself in knots wondering what other people thought or entertain useless feelings like regret.

What happens in Aurelia stays in Aurelia. Or, more precisely, what Aurelian Selene does is her own business. She was tired of existing in the land of what-if worries and why-didn't-I regrets. What if she just lived in the present?

After packing her things, Selene found everyone in the front yard. The air seemed charged with a feeling she couldn't name. Sam's head was bent and Eldridge stared up at the sky. Brunie was grooming her feathers. The screen door snapped shut behind Selene as she came outside.

"Sorry to keep you waiting," she said.

"Samael insisted you should go as soon as the sun rose, and I can't say I blame him. How do you feel this morning?" Brunie asked.

"No lasting damage. Is everything all right with you both?"

"We're fine," Brunie said. "I've packed you a breakfast."

"More like breakfast, morning tea, lunch, and dinner," Eldridge said, pointing at the bulging switch pouch hanging from Sam's shoulder.

A gust of wind ruffled Selene's hair, causing Brunie to motion to the sky. "My Harpy senses tell me a storm's coming, but not tonight. Maybe tomorrow or the next day. It's going to be a big one. You and Sam will need to make preparations."

"Thanks for the heads-up. I'm sure we'll figure something out," Selene said. "Are you sure everything is okay?"

"We're just sorry to see you both go," Eldridge said. "And that your visit had to end the way it has. We would have liked to show you more of Snowmelt and the wonders of our world before you return home."

Then Brunie was in front of Selene, extending her arms. "I guess it's that time then," she said before pulling her into a tight hug. "Safe travels, lovely girl. Farewell."

Selene hugged her back. "It's been wonderful to meet you both. I can't thank you enough for last night."

Brunie peered at her with her owl-like eyes. She cocked her head and made a little coo before patting Selene's cheek affectionately. The gesture was sincere, so heartfelt it made Selene's chest constrict. How often had she craved a simple touch like that from her father? Or wished her mother would look at her in a way that made her felt *seen*, instead of assessed? She wished they could stay longer, but Sam seemed anxious to go.

Stepping away from Selene, Brunie moved toward Sam then gestured for him to bend down. Playfully tugging on a lock of his hair, she said, "I have a strange feeling that it will be a long time before you visit again. Take care of yourself, demon. And your Selene. We'll always be here for you." Her hug for him was strong but brief as if she couldn't bear to stretch their goodbye out further. Sam mumbled something Selene couldn't make out.

Next, Eldridge approached, and Sam knelt to the ground. Putting both palms on Sam's shoulders, Eldridge said, "I'm proud of you, lad. I know you will make me proud too. You've always done the right thing when given a choice." Then the Goblyn hugged him.

"Thank you for... everything," Sam whispered as he gently held the Goblyn.

"Ah, come now, we'll see you again soon, eh?"

Abruptly Sam pulled away and stood. He ran a hand through his hair in that way Selene knew meant he was struggling to control his emotions. "Brunie's right, it may not be for a long time."

Eldridge looked suspicious, but he didn't push further. Turning to Selene with arms extended, he said, "You'll take care of our lad, won't you? Don't let him frighten you with that temper of his."

Selene bent to meet his embrace. "That temper saved my life last night."

"I suppose it did," Eldridge chuckled, then squeezed her hard. "Be careful. But also be bold, and be brave, my girl."

"I will," Selene said, squeezing back. When they broke apart, she looked up at Sam, but he had already turned away. Taking one last look at Azuresong Pastures, Selene waved goodbye.

As Selene followed Sam over the green hills surrounding Azuresong Pastures, he walked so fast she had to practically jog to keep pace. It was obvious that he was feeling down about leaving Brunie and Eldridge, but that didn't stop her insecurity from rising up. Again, she wondered if she had done something wrong last night. He had seemed pretty damn into it, but maybe it wasn't the same toe-curling, world-rocking experience for him as it was for her. Was he now trying to put some distance between them? She wasn't sure how to broach the subject, so she decided to start light.

"That's quite a lot of muffins Brunie gave you," she said, pointing to the switch pouch. "Do I see honey tarts in there too? How do we know they won't all end up in Queen Thema's kitchen by mistake?"

Sam didn't reply at first, only handed her a muffin. Then he said, "Yes, there are honey tarts. And one muffin did end up at Queen Thema's. Until I turned the switch pouch inside out so nothing could travel in or out of it."

"I see," she said, feeling silly for trying to engage him to talk about muffins. She chewed as they walked. "Brunie and Eldridge are such wonderful people. I'm so glad I got to meet them."

"As am I."

"It must be hard to leave them. I'm guessing that's why you seem sort of... off this morning," she said carefully.

He didn't respond for a moment then said, "Saying goodbye was difficult. Especially when I don't know when our paths will cross again."

"Why don't you stop by on your way back to Queen Thema's? After you've gotten rid of me," she said. Since he was acting so ambivalent about what they did last night, she didn't want to seem clingy.

"After I've gotten rid of you?" he repeated.

"Once I've gone home. You can do whatever you want once I'm out of the picture." She tried to use a light tone to hide the dread and confusion she now felt about leaving.

The curve of Sam's horns expanded slightly. "Are you that anxious to go back to Gaia?" he asked.

"Well, it's my home."

Sam's mouth tightened "What if you had other options?"

"What options?"

"You could live in... other places. Better places. With those who would appreciate you."

"What places? What are you talking about?"

"What sort of life do you dream of?" Sam demanded, stopping in the middle of the dirt path they followed. "If you could choose any life for yourself, what would it be?"

"I don't know."

"What about endless wealth, eternal comfort, power, and status?

If you could live like royalty and be treated like a princess, would you choose that?"

Selene hoisted her backpack tighter to her shoulders. "I've never been the princess type. Why are you asking me this?"

"If you could live in a place where you would be treasured and adored with every whim met, wouldn't you want that? You'd never get sick, never feel sorrow. Instead of mundane routine, endless obligation, and tending to your Kevin P. Norton on Gaia?"

"This conversation has turned very weird. Can we keep walking?"

Sam didn't move. "Just tell me, what sort of life do you desire?"

Selene averted her eyes. His question poked right into a tender spot—one she didn't even know she had. "I-I don't know. I've never thought about it, to be honest."

"You've never thought about what life you want?"

The answer thudded deep in her chest. *No, I haven't.* She hadn't allowed herself to think about her own wants since she was very young. It had always been pointless. Unless her desires were convenient or matched up with someone else's, dwelling on what she wanted was a recipe for disappointment.

It was the reason Kevin believed his favorite restaurant was her favorite too, and why she had attended her father's alma mater instead of going to college out of state. It was why she had grown up with a bedroom painted with the same gray used in her mother's kitchen remodel instead of the lavender shade she had begged for. Not ever getting what she wanted had put her into a career she didn't love, living in a city she'd never left, spending all her free time doing favors for other people.

"I guess I want a life where I'm happy," she said vaguely.

"Happy, how?"

"Healthy. Safe. Normal things."

"Good health and protection, yes. What else?"

She gritted her teeth, annoyed at his questioning, but more annoyed at herself for not knowing how to answer. "Travel," she said, considering. "I'd like to travel more. I've never even been out of the country before. Well, I guess Aurelia counts. But I'd like to go to other places from my world. England, Japan, New Zealand, France, Peru."

"What else?" Sam asked, starting to walk again. She followed behind, ducking as she stepped under a tree branch.

"Not worrying about money would be nice."

"I see. What sort of surroundings would you like to live in?"

"Maybe somewhere with cooler weather since Nashville can get so humid. I don't even know where that would be, though."

"Health, safety, travel, wealth, temperate climate," he said, as though he were compiling a list.

"That sounds weird when you say it like that. I don't crave wealth, I crave security. And... freedom. I guess I crave freedom. To just do whatever I wanted without having to worry."

"Worry about what?"

"Lots of things. What people think of me. What my family needs. Whether or not I can afford something."

"I see. What other things do you wish for?"

"I don't know! How about a new car, a lifetime supply of chocolate, and world peace," Selene said impatiently. "You seem very serious about this. Why are you so interested?"

"Just passing the time."

"Uh-huh. What about you, then? What's your ideal life like?"

"Very simple. I would have complete control over myself and my life's path."

"What do you mean?" Selene asked.

"Just what I said."

"You can't get off that easy. What about your ideal house, climate, job, and all that?"

"I care little for those things. I only wish to indulge in the rights and gifts owed to me by fate."

"How can you control all parts of your life, but also believe in fate?"

"It is the way of my people," he replied simply.

"What does fate owe you?"

He paused to look down at her. "Vengeance, then victory. To claim what's mine."

His dark eyes glimmered. And although she had no idea what he was talking about, she felt herself blush.

CHAPTER 31

Selene puzzled over Sam's talk of fate's gifts for the rest of the day, but shied away from asking him more about it. She was too reluctant to receive another interrogation about her non-existent hopes and dreams. Also, she was tired. The events of last night were catching up with her and her shoulders and feet ached. When nightfall came, she welcomed it, despite the danger it brought.

After following a rough path through the trees, they found a suitable spot to make camp under the moonlight. Selene was about to inflate her tent when Sam froze. His head cocked to the side, listening.

"What's wrong?" she asked. Then she heard something too. A soft whimpering up ahead, but not an animal. More like a woman crying or moaning in pain. A sob, then short hiccups, followed by another sob.

Goosebumps rose on Selene's arms. "It sounds like someone's hurt."

Sam extended an arm. "Stay behind me. It could be anything."

They crept closer. Sam moved silently through the trees, but

Selene's footsteps weren't as graceful. She winced when a twig snapped loudly under her boot.

"Who's there?" a feminine voice called out. "Hello? I-I need help. Please. Someone attacked me and... my ankle, I think it's broken," The voice was thin and pleading, but also eerie. Something about the sound that made Selene break into a sweat, despite the night's chill.

Sam halted his steps, causing Selene to nearly collide into him. His nostrils flared as he looked around, sniffing the air.

"Violet water... " he whispered. "Margery?"

"Is that you, Samael? Oh, thank God!"

Selene recognized Margery's unmistakable voice. What on earth was she doing here?

"Where are you?" Sam asked.

"I'm here! Behind this tree. Help me, please! I'm hurt."

He stood still for several moments, as though weighing whether or not he should go to her. After tightening his fingers around the largest knife on his belt, he said, "We're coming."

They quickened their pace until Selene saw a figure in red sprawled on the ground under a huge tree. Her heart picked up at the sight of the vampire, even though Margery was clearly incapacitated. Her scarlet cloak twisted over her torso, while one booted foot was tangled in a gnarly tree root. Margery rose up onto her elbows, black hair streaming behind her.

"I'm so happy to see you! It's a miracle!" Margery said.

"What happened?" Sam asked.

"I tripped on this root, and now I can't seem to move. Oh Samael, will you help me? It hurts so much."

Sam whispered to Selene, "Stay back," and gestured for her to huddle behind a nearby tree. Then he slipped off his backpack before slowly approaching Margery. From Selene's vantage point, she noticed that although Margery appeared to be crying, no tears leaked from her eyes. The heavy layers of foundation on her face weren't tracked with moisture, and her thick eye make-up was perfectly intact. A perk of being undead, she thought.

"Why are you here alone? Is the Padu near?" Sam asked.

"I've left it to strike out on my own. But I guess someone didn't like that so, they sent a brute to attack me! Why?" she sobbed. "I tried to run away from him, but then I fell."

"You cannot stand?"

"Don't you think I would have gotten myself out of here if I could?" She flexed her knee to demonstrate that her foot was immobile. "I'm all twisted up. Will you help me?"

Sam looked back to Selene before stepping closer to Margery. "Have you fed recently?"

Margery released an exasperated cry. "Mercy me, Samael, I'm not looking for a snack! Can you not put aside your prejudice against my kind for one moment? What would your little Nereid girl over there think of you, failing to provide aid to a helpless woman?"

Margery's words seemed to have their intended effect on Sam. "Fine. I'll have a look," he said, then crouched to examine her ankle. The moon glowed brightly in the sky, and the sight of Sam's hands on Margery's velvet boot made Selene strangely jealous. And deeply uneasy.

"Is it broken?" Margery asked.

"I don't think so, just twisted and trapped in these roots. Let me cut them away, and you can be off."

As Sam pulled out his knife from his belt, a slight movement in the tree branches above caused Selene to look up. Squinting through the thick foliage, she could make out something dark crouched on a heavy branch. It was too big to be a bird and the wrong shape for a forest animal. Alarm bells went off in her head.

It was a man.

The hair lifted on the back of Selene's neck. Was this Margery's attacker? Hiding right above her up in the tree all this time? Selene called out a warning just as the figure sprang from the branch. It landed on the ground next to Sam. Selene could see it was a well-built male, with greasy, slicked-back hair. He wore a long black cape, and in his pale hand was an enormous wooden club, dotted with protruding nails.

Sam drew back, but before he could fully react, the sickening sound of a *thud* rang through the forest. The figure's club had made contact with Sam's head, and the impact sent the big demon reeling back. His body hit the grass with a force so strong Selene felt the ground vibrate under her feet. A shocked cry burst from her lips.

She watched the figure stand over Sam before striking him in the head a second time. As Sam struggled to sit up, Selene could see that the blows had caused an inch-long crack to appear across the lower half of his left horn. There was also a deep gash on his forehead, which began to stream with blood. Sam moaned with pain as his head swayed. Weakly, he tried to thrust his knife at the man but was met with empty space. Sam raised a hand to his horn then collapsed back on the ground.

Selene stood frozen behind the tree, staring dumbly at the scene before her. *Get up, Sam, get up!* Yet he did not rise.

The creature circled Sam, then nudged him with his club. There was no movement. With an eager cry, he leaped on top of Sam's chest then threw his head back to reveal a pair of vampire fangs.

"No!" Selene cried, breaking out of her temporary paralysis to run toward them. But as she did, Margery deftly untangled her foot from the tree root and popped to her feet. She sprinted toward Selene and shoved her to the ground.

Margery made a disgusted sound and smacked the back of the vampire's head. "You idiot, stop wasting time!" Pointing at Selene, she said, "She's the one we want!"

White-hot fear coursed through Selene's veins. For a second, she was beset with the ridiculous urge to look behind her—just in case there was some other "she" they were referring to. Surely these two monsters couldn't have set this trap for her alone.

"I only need a taste," the vampire said.

He drew his tongue over Sam's bloody cheek. The sight was so revolting Selene wanted to turn away, but then then vampire began to gag. Violently. Crimson blood trickled down his thick jaw. He slid off Sam's body to writhe on the ground. Coughing and spitting, he wheezed, "His blood! It's... it's like acid!"

"It's demon blood, you fool," Margery cried. "You've just poisoned yourself."

The vampire began to vomit in the grass. The smell was so noxious Selene pressed a hand to her mouth, fearing she might join him.

Margery watched him, then said with exasperation, "Look at you. What good are you to me like this? Oh, forget it," She reached inside a fold in her red cloak and pulled out a polished stake. It was about eight inches long and made of dark wood. "I knew I should have done this alone."

The vampire tried to crab-walk away from her, but Margery advanced toward him. Then she drove the high heel of her boot into one of his hands, pinning him to the ground. Crouching before him, she flashed a smile that showed her yellow fangs.

"Don't—" the vampire begged.

"Don't what?" Margery teased. With brutal efficiency, she placed the stake above his heart then drove it in deeply with the heel of her hand. "Nighty-night!"

The vampire's body tensed, then crumpled. He fell back into the grass before the light in his eyes winked out. Television had led Selene to believe vampires disappeared in a poof of ash when they met their final end, but it wasn't true. She took in the lifeless vampire before turning her gaze to Sam. Oh God, was he dead too?

A nauseating *squelch* pulled her attention back to the threat at hand. It was Margery, pulling the stake out from the vampire's chest. Margery cleaned the wood with a handkerchief, humming softly to herself. When she was done, she twirled it like a baton then tucked it back into the folds of her cloak.

"There," Margery said, winking at Selene. "Now it's just us girls."

CHAPTER 32

Margery pursed her bloated lips. "Are you trembling, darling? I'm not planning to hurt you. I need you alive."

"What do you want with me?" Selene asked. She was still sprawled on the ground after Margery pushed her.

Margery looked surprised. "To claim my reward, of course. You're a very popular girl. A true treasure."

"Me? Why?"

Margery wagged a bony finger. "I knew you weren't a Nereid back at Padu. And Samael said it was just your soap I scented—naughty boy! Tell me, how did you get to Aurelia? Did one of the queens bring you through as Lilith brought us?"

She knows I'm human. Selene swallowed. Why hadn't she probed Arkaya further about why she had to disguise herself as a Nereid? Was it to protect her from vampires?

"No. Lilith didn't bring me," Selene said.

"Then how did you get here?"

"I... I fell through a puddle."

Margery moved closer, her gray eyes gleaming. "What's it like back home? It was 1899 when I left. Why it must be over two thousand by now! Is everything run by automatons?"

"I... I..." Selene trailed off as she thought about what to do. Desperately, she tried to remember any moves from that self-defense class she took at the Y years ago. Besides yelling loudly enough to make a scene, all that came back was the instructor's insistence that women have more power in their lower bodies. Kicking was better than punching.

Margery's painted-on eyebrows drew together. "I asked you a question, human. Is everything run by automatons or not?"

"Uh, sort of," Selene said. Her eyes darted around, searching for a weapon of some kind. The ground was bare of branches or sharp sticks. The club that was used on Sam had been tossed about fifty feet away. "We have machines to clean the house called vacuums. Carriages that don't need horses and everyone talks to each other through little glass rectangles."

Margery looked interested. "Are there cities underwater?"

"No."

"Do you have flying mailmen? I saw a postcard with such a thing once."

"Not quite," Selene said. She tried to ease back against a tree, mentally cataloging the various ways she knew to kill a vampire. Sunlight, fire, removing the head—none of those were viable at the moment. She vaguely remembered something about silver, but judging by the amount of silver-set jewels Margery wore, it was a myth. Her eyes darted to Sam, and a lump rose in her throat. She tried to see if his chest still rose and fell, but she couldn't tell for certain. Maybe if she humored Margery for a bit, Sam would wake up and end this.

"Airplanes," Selene said. "No underwater cities or flying mailmen, but we can fly hundreds of people anywhere in the world in big machines called airplanes."

"Really?"

"Of course. You can fly from New York to Los Angeles in about six hours," she said, while another nugget from her self-defense class came back her. *Always go for the eyes.* Selene's fingers clawed at the ground for a handful of dirt, but she only came up with limp blades of grass.

"How many live on the moon?"

"None. Not yet, at least. We're doing a lot of research on Mars, though."

"Mars! Amazing," Margery said. The vampire reached down to wrap her cold fingers around Selene's forearm. "Come now, stand up. You'll tell me more as we journey to my king's castle."

Selene was abruptly pulled to her feet, swaying from the strength Margery used to jerk her upright. She tried to pull her hand back, but Margery only tightened her iron grip.

"That hurts. Let go," Selene protested, but Margery tugged her close so that their bodies were nearly touching.

"Oh... ohhhh, your scent," The expression of ecstasy that transformed Margery's face was terrifying. She leaned in to sniff, then brought Selene's hand up to nuzzle her wrist. "You smell delicious."

"I said, let go."

"How long it's been since I tasted human blood..."

"You said you wouldn't hurt me."

"I wouldn't dare spoil my prize." Margery's pupils were blown, making her appear ferocious. "But all the same... one little taste wouldn't hurt."

"No! Let go of me!" Selene tried to yank her arm back, but Margery was too strong.

Licking at the skin of her wrist with a tongue that felt both slimy and gritty, Margery quivered with pleasure. "You're right. It's too risky to feed from the vein. I've never been known for my control," she chuckled. She dragged her lips over Selene's palm, then twirled her tongue around the fleshy end of Selene's thumb.

"Here. I'll take a teeny-tiny drop from here. Just to put a spring back in my step. It wouldn't turn you—it would only be a pleasurable pinch. No one has to know. Julian had it all wrong with his blood wagons. Blood isn't better when it's tormented. It's much sweeter when both parties are in agreement."

"I don't agree!"

Margery's expression flashed from hunger to madness. "You don't know what it's like! To only feed on these Aurelians and their inferior blood... it's agony! I'm so hungry, always hungry. I drink and drink, but I'm never full."

"Get away from me," Selene tried to pry Margery's fingers from her arm.

"Quit squirming, will you, darling? Just let it happen."

"No! You can't do this!" Selene's muscles were trembling from the strain of trying to pull away.

"Yes, I must!" Margery shrieked, her voice echoing through the trees. "I NEED YOU!"

The last three words were shouted with wild desperation. But to Selene, they could have been whispered, and the effect would've remained the same. Her body stiffened before an unnatural calm took hold of her. While the trees around them rustled, everything seemed to move in slow motion.

I need you.

She rolled the phrase over in her mind, feeling the weight of the words. The entreaty, the implication. The obligation.

I need you.

How many times had she heard that before? How many people in her life used that phrase to manipulate her?

I need you, her boss always repeated before a board meeting. When she'd be stuck working all weekend on *his* PowerPoint presentation. "You're so much better at it than I am," he would say over his shoulder before walking out the door at 4:00 on a Friday.

I need you, Kevin would whine before each of his shows. He needed her to manage the merch table, coordinate with the venue, and set up equipment. It didn't matter how Selene felt about it or what other plans she had made.

I need you, her mother would say when she was too drunk to

stand. When she instructed Selene to tell the police they had been rehearsing a play after the neighbors called to complain about all the yelling.

I need you, her father had begged when the twins wouldn't stop crying. When he had to travel for weeks at a time and told Selene she was in charge of the household.

I need you. She had heard those words spoken to her all her life. But this time was different. This time, instead of making her feel guilty and selfish for looking after her own desires, they caused something deep within her to shift. A part of her that had been long buried gasped and trembled. It rose and stretched itself up. Vibrated and cracked, breaking loose from its bonds. Soaring up inside of her like a whirlwind.

Fear turned to anger. Anger deepened to rage. Rage grew into fury. It flowed through her veins like lava. Burning her from the inside with its intensity. She was tired of being needed. Tired of giving others her time, her expertise, her energy, her attention. Always without ever getting anything in return. And now, here was Margery, wanting to take her most precious asset.

Her blood.

Her vitality.

Her very life essence.

No. It would not happen. Not today. Not ever again. She was done with vampires—both the metaphorical kind and the one standing in front of her.

Remember your anger, the Harpy had said. *Feel it, use it!*

Moonlight cast odd shadows over the ground and illuminated Margery's unnatural face. Her sickly gray tongue swirled around Selene's thumb before her lips pulled back from her fangs...

Without hesitating, Selene used all that rage—that pulsing, throbbing power—to kick Margery in the gut as hard as she could. It was a strong blow and effective. The vampire's face was surprised as she fell back onto the ground. Her hold on Selene's arm broken at last.

"You bitch!" the vampire cried.

Margery's red cape fell back to expose the stake on her belt, and Selene jumped for it. Margery rolled to her side, shoving Selene away, but Selene moved faster. Possessing a strength of will she didn't know she had, Selene reached for the stake at Margery's waist, but her fingers met empty space.

"How dare you!" Margery shouted as she pushed Selene away and rose to her knees. "I was kind to you! Now you're trying to stake me?"

"Fuck you!"

Margery grabbed Selene's hair and yanked back, exposing her throat. "I could make you my slave, human! You think I won't? You're nothing but prey to me." Selene reached back to dig her fingernails into Margery's hand. The way the flesh gave away and oozed under her nails was horrifying.

"That hurts!" Margery cried and let go. Selene moved to her hands and knees to kick out behind her. Her heel made contact with Margery's chest and sent her sprawling back. Selene didn't know why she had stuffed down her rage for all these years—it felt incredible to let it run wild.

The vampire wheezed, then grabbed Selene's foot to flip her onto her back. Margery tried to grab Selene's arms, but as they wrestled, her stake brushed Selene's knuckles.

"Give up! Give up and accept your fate," Margery cried.

Selene struggled dramatically so that Margery wouldn't notice how she was working the stake up to slip out of the vampire's belt. Deftly, Selene curled her fingers around it once it was free. But just as Selene tried to raise her arms to drive it into Margery's chest, the vampire straddled her waist. Quickly, she pinned Selene's upper arms to the ground with her hands. Selene tried kicking her legs to jostle Margery off, but it didn't work. It barely moved her. Margery might be old, but she was very strong.

"Little bitch. You think you can beat me?" Margery spat. But then her eyelids grew heavy, and her expression became desirous. "Look at your lovely face so flushed with blood... "

Selene attempted again to free her arms, but Margery's grip was too strong. Her panic rose. Was she actually about to be bitten? Turned into a vampire or drained to death? She looked left then right for an escape, but there was no way out. Sam's body remained still, making her heart ache. She desperately wished she weren't such a puny human at that moment. If only her demon would wake up to come tear off Margery's head. Or stake her, set her on fire, toss her off a cliff, Selene didn't care. Even the shadows would be helpful at this point.

Instantly, in her peripheral vision, Selene saw several black masses tumble from the trees and rise from the ground, as if on command. Pulsating and swirling like black fog, they hovered above the ground before rolling together into a hazy cloud.

The shadows! Sam was sending the shadows to help her!

They swooped and rose to float above Margery's head. Selene watched them throb for a moment, uncertain of what action they were about to take. Their touch didn't hurt, she knew that from when Sam had them surround her in Snowmelt. So why had they come? Suddenly, her self-defense instructor's voice pounded in her ears—*always go for the eyes.* And as though she had uttered a command, the shadows dropped to cover Margery's face, poking at her eyes and obscuring her vision.

Margery shook her head to dislodge the vaporous shapes. "What is this?" she demanded. Her wig now sat crooked on her head. "What have you done?"

If only the shadows could grow murkier, Selene thought, to infuriate Margery even more. A tingly chill brushed Selene's cheek before surprisingly, the shadows grew deeper and more opaque right before her eyes. More dark masses joined the writhing black cloud, intensifying its color.

The vampire let out a frustrated scream until finally, Margery let go of Selene's arms. "Get these off of me!" she cried, waving at the air around her face. "You think a few little shadows can stop me? I'll drink you dry!"

Margery bared her fangs, obviously planning to bite at whatever part of Selene she could reach. But Selene's reflexes were too quick. She positioned the stake in her hand to point up—so that Margery fell straight upon it.

Through the shadows, Selene watched Margery's expression turn from rage to surprise to confusion before falling into an expression of deep peace. Her body spasmed then slumped down over Selene's. She was utterly still.

Selene laid motionless with Margery's body draped over hers, too afraid to move. She couldn't have been lucky enough to hit her heart, could she? When nothing happened after several moments, Selene nudged the vampire and got no response. Using all her strength, Selene rolled Margery's body away and sat up. Death was undeniably written across the vampire's face.

She had defeated Margery. Killed her, in fact, thanks to Sam's help. Selene examined her hands, expecting them to be covered in vampire blood, but they were clean. It had all happened so quickly that Margery's clothes had absorbed most of the blood leaking from her chest.

The shadows were still swarming over Margery's sallow face, causing Selene's heart to swell with gratitude for Sam. Even gravely injured, he protected her. Yet, as she looked around expectantly for Sam, her insides plummeted. He was lying in the same position as when he fell—unconscious and unmoved.

Selene scrambled toward him. The bloody gash on his forehead and the horizontal crack that nearly bisected his horn was horrifying. Placing a hand on his shoulder, she whispered, "Sam?" He didn't respond. She stroked his cheek. "Sam? Please come back to me." He failed to wake up.

The terror of possibly losing Sam was staggering. How could something so simple as a bump on the head incapacitate her unbeatable demon? Maybe the club was embedded with magic, or poisoned somehow. Or was damage to a demon's horn very serious? She wished she had asked him more about things like that. Like what it meant to be a demon, how it felt to live in his body, and the strengths and weaknesses of his kind. There was so much she wanted to know about him that she hadn't asked—would she get the chance now? She wiped at the tears filling her eyes and looked around the forest, not knowing what else to do. Hopelessly, she turned toward the shadows writhing over Margery and cried, "What do I do now?"

Her voice made them stir and rise toward her. They hung in the air in front of her, almost expectantly, like a dog awaiting its master's command. She gaped at them for a moment then experimentally, imagined them moving to envelop a nearby tree stump.

Before she could blink, they obeyed her wish.

CHAPTER 33

Pain. Raw, throbbing pain consumed Sam's body. It was as though he was suspended in darkness, unable to see, hear, or focus on anything outside of the torment radiating from his head. His life force was weak, damaged. Yet he couldn't remember how he had come to be in such a state.

Vaguely, he registered something cool touch his face, then it was gone. He wanted more, but he couldn't seem to form the words to ask. The touch came again—soothing and welcome. Slowly, the darkness began to lift.

"Sam?"

A voice was calling for him. He wanted to drown in that soft lilt and bask in the cool touch. Yet his throat felt closed, cut off from speech, and his body was depleted of strength. If he concentrated very hard, perhaps he could open his eyes. His lids were heavy, yet after a moment, his right eye fluttered. Forcing the lids to open fully, a figure began to take shape before him.

"Sam! You're alive!"

It was Selene leaning over him. It had been her touch, her voice. He should have known. Her forehead was furrowed with concern. He wanted to soothe her, to assure her he was all right, but the only thing that came out was, "Selene."

Some of the tension in her expression eased. He blinked again and wondered why he couldn't open his left eye. Raising his hand to rub it, Selene stopped him, then threaded her fingers through his.

"No, don't move," she murmured. "Just rest for now."

His fingers tightened around hers and Sam noticed there were bits of twigs and grass in her hair. "Where am I?" he asked.

"We're in the forest. I'm not sure where. About a day's walk from Brunie and Eldridge's."

"What hap—" Before he could finish his question, a flood of memories came back to him. Margery sprawled on the ground. A rustle in the trees. A figure in black before him, then an agonizing blow to his head and horn.

"Vampires!" he cried. Panic surged as he moved to sit up, but she gently pushed him back to the ground.

"Shhh. They're gone now. We're safe."

"Gone?"

"Yes. Dead. Margery killed the one who attacked you, and then I... I killed Margery."

"*You* did?"

Selene nodded. "The trap they set was for me. She was trying to take me away somewhere, to a king's castle, she said. For a reward? I don't know. But she wanted to bite me first. We fought and I staked her."

Sam couldn't hold back a smile, even though it made his face ache. If he weren't so weak, he would have kissed her at that moment.

"So brave," he whispered.

Because the light of the forest was strangely bright, he saw her blush. Then her lovely face turned serious. "Sam, your horn is cracked."

"Ah," He reached up to touch it and winced. "So that's why I blacked out."

"Is it very serious? What does it mean?"

"It's a vital organ. For demons, our horns are attuned with our life force." His voice was becoming stronger now. "They can be our greatest weapon, but also our greatest weakness."

"Should I find a healer?"

"No, it will mend on its own." He spotted movement from the corner of his eye. It was a mass of shadows spiraling around a tree stump. "What are the shadows doing?"

Selene followed his gaze. "Oh, yes, I think I'd be dead without them."

"Why are they here like this?"

"You didn't send them?"

"No."

Selene frowned. "They came anyway. Margery had pinned me down and I thought about how it would be good for the shadows to block her eyes. Then they just... appeared."

"They followed your command?"

"Yes. I thought about where I wanted them to go, and they did it."

Sam sat up. After the first wave of dizziness passed, he said, "Show me."

Selene extended her arm then closed her eyes. In a flash, her entire limb was obscured by black mist.

"Amazing," Sam said. They both watched the shadows chase up and down her arm then bump against Selene's neck like a cat seeking affection. "They like you."

"I like them too. But how do I get them to go back to normal?"

"Go home," Sam commanded. Instantly the shapes dispersed and the forest darkened.

Selene watched them dissipate. "Do they come when someone's in trouble or something?"

"No. Definitely not."

"Why do you think they came for me?"

"I'm not certain," he said, but it was a lie. He knew the reason they had come, yet he wasn't ready to tell Selene.

They recognize you as my mate.

The thought made him want to roar with pride, despite his injuries. There was no question that she was his fated one now. No creature he had ever met was able to control the shadows, outside of his parents. His mother, a Shadow demon, used to delight him with dark shapes conjured up against the wall of his bedroom. His father would sometimes join in; creating misty hellhounds to playfully chase the ghouls his queen had created. King Asmodeus explained that although shadow control wasn't one of his gifts, the shadows naturally obeyed the consort of those that ruled them.

Sam looked around and said, "Let's just make camp here."

"But the bodies," Selene said, gesturing behind her.

"Their scent will act as a deterrent to other vampires. They'll be nothing but dust come sunrise."

"All right. But I want you to sleep with me," Selene said, then corrected herself. "Just sleep! That came out wrong. I meant, sleep next to me in the tent. No hammock. So I'll be there if you need help. Head injuries can be serious."

Sam raised an eyebrow. "As much as I would enjoy a night of *not* sleeping in your tent, rest will accelerate my healing. I would be delighted to sleep next to you."

Selene set the tent to inflate. Once it was fully expanded, she helped Sam duck inside, careful to not bump his horns on the low ceiling. Then she eased him down to the thick padded floor. After switching on a lantern pulled from her pack, she began to clean the dried blood from his eye with a cloth dampened by her drinking water.

"Wow, it looks like the gash on your head is already closing over," she said, peering down at him.

"Demons heal quickly."

"What about your horn? Should we bandage it?"

"Yes, so the crack doesn't spread," he said.

"What would happen if it did?"

"My horn could snap off."

"Ouch," Selene winced.

"The pain would be unimaginable. But fear not, I can already feel it knitting back together." He chose not to mention that the loss of his horn could be an injury he might not survive. She had worried about him enough for the night.

Selene rummaged through her backpack until she pulled out a red square of cloth that Arkaya had enchanted to deter insects. Gently, she wound the cloth around his horn then leaned back to examine her handiwork. "There. What else do you need to get ready for bed?"

Sam closed his eyes, reflecting on all the nights he had dreamt of being alone with Selene in her tent. And now here he was, barely able to lift his head. But that didn't mean he couldn't still be close to her. He didn't have to let his injuries deny him every pleasure he craved.

Opening his eyes he asked, "Will you help me undress?"

"Uh... sure. Of course," Selene said, feeling shy. She started by pulling off his boots and setting them aside. Next, she moved to undo the silver buckles running down the front of his leather vest. After helping him sit up, she peeled the vest off his massive shoulders and folded it as best she could. She was trying to act casual, but her hands trembled.

She eased his arms out of his tunic until the garment pooled around his neck. Glancing down at the ropes of corded muscle wrapping around his torso, she bit her lip. It was the first time she had seen him without his shirt and the sight was... compelling. The number of scars he bore from his years in the wagons was gut-wrenching, but his body was gorgeous. Powerful. Primal. She knew it wasn't the appropriate time to drool over his muscles, but she couldn't seem to help herself. Each time her hands accidentally skimmed over his skin, she wanted to linger.

Careful not to bump his horn, she guided the tunic over his head. She glanced at his lower body with uncertainty. "Your pants... should I?"

The smile he gave her was coy. "Best to leave those on."

"Right," she said, feeling equal parts relief and disappointment. "What about your bedding? Is it all in your backpack?"

"Yes." After she covered him with his huge red-fringed blanket Sam asked, "What do you need to do to ready for sleep? You've done enough fussing over me."

"I-I just have to change into my nightgown." The thought of stripping down right there in front of him made her stomach flutter. She considered sleeping in her clothes, but the smell of Margery's awful perfume lingered on her.

After digging her nightgown out of her backpack, she unzipped her hoodie and tossed it to the floor. He had seen nearly everything last night, she told herself. How was this different? She slipped off her boots and socks, then turning her back, shimmied out of her jeans. She could feel the weight of his gaze on her back, making her tighten her fists at the hem of her t-shirt. Quickly, she pulled it off so that she was clad only in her bra and panties. When she reached back to unhook her bra, his husky voice made her pause.

"Selene."

She glanced over her shoulder. "Yes? What's wrong?"

"Turn around."

"Why?"

"I just want to look at you. Please."

Dropping her hands, she slowly turned to face him. Although it was dark in the tent, the lantern illuminated part of his face. His eyes were hungry, roving over her like a caress.

"Keep going," he said softly.

Keep undressing? In front of him? She swallowed as her apprehension grew. Since she and Kevin were a strictly lights-off couple when it came to sex, this was unfamiliar territory for her. Was the lantern bright enough to show the silvery stretch marks snaking across her thighs? Would Sam notice how her stomach wobbled when she moved?

Dropping her eyes, she reached back to unhook her bra. When the straps slid off her shoulders, her nipples tightened in the cool night air. Tossing her bra down with the rest of her clothes, she kept her eyes lowered as she pushed her underwear down and stepped out of them. Then drawing in a deep breath, she raised her chin to face him.

When his eyes raked up and down her body, it took all her willpower not to grab her nightgown to cover herself. She watched his lids go heavy, but she wasn't sure how to describe his expression. It was not disgust or judgment as she had feared. Instead, it was heated, practically searing. But also... awed? He stared at her as if he were looking at something breathtaking like a sunset, a priceless painting, or rare gem. No one had ever looked at her like that. It made her blood catch fire.

"You're so beautiful," he whispered. The feeling of being admired, being appreciated in this way was so foreign that her first instinct was to protest. She wanted to deflect his praise with a dig about the width of her hips or the dusting of hair on her legs, but stopped herself. Fondly remembering a time when Queen Thema's response to a compliment was "I know," Selene went for a more gracious approach.

"Thank you," she said softly.

He held out his hand, beckoning her. "Come here. Sleep beside me like this."

"Naked? But—"

"I want to feel you against me," he interrupted. "Without any barriers. It will help me heal."

My God, that man melts my butter.

After switching off the lantern, she lay down beside him. She rested her head on his chest so that her hair spilled out over his shoulder. He curled his arm around her back, tucking her against his side. After settling the blankets over them, he asked, "Are you comfortable?"

The power of speech seemed to have evaded her. Her thoughts were muddied, as every spark of awareness she possessed was awash in sensation—the clench of his strong arm around her, the feel of his heart beating under her palm, the smoky pine scent of his skin. They fit like two puzzle pieces locking into place.

"Selene? Are you comfortable?" he repeated.

"I am."

Sam squeezed her closer. "This is nice."

"Yes," Selene agreed softly. But nice wasn't the right word. It was completely inadequate when describing the warmth, the over-whelming *bliss* of having her body nestled against Sam's. Skin to skin, just as he had wanted. There was only one word to describe how it felt being so near to him. How free she felt at that moment, how grateful. One word to describe the change in her since coming to this realm. The feeling of power, of strength she had, even though it seemed she was not without enemies.

It felt *right.*

CHAPTER 34

ap, tap, tap. Sam awoke the next morning to rain tapping on the roof of Selene's tent. The air was thick with moisture, the light muted from the dark clouds brewing outside. A storm was coming, just as Brunie had predicted.

They should arise for the day, Sam thought. Go to higher ground; find an inn or a tavern to hole up in until the storm passed. The tent was sturdy, but not strong enough to withstand heavy winds or lightning. They should leave now, while it was still early and the rain was soft.

Yet he didn't get up. He refused to move. There was no way he was cutting this moment short. Rolling over, he pulled Selene toward him. She nestled against his chest. They had spent the whole night together with their bodies intertwined. He traced his fingers up and down her back, marveling at the healing touch of his mate. Last night he had been too tired and injured to let his hands rove as he would have liked, but he was awake now—and feeling very much recovered.

Possessive rage gathered within him as he considered how easily he could have lost her last night. It was terrifying to think that he had left her unprotected. He should have scented the other vampire in the tree or suspected that Margery was up to something. Instead, he had been too rash, too trusting. He had never expected to have his kindness to Margery repaid so cruelly.

Selene had proven herself admirably, though. Not only was she unflappably calm, she was also brave and resourceful. Yet, now that he was certain she was his fated mate, Sam was even more troubled. He knew she enjoyed his company, but how would he make her understand how deeply their bond went? Since a demon and a human pairing was unknown to him, it would be even more foreign to her.

In the Underworld, he could give her everything she desired—wealth, protection, good health—but would that be enough? As his mate, she would receive her own title as Princess of the Underworld and be treated accordingly. Perhaps her gratitude for such a life would make her love him. Or at least learn to, in time.

Yet he wasn't satisfied with that. He wanted her to cleave to him now, not later. He needed a way to woo her, to win her affection in *this* realm. Or even better, bind her to him. Something permanent and powerful enough to go beyond a human's comprehension of such matters. One that would compel her to welcome her descent into the Underworld, especially when the growing vampire threat left little time for an extended courtship.

Claim her.

There was only one answer, and it was obvious. He needed to bed her while reciting the ancient incantation that would unite them as one. Normally, such a ritual was performed with vows spoken by both parties, but since Selene was not a demon, he would speak it alone.

Imagining it made his pulse quicken. When they were together in Brunie's kitchen and then the attic, his body had screamed to mark her with his scent, his seed. How desperately he had wanted to drive his body into hers, yet he was so concerned about hurting her, he hadn't fully considered all the implications of their first joining—or how powerful it would be if he spoke the binding chant during it.

Meditatively, he began to stroke her hair while planning his seduction. Although he was anxious to complete their bond, she deserved better than to be claimed in a tent stained with two moldering corpses nearby. He would find an inn along the way, one with a lavish suite where he could take his time with her. A quiet place that wouldn't trigger his instincts. The men of her world had obviously not appreciated her nature or understood how to properly tend to her, but he did. His mate was a sensual creature—passionate and responsive. As long as he could manage his instincts and stay in control, she would soon be his.

"Are you awake?" she whispered, pulling his attention back to the moment.

"Yes."

"How's your head?"

Sam touched his horn. "Better. Much better, actually."

"Good."

"What about you? How are you feeling?"

"All right," she said, but her tone was somber.

"You seem troubled."

"I feel like I should have more guilt about last night. I mean, I've never killed anyone before—"

"You acted in defense," he said vehemently.

"I know that. Sort of. It's just a weird thing to wrap my mind around."

"As a vampire, Margery was already dead."

"Yes, but I keep thinking about how the stake felt in my hand. When it went into her body and she fell on me... " She blew out a breath. "It's not something I'd like to do again."

"You won't have to. Ever."

"She said a lot of strange things to me. What do you think she meant about claiming her reward? And taking me to see a king? I thought queens ruled Aurelia. She knew I was human and didn't want to drink me fully, she wanted me alive."

"She was old, and her mind had gone," Sam said, careful to ignore her other questions about Margery's intentions. "Had she bitten you, she would not have left you alive."

"Yes, somehow, I knew that." She shifted her hips. The motion pressed her breasts into his side, making his already stiff cock strain against his trousers. "But still, why would she—"

"Don't dwell on it. Her words sprung from madness," Sam said quickly. "I'm sorry I left you to face her alone."

"You couldn't have known what would happen. I'm just glad it's over, and you're okay. It was the worst night of my life, and I didn't think anything could top the vampire attack in Snowmelt."

"Only good times lie ahead," he said, pressing a kiss to her forehead. He began tracing circles on her lower back. Even though he had just rejected the idea of claiming her in the tent, the drive to soothe her was undeniable. If he could use his hands and mouth to pleasure her, perhaps she could forget for a moment. Then they would be on their way.

His voice dropped an octave as he murmured, "Do you need... distraction?"

"Do I need what?" Then as realization seemed to take hold, she said, "Oh."

Slowly, he drew his hand over the curve of her hip under the blanket, then up her ribcage. He repeated the motion in the opposite direction while waiting for a signal from her, a sign, a word of encouragement...

"Yes," she breathed.

He didn't hesitate. Pushing her onto her back, he bent and took her mouth. Flicked his tongue against her lips so that she opened to him. She swirled her tongue around his, meeting his every stroke, then tangled her hands in his hair, tugging softly.

He deepened their kiss. She arched her back, making him very aware of the way her breasts jutted against his chest. His shaft jerked painfully against his pants, and he pulled back. Softened his kiss to make it less frantic. He cupped the underside of her breast, feeling much more confident about how to touch her now. When his thumb rubbed over the taut peak, she moaned. Aching to taste her again, he licked his way down her body. The feel of her warm flesh on his lips and tongue was addictive. Softly, he blew against one pearled nipple until she began to squirm.

"Sam, please," she said.

He drew a nipple between his lips, and she made a small sound of delight. He sucked hard before flicking his tongue back and forth. With his other hand, he stroked her opposite breast, careful to keep the pressure he knew she preferred.

Selene's hands roved up and down his back, squeezing his clenched muscles and stroking his heated skin. She was careful to avoid his injured horn but caressed the other one with sweeping touches that made him groan, causing the edge of his teeth to scrape against her breast. Her hips bucked as she cried out. Sam pulled back to search her face.

"Was that too hard?"

"No, no it was... I liked it," she panted. "More."

That one word made his claws shoot out then retract. Feeling as though his control was slipping, he paused to collect himself. Staring down at her, he took in the striking contrast of their bodies pressed together. Everything about her was lush and feminine, while his flesh bore the marks of combat and pain. Oftentimes it was his body, not his instincts that made him feel the most out of place in Aurelia. His stature was too big, his features too angular, his horns and claws too sharp to ever feel truly at home among the races of this realm. Yet he didn't feel like an outcast with her.

She wanted more? He would give her more. He would give her everything. The life she craved, the home she desired, the pleasure she needed.

Skillfully. Tenderly. Mercilessly.

Selene wet her lips when she saw Sam's gaze turn from lustful to something darker. He was staring down at her like a starving wolf watching his prey, or a hungry lion scenting blood. Ready to pounce and devour.

And damned if she didn't like it.

His hand crept down her neck to stroke between her breasts, then over her stomach. Lingering for a moment, his hand moved lower until it rested at the triangle between her legs.

"Show me how you like to be touched here," he said against her lips, cupping her damp heat.

"Sh-show you?"

"Guide my hand."

"But your claws—"

"I'll keep them sheathed. I swear it. Show me."

Selene swallowed. It was unnerving to be asked for such a bold thing, but Sam's voice was commanding. Compelling. There was no room for embarrassment, not when it was just the two of them.

She parted her thighs until he was touching her fully, intimately. The feel of his big fingers pressed against her wet folds was heady, and she noticed him close his eyes briefly as if overwhelmed by the sensation too. Reaching down, she took his index finger and placed it on her swollen clitoris. "Rub right here. But slowly. Gentle and steady." She guided his hand in a circular motion.

His eyes glittered as he watched her face then looked down at where their hands met. "Like this?" he asked as he continued the motion. Selene hips rose to meet each of his strokes. Her breathing became ragged.

Reaching out, she began to stroke all of the interesting dips and bulges of his chest. He had so many scars; most of them appeared to be knife wounds or burns. As much as they pained her to see, she also found them incredibly sexy. Each one was a testament to his resilience—a tangible mark that symbolized the strength he had to rise above the trauma of his past.

She trailed her fingers down to the bulge in his pants. He inhaled as she ran her hand back and forth over the leather that hid him from view. When she said she needed more of him, she didn't mean just his magic hands. She was certain that his cock would be just as magnificent as the rest of his body, and right now, she wanted to see it. Touch it. To lick and suck up and down its length. Imagine how it might feel plunging inside of her and filling her with throbbing heat. The mental image made her bite back a cry.

Wait.

Were they only messing around here, or was she actually about to have sex with a demon? Brief whispers of logic brushed through her mind. Could she get pregnant? No, it was fairly unlikely with her IUD. Demon STIs? Probably not since she was fairly certain he was a virgin. So the practicalities were taken care of, but what about the emotional part?

Did she really want to have a demon fuck her right at this moment? In the middle of nowhere, steps away from the vampire she killed?

Yes.

Because it wasn't just any demon. It was Sam. He was *her* demon. And right now, she wanted everything from him.

She fumbled with the laces of his pants. "Sam... take these off. I want to—"

"Can I bring you to come like this?" he interrupted, never deviating from the technique she had demonstrated with his hand.

His question made her eyelids flutter. "Oh, yes."

Okay, so she would just let this first orgasm happen, then they would have sex. The anticipation of Sam inside her gave way to a deeper desire than getting off. She wanted to be *filled*. Needed it at that moment. Drawing from her remaining depths of sanity, she said, "Sam, let me show you something else. Another way I like to be touched."

She grasped two of his fingers to position them right outside her opening. Then while biting her lip, she slid them into her wet heat.

"Selene!" he moaned as his hips jerked against her. Despite his injury, his horns grew longer, and she thought she saw the color of his eyes flicker. But her mind was so overwhelmed with desire she could have imagined it. Body trembling, he squeezed his eyes shut and ground his jaw. When his eyes opened again, the irises were no longer brown. They were deep red.

She showed him how to ease in and out of her. Gradually increasing the rhythm until the pleasure was too much. She dropped her hand from his, happy to let him do whatever he wanted. Helpless to do anything but accept.

"Oh, God, Sam, it's so good."

When he groaned and dropped his head, Selene registered that something was off. His body was changing, growing as she had seen it do when he was violent. But as the tension in her body climbed higher and higher, she was mindless to anything but sensation. The warmth of Sam's body against hers. The damp air swirling around her bare skin. The glide of his fingers filling her deep within.

Her muscles began to shake. Her body was coiled up tighter than she had ever thought possible. But when his thumb brushed over her clit, it was over.

The heat that had been pooling in her belly rose up to burst with a frightening intensity. A scream ripped out of her as the first spasm took hold. The force of it made her shake with ecstasy. Wave after wave of unbearable pleasure coursed through her. Over and over until her bones felt liquid.

Then she heard a growl. She opened her eyes to see Sam kneeling over her like an ancient god. He looked crazed—eyes red, horns extended, with a crimson sheen to his skin. Yet she wasn't afraid. She could sense how desperate he was for her, and she wasn't going to deny him. This was going to happen.

She tugged on his pants again. "Sam, I want you. All of you. Right now."

He shook his head, clenching his fists so hard she feared he'd crush his own bones. "No, we should stop."

"I don't want to stop."

"Not here," he bit out. "Later."

"No, I can't wait! Please, Sam, I want you inside me." She rolled her hips as though to beckon him, but the motion seemed to make any remaining control he had snap.

With a defeated groan, he threw his head back and roared. Suddenly, she felt her body being jostled. "Spread your legs," he commanded, tone thick with authority. As she complied, something sharp bit into both thighs when he kneeled between her legs. His voice was guttural as he looked down at her.

"Mine."

CHAPTER 35

As Sam stared down at Selene, logical thought fled. Instinct eliminated hesitation. Determination replaced uncertainty. A force greater than lust spurred him on. He would give his mate what she desired and claim what was his.

Yes. Here.

Though he had intended a lavish seduction for her claiming, he could tantalize her in a fine bed with silken sheets another time. If she needed him at this moment, he wouldn't delay their joining further.

Now.

His vision hazed with demonic power. He pulled at the fastening of his pants and when he was unable to loosen the laces, he tore the fabric apart, releasing his length to her eager gaze. He was on fire for her, shaking with need. Barely in control.

At last, to know this pleasure.

But the relief he felt at having his heavy erection freed from its confines was short-lived. When he positioned his body over hers, the tip of his shaft brushed the soft curls of her sex. His body tensed, and his eyes rolled back in his head.

Defeated.

His back bowed when the pressure within him could no longer be restrained. He began to ejaculate—hot ropes of semen erupting from him to lash against her belly. Waves of bliss rolled through him upon the release, even as he knew it meant failure.

It was over. Before it had even begun.

Once the last tremors had left him, he sat back to wipe the sweat from his brow. Shame rose in his throat, making it ache. He had always worried it was his strength or rough handling that would put her off. He hadn't considered failing her in this way. *Couldn't last.* No better than a pimpled youth or a human man such as Kevin P. Norton.

"Forgive me," he mumbled, using his discarded shirt to wipe away the seed soiling her perfect skin.

"For what? It's okay," she said, sitting up.

"I didn't mean to... " He trailed off while tucking himself back into his ripped pants. "I'm sorry."

Would he ever be fully in control of his body and its drives? The humiliation he felt at being unable to perform for his mate was making him feel suffocated.

He shot to his feet, reaching toward the tent's exit for fresh air. But then he heard a ripping noise, like cloth tearing. The entire tent began to wobble and lurch around them, like an earthquake. It the ground wasn't moving, though—it was the walls around them.

"Oh no, the tent!" Selene exclaimed. Next came a hissing sound, and Sam felt cool air on the top of his head. Rain clouds appeared above him, and he realized that in his haste to escape, he had shredded the top of the tent with his horns. The whole structure began to deflate. Selene wrapped the blanket around her shoulders and stood. The tent fluttered down past their heads with a *whuff* of air, pooling at their feet.

Sam stared at the ground, astounded by the extent of his ineptitude. Selene would undoubtedly want to leave him now. Not only was he a terrible lover, but he couldn't even keep her adequately sheltered. When he raised his gaze, he was surprised to see her entire face flushing red. Her eyes shone with unshed tears, and her mouth was pressed into a thin line. When he took a step toward her, an explosive sound burst from her lips, making him pause.

It was laughter.

"Oh, my God! I can't believe that just happened! Whoops!" Selene cried. She wasn't sure why the situation struck her so funny, maybe it was all those post-orgasm endorphins, but her shoulders shook until she was nearly doubled over. When she straightened, Sam was scowling at her.

"You didn't think that was funny? It was just so... unexpected!" Wiping the tears of mirth from her eyes, Selene said, "The hazards of demonhood, huh?"

"The tent is ruined."

"I should say so. But what a dramatic exit it had!" she said as another wave of giggles overtook her. It felt good to laugh, especially after everything that had happened last night. Sam did not share her amusement, though. He was looking at her as if she had grown three heads.

Clearing her throat to regain some composure, she said, "Whew, sorry about that. Is your horn okay?"

"It's fine."

"That's good," she said, smiling. But Sam continued to stand unusually stiff like he was waiting for something. She put her hand on his arm. "The tent doesn't matter. I can sleep outside."

"You can use my hammock."

"All right." *Or we could share your hammock.* She would not object to another round like what they had just shared. In her wildest imaginings, she hadn't thought sex could be that good. And they hadn't actually even had sex! Demon in the sack, indeed. *That* was what she had been missing for so many years. Passion. Intensity. Abandon.

Sam pinned her with a gaze that felt very serious. "Selene, about what happened... before I destroyed the tent. I'm sorry. I should have kept control. I should have been able to last longer."

Ah, there it was.

He was embarrassed about finishing too soon. She wasn't upset about it, especially since he had taken *very* good care of her before. In fact, seeing him so undone for her was pretty hot. She tried to keep things light. "You're sorry for giving me the most amazing, mind-boggling orgasm I've ever had? Because I'm not."

"No, I mean... after that."

"I know what you mean. But there's nothing to be sorry about."

"But I—"

"Stop," she interrupted firmly. She was not going to let him spiral into a fit of self-loathing, nor was she going to spend hours reassuring him. "Sam, I know that control is important to you, but I need you to listen to me. More importantly, I need you to *believe* me. I liked everything that happened. I wasn't disappointed. We can try again later. If you want to."

The wariness in his eyes was replaced by relief. Closing the distance between them, she rested her cheek against his chest. Instantly, he crushed her to him, his fingers tightening in the blanket she wore.

"I want to," he said raggedly.

She sighed. What a wonder he was. So different from what she had expected when they set off on this journey together, in the best way possible. As they stood together, she had a small but powerful realization.

I don't have to go home. I could stay in Aurelia with him. Forever.

When rain began to fall again, she reluctantly pulled back from his embrace. Nudging the lumps under the tent canvas, she said, "I need to get dressed. Can you pull out our things?"

Sam pulled the canvas apart as if it were tissue paper and tossed his backpack out after hers. Selene let the blanket fall, not caring that she was buck naked in an Aurelian forest, and got dressed. Sam did the same.

Selene gestured to the ruined tent. "What should we do with it? It doesn't seem right to leave it behind."

Sam pulled on the tab that usually collapsed the tent. It sputtered and whirred for a bit before folding in on itself. Despite the damage, it compacted as neatly as ever. "We'll just take it like this." Then he looked sheepish and said, "I suppose it was a bit amusing when I tore it."

She grinned at him. "It was! Maybe we should stick corks on the end of your horns for safety." When she was rewarded with the rusty sound of his chuckle, she said, "I like seeing you smile."

"Then, for you, I'll do it all the time," he replied huskily. The sound of distant thunder made him look up. "We should get moving. There's a town called Twyzel about a day's walk from here. Hopefully, we can make it there before the storm hits."

"What's Twyzel like?"

"Full of vampires," he said with a glance at the remains of Margery and her companion. They were now empty clothes after the muted sun had turned them to dust. "We're about to enter Goblyn country."

CHAPTER 36

Selene and Sam walked for hours in dreary weather until lightning started. Sam led them to a cluster of caves and ducked into a few seeking refuge. Selene waited for him under a shallow rock ledge, getting soaked by sideways-falling rain. Finally, Sam emerged, beckoning her to follow him to shelter.

"It's a steep hike down, but it's protected," he said, shouting to be heard over the rain.

Selene followed him through an opening in the rock then pulled out a lantern from her pack. When she switched it on, the light revealed a narrow passageway in the rock.

They set off with Sam in front and Selene behind. It wasn't a pleasant trek; a few bats were startled by their presence, and the slippery floor required close attention. Eventually, they heard the sound of rushing water. Sam pointed to a dark opening ahead. "It's here. There's even a waterfall."

He led Selene over a ledge that stretched above a vast cavern. Lifting the lantern, Selene looked around, surprised to see how big it was, almost like a ballroom. Rock columns shot up from the earthen floor, and the stone formations draped across the high ceiling looked like huge swathes of lace. It was chilly within her rain-soaked clothes, but not unbearable. Through a crescent-shaped opening on the far side of the space, Selene could glimpse a pounding waterfall.

"It's perfect," she said as Sam helped her climb down.

"Someone must have used it for shelter years ago. There's still a fire pit and bits of wood."

"How long do you think the storm will last?"

"Could be days. I'll send for some more lanterns in the switch pouch. We can use the waterfall for drinking and bathing. The only thing I'm not certain of is bedding."

Selene eyed the dirt floor. "We could use what's left of the tent. The padded floor is still good, like a giant mattress."

Sam's eyes darkened as he met hers. The unspoken tension of being alone together for days, with nothing to do, crackled. "As you wish."

~

Sam was pleased with the shelter he had found for them, but he wished there was a warm spring nearby instead of a freezing water-fall. They both took turns standing near its spray to wash their bodies of the dirt and dust. When Sam helped Selene wash her hair, he considered how much more pleasurable the activity would be if they were both nude, but such delights would have to come when it wasn't so cold. When they finished bathing, Sam built a fire and they changed into fresh clothes.

Selene emptied the switch pouch of all the food Brunie had packed, while Sam dashed off a note to Queen Thema requesting more lanterns. When he finished, Selene was chewing happily, a thick slice of bread in her hand.

"Good?" he asked.

"Mmm-hmm," she answered. "I didn't realize how hungry I was."

Eagerly, he said, "In the Underworld, the demons of Gluttony specialize in cravings. If someone wants a specific food, they only have to imagine it as they recite an incantation. No matter where they are, the demons of Gluttony will hear you and prepare it."

"Really?"

"Yes. Even if they have never prepared the dish before, they use your memories as a recipe."

"That's wonderful! Did you do that much as a child? I'd be summoning cake and ice cream every hour."

Sam explained that he was not allowed to command other demons until he became of age. However, if he were able to, he would have asked for an endless supply of his favorite cinnamon sweet buns, which made her laugh. As they ate, Sam told her stories about imps, hellhounds, and the Sanctum of Agonizing Rectitude. She asked about the landscape, and he explained that it wasn't all fire and brimstone. There were places of great beauty within the subterranean realm, as long as you weren't expecting sparkling beaches or sunny pastures. Her surprise at this made him pause. What else had her kind gotten wrong about his?

"What were you taught about demons?" he asked.

She tucked a strand of hair behind her ear, seemingly reluctant to speak.

"I'm curious," he urged.

"Most humans think they're pure evil. Possessing people, stealing souls for Satan, causing chaos, that sort of thing."

"Hmm," Sam replied, intrigued by her assessment. "Only the ones summoned by ritual stay in your world. And nothing is pure evil, as nothing is pure good."

He explained how even though demons cared little for convention, there were certain rules that they were strident about. This made the Underworld quite an orderly place, free from the violence her kind believed was rampant there.

Yet there was one thing she had said that made him pause. "Who did you say we steal souls for?" he asked.

"Satan." When he gave her a puzzled look, she prompted, "The devil, ruler of hell, prince of darkness, fallen angel and all that? Father of Lies? Isn't he, like, the boss?"

"Father of Lies? Ah, you must mean my uncle Lucifer. Does he tell humans that he rules the Underworld? Typical of him."

"So it's not true?"

"Lucifer is a minor demon who governs lies and falsehoods. My father rules the Underworld. King Asmodeus, the Venomous One, alongside my mother, Lamia, Queen of the Night, and Maiden of Desolation."

"Wow, so that makes you a prince," Selene said. "The prince of darkness!"

He shrugged, trying to appear unbothered though her words brought on an emotion he couldn't name. He had meant to impress her with tales of his world, but the reality of his impending home-coming brought up new insecurities. Was he still considered a prince? Or had he been gone so long no one even remembered him? Would his family accept him and his human mate once they returned? Or would they want to punish him for all the lives he took in the blood wagons?

Before he could further dwell on his thoughts, the switch pouch expanded with one of the lanterns he had requested. Selene pulled it out, and another followed. Then another, until they had ten lanterns, enchanted by Arkaya to glow with the flip of a switch.

While Selene covered their remaining food, Sam spent a consid-erable amount of time making their bed. He knew he should spend the night resting, yet even after such a physically grueling day, he did not feel tired. Not when his mate remained unclaimed. Once he pulled the bedding from his pack, he carefully spread it out over the tent floor and adjusted it repeatedly. Then he moved the lanterns so that they surrounded the bed, illuminating it like an altar.

When he finished, he said, "It's probably quite late. I guess we should go to sleep." He swallowed thickly. "Unless you're not tired...
"

"I'm not tired," she replied, meeting his eyes. She began to twine her fingers in her hair then rose to her feet. Reaching out, she took him by the hand and pulled him toward her. "Let's just lie down for a moment."

She tugged him down to the makeshift bed. He wrapped one arm around her shoulders, and she pressed to his side. Though he had found great comfort in this position previously, he did not feel that now. Only desire. Instinct. Thick with urgency. They laid together quietly until, at last, Selene's voice echoed through the cavern. "Sam..."

"Yes?" he answered quickly.

"It seems like we're going to be here for a few days."

"I know."

"I was wondering if... " she trailed off.

"What?"

"I liked what we did in the tent this morning. Would you like to do... more?"

"I want to do everything," he blurted out.

"You mean you want us to—"

"Yes. Yes, all of it. Tonight," he interrupted. *Right now.* He didn't mean to sound so impatient, but he wanted to make his intentions clear.

The look she was giving him caused his already pounding heart to quicken, even as the trust shining in her eyes made him uneasy. She was expecting that he would take care of her. He needed to tell her the truth.

Staring up at the black abyss of the cavern ceiling, he said, "Selene, I need you to know something."

"What?"

"I-I've never been... with a female... "

She leaned over to kiss him briefly, which was a surprise. He kissed her back until she whispered against his mouth. "I know, Sam."

He stiffened, hating how his inexperience must have been painfully obvious to her. She placed her hand on his chest. "I only knew because Eldridge hinted at it. And of course, there wouldn't have been time for such things when you were in the wagons."

"Being with me could be... different from other males. I don't know if I can be gentle."

"Who said I wanted gentle?"

"Females like gentle," he explained. "And slow."

She arched a brow at him. "Not always."

"But my size. You're so small. I fear hurting you."

"I'm tougher than I look," she said. He opened his mouth to air his worries further, but she cut him off. "Sam, tell me this—if I say that something hurts or ask you to stop, will you do it?"

He gave her an incredulous look. "Of course, I will."

"Then, it will be fine." He felt humbled and terrified by the amount of faith she had in him. She must have sensed his unease because she added, "I just want to be with you. It doesn't have to be perfect. We'll figure it out together."

CHAPTER 37

S am's fear began to dissolve with Selene's reassurance. She made their joining sound so simple, so natural. Perhaps it really could be. He didn't want to wait anymore. This was happening.

Rising onto his elbow, he cupped her face and kissed her. Softly at first, but it soon turned fevered. Rapturous.

His hand skimmed down her body. Their kissing intensified when he slipped his hand beneath her shirt. Her flesh was hot and so incredibly soft. She sat up to pull off her shirt then the rest of her clothes until she was fully naked before him.

The lantern light gave her skin a pale, golden glow. Sam sighed. How grateful he was to have been gifted with such a mate. Despite all of the pain he had been through in Aurelia, it had ultimately brought him to her. Finally, fate had looked upon him with favor.

There was so much he wanted to tell her but couldn't. At least not at that moment. But he could express how he felt for her in other ways. He didn't have to use words to make her understand that they were meant to be together. He only had to stay in control.

Selene ran her hands over his bare chest, and he pressed his thick erection against her side. When her fingertips brushed against one of his nipples, Sam gasped at the jolt of pleasure. She did it again while he kissed his way down her neck to close his lips around one taut nipple. Sucking hard, he used his other hand to dip between her legs. His cock pulsed hard when he found her wet for him, and she shuddered as he brushed his thumb against the spot he knew she liked best.

His control was starting to ebb. She dragged her nails up and down his back, and he growled. His touch became rougher as he became absorbed with pleasure, causing him to pause.

Breathe. Focus. Control.

They had barely started, and already he was losing himself. He wanted to drag out this first time, to savor her. He had planned to make her come at least once before the act because he feared he wouldn't last for more than a few moments. But the pressure within him was too strong. He had a driving need to get closer to her—as close as two bodies could be.

"Selene... I know we just started, but... I don't think I can wait anymore... need to... "

"I can't wait either," she moaned. "I'm ready."

Although Selene trusted Sam, her apprehension rose when she saw the way he took off his pants. *Tore* off his pants, more precisely. He didn't even unbutton them. He literally gripped the front with his claws and ripped them off his body.

Whoa.

Since he was worried about hurting her, she was going to suggest that they start with her on top. The way he moved between her legs quickly quelled that idea. He seemed to have very specific plans for her and knew exactly how he wanted their first time to unfold. His muscles had grown larger, making her keenly aware of the differences in their physical strength. His hands were shaking while his broad chest heaved. And that demon cock of his... well, she suspected she was going to have trouble walking tomorrow.

Carefully, he leaned over her on outstretched arms. When he settled between her thighs, his shaft made contact with her core, and he trembled. Then cursed. Then snarled as she shifted her hips so that he slipped along her wet folds. His eyelids fluttered as he moved against her, and Selene was certain he was battling the urge to come.

Knowing they shouldn't delay this any further, she reached down between their bodies to guide him into position. He looked down, and for one heart-stopping second, their eyes met. What she saw took her breath away.

His irises were fully red. Smoldering. Lines of tension branched around his eyes and the corners of his mouth. His skin had deepened in color, and he was covered in a light sheen of sweat. The lanterns and firelight gave the space around them an eerie orange glow. The reality that she was about to be fucked by a demon couldn't have been more apparent.

But although Sam's body was built to inflict vengeance, she knew how hard he was trying to be tender. His claws were out, and the muscles of his neck were corded, yet he wasn't shoving himself inside of her. He was trying to go slow, trying to make it good for her. The way he was looking at her made her feel like something deeper than just sex was happening between them—as though when it was over, she would never be the same.

"Yes, Sam. Now," she breathed.

With a moan, he pushed into her.

He was so big that her body was only able to accommodate a few inches with that first thrust. This seemed to surprise Sam because he instantly froze. He looked confused as he tried to press further, and she winced. Panic-stricken, he cried, "Selene, I'm too... this won't work!"

"It will," she breathed, already overwhelmed by the fullness within her. "It's fine. You're doing great. Just... go slow. Can you do that?"

He nodded tightly. She could feel his body shake as he sank his hips deeper. He must be desperate to thrust deeply, she thought. He was probably only halfway in now, and the stretch within her burned, but she didn't want him to stop for anything. Especially when the way he was moving made his pelvis bump against her clit. This was about to get *good*.

"A little more, Sam," she said, wriggling her hips to take him deeper.

"Is it hurting?" he asked, his voice gone gravelly.

"It's getting better," she whispered. "Keep going."

Instinctively, she knew they didn't have much time before he went wild, and that seemed to drive her arousal up further. He pushed into her again, and it felt much better this time.

When he was finally, fully seated within her, he groaned. Then let out a long sigh that sounded almost like... relief?

It was a strange noise, but one that Selene felt deep within her bones. Without words, she seemed to understand the sentiment behind it because she felt the same way. As if she had come *home*.

"More?" he asked in a voice that didn't sound like his own.

"Yes, Sam," she moaned. "Don't hold back."

The pleasure.

Sweet oblivion, he had never imagined anything could be so good. The slick clench of her flesh around his cock. Hot. The way she moaned his name. Lush. It was nothing short of bliss.

Slowly, he slid back, then pushed forward. Another consuming wave of pure ecstasy hit. He did it again, harder this time, and looked down to gauge Selene's reaction. Her lips were parted, and her head was thrown back. Sweat dampened her skin. She did not appear to be in pain, so he thrust again. And again, until he found a driving rhythm.

She drew her knees back further, giving him deeper penetration.

The pressure to come was even more intense now, and he knew his control was ebbing. Already his skin had flushed, and his horns had grown larger, but he could take it. As long as she didn't do anything to ratchet up his arousal any further, he could stay in control. He would absorb the calming influence of his mate until they were both completely satisfied.

He glanced down, concerned that he wasn't touching enough of her. He needed to make sure she was covered in his scent. Her eyes were closed, and her breasts quivered with each of his thrusts. Her rose-colored nipples were so tight he couldn't resist bending to suck one in his mouth roughly.

"Oh, God!" she cried and dug her nails into his back. The sound made his vision blur red.

No! Stay in the moment!

He released her nipple and buried his head against the side of her neck, helplessly bucking against her. She met each one of his thrusts, and he could hear her panting breaths in his ear. He wondered if she was close. The thought of her coming around his cock, bathing him in her wetness, made him even more manic. He snarled against her.

He could feel her body tense. Her nails sunk into his back, while her other hand reached up to grip his uninjured horn as if she needed something to hold on to. The feel of her hot palm against his sensitive horn shot bolts of lust throughout his body.

Suddenly, her back arched, and she cried out, "Sam!" Then... he felt her release. Her inner walls clenched around his shaft. Rhythmic contractions followed, so intensely pleasurable that his eyes rolled back in his head.

His control shattered.

More.

As his mate writhed and moaned, he rose to his knees.

Deeper.

He gripped both her hips to lift her body up to his. Her head and upper back remained on the bed as he began to pound against her. Hard.

His claws dug into her flesh as he slammed into her, lost to anything but pleasure. But it wasn't enough.

Closer.

He needed to get closer. Consume her. Brand himself on every inch of her body. There was still something he lacked; something left undone.

Claim her.

Dark shadows hovered around them but retreated when he snapped his teeth at them. His mate was moaning again. She had placed her hands over his and was meeting each of his brutal thrusts with an ecstatic expression. Vaguely, he wondered why he had ever been so worried about frightening her. A demon's mate would naturally revel in his ferocity, just as he thrilled to her passion.

He felt his seed rise. The time was now. He had to say the incantation right as he climaxed, so that the magic would bind them. He had read the words often enough when he played among the scrolls held in the Hall of Demonic Canon as a child.

Using a language so old it was imprinted on his very essence, he spoke the ancient words.

As is the will of fate, I claim you as my mate.

His ejaculation shot into her like an eruption. Throwing back his head, he released a bellow that he was certain must have echoed throughout the whole of Aurelia. His back arched as he emptied himself into his mate's precious body. Demon magic shimmered over them both like a silver mist. Her beautiful face looked dazed at the effect.

In a blinding rush, he felt a surge of sensations. Euphoria. Possessiveness. Gratitude. *Connection.* The feeling of finally being given water after a lifetime of thirst. Everything he had ever longed for, everything he had ever wanted was now his. It was as if their bodies were no longer separate, but joined as one.

Mine.

Forever.

When it was over, his body sagged. Gently, he lowered Selene's hips to the bed then collapsed over her. One of her arms snaked around his back, while the other stroked his hair. They were both breathing heavily, perfectly in sync.

He felt utterly replete. He had done it. The mating bond was in place. Now she would understand that they weren't ever to be parted. She would remain at his side for eternity.

Dimly he was aware that his weight might be crushing her, so he rolled to his side, pulling her with him. He leaned back to study her face. Her hair was wild, and her cheeks were pink. A smile curved up the corners of her lips. Never had he seen her look more beautiful.

"Wow," she said.

He kissed her temple and gathered her close. There was nothing to describe how he felt at that moment. It was a mixture of elation, triumph, relief, and deep satisfaction. The feeling spread all over his body but was concentrated most intensely in his chest. His heart. His love for her was so deep, so consuming that it ached in the best way.

The future held nothing but hope. All he had to do was kill Zaybris. Then everything he had ever wanted would be his.

Theirs.

CHAPTER 38

*D*amn, *my demon has stamina.*

It wasn't until after Sam was gearing up for a fourth round, this time to try a position he had seen drawn in a book, that Selene pleaded for a time out.

"I'm only a mere mortal," she cried, guzzling from her water bottle. Her ab muscles were already twitching from strain. "Can we take a little nap? Then I'll be ready for more."

"How much more?" Sam asked, nuzzling her neck.

"At least two more times, maybe three if you ask nicely."

His breath was warm against her ear. "Don't I always ask nicely?"

She smiled at him. "Actually, that's one of your best qualities." He smiled back and they both gazed at each other for a moment. A rush of happiness made her want to sing. *So this is love...*

Sam kissed the tip of her nose and said, "Get dressed, then. I'll fill these up." He grabbed their water bottles and headed toward the waterfall. Selene watched him go, unabashedly admiring his perfect butt before she donned a pair of light cotton pants and a T-shirt.

Movement to her left made her turn. She glanced over and saw the switch pouch had expanded. Inside, she found a warm, covered dish that looked like a gourmet meatloaf. Although they still had plenty of food left from Brunie, a hot meal in the chilly cave sounded wonderful. Having meals delivered this way made Selene wonder if she stayed in Aurelia, could she and Sam work out a deal to continue getting meals from Thema's kitchens? Who needed cooking when there was magic? The thought of sharing a meal across from Sam every night for the rest of her life was intoxicating.

When Selene slid the pan out of the pouch, a scrap of paper fluttered to the ground. It was a handwritten note. She bent to pick it up. The penmanship was ornate enough to shame the calligrapher her mother used to address party invitations. But before she could marvel at the writer's talent for lettering, Selene's eyes caught on her own name. Helpless to resist, she crouched near the lanterns to read each word.

To my loyal Samael,

Zaybris knows of our plan and has commanded all vampires in the realm to find Selene. If she gets taken before you can offer her up, so be it. There's other bait to be had, and more than one way to possess the stone. Victory is near. I can feel it. Once my sister is found, the celebrations will echo all the way down to you in the Underworld. — Thema

Selene gasped. She read the note a second time. Then she reread it a third time and a fourth—trying to make sense of it. Her hand began to shake.

Sam's voice came from behind. "Here you are, fresh water for your exertions."

"Sam?" her voice was barely audible. She couldn't seem to focus on the paper. Her vision was swimming. "What's this?"

"What is what?" he asked, pulling on a fresh pair of trousers.

"This note. From Queen Thema."

Snatching the paper from her, he quickly scanned it before tossing it into the fire. "It's nothing," he said, but his expression was dark. Guarded.

When Selene looked at him, there was a rushing sound in her

ears. She tried to stand, but her knees shook, causing her to sink back onto the ground.

"I'm... bait?"

Sam rubbed the back of his neck, wishing he could give Thema's neck a good squeeze for her carelessness at that moment.

"It's nonsense," he replied. "Just ravings from an old queen."

"What does this mean? What is she talking about?" Her voice was panicked.

"It's nothing to get upset about. Come here."

When she stood, he tried to hold her, but she drew back. Her face was stricken, and her eyes were wide. Sam considered his options.

He could continue lying to her, which would save her from undue stress and worry. There was no reason for her to know their relationship was based on lies—not when their love was clearly destined. He could confess everything later, once Zaybris was dead, and they were safe in the Underworld.

Or he could begin their relationship with the truth. Thema's note was the last way he wanted her to find out, but the evidence was pretty damning. If he wanted their love to be built on a solid foundation, he shouldn't hide anything from her. The choice was clear. He only hoped he could find the right words to make her understand.

"Sit down," he said, gesturing to the bed. "I-I have much to tell you."

"I'd rather stand."

"All right, but I must tell you the full story before you react. Do you understand?"

"Start talking."

Clenching and unclenching his fists, he began. "Queen Thema has been desperate to find her sister Queen Lilith ever since she went missing. She's hired trackers and enchantresses, but none were ever successful in locating her. When Thema heard that a vampire—

Zaybris—had a traveler's stone, it clouded her judgment. The stone has many properties. One is finding lost people."

"What are the other properties?"

"Inter-dimensional travel," he said. "Queen Thema asked me to find Zaybris and take the stone from him to reveal her sister's whereabouts. He has many guards, and we knew getting close would be difficult. We had to offer him something he wanted."

Selene hugged her arms around her middle. "What did he want?"

Sweat had begun to bead on Sam's forehead. "Human blood, living blood was what he wanted most and... you had just arrived. We needed a way in. Queen Thema didn't think his guards would allow me to see him alone, so Queen Thema told Zaybris she wanted to give him a gift."

"And that was me," Selene said, her voice wavering.

"Your presence would allow me to face him directly and take the stone. But you were never in danger! We never intended for him to actually take you! It was only a ruse to gain entry. Quite innocent, really."

"So innocent you couldn't tell me about it beforehand?"

"I'm sorry," Sam said.

"Oh, God, that's why the vampires came to Snowmelt. And Margery too. They wanted me. My blood!"

"No. Well... yes. They wanted to deliver you to Zaybris themselves." Sam jerked his fingers through his hair. This conversation was going terribly. "I know our plan seems cruel, but I would never let anyone cause you harm."

"How generous," she said caustically.

"It's the truth."

She stared into the fire then said, "And if this plan worked? If you got through to Zaybris to take the stone, then what?"

"Then I would kill him to take the stone, and my vengeance."

"Your vengeance," she repeated.

"I have waited many years to face Zaybris."

"Wait, you know him?"

Sam swallowed. "Yes. Zaybris is the vampire that kidnapped me."

Even in the cavern's dim light, he saw her go pale. "Well, well. This just keeps getting better and better."

"The traveler's stone would transfer ownership to me upon the vampire's death. I vowed to Queen Thema that I would use it to locate her lost sister. I would have my vengeance and she would have answers."

"But the note says you'll be in the Underworld," Selene said. The way her expression changed from shock to scorn made bile rise in his throat. "Oh, now I see."

"No, it's not how it seems—"

"I think it's exactly how it seems," Selene cut in. "You were going to kill Zaybris and use this magic stone to take *yourself* back to the Underworld. Leaving me to fend for myself in Aurelia. That was the real plan all along, wasn't it? How could I have been so stupid?"

Her refusal to see anything but the worst of the situation made his anger rise, but if there were ever a time for him to stay level-headed, it was now. Straightening his shoulders, he approached her slowly, careful to appear unthreatening. He took her hands in his. Softly, he said, "It was a dangerous and foolish strategy. I see that now, and I'm sorry for deceiving you. But when things between us changed, I made a new plan."

Her eyes narrowed. "What plan?"

"Once I killed Zaybris and the time came for me to return to the Underworld... " he paused. Lifting her hands, he pressed his lips against her knuckles. "My love, I planned to take you with me."

Selene snatched her hands back, recoiling. "You were going to kill me?"

"No! No, of course not!"

"You said the Underworld is for dead people!"

"I would take you using the stone. You would live as my human consort," he clarified. "Selene, you are my fated mate. The one I hold up above all others. This means you would be free to roam the

Underworld without actually dying. Or you could become a demon in time. Such things are possible."

"Are you serious?"

"Yes. I claimed you as mine last night."

"*Claimed* me!" Her outrage at his words was clear. "What the fuck are you talking about?"

Her reaction to news of their sacred bond made heat flush through his body and his vision cloud red. This was going all wrong. So wrong that it was causing his demonic urges to rise to the surface. He forced himself to remain in control. *Patience.* How could he expect her to understand the significance of the mating bond instantly? He had to use the right words to make her see.

"We share a bond that cannot be broken. Of this, I am certain. You'd be treated as royalty in the Underworld. Never grow old or die of illness. I would give you everything."

"Except a choice!" Her shoulders hunched as she looked away. "I'm never going home, am I?"

"Selene... "

"You would do to me what Zaybris did to you?"

Sam flinched at her accusation. "No! This is nothing like that! You're my fated mate! We are connected in a way that transcends all other bonds. Where I go, *you* go! Forever!"

The pain in her face made him want to howl. He was failing. Saying all the wrong things, and she was slipping away. He could see it. Had the mating incantation failed? He knew he had recited correctly, and he had *felt* something shift between them. Why hadn't she felt it too?

Her eyes were downcast when she said, "I can't believe how trusting I was. I thought Queen Thema cared about me. I thought you did too, but I was just a pawn. Bait."

"Selene, I love you," he said desperately. "But I have to go home, and killing Zaybris is my only chance."

The rush of the waterfall and crackle of the fire were the only sounds filling the cavern for several moments. Finally, Sam said, "Come with me, Selene. Please."

"Why should I?"

"Because I can't be without you. You calm me. You bring balance to my instincts—a peace I've never known."

"How do I do that?"

"Just your presence as my mate. You are like balm to the chaos within me."

Selene rolled her eyes. "Whatever."

"It's true. Please believe me." Sam took a step forward, holding out his arms to her. He drew a breath before proclaiming, "Selene, I need you."

Her head snapped back, and the coldness he saw in her eyes felt like a slap across his face. Her voice dripped with spite as she said, "You *need* me?"

Instantly, he knew it had been the wrong thing to say.

Grief threatened to overwhelm him as he realized that for her, the prospect of spending eternity with him wasn't a joyous one. She was angered by it. Disgusted. She didn't care about his status as prince or his ability to cradle her in luxury. She saw him as another leech who only wanted to *take* from her and use her gifts for their own gain. Just like her family. His continued failure to present himself as a worthy mate ignited his aggression.

"Enough of this," he said as the tight hold on his instincts broke. He strode forward, crowding her until her back pressed against the cave wall. He could feel his horns expand, his body increase in size. He placed his hands on either side of the rock behind her, not caring if he frightened her now. Let her see what the idea of being without her did to him. She should know what it looked like when a demon was denied.

Selene's eyes were unfeeling as she looked up at him. "Step back. You're not pulling this demon intimidation crap on me."

He didn't do as she asked, mainly because he feared she would run from him. His voice dropped an octave as he stared down at her.

"You can be angry with me for as long as you want. But know this—nothing can keep me from you."

"You're a monster," she whispered. Sam feared he had gone too far. Just before he pulled back, he heard the sound of footsteps behind them.

Suddenly, a voice called out, "Oh my heavens! Are we interrupting a lover's quarrel?"

Sam whipped around to see a pale man with long, white-blonde hair standing at the cavern's entrance. He was cloaked in black and flanked by six vampires, each staring at them with a triumphant smile.

Zaybris.

CHAPTER 39

Adrenaline surged as Sam let his demonic instincts consume him. He pushed Selene behind him and roared. The vampire had caught him by surprise, but the need for vengeance focused his mind. *Time to end this.*

"Hello again, little abomination!" Zaybris called, pausing to brush dirt from the shoulder of his velvet cape. "Queen Thema failed to mention it would be you bringing me my prize. Look how you've grown! Yet you still have your mother's eyes." He waved a hand at his guards, "Restrain him."

Six guards jumped down from the rock ledge to lunge at Sam simultaneously. They tried pushing him to the ground, but Sam was too strong. His fists shot out, punching and tearing at whatever body part he found. The vampires clawed at his bare chest, but he refused to move. If they took him down, Selene would be exposed. He tried to get a hold of their heads, but battling six opponents at once was difficult. Vaguely, he was aware of Zaybris coming toward them.

"My, you are lovely," the vampire said to Selene. "So fresh, so full of life."

"Don't touch her!" Sam shouted.

"Such protectiveness," Zaybris said.

"Run!" Sam said to Selene, but she was cornered between Zaybris and two boulders.

Zaybris looked toward his guards and made an impatient noise. "Surely you should have taken him down by now. What's that cloth around his horn? Go for that, you fools."

Sam couldn't keep the panicked, "No!" from escaping his lips. He head-butted the first vampire that reached for his horn, but another one leaped on his back. Sam moved to shrug him off, but not before cold fingers curled around his injured horn. The pain that shot through him was so intense he cried out. Stumbling, he heaved his back against the rock wall, hoping to dislodge the vampire.

It was then he heard a *SNAP*.

White-hot misery coursed through his body. Throbbing, savage agony. His knees met the cavern's floor before he fell facedown into the dirt. A scream sounded behind him. His eyelids slid shut as blackness threatened to overtake him. He fought it back. *Must protect Selene.* Rolling to his side, he watched helplessly as his greatest enemy approached his mate.

"Well done, let him suffer!" Zaybris said to his guards. "He'll be dead in minutes without that horn. Leave us now. My prize and I will be traveling a different route." He said, fingering the white stone suspended around his neck.

The vampire guards drew back, leaving Sam collapsed on the ground. One of them tossed something long and pointed at him, which landed near his head. In his delirious state, Sam first thought it was a tree branch. When he realized he was at eye-level with his own horn, revulsion set in. He fought back the nausea, along with the emptiness nudging at his consciousness.

Through blurred vision, he saw the guards run toward the cavern's exit then disappear. Sam tried to focus on Zaybris, who was speaking to Selene with impatient gestures. Even though she must be terrified, she wasn't cowering. Shadows swirled around her as they argued. The vampire reached out to grab her arm, but Selene pushed him back. The motion sent a whiff of Zaybris's scent toward Sam—the unforgettable odor of rot and dust. It filled Sam's senses, instantly bringing him back to the night he was kidnapped.

He remembered the fear, confusion, and terror he felt when he saw a vampire standing over his bed. Selene would be suffering those same emotions right now, plus the pain of his own betrayal. He had been a fool—a greedy, selfish fool who didn't deserve a mate such as her.

Voices drifted toward him. Selene's then Zaybris's, but he could only make out snatches of what they were saying.

"Get away from... "

"Margery's clothes... your scent drew me... "

"I won't leave... "

"Savior of my people... "

"Sam... "

"...my castle... to serve... "

Their bodies swam in and out of focus, and Sam gave himself an inward shake. The enemy was here, within his grasp. He couldn't lose now. Zaybris needed to die for vengeance, but more importantly, Sam needed to protect his fated mate. He had already caused enough pain, and he wouldn't fail her again.

Drawing from the depths of endurance, Sam felt around the dirt until he found his discarded horn, then gripped it tight. It felt dead in his hand and very wrong—like holding one of his own limbs. Though his strength was failing him, now he had a weapon. This wasn't over yet.

Give her what she desires most.

Weakly, he sat up, just as Zaybris was telling Selene about all the fine gowns she would be allowed to wear. Sam focused on the vampire's black shape while he climbed to his feet. Then quickly, before he let his weakness and pain consume him, Sam lurched toward the two of them and tackled Zaybris to the ground. It was more of a well-aimed fall than a strategic attack, but it achieved its intended effect. Restraining the vampire with the weight of his body,

Sam tightened his grip on his broken horn before lifting it high. Then, calling on every last reserve of strength he possessed, drove it down into the vampire's chest.

Zaybris screamed and bucked, but Sam didn't move. He twisted the horn, relishing how the vampire's face contorted with pain. Zaybris coughed and panted until finally, his undead body stilled. Sam watched as his eyelids slid shut, and his pale face relaxed. He savored his bittersweet victory for only a second before gripping the traveler's stone and looping it off Zaybris's neck. Sliding off the vampire's body, Sam collapsed on the ground.

Instantly, Selene was at his side, and he smiled weakly. He had done it. Protected his mate, found vengeance from his greatest enemy, and claimed the traveler's stone as his own. Yet he could not bask in his victories yet. There was one more task he must complete.

He pressed the traveler's stone into Selene's palm. "Take it."

When she only gaped at him, Sam thought perhaps she didn't hear him. He tried speaking louder, even though the effort pained him. "The stone is mine now, but I gift it to you. Take it!"

"Oh, Sam, I—" she cried.

"Go home. To Gaia," he interrupted. "I'm sorry I tried to force you. To be with me. It was selfish. And cruel," his words were starting to slur now, but he wanted to make sure she understood. "I don't care about... Thema's sister. The stone is yours now. Touch it and think of your home. Go."

"But—"

"Hurry," he whispered. "Before more vampires come. Be happy. I love you. I'm sorry."

Her beautiful face was marked with anguish. It was becoming harder to keep his eyes open, and her image wavered in front of him. Suddenly, her body was jerked back. Panic flooded Sam. He looked up to see Zaybris standing over him, one arm banded around Selene to restrain her. Sam's own black horn protruded from the vampire's chest. He watched Zaybris pluck it out as if it were only a thorn.

"Ouch! You're lucky I don't breathe," Zaybris said, before tossing the horn clear across the cavern. He coughed then said, "Did you think your filthy horn could kill me? Wood is the only thing that can stake us, made from Earth's creation. But only when it hits a vampire's *heart*, hell-spawn, not a lung."

Zaybris then used his free hand to pry the traveler's stone from Selene's grip, though she didn't make it easy for him. Once the stone was free, Zaybris looped it around his own neck then laughed. It was a vile, slippery sound.

"Aww, poor demon! Isn't this poetic? What agony to be parted from your beloved!" Zaybris bent to lick Selene's neck, making her shudder. Sam made a strangled sound as he tried to grab at Zaybris's boot. The vampire quickly stomped down on his hand, breaking several small bones.

"What's the matter? You don't like having something dear taken from you?" Zaybris's smirk shifted to fury. "This is the misery I live with each day! Now, you can feel the pain I felt when Lilith left me to be with your father. And why I went all the way to hell to try to retrieve her!"

Then with a triumphant smile, Zaybris closed his eyes and squeezed the traveler's stone. In an instant, he and Selene disappeared.

CHAPTER 40

The transition through dimensions unfolded just as Selene had remembered. The smell of ozone came first, followed by the sensation of being pulled. Then came the bone-melting squeeze, before ending with the feeling of being dropped from a great height. Though the journey from Rugby to Aurelia had felt like it lasted only a minute, this time, her experience of disappearing and reappearing into another place seemed to stretch on for hours.

When the sensations cleared, she opened her eyes. She was indoors, staring at a stone wall. The air was musty and dank, with a touch of something sinister like... sulfur? Or was it smoke? There were no sounds except faint creaks echoing above, like footsteps. Vaguely, she wondered why she couldn't move her arms. A groan sounded next to her, and the pressure restraining her arms lifted.

She sat up, realizing that she was in a room. A bedroom, more precisely, lit with electric wall sconces. She was lying on a tapestry rug spread over a marble floor. In the room's center stood a twin-size bed with linens the color of red wine, while a cold fireplace sat in the corner. The bed, desk, and nightstand furnishings were heavy but small, as if scaled for a child. A thick layer of dust covered the decorative carvings of skulls on each piece.

"This isn't my castle!" cried a voice beside her. "Where am I?"

She turned to see Zaybris lying on his back, rubbing his eyes. A burst of adrenaline cleared her foggy mind, and she scrambled away from him. Moving toward the bedroom door, she pulled the handle. Logically, she knew there could be any number of fearful things outside, but at the moment, all she could think of was escaping Zaybris. She pulled and then pushed at the door, her muscles straining with effort. Yet, no matter how hard she tried, the door didn't budge. It seemed to be locked from the outside.

Where are we?

She watched Zaybris rouse to look around the room. His eyes landed on Selene briefly, but he didn't seem to register her presence.

"This looks like... this is... " His dropped his head. "Her face... I was thinking of her face."

Creeping away from the door, Selene wedged herself in a corner on the other side of the bed. She watched the vampire rub the hole in his chest, and instantly her thoughts went to Sam. The image of him lying alone on the cavern floor, unconscious and with only one horn, made her stifle a sob. Was he dead? Could he escape? His betrayal had cut deeply, but that pain paled in comparison to the possibility of his death.

Her heart ached when she remembered how his face looked when he gave her the stone. Although his body was battered and broken, he was so proud. He genuinely wanted her to use it. He wanted her to go home, even though, for him, it meant losing everything. He said he loved her, and she believed him.

Yet his deception combined with his degrading talk of "needing her" made her feelings for him less clear. She had been so angry when he had acted like taking her to Underworld was the gift of a lifetime, and hurt when he revealed that he had "claimed" her as his mate. As if she were no more than a piece of luggage.

So why does the thought of never seeing him again make me want to die?

Zaybris eased himself against the wall opposite her. Squeezing back tears, she straightened her back, ready to assume a fighting stance even though it seemed ridiculous in her braless and barefoot state. Now wasn't the time to sort through her complicated feelings for Sam. Not when she was locked in a room with a thirsty vampire.

Seeming to remember Selene was there, Zaybris looked at her earnestly. "Your beloved demon. He had his mother's eyes." He gestured to the stone around his neck. "That's why we're here. I was thinking of her as I looked at him."

"Where are we?"

Zaybris coughed, then gave an odd smile. "The Underworld."

Selene reeled back. She touched the stone walls, noticing that the smell of sulfur seemed more prominent now. Did that mean she was dead? Were they both? The dead didn't have pounding headaches or racing hearts, did they? She held out her hands, half expecting to see decayed flesh or prominent bones, but they looked normal.

Zaybris gestured around them. "This is the demon spawn's room. This blasted stone returned me to the spot where I took him."

She looked around the room. They were in Sam's world, his home. In his own room where he must have played and slept before he was taken. The fact that it obviously had not been touched since young Sam had occupied it was heartbreaking. What terrible irony it was that she should end up here instead of him.

Zaybris laughed bitterly. "Fate has an absurd sense of humor. Don't you think, human? Lady? What was your name again?"

"Selene."

"I am Zaybris, your new ruler," he said. "I meant to take you to my castle to be honored as a giver of life, yet here we are. Intriguing, don't you think? I had always believed I was destined to regain Lilith's favor by ruling in her stead, but perhaps I was sent here to win her another way."

Without waiting for her to respond, Zaybris tried to stand. His legs were shaking, and each movement seemed to pain him. When he reached out to the desk chair for support, he lost his balance. Both he and the chair fell to the ground with a large *bang*.

"Hmm. It appears our journey has weakened me considerably," he said, rubbing his back. "Not to worry, though. Come here, Selene. I need a drop of your blood."

Before Selene could protest, footsteps pounded outside the room. She pressed back into the corner. Sam had told her that the Underworld wasn't all fiery pits and lakes of lava, but what if things had changed? Would the demons here help her escape, or was she about to be roasted on a spit?

The bedroom door flew open. It revealed an elegant woman with dark eyes and gray wings. She had pearlescent skin, tinged with green and copper, and waist-length auburn hair. She wore a fitted black dress with bell sleeves and tiny buttons down the front. A silver crown made of spikes rested above her pointed ears.

When the woman looked at Selene, her eyes were surprised. The woman's gaze whipped over to Zaybris, and Selene watched her beauty transform into something terrible and frightening, like a vengeful queen from a fairy tale.

"You!" the woman cried, pointing at Zaybris. "How dare you show your face in the Underworld! Where is my son?"

"Lilith, my love," Zaybris said, walking toward her on his knees.

Lilith. Selene's skin tingled as she realized she was staring at the lost queen of Aurelia. Who was also apparently Sam's mother? The resemblance was clear—both in the set of her mouth and the tone of her skin. She wasn't much taller than Selene, but her bearing made Selene feel like a child cowering before a giantess.

Zaybris moved to wrap his arms around Lilith's legs. "Sweet Lilith, destiny brings us together so that we may never again part."

"Don't call me Lilith!" She kicked him hard in the chest. "I gave up that name when I began my new life just as you did, *Lawrence.* Tell me where my son is!"

"W-what should I call you?" Zaybris asked, brushing his hair out of his eyes.

She placed her hands on her hips, causing the sleeves of her dress to billow. Wispy shadows chased around her skirts. "I am Lamia now. Queen of the Night and the Underworld. The Maiden of Desolation, and first Shadow demon of her kind. Mate of Asmodeus, king of the Underworld and mother to Samael, the lost prince of Vengeance. Now I command you to explain to me why this room was filled with your stench the night my son disappeared!"

Zaybris swallowed. "I didn't think anything could top your Goblyn beauty, but how lovely you are as a demon now. More humanlike. Was the transition painful?"

The queen kicked him again, this time in the stomach. "It was glorious," she shot back, then turned to look at Selene. "Who are you?"

Selene's adrenaline was off the charts, yet she tried to appear calm and unthreatening. "Queen Lilith—I mean Queen Lamia, my name is Selene. I was in Aurelia, but Zaybris took me here. I-I know your son."

The queen took a step closer. "I can smell him on you." Her eyes brimmed with tears that she quickly blinked back. "Samael is in Aurelia?"

"Yes," Selene said.

"Has he been there the whole time?"

Selene nodded. "Since Zaybris took him as a boy."

Queen Lamia closed her eyes and murmured, "I was sure he was in Gaia. We've spent decades searching for him. And for Zaybris." When her eyes opened, they glowed red. "Oh you despicable leech, I always knew you took him. I just didn't think you would be so cruel as to take him to Aurelia."

Zaybris shrugged. "You give me too much credit. I merely thought of the only other realm I knew, besides Gaia, which was Aurelia."

"A closed dimension," Lamia said.

"Not to me. I can go anywhere I wish now."

"Then take me to him at once! How did you even come to the Underworld without being dead?"

Zaybris carefully rose to his feet then gestured to the stone suspended around his neck. "A traveler's stone. After you left, I spent years searching for a way to rescue you. Then I met a man who had used a traveler's stone to transport himself from Atlantis dimension to Aurelia. I killed him for it, so it now belongs to me."

"Rescue me?" Lamia asked. "Yet, you chose to abduct my son instead."

"I didn't plan to," he spat. "When I arrived in this foul place, I followed your scent, which led me to this room. When I saw a young demon sleeping in that bed with your features, I... I became enraged. I couldn't believe that you had chosen to breed with... with..."

"My fated mate?" Lamia supplied.

Selene's breath caught at the familiar term *fated mate*, but before she could dwell on it, Zaybris said, "I saw that you had built a life in the Underworld. Without me. So I did the only thing I could think of to make you notice me. *I took your child.*" A smirk overtook the vampire's face. "I wanted to hurt you as you hurt me. To take something dear to you just as your demon lover took something dear to me. I was your most trusted advisor, yet you spurned me for a fiend you barely knew."

Lamia laughed. "I knew Asmodeus long before you met me. You have him to thank for your relocation to Aurelia. He didn't like how your kind violated the line between human life and death on Gaia and asked me to intervene. We fell in love, and—"

"Then he coerced you to leave me! Or did he possess you to choose his wickedness?" Zaybris demanded. His knees trembled, causing him to fall back onto the edge of Sam's bed.

"It was you who coerced me!" Lamia shouted. "I was already with child when you tried to attack me. I was preparing to leave Aurelia to live in the Underworld, planning for the protection and care of my people. I hadn't even had a chance to tell my sisters yet.

And then that night when I saw how crazed you had become, how possessive, I was frightened. Asmodeus didn't want me to live with him until I was ready, but I couldn't risk staying near you another moment. I transported myself to Gaia where Asmodeus took me to his home."

"It's all in the past now. I forgive you for leaving me. Won't you forgive me too?" Zaybris pleaded.

"Absolutely not! Now take me to Samael at once!" said the demon queen. She drew herself up to spread her wings, and Selene tensed, certain she was about to see Zaybris burst into flames or get turned into a toad before he could take the queen anywhere. The shadows around Lamia's skirts grew more menacing. Then a roar from outside the bedroom made them all turn. Heavy footsteps shook the room like an earthquake.

Selene gulped as an enormous demon filled the doorway. He stood at least seven feet tall, eight if you counted his great black horns. They were gnarled and thick as tree branches, rising from the top of his bald head to point forward menacingly. Upon his brow was a crown of spikes similar to Lamia's, but his was chipped and battered like he had used it as an actual weapon. His goat-like legs stamped the floor as though he were about to charge. His expression was dark as a thundercloud.

There was only one person this could be—Asmodeus, king of the Underworld.

CHAPTER 41

I f Zaybris still had the ability to soil himself in fear, he was certain he would have done so at that moment.

After his transformation to vampire, Zaybris had happily relinquished his habit of comparing himself to other men. There was no need to lament that he wasn't wealthier, stronger, or as cunning as he wished to be—not when his superiority had been divinely ordained. However, as he stared up at Asmodeus, all his mortal insecurities came flooding back.

This wasn't exactly the gruesome devil he had always pictured. Despite his cloven hooves and blood-colored skin, the king of the Underworld was quite... handsome. He had a strong jaw, prominent cheekbones, and teeth so white they gleamed through the darkness of the room. He wore dark leather trousers and a cape secured by two skulls curved around each shoulder. His chest was bare—obviously an arrogant effort to show off his chiseled physique.

"Who dares to disturb my son's room?" the demon king boomed.

"It's who we've always suspected took Samael," Lilith said.

"Zaybris," Asmodeus growled. "Where is my son?"

"Aurelia," Lilith said. Though her expression was fierce, her voice wavered.

Asmodeus bared his teeth. "You mean to tell me that after the decades we spent sending out demon trackers, hiring enchantresses, consulting seers, and bargaining with nobility to find Samael, he was in Aurelia? All this time?"

Zaybris shifted his weight and shrugged.

Asmodeus released a terrifying howl. "And now, vampire, here you are. In my realm at last. Ready to receive my wrath." He began to charge toward him until Lilith pulled back his massive arm.

"Wait," she said. "He's not dead. He controls a traveler's stone."

This seemed to make the demon king even angrier, causing his body to shake. For a fearful moment, Zaybris braced himself to be staked or beheaded until he remembered demons weren't allowed to kill. Only punish. The thought should have brought him comfort, yet when Asmodeus stepped forward, Zaybris held his hands up defensively. The fiend did not strike him down, though. He only took Lilith's hand into his great clawed one.

"Take us to Aurelia," Asmodeus said to Zaybris.

"No," Zaybris said, struggling to push back his fear to remain in control of the situation. "Soon, I will take *Lilith* back to her native lands, but I'm far too weak now. I need human blood to refresh myself." He gestured toward Selene, who was cowering like a frightened rabbit.

Asmodeus's eyes flickered to Selene then back to Zaybris. "Take us. To see our son. Now!"

Zaybris straightened his spine. "Your son is dead."

"Liar." Asmodeus's red eyes narrowed. "You think I wouldn't know if my own son had entered the Underworld?"

Drat. Zaybris hadn't considered that. So the little monster was still alive, for now. No matter. If the demon still lived by the time he and Lilith returned to Aurelia, Zaybris could gain favor by gifting her with a reunion.

"You will take us to him right now," Asmodeus said, grabbing Zaybris's arm roughly.

"I told you I can't! Watch if you don't believe me," Zaybris said. He tapped the stone, whispering *Aurelia,* but nothing happened.

"Try again!" Asmodeus roared.

"Dimensional travel takes a great deal of personal energy! And I'm not one of your imps you can order about," Zaybris said.

"Have my sisters been taking care of Sam?" Lilith asked unexpectedly. "What did they say when you told them I left?"

When Zaybris looked at Lilith's face, his fear and anger softened. Her flowing hair was still the color of autumn sunsets, while her eyes remained obsidian pools that he yearned to drown in. He knew she was upset with him, but surely she retained some fondness for their time together. Her mood would pass with time. Once he proved himself worthy, all the heartache he had endured would be worth it.

The demon growled. "My queen asked you a question."

Zaybris wet his lips. "The Aurelian sisters were understanding... "

"Understanding?" Lilith said.

"He's lying," came Selene's voice from behind him. "He never told them anything."

The audacity! He hadn't harmed one hair on the human's head, and yet she betrayed him. Did loyalty count for nothing in the modern age?

"How dare you!" he cried.

"He didn't tell them?" Lilith repeated.

Selene shook her head then said quickly, "No one knows what happened to you. In Aurelia, you're called the lost queen. They've been searching for you for years—"

"I'll be taking some of that blood now!" Zaybris said before baring his fangs. He tried to launch himself across the bed to grab Selene but was pulled back. Something strong clamped around his throat, causing his teeth to clatter painfully. Then he was lifted in the air, his back pressed to the stone wall by the demon king. Although

Zaybris had held many victims in this same position, he was sure none of them felt as vulnerable than he did at that moment.

The scent of Asmodeus's breath was metallic and sharp. "Threaten her again, and I pull out every tooth from your skull."

"You never told them," Lilith said softly. For a moment, Zaybris regretted the pain the admission seemed to cause her. Yet now wasn't the time to show any sentimentality. He had to show her what a strong and true ruler he could be.

"I don't have to explain myself to inferiors," he retorted, struggling in the demon's grip. "Lilith, don't you see? It's fate that has brought me back to you. With this human's blood, I planned to revitalize the vampire race to show you what a true and just king I could be. Let me rescue you from this dark abyss. Come with me! Let us return to Aurelia to rule *together*."

Lilith rubbed her temples then turned to the king. "Oh, Asmo, I can't even bear to look at him."

"Go then, beloved, I'll take care of this," the demon replied. He peered closely at Zaybris. "Ah, vampire, what a quandary you pose. I can't keep you here against your will, but if I could, I would first tear off all of your fingernails..."

Asmodeus began to describe all the fearsome ways he wanted to torture him, but to Zaybris, the demon's voice fell away. He watched Lilith trace her fingers across the footboard of the child-size bed. Then she repeatedly extended and retracted her wings in a gesture he recognized from their time together as agitation. Her expression was lost.

Zaybris thought back to all the times the Goblyn queen had asked for his advice. The moments they had shared alone in her study—discussing plans for housing, blood donations, and sunlight protection. She had been joyous then, excited about the opportunity to give his people a home and serve as their benevolent queen. Yet there was no spark in her eyes now—only deep sorrow. In an instant, all his efforts felt hollow. The truth of his situation fell upon him like an ax.

She doesn't care about my plan.

Heartache made a lump rise in his throat against the pressure of Asmodeus's hand. All that he was doing was pointless. Why should he carry on the effort of trying to revitalize his people if it made no difference to her? She wasn't going back to Aurelia. Lilith had turned her back on the realm to live in the Underworld. Now she was queen of an entire dimension, not just a small territory. Could he hold all of that glorious ambition against her?

No. Not when her drive was one of the things he loved most about her. And if he truly wanted to be with her, he needed to make a sacrifice. A grand romantic gesture.

There is only one destiny for me now.

Squaring his shoulders as best he could while dangling in the air, Zaybris said, "I will endure any punishment that awaits me, great king."

Asmodeus looked surprised. "Is that so?"

"Yes. I am choosing to stay here in the Underworld."

The demon chuckled. "Are you, now?"

Zaybris tugged at Asmodeus's muscled forearm. "Let me down, will you? I swear I won't cause any trouble."

"Words are binding in my realm," Asmodeus said.

"I understand. Please!"

The king glanced at Lilith, who inclined her head. Abruptly, Zaybris was dropped to the floor. The impact made his chest wound throb, but he wouldn't let the pain keep him from what he needed to say.

"Lilith, my darling, my queen, I would rather live an eternity in this wretched place than be parted from you again." Zaybris reached up to close his fingers around the traveler's stone and pulled it off its chain. Lurching across the room, he came toward Selene and shoved the stone into her hands. "Take it! I don't need it anymore. Go on, take it!"

The stone dropped into Selene's palm. She looked at him and he nodded vigorously, closing her fingers around it. "A traveler's stone can be taken by death or gifted in charity. I relinquish my claim and gift it to you. Use it as you wish. Let it lead you to your fated mate just as it led me to mine."

Puffing out his chest, he turned to Lilith and dropped to one knee. "My queen, I pledge myself to you. To serve you in whatever capacity you desire, here in the Underworld."

He felt euphoric as the vow left his lips. *This* was the reason the stone had taken him here. *This* was how he was meant to spend the rest of his days. Everything made sense now. Zaybris waited expectantly for Lilith to react, hoping she might embrace him or gift him with a smile. But instead, her eyes turned cold.

"Take him away," she said to Asmodeus. Then after shooting an envious look at the stone clutched in Selene's hand, she added, "And make preparations for us to travel soon."

CHAPTER 42

Upon first contact, the stone felt cool and tingly in Selene's hand when Zaybris pressed it on her. But as soon as the vampire told her it was hers, her palm began to grow warm. A bright light glowed between her fingers, followed by a burst of energy. It rose from the stone then dropped to settle like liquid gold rushing through her veins. The sensation was pleasant, and jarring enough to keep her from processing the magnitude of what Zaybris had just given her.

Unlike when Sam tried to give her the stone, this time, she knew it was *hers*. She looked back at Zaybris, sure he was about to snatch it back from her, but he had already left her side to grovel at Queen Lamia's feet.

"Let's go, vampire," King Asmodeus said before hoisting Zaybris over his shoulder like a sack of potatoes. He turned to Queen Lamia. "Where do you want him, my treasure? The Sanctum of Agonizing Rectitude or the Hall of Eternal Torment?"

"Your choice," she replied wearily. She smoothed her long hair in a gesture that made Selene think of Queen Thema. She wondered how Sam would react if he knew he had actually served as a guard to his aunt.

"Let's start with some eternal torment, shall we?" King Asmodeus said.

As the king moved to take Zaybris from the room, he paused to address Selene. His gaze was just as penetrating as Sam's could be, yet more uncomfortable—as if he could see every mistake Selene had ever made and hear every lie she ever told. Her first instinct was to wither and cringe, but she lifted her chin. Although she had scoffed at Sam's "fated mate" idea, she was suddenly desperate to meet Asmodeus's approval.

The demon's voice was kind, though his expression failed to reveal his opinion of her. "The Underworld welcomes you. We've never had a living human visit, but no harm will come to you here. You can't stay long, though." His face split into a lopsided smile that was undeniably charming. "Unless you wish to become one of us."

Selene swallowed. "Thank you."

"No harm will come to me, too, right? As a guest of Lilith," Zaybris cried over King Asmodeus's shoulder.

The demon chuckled and squeezed the back of Zaybris's knee. "Her name is Lamia now. And don't worry, you'll only get what you deserve," he said, giving Selene a wink.

Turning at Queen Lamia, Asmodeus asked, "All right, beloved?"

"Yes. Go now. I need a word with this... Samael's human."

The demon kissed his mate on the forehead then strode out of the room with Zaybris dangling over his back.

Queen Lamia inhaled as though gathering herself together. "You must be exhausted. Please, sit. Tell me more about Samael and how you came to be in Aurelia. Then you will take us to him."

Selene sat down on Sam's bed, and Queen Lamia moved to stand in the open doorway. "Asmo, wait," she called out to the king. "Will you send for some refreshments for us?"

"Lemonade?" King Asmodeus called back.

"Yes, thank you. And cakes."

Selene would have laughed out loud if she weren't so drained. *Lemonade?* Of all the refreshments to be served in the Underworld, he had offered lemonade.

Instantly, the word made her think of serving drinks at her mother's parties. Slicing and juicing lemon after lemon with Cass until their hands ached. No matter the occasion, lemonade and sweet tea was always a staple at her mother's events. She would rather die than thwart Southern tradition, Cass had joked.

Her sister's face appeared in her mind, and Selene wondered what she was doing right now. Their time together in Rugby seemed like a lifetime ago. What month was it back home? What season? An image of Rugby's quaint library covered in snow came to her, followed by the Gentlemen's Swimming Hole dotted with ice.

An odd buzzing started in her hand. It spread up to her arm then across her whole body. The familiar smell of ozone hit her nostrils, and it felt as if the room was spinning.

She looked at Queen Lamia, panicked. "Something's happening... "

"The stone! Let go of the stone!" Queen Lamia shouted.

Selene looked at the stone in her hand. She tried to pry her fingers apart as realization dawned. But it was too late. Her body lurched and twisted like she was being pulled inside out. Queen Lamia's desperate face swam before her, gripping her shoulders and begging her not to go.

Then everything went dark.

CHAPTER 43

S am awoke in agony. He thought the throbbing pain where his horn used to be had blurred his vision black. After a moment, he realized he was wrapped in the darkness of the cave.

"Selene?" he tried to call out, but the words turned into a cough that wracked his broken ribs. The sound echoed through the walls of the cave. He listened intently for a reply or the presence of Zaybris's guards but only heard the rush of the waterfall and his own heartbeat reverberating in his ears.

I failed her.

He reached out to feel the ground around him, at first encountering only dust. Then his hand bumped against something made of glass and metal. His fingertips explored the object until its shape came to him. It was one of the lanterns from Queen Thema's castle, now broken. They had all been smashed to pieces, he realized. Finding his way out of the maze that had led them in felt impossible without light. Still, he had to try.

Carefully, Sam attempted to stand but collapsed face-first onto the ground. He knew his life-force was ebbing away, but he wouldn't fail Selene a second time. Zaybris must have taken her to the Goblyn castle with the traveler's stone, he reasoned. The vampire was probably putting her in chains right at that moment or harvesting blood from her veins. The thought filled him with such terror and rage it gave him the strength to roll to his side. There, he could see light coming from the rock opening to the waterfall. A way out. Slowly, he used his elbows to inch his body closer to the waterfall and the sliver of sunlight reflected.

At last, he was able to peer over the cliff edge to see what was below. The waterfall flowed into a river, one he knew flowed toward the Goblyn castle. The drop was steep, not much less than the tower's staircase that led to his chambers at Queen Thema's castle. He considered climbing down the crag, but his hands were bloody and raw from fighting. Yet, he knew there was no other way out.

Without stopping to consider the dangers, Sam dove over the cliff's edge. Wind and water rushed past him as he fell, whipping his hair around his broken horn. The resonance of the waterfall pounded from all directions. The murky depths of the river below came toward him faster and faster until he was plunged into a shock of cold water.

He let himself sink for a moment, relishing how the icy water soothed the pain of his injuries. Numbness overtook his body. Feebly, he tried to kick against the water's pull, but his feet felt heavy.

He needed air. Instinctively, he opened his mouth to breathe, and river water rushed in. The more he tried to expel it from his mouth, the more it filled his lungs. Twisting and turning, Sam tried futilely to take a breath, but he was too far below the water's surface. Down and down he sunk until the motion in his limbs stilled. His eyes slid shut, and his head tilted back.

I'm dying.

Demons in the living realm couldn't die of sickness or old age, but they could still perish if their vital functions were compromised. Sam thought again about how he had failed Selene. Betrayed her. Lied to her. He had failed Queen Thema too. He had done almost nothing of worth or honor in this life. He had squandered the love of his fated mate and would now be exiting the living realm with his vengeance for Zaybris unfulfilled. At least he would soon be reunited with his parents.

Sam's heart slowed, and his attempts at breathing stopped. Just before he slipped into unconsciousness, he felt something large swimming behind him. It swam again past his side, then he felt pressure around both wrists. Without warning, Sam's body was jerked up and pulled through the water at top speed. He felt his head breach the water's surface and air race over his face. Then he was flipped onto his back and pulled through the water again as though he were a heavy fishing net. Finally, he felt the bite of river stones against his back and the sun beating on his bare chest. He was no longer in the water but on land.

Sam rolled to his side, vomiting up water and gasping for breath.

"Easy now. Breathe into this," Sam heard a voice say. Something hard and round was pressed to his lips, and glorious, clean air filled Sam's mouth. Greedily, he breathed it in. Feeling rushed back to his limbs and the haze in his mind began lifting. Then suddenly, the air-delivering device was ripped away from him.

Sam made a noise of protest and turned to see someone peering down at him. It was a Nereid, a male with patches of gold-scaled skin. The top half of his body was muscular flesh, but below his waist, he had a golden fishtail instead of legs. Down the middle of his head, strands of blue and green hair were woven together in a braid.

"Slow down, or you'll be even worse off," the Nereid said, holding up a long, slender seashell. The end of his ruffled tail splashed rhythmically into the riverbank. "This shell is enchanted to deliver air, but too much can be deadly."

"Thank you," Sam rasped.

The Nereid smiled broadly, displaying a row of sharp white teeth. "I knew it was you."

Sam wiped water from his face. "What?"

"You're Samael!" The Nereid said his name like a victory cheer. "What happened to your horn?"

"Do I... know you?"

The Nereid shook his head, "No, but you saved my life many years ago. My name is Kye." His tail rippled, sending droplets of water into the air. "When I was young, a group of vampires tried to get me to fight for them. They took me from my waters, made me don legs, and locked me in a wagon."

Sam nodded weakly.

"On the night I was supposed to fight, you set fire to everything and freed me. It was amazing! I always wanted to repay you. And then today, you just showed up! In my river! What are you doing here?" Kye said.

"I've been injured." Sam tried to sit up, but the motion made him dizzy. "I was trapped in a cave above us and escaped over the waterfall. I'm trying to get to the Goblyn castle."

"What for?"

"My mate," Sam said thickly. "She is being held there against her will. By vampires."

"Oh no, we can't let that happen," Kye said. He began twisting his torso in a stretching motion and rolling his shoulders. "I'll take you to her. There's nothing I hate more than vampires."

The fear of what danger Selene could be facing at that moment made Sam's words come slowly. "No. I can't swim now. I'm too weak."

"Yeah, I know," Kye replied. "Don't move. I just have to grab something from home." Quickly, the Nereid dove back into the river. A few minutes later, a thin boat-like structure shot to the surface, followed by Kye. He emerged wearing a chest harness made of netting with two thick straps secured to the boat at his back.

"Climb aboard," Kye said.

Sam crawled on his hands and knees toward the water. When he gripped the boat's edge, black spots clouded his vision. He felt Kye come up behind him and unceremoniously push Sam in until he was lying with his back against the shell-like bottom of the boat.

"Hey, sorry about that, but I had to get you in somehow," Kye said cheerfully. "Just relax. I'll get you to your mate soon."

With a splash, Kye dove underwater and began swimming at a fantastic speed, pulling Sam behind him. The steady motion made it impossible for Sam to keep the darkness fogging his consciousness at bay. He couldn't say if the journey between the waterfall and the Goblyn castle took two minutes or two days, but the next time he opened his eyes, Kye was poking his shoulder.

"Samael, wake up. We're here!"

He sat up, noticing that the rest he had gained made his head feel clearer. The sun was setting, and the air was cool. When he laid his eyes on the Goblyn castle before them, vengeful anger strengthened his will.

I'm coming for you, Selene.

Gingerly, Sam hauled himself out of the boat. "Thank you, Kye. You have my gratitude."

"It was my pleasure." Kye bobbed in the water and gestured to the castle. "It's pretty grim in there. You need a hand? I haven't been on land for a while, but I could change into legs."

"No, you've given me enough help," Sam replied. "This is my vengeance to take."

Kye shrugged. The motion flipped his blue and green braid over his shoulder. "I'm glad I could help. Now we're even, demon!"

"We are. Farewell, Kye."

"Bright blessings," Kye replied. Sam watched the Nereid wave and then swim away, dragging the boat behind him. Sam was grateful that his time in the blood wagons had brought him such a boon.

Slowly, Sam approached the decrepit castle. No lights were shining in the windows, and it looked like no one had inhabited the castle for decades. The outer gardens and orchards were so over-grown Sam nearly walked straight into the iron gates defending the castle's entrance. No guards stood outside, which Sam found odd. Wouldn't Zaybris be more careful to protect himself? Perhaps the vampire assumed Sam was dead and wouldn't be coming for Selene.

Wrong.

The rusted gates opened easily with a push. Sam crept toward the large oak entry doors that bore a brass plaque depicting a bat in flight—Queen Lilith's royal crest. One door was ajar, and Sam slipped in. He tensed for a surprise attack. Nothing happened. Only the sound of his ragged breathing filled the empty entry hall, then the scuttle of a mouse disappearing under a loose floorboard.

"Selene!" Sam shouted repeatedly. Each time he paused to see if he could somehow connect with her through their bond and find where Zaybris had hidden her in the castle. He waited for some kind of response, either by sound or internal feeling, but nothing came. Enraged with fear and desperation, he began tearing through the castle. With what little strength he had, he started opening doors, searching each room he encountered, and even destroying bookcases and walls in search of secret passages.

Panting with exertion and covered in sweat, Sam finally made it up to the throne room on the top floor. He had found nothing in every space he searched but bats and cobwebs. Everything stank of mold and dust, leading him to a heartbreaking realization.

Her scent isn't here.

Even if Zaybris had hidden her someplace, Sam was certain their bond would make him able to catch her scent. She wasn't in the castle. Sam didn't know where she was. Every bit of rage and frustration rose and came out of him in an ear-piercing roar. Before the throne of the lost queen, Sam fell to his knees and dropped his head in his hands.

"We don't have any gold," a voice called out. "There's nothing here of value."

Sam's head whipped up. A well-dressed but tired-looking vampire was watching him from behind a table Sam had overturned. Sam shot to his feet and charged toward him.

"Where is Zaybris? Where did he take the human?"

The vampire's mustache twitched fearfully. "I don't know. Zaybris left with some guards a few days ago. I haven't seen him since."

"Do you know of the human he sought?"

"He went out to find her but planned to return here. Do you wish to drain her too?"

"She is my mate! I have come here to save her and destroy Zaybris! Where is he?"

The vampire held up his palms defensively. "Please, I am no ally of Zaybris, and I don't wish any harm to come to your mate. But I don't know where he took her."

Sam took a step forward. "How do I know you're not lying?"

"Waldron speaks the truth," a new voice called out. "Zaybris isn't here. Have you come to rescue us?"

Sam turned and saw a petite Goblyn in a pink dress hovering on leathery wings. More Goblyns began to emerge from dark corners and around doorways. A few vampires shuffled out, looking more weary than fearful.

"Where have you all been hiding?" Sam asked. "Is Zaybris there with you?"

"He isn't here, and may he never return," a vampire said in a rasping voice.

"Does your kind not serve him?" Sam asked. "Why are you all here if he is so despised?"

The Goblyn in the pink dress floated closer to Sam. "This is our home. Please, sir. Can we bring you something to eat or drink? At least let our healer dress your wounds."

The vampire called Waldron said, "Zaybris is nothing but a tyrant. Our kind has been lost without Queen Lilith, but when Zaybris returned, he didn't bring order and integrity as he promised. He only riled up the greediest among us."

"To serve his own needs," another vampire echoed.

Sam eyed them cautiously. The rush of adrenaline that had

propelled him into the castle was nearly spent, and his legs were shaking. It seemed that neither Selene nor Zaybris were in the castle. Although part of him was compelled to search all of Aurelia for Selene, he knew he was far too weak.

Zaybris could have taken Selene as far as the Vowa territory with the stone, which would take Sam weeks to reach, and doing so was a poor strategy when Zaybris could return her to the castle in a blink. The feeling of powerlessness he had was overwhelming. It wasn't wise to trust these strangers, but they posed no threats to him and seemed truthful in their hatred of Zaybris.

"You truly believe Zaybris means to return here?" Sam asked Waldron.

"It was his intention, yes. He had prepared a suite of rooms for her and... ah, well... devices to collect her blood."

Sam growled, and when his knees threatened to buckle, Waldron swept a chair under him.

"Sir, please sit and rest. May I ask your name?" Waldron said.

"Samael."

"Welcome to our home, Samael. We will do whatever we can to reunite you with your human."

Sam nodded weakly, resigning himself to living with the agony of waiting. He patted his side in search of the switch pouch before realizing it was left behind in the cave. "Do you have any means of communication here? I need to get a message to the Malkina queen."

Waldron reached into the pocket of his tweed suit jacket. "We have this crystal that once contained a message from Queen Thema. Would that do?"

"Yes." Sam took the crystal and considered how to phrase his message. He had to tell Queen Thema of the disastrous end to their scheme and demand that she organize a massive search among the queens for Selene. Unwanted images of Selene lying still and pale with death came to him, inducing panic. What if Zaybris had been so greedy that he drained her? What if he had beaten her or violated her? What if she was somewhere crying out for him, but he couldn't hear her? Surely he would feel it if she had died, Sam reasoned. Zaybris needed Selene's living blood. It was in his best interest to keep her healthy and whole.

Sam asked the Goblyns if they could bring him some water and food. He clutched the crystal and tried to transform all his fear, regret, and despair into determination and strength.

It's not too late for us, Selene. It can't be.

CHAPTER 44

Selene awoke, lying on her side. Something wet and squishy was pressed to her face, and her head was throbbing. Every muscle quivered with fatigue. When she breathed in, the air filling her lungs was humid and warm. It smelled of dirt, grass, and trees. Vaguely, her mind registered she was above ground.

There was pressure on her shoulder like someone was shaking her. The motion made her head hurt even more, and she tried to pull away. She cracked open her eyes and saw a dark figure crouched over her.

"Sam?" she croaked.

"Selene, what's happened to you?" a voice replied. "Did you hit your head? Should I call 911?"

The voice was familiar, but she couldn't place it—like a forgotten word hovering on the tip of her tongue. She rolled to her back and saw a woman's face loom over her. She had crystal blue eyes, a messy bob haircut, and was dressed in black. It took Selene a moment to realize it was her sister. What was she doing in Aurelia?

"Where's Sam? I have to help him, Cass." Selene tried to sit up, but Cass pushed her shoulders back.

"Oh no, you need to stay put. I think you have a concussion."

"He's hurt," Selene tried to explain to her sister while squirming out of her grip. "He could die. We have to find him."

"Who's Sam?" The worried look on Cass's face deepened. "Just rest for a sec."

The image of Sam alone in the cave, bloodied and beaten, came to Selene's mind. How would she find him again in that maze of cave tunnels? Fear for him made tears fill her eyes.

"Let me up! We have to get to him! I can't just leave him there," Selene pleaded. She tried to push Cass's hands away and noticed how she was clutching something in her hand. A shiny white stone, wrapped in odd-colored wire and hung from a leather cord, filled her palm.

A memory tugged at her mind, reminding her that stone was important and needed to be protected. She shoved it into her pocket, then sat up. Something was buzzing through the air, miles above her head. Was that a Harpy? Maybe it was Brunie, coming to help her or even Pydiana swooping overhead. Selene looked up at the figure in the sky. Then she realized it wasn't a Harpy at all.

It was an airplane.

She went dizzy for a moment, and then looked from side to side. The trees surrounding them were smaller, nothing like the grand forestry of Aurelia. A robin perched on a nearby rock took flight when a squirrel startled it away. Selene looked at her sister, down at the puddle she was sitting in, then up at the sky.

"Where am I?"

"You don't remember?" Cass asked. "We're in Rugby."

It was as if a boulder of ice dropped into her stomach. All at once the events of the past 24 hours came to her in rush, like images of a movie on fast forward. The Underworld, Zaybris, Lilith/Lamia, the stone. How her thoughts had gone to Rugby and Cass just before the stone began to buzz...

"The stone took me home," Selene whispered.

"No, honey, you're not home. We're in Rugby, remember?" Cass said. "We hiked down here to watch the sunrise."

Selene blinked, realizing Cass was wearing the same striped leggings and black Lycra jacket she had last seen her in. Her camera was on the ground nearby. "What day is it?" Selene asked.

"Sunday."

"When did we drive here? Is it the same day?"

"Same as what? We got here yesterday. What happened to you?" Cass said. She gestured at the trail down to the water. "I was only gone a few minutes. Did you slip on these rocks or something?"

"I... I don't know."

"Where's your stuff? And what happened to your shoes?"

Selene extended one leg to see that she was barefoot. The soles of her feet were caked with dust from her time with Sam in the cave. The sulfuric scent of the Underworld clung to her T-shirt, and now she was covered in mud from Rugby, Tennessee. She rose to her knees.

"Hey, I said don't move—" Cass said.

"I'm fine," Selene lied. "I just need to get my bearings."

"Drink some water," Cass said. Selene's hands shook as she took the bottle. After a long drink, Cass reached out to tuck a lock of her older sister's hair behind one ear. It was a gesture that Selene had done to Cass countless times when she was younger, especially when she was upset. Tenderness made the tears that had gathered in Selene's eyes for Sam spill freely down her cheeks now. All the worry, confusion, fear, and pain she had just been through came to the surface in a torrent of emotion.

I'm really home.

She pulled Cass into a tight hug and began sobbing into her shoulder.

But what about Sam?

"Now you're really scaring me. What's going on?" Cass said.

"It's... it's good to see you," Selene mumbled.

They continued to hold each other until Cass said, "Tell me everything you remember."

Selene sniffed and looked into her sister's worried face. Her first instinct was to tell Cass the truth about everything, but even her through her haziness, she knew how outrageous it would sound. The idea of explaining what had just happened to her made Selene start to doubt her own perception of reality. Demons, Harpies, vampires, cat people, other dimensions—how could it all be real? Was it just an elaborate dream?

"I must have slipped over in the mud," Selene said slowly, before taking another drink from the water bottle. "Can we go home?"

Cass nodded. "Yes, but we're finding you a doctor first."

After they both changed clothes and collected their things from the guest house, Cass drove Selene to an urgent care clinic about 30 miles away from Rugby. Selene had resisted going at first but realized she needed to know if something was wrong with her.

Selene made Cass stay in the waiting room then told the doctor her symptoms were memory loss and confusion. He asked if she'd been through any stressful events lately, like a job loss or break up, which made her burst into tears. With a knowing nod, the doctor reassured her there were other fish in the sea and encouraged her to try online dating. He performed all the necessary tests, then revealed she was suffering from dehydration, but otherwise in perfect health. He speculated that a reaction to her new allergy medication might have caused her disorientation, but there were no indicators of head trauma. She was relieved, but also troubled to not have a reasonable explanation of her experience.

Cass drove home while Selene dozed. Once they arrived at Selene's apartment, Cass took her luggage and helped her upstairs. It was unnerving to see the apartment just as she had left it. From the pile of mail on the coffee table to the dirty cereal bowl she'd left in the sink, nothing had changed. While Cass went to find her fresh pajamas and start the shower, Selene stood in the living room, trying to absorb all that had happened.

In the distance, she could see the Nashville skyline through her balcony door. She opened the glass slider, noticing how different the air was here—thicker, dirtier. She could smell the exhaust from the cars passing below and smoke from her neighbor's barbecue grill. Her hands tightened on the balcony rail.

What now?

Swallowing thickly, she wondered if Sam was still alive. How much time had passed? When Zaybris took her from the cave, she was sure Sam was close to death. It was a miracle that King Asmodeus had said he wasn't dead, but what if that had changed? Had Sam passed on to the Underworld? Or was he still lying in the dark cave—injured, alone, and sick with worry about her? Impulsively, she reached for the stone in her pocket, ready to try transporting herself back to him. But before she could visualize his face or wonder if the stone still worked, she paused.

Do I want to go back?

Snatches of the fight they had before Zaybris arrived ran through her mind.

Queen Thema's note.

Sam's lies.

The word *bait.*

Sam telling her only *she* could calm his violence. How he needed her to do so.

Anger simmered along with deep hurt. She had felt so stupid when she found the note, so betrayed. Especially since up until that point, she had thought she loved Sam. She was even thinking about staying with him in Aurelia before she learned everything about their relationship was built on a lie.

Cass called out to say the shower was hot, and Selene turned numbly. She should be elated right now, especially since she success-fully avoided being turned into a living blood bank. This was what she had wanted—a way home, a reunion with her family, a return to normal life. Aurelian Selene was gone, long live Ordinary Selene.

Maybe it really was all a dream.

CHAPTER 45

Selene slept all through Monday, and into Tuesday. She was plagued by dreams of an anguished Sam running through a castle calling her name, and the feel of Zaybris's tongue on her neck. Cass made brief appearances at her bedside, and Selene was comforted by having her sister take care of her for a change. Vaguely, she remembered Cass leaving for work. When she woke again, Kevin was standing over her saying, "You're still in bed? It's nearly dinner time."

Selene sat up groggily. "I guess I overslept. What day is it?"

"Tuesday. Your boss has been blowing up my phone looking for you. Why didn't you call in sick?"

'Oh, I... " It took Selene's brain a minute to recall that she had obligations and responsibilities in this world. "I didn't think about it."

"Where's your phone? You must have a million texts from him." Kevin asked, gesturing at the empty space where her phone normally charged on the nightstand.

Selene frowned, trying to remember what her phone even looked like. The last time she could remember seeing it was within the backpack Arkaya had given her, which was now on the floor of the cave. Next to Sam. The image made her breath catch.

"I lost it," Selene said. "Cass and I went to Rugby and must have dropped it when were hiking." She paused then asked, "Why are you here? I thought you were touring."

Kevin pushed a lock of his chin-length hair from his face, and Selene wondered when he had last shampooed. "We're back for a week. The drummer's tendinitis was bothering him. I landed a gig at Maynard's Tavern on Saturday though. You'll help me out for it, right?"

"I guess," she replied sleepily.

They stared at each other while Kevin fiddled with his silver thumb ring. Then after a moment, he sniffed, "I thought you'd be happy to see me."

"Mmm hmm," she said, then rolled over to face away from him and fell asleep.

It was nearly 6 a.m. when Selene woke again. Kevin had climbed into bed next to her at some point and was snoring softly. So many times she had thought about how she'd feel upon returning home, but the reality was just... meh. It was good to see her sister, and she wanted to see Evan soon, but she wasn't as relieved at being home as she expected.

The automatic coffee maker switched on in the kitchen, reminding Selene that she should be getting up for work now. The idea made her want to groan. Spending her days filling out forms, sitting through boring meetings, attending webinars—all of it felt so pointless compared to how she had been living in Aurelia.

What would her life have been like if she had stayed? She pictured a quaint little cottage like Brunie and Eldridge's, with smoke puffing out the chimney and flowers bursting from the window boxes. She would spend her days going on long walks, reading, and growing vegetables, and her nights locked in Sam's arms. He would do manly things like chop wood and hunt for food, but still help with the dishes and pick up his dirty socks. Maybe she could open a little bookstore or start a library wherever they settled...

Stop.

Rolling over, Selene remembered that Sam's plans for their life together were very different. He had wanted to leave Aurelia as soon as possible and take her to the Underworld. Lock her away where she'd be his little pet since he had "claimed" her as his mate. What did that even mean? That she existed to soothe his dark moods or hop into bed whenever he felt like it? Whenever he *needed* her? The thought made her tense with anger.

The aroma of coffee drifted through the apartment, and Selene slipped out of bed. She poured herself a cup, spurning her usual artificial sweetener for real sugar, and gazed out the window. It still wasn't clear to her if her time in Aurelia was real. The vividness of the experience faded with each minute she connected with the real world. A hallucination seemed the most plausible explanation. Perhaps there was a gas leak nearby that had given her strange visions. Or maybe the doctor had been right about her allergy medication.

Would she ever really know?

The thought of always living with such uncertainty was devastating. Yet sleeping all day and moping wasn't going to cure her. Maybe a return to her routine was what she needed to refocus— something to occupy her mind and give her some perspective. After finishing her coffee, she started the shower to get ready for work.

Once in the office, it took her a while to remember the context of the emails in her inbox. Her boss had been understanding when she explained how she'd lost her phone and gotten sick in Rugby. The hours dragged by, and her back ached from so much sitting. When her lunch hour came, she was grateful for an excuse to pop out and buy a new phone.

It took longer than expected at the cell phone store, and she was starving by the time she finished. She stopped by a barbecue place to grab lunch, and while she waited in line, the hair on the back of her neck began to rise. It felt like someone was watching her.

She looked around the restaurant, but everyone was glued to their phones or occupied in conversations. The feeling continued until her eyes landed on a tall man leaning on the wall near the restrooms—staring directly at her. He wore a black button-down shirt, indigo jeans, and a silver skull-shaped belt buckle. The cowboy hat he wore gave him away as a tourist, but he didn't seem lost or taking in the local flavor. There was something predatory in his lean, casual stance.

Their eyes met, and his mustache twitched with a smile. He touched the brim of his hat and nodded. It was an old-fashioned gesture, but before Selene could respond, it was her turn in line to order. She could still feel the cowboy's eyes on her as she paid, but when she turned around, he was gone.

Back at the office, she stared at the clock until it reached 5:00, then practically sprinted out the door. As she drove home, she thought about the cowboy, wondering why she felt strangely drawn to him. It wasn't just because he was tall, dark, and handsome—there was something more. Thoughts of him dissipated though, once she got home and gratefully found the apartment empty. She flopped onto the couch, relieved to at last have some time alone.

After finding nothing on TV, she picked up the pile of cardboard coasters stacked on the coffee table to shuffle them absentmindedly. They were emblazoned with lyrics from Kevin's moderately successful song, "He Died of Poetry," and used as giveaways for fans.

She thought back to the night when they first heard that song play on the radio. They'd been driving back from a Nashville Sounds baseball game, and both of them had screamed when the DJ introduced it. Kevin had been so excited he immediately wanted to visit a tattoo parlor to get the title memorialized across his forearm. Selene stood by as he got inked, checking his social media, and reporting back with all the new followers. She had been thrilled for him, but also gratified to see the work she had done pay off. It wasn't easy building his platform, making contacts, and learning about the music industry, but that moment seemed to make it all worthwhile. For months after, he would dedicate the song to her at shows. The recognition made her glow.

I miss those times.

She thought about all the little victories they had celebrated as a couple. In the beginning, they used to have a lot of fun together. Kevin wasn't a bad person; had she been too hard on him? Was it fair to compare a regular guy to a towering, muscle-bound Vengeance demon? Especially one who may or may not have been a hallucination?

Placing the coasters down, she stretched out on the couch. Maybe Kevin did just want some space to focus on his career. All relationships took work, and this could be a new beginning for them if she were open to it. It was worth considering.

The rest of the week went by quickly. Selene felt like she had something akin to jet lag and kept falling asleep on the couch in front of the TV each night. Cass texted her a few times to see how she was feeling, and Selene feigned normality. Work was as dull as ever, peppered with a few awkward moments when she unexpectedly found herself walking out of a meeting that had dragged on too long and confusing her boss by flat-out refusing his requests to work through lunch.

Kevin spent most of his free time rehearsing at a friend's house for his gig, so they rarely saw each other. When they were home together, Selene tried to be positive but found herself barely able to hold a conversation with him. He always seemed to be whining about something or fishing for reassurance. She went along as best she could, but her thoughts kept straying to the stone she had clutched in her hand in Rugby—now sitting in her jewelry box. A few times, she had taken it out to look at it, wondering if it was truly pulsing with energy or just her imagination. One time she even thought she saw an image of Sam's face glinting on the stone's shiny surface, but the surge of grief it caused made her quickly put it away.

On the day of Kevin's big show, he left in the morning for one last rehearsal. Selene spent the day running errands until she found herself unable to resist the call of her cozy bed for a quick afternoon nap.

She was awakened by the words, "Are you serious, Selene? Why isn't my stuff ready?"

Kevin stood by the bed, glaring at her with his hands in a "what gives" gesture. The clock showed it was nearly 4 p.m. but it took Selene a moment to understand why he was so offended. Then she remembered how she usually had all his merchandise organized and packed up by the door before his shows.

"Oh, sorry. I haven't been feeling well lately," she said.

"I have to be at Maynard's in an hour," Kevin said.

"I know, just give me a sec to wake up." She rose from the bed then began brushing her hair.

"You don't look sick," Kevin muttered. He started to pace, stroking his goatee impatiently. "Could you hurry it up a little?"

"Sorry, I'll be ready in a few minutes." She began gathering her hair back into a ponytail.

"You know this show is important to me. There might be industry people there."

"So you've said."

"You had all day to pull everything together."

Selene's eyes narrowed as she watched him in the mirror hanging on the wall. "I told you I haven't been feeling like myself this week."

"How convenient."

"What's that supposed to mean?"

"It's just that... well," Kevin plucked at the beaded bracelets around his wrist. His eyes were accusatory as they met hers in the mirror. "It would be nice if you could support me for once!"

Selene paused as the words rang her ears. Slowly, she set down her hairbrush and turned to face him. "What did you just say?"

"You heard me. This is my dream we're talking about, and you're acting like it's nothing." He kicked the footboard of their bed.

"That's not true," she said.

"Then show me that you want me to succeed here."

"I'm trying—"

Kevin stepped closer to take her hand. "Try harder, Seleney."

Selene jerked her hand out of his grip. Anger ripped through her like a shot—more urgent and closer to the surface than ever before. It sizzled through her veins. She leveled her gaze until Kevin paled and looked away. Then she pushed past him to march into the living room. She began to grab handfuls of merchandise from the stacks of CDs, LPs, stickers, and coasters littering the room.

"Forgive me for neglecting my duties!" she snapped while tossing Kevin's things into a plastic bin near his guitar case. From the corner of her eye, she thought she saw a black shadow dart toward her, but it dissipated when Kevin followed after her.

"Hey! Be careful. Aren't you going to inventory those?"

"Are you going to dock my pay?" Selene continued filling up the bin. Her skin felt hot, though the air conditioner was on. After all that she had done for Kevin, she couldn't believe his nerve. *It's never enough.* Seeing so clearly how he was trying to manipulate her felt as though she were waking up from a long sleep.

She went to the coat closet and pulled out the metal cash box she used for making change and threw it against the carpet. How many shows had she lugged that thing around? She even carried it into the bathroom with her to prevent someone stealing Kevin's "hard-earned" profits. Next, she grabbed the folding table with the wobbly leg and set it near the front door with a *thud*.

Finally, she picked up the big vinyl sign leaning against a wall with the KEVIN P. NORTON logo she had commissioned. Shoving it into Kevin's chest, she said, "All done!"

He swallowed. Carefully, he took the sign from her hands then set it on the floor. "What's wrong with you?"

"I'm done being your manager."

Kevin gaped at her. "What do you mean?"

Gesturing around, Selene said, "This. Coordinating your schedule. Running your social media, booking your shows, hauling your gear. I don't want to do it anymore."

Kevin's mouth open and closed, but no sound came out.

"I quit," she said.

He looked shocked. "But... I thought you loved my music."

"This isn't about your music."

"I don't understand."

"It's about my time. You wanted a break, so here you go."

The confusion in Kevin's face turned to a sneer. "What's your problem? You've been weird all week."

Selene laughed. "Oh, have I?"

"You used to like helping me. I don't understand what's changed."

She was about to say something caustic, but the hurt in his eyes made her pause. Her anger ebbed as she took in how pitiful he looked, standing there in his best vintage t-shirt next to a sign bearing his own name. She considered that it was an abrupt change for him to take, after she spent so much time working for him without complaint.

"I'll show you how to do everything," she said. "We can take it one thing at a time."

"But you're so much better at it than I am. And what about tonight?" Kevin's voice was panicked. "You know how important this show is for me. I can't do everything by myself!"

"Take a breath. I'll help tonight. But after this, things have to change."

He nodded. Selene smiled, feeling more awake than she had all week.

CHAPTER 46

Hours later, Selene found herself dutifully clapping from her usual spot at the back of Maynard's Tavern. Kevin was on stage, dripping with sweat, and strumming his guitar. When he got to "He Died of Poetry," Kevin made a big show of dedicating it to her. Selene waved from behind the merch table and tried to appear gracious. The display was a bit excessive, but she was grateful to see him show some appreciation.

The artist appearing after Kevin had a much bigger following, so Maynard's was beginning to fill up before Kevin left the stage. It was the usual crowd of Nashville locals—women wearing sundresses with chic hats, the men dressed in ripped jeans and old concert shirts. But as Selene watched the people file past her, goosebumps broke out on her arms. There it was again, that feeling like someone was watching her.

She looked around the bar until she spotted the source—a tall man leaning against the retro jukebox. *The cowboy.* He was wearing the same clothes he wore at the restaurant, and when their eyes met, he nodded. She gave half a smile, then kicked herself because he seemed to have taken it as an invitation to approach her.

"Evenin', ma'am," the cowboy drawled in a deep voice that added to the whole outlaw vibe he had.

"Uh... hello." He smelled like gunpowder, but his smile was engaging. Selene wasn't sure what to make of him.

"You come here often?" he asked.

Seriously?

"Sure, when my boyfriend plays. Did you see his set just now? We have some things for sale here," Selene said, motioning to the table. The word *boyfriend* tasted like poison in her mouth, but she wanted to make sure this guy knew she wasn't interested. "Or you can sign up for the Kevin P. Norton email list—"

"Lady, you don't have to play games with me," the cowboy interrupted, his brown mustache stretching into a smile. The way he said *lady* was strange. Like it was a title. He looked at her expectantly. "Since I saw you the other day, I've been trying to track you down. Glad I found you tonight."

"Excuse me? Do I know you?"

After a moment, he frowned, then looked left and right. Bending forward, he gripped the center of his hat and lifted it slightly—just enough to reveal something that made Selene gasp.

Two horns.

They were brown and squat, nestled within his dark hair. These horns were much smaller than Sam's, like the ones you'd see on a baby cow. Selene dropped her gaze to meet the cowboy's eyes. As she did, they flicked from hazel to bright red. His grin was conspiratorial.

Demon.

Selene felt stupefied. A real demon! Here? But he looked so normal! Sort of. Unable to help herself, she blurted out, "Y-you're not from around here!"

"No, ma'am. I'm from down south," he said, pointing at the ground. "Deep south."

"How did you get... up north?"

He crossed his long arms. "The usual way, by a summoning. I

was called here in 1865 by a seance," he said, then extended his hand. "Halphas, demon of Delusions. But I just go by Hal in this realm."

Selene grasped his hand and shook. His grip was strong and reassuring. For some reason, it made any anxiety she had about him melt away. "I'm Selene Riley. Just... Selene."

"A pleasure, Lady Selene." He surveyed the bar eagerly. "Is your mate here? I'd love to meet him."

Selene's mouth went dry. "M-my mate?"

"Forgive me, is it a she?"

She quickly glanced at Kevin, who was chatting near the stage. "I'm not... he's—"

The cowboy cut her off with a laugh. "Come on now. I know for damn sure it's not that pipsqueak you're selling trinkets for."

She swallowed. "What makes you think I have a mate?"

"Lady, you've got demon glittering all over you. Down to your aura. You've been claimed. And quite thoroughly," he said with a wink.

Selene's face heated.

"Aw shucks, I didn't mean to be so crude. I've just never met a human mated to a demon before. I've always wondered if it was possible. Hoped it was, to be honest."

"You can *see* his claim on me?"

"Clear as day."

Hal's words buzzed through Selene like an electric current. She bit her lip as sadness, regret, confusion, yearning, and deep heartache tightened in her chest.

Suddenly, the area around them fell dark, as though a light bulb directly above them winked out. All at once, it became difficult to see anyone else. Shadows cloaked the two of them.

"What in tarnation—" Hal said. A cluster of black shadows swarmed above them then curled around Selene's shoulders like a shawl. Her mouth opened in surprise while Hal chuckled. "Ah, I see. Now that's a rare trick! You must have learned that from your fella."

Hot tears pricked at Selene's eyes. The dark shapes seemed to pick up on her emotions and pulsed more strongly. They chilled her skin, but their presence was comforting.

Is your mate here, he had asked.

You've been claimed.

Her experience in Aurelia *was* real; she didn't have to fool herself anymore. All the anxieties she had about her ability to separate fact from fiction were swept away. Hal and the shadows weren't a hallucination, which meant Sam wasn't either.

Relief hit her along with a wave of longing for her demon so strong she sagged in her seat. Selene wiped her eyes then waved the shadows away. Hal was watching her with concern.

"Hey, why the sad face? Has your mate been cruel to you?" He punched a fist into his palm. "Where is he? I'll straighten him out."

"He isn't here," she said quietly. "We're... separated."

Pulling up a chair, he said, "Did y'all have a quarrel?"

"It's complicated."

"Can't be all that bad, can it?"

"I don't know," she sniffed. "I'm not even sure he's alive."

"Of course, he is. I wouldn't be able to see his claim if he wasn't."

"Really?" she said, feeling as though a great weight had lifted from her chest. "I'm glad to hear that."

"Is that all that's troubling you?" Hal asked.

"Yes. No. It's more than that. He...he had some plans that I didn't agree with. And said some things—" She shook her head, remembering how Sam had used his strength to intimidate her in the cave. How could she love a man who acted that way? It was ridiculous to cry over someone who wanted to claim her like a piece of meat.

"Anything I can do to help?" Hal asked.

She considered the demon. Even in the dim bar lighting, she could see the rim of red around Hal's hazel irises. If anyone could help her translate the mysteries of demon matehood, it was this guy. "May I ask you a question?"

"Of course," he said.

"What does it mean for a demon to call you his mate? To claim you?"

"He didn't tell you?"

"No. I think he meant to, but there wasn't time."

Hal nodded, and Selene was grateful he didn't ask her to elaborate. "Our kind believes that fate matches us with another to increase our power. If you're his mate, then he can share his strengths to enhance your abilities, while you do the same for him. It looks like that's already happened with the shadows."

"But what about the claiming part? Does it mean I'm like, his property?"

Hal threw back his head and laughed. "I take it you've never met any female demons, huh? They would never stand for that."

"Then what does it mean?"

"It just means he's felt the bond and wants to be yours. He wants other demons to know that you're his mate, and not to be trifled with. But that doesn't mean you have to accept his claim. Oh, that must be the problem. You haven't claimed him, have you?"

"I can do that?"

"Yep. Our kind believes in fate, but we also believe in free choice. He can claim you all he wants, but until you claim him, the mating bond isn't fully in place. He really should have told you these things. Has he taken on any traits of yours?"

"I'm human. I don't have any traits worth sharing."

"Now, that can't be true."

She reconsidered. "Actually, he said I calm him."

"My, my." Hal raised his eyebrows. "That's a precious gift to a demon."

"Is it?"

Hal nodded.

Selene slumped in her chair. "It sounds like a lovely sentiment, but I don't want to be in charge of his emotions." Her gaze bounced around the bar anxiously. "I can't take that on. I don't want to."

Hal adjusted his hat. "No, no, no. He's got it all wrong. Mates help bring their partner's inner qualities to the surface—they don't control those traits. Have you felt differently since meeting him? Acting in a way that people say isn't like you?"

"I've been a lot angrier," she said. "My tolerance for BS is gone."

"Do you think that came directly from him? Or was that anger within you all along?"

"Definitely within me," she said thoughtfully. "It always felt trapped, though. Bottled up. For decades."

"Exactly." Hal smiled. "Your mate pulled the cork on that bottle. You did the same for him, but with a different emotion."

Selene considered his words. She was going to question him on the topic further, but found herself asking, "How does a human claim a demon? Do we have to live in the Underworld?

"Not unless you want to," Hal said then shrugged. "I'm not sure how the claiming works with non-demons, honestly. But I do know this—the first step is to decide you want to. What is it that you want, Lady Selene?"

Her jaw tightened. She thought back to that day when Sam asked her about her ideal life. "I hate that question."

"Why?"

"It's not easy to answer. There's a lot to consider."

Hal gave her a skeptical look. "Is there?"

"Always."

Then shaking his head, he said, "Darlin,' I'm feeding on your delusion right now."

Before Selene could reply, Kevin was at her side, nudging her with his elbow. "How much have I sold?"

"Nothing yet," she replied, bristling at his touch.

"Not quite," Hal said, rising to his feet. He tapped his finger on a CD. "I've got to mosey along to see more acts tonight, but I'll take one of these. It will help sustain me when I can't get out to see new talent." He pulled out a hundred-dollar bill from his pocket and handed it to Selene. "Keep the change."

"Wow! Thank you. I'm so glad you enjoyed my set!" Kevin gushed. "I love your hat. Are you in the music industry?"

Hal smirked. "Thank you, son. I'm no big wig, just a fan of aspiring musicians. And as for your music, let's just say it... fed my soul."

"That's really profound," Kevin replied with a hand over his chest. "It's my honor."

Hal clapped him on the back. "Keep trying, boy. Always keep trying." Then touching the brim of his hat, he whispered to Selene. "Dark blessings to you, Lady."

Kevin looked puzzled while Selene smiled and said, "Thank you, Hal. You've given me a lot to think about."

"Don't think, just feel. If there's something you want, claim it." Then he gave her a small salute and turned to walk out of the bar.

Kevin flopped into the seat Hal had occupied and began drumming his fingers on the table. "He was interesting. Did you hear what he said about my music? Fed his soul."

"Yes," Selene murmured. As Kevin blathered on about music and souls, she stared at the jukebox where Hal had been standing. Suddenly the answer to the question she hated most wasn't so complicated anymore.

She thought about all the experiences she had wanted as a child but wasn't allowed to have. Summer camp, weekend sleepovers, studying abroad. And then as an adult—out-of-state college, travel, adventure, a partner who listened to her and respected her desires. She always had an excuse for not taking what she wanted. Not enough PTO hours, too expensive, more trouble than it was worth, too disruptive to her family, too unrealistic to hope for.

But if she took all of that away—eliminated all of the complications and self-imposed barriers? Then what did she want?

The truth spread throughout her limbs like effervescent bubbles. Bright, fresh, and real.

I want to be with Sam.

There was simply no other option for her. She had to go back to

Aurelia. She wasn't going to be Sam's emotional crutch in the way he seemed to think she was, but she had to see him. At least talk to him. She had a stone that could take her anywhere! If Sam couldn't accept her terms to be the partner she wanted, then she could say goodbye and come home. But at least she would know. Then she could move on. It was pointless to waste another moment.

Turning to Kevin, she said, "We're breaking up. I wish you the best, but it's over."

CHAPTER 47

The drive home from Maynard's was tense, but Selene held firm to her decision. Kevin tried several tactics to get her to reconsider, but Selene never wavered. Eventually, she told Kevin his bargaining was useless since she was moving out of state.

"Where?" he had asked.

"I'm going to... " How to explain that she was going somewhere unreachable? A remote village in Alaska? A tiny island in the Pacific? Impulsively, an idea popped into her head. "An eco-village. I want to live off the grid."

"Are you serious?"

"Yes. You know how important recycling is to me," Selene replied, chuckling to herself. Their ongoing fight about Kevin's habit of throwing paper into the trash instead of the recycle bin was paying off. She spouted a few platitudes about connecting with the earth and getting away from it all until they reached the apartment. Once inside, she told him he needed to sleep on the couch, and she closed the bedroom door.

The next morning, Kevin was gone when Selene woke so she started planning her departure. A few experiments using the stone to transport herself from room to room in the apartment had taught her it was best to visualize the physical space where she wanted to appear. She figured Sam had probably gone back to his life at Queen Thema's, so that was where she needed to focus. She wished she had seen inside his bedroom so she could imagine herself there. Surprise! But she also didn't want to scare him, so maybe she would just turn up outside the castle gates.

She hated to think how worried he must be about her. He had no idea where Zaybris had taken her or what he had done. He soon would, though. She would explain everything, including how his own mother was Lilith, the lost queen herself. He would be so relieved and happy. Queen Thema would finally have closure as well.

Selene considered Queen Thema while she cleaned out her closet. She hadn't fully resolved her feelings about the Malkina ruler. On the one hand, she felt furious and betrayed to have been nothing but a means to an end. Bait to further the queen's own agenda.

Yet, Selene could sympathize with her motivations. If something had happened to Cass or Evan, wouldn't she exploit every advantage to find them? The queen was definitely an opportunist, but Selene didn't think she intentionally wanted her harmed. The whole thing was deeply wrong. However, she couldn't shake the fact that if Thema hadn't concocted her plan, she might have never met Sam.

Queen Thema was going to get a piece of her mind, Selene resolved. But she didn't want to focus on her grievances at the moment. Right now, it was only Sam that she craved.

Tomorrow. I'm going to see him tomorrow!

Her excitement was cut short by a tide of guilt. The reality that she would soon be saying goodbye to Cass and Evan was excruciating. Would they hate her for this? She hoped the stone would allow her to check in periodically. Would they be okay without her?

While she pondered these questions, a family photo slipped out from between the pages of a book she was sorting. It was one her father had taken at Christmas when Selene was about fifteen and the twins were ten. Evan and Cass stood proudly next to two new bikes, and Selene modeled the plaid robe she had received. Her mother sat in an armchair behind the Christmas tree; her face deliberately turned away from the camera. In the corner of the photo, a sliver of her father's finger touched the lens.

There weren't many photos from her childhood, so Selene studied the picture for several minutes. When she realized how the image summed up the dynamics of their family, a lump rose in her throat.

It had taken her a long time to accept her family's dysfunction. She had an absent, workaholic father and a co-dependent mother with substance use disorder. They would never be like the families on TV or the families of anyone she knew. Selene had done her best to protect Cass and Evan, but now they were grown. It wasn't her job to nurture them anymore. It was never her job to begin with.

Selene placed the photo in the pile of things going to Aurelia, yet she kept coming back to the face of her fifteen-year-old self. She wished she could hug that sweet girl and tell her not to lose hope. She would tell her to stop trying to please everyone because it would never be enough. It was okay to disappoint people and let them go, if necessary. She wanted to tell her how one day she would find someone who only wanted her to be happy and would give her the freedom to discover what she wanted.

She would make young Selene understand the lesson it had taken her thirty years to uncover—she didn't have to be bound by anything but her own desires.

Selene decided it would be best to break the news of her upcoming "move" by taking her family out to dinner. If they were in a public place, she reasoned there would be no yelling, and there would be a clearly defined start and stop time to the whole experience.

She had reserved a private room at a Middle Eastern restaurant near her apartment. Selene was the first to arrive, and her nerves were humming. Get it together, she told herself. *If I can kill a vampire, surely I can break this news.*

Eventually, she heard the click-clack of high heels approaching. Then there was her mother, standing before her. She wore a sleeveless dress and had pinned her blonde hair up to show off the designer scarf around her neck. A frown pulled at her mouth. Still, Selene felt gratified to see her mother after so long.

"Hey, Mom," Selene said. She hugged her, breathing in the familiar scent of Chanel No. 5 perfume.

Vivian stiffened at the uncharacteristic affection. "You look different. Have you been using that serum with the green tea I gave you?"

Selene had no idea what product her mother was referring to. She had a drawer full of rejected skincare items her mother had given to her and Cass when they failed to achieve the desired results. "Yes," she lied.

"Well, it's working," Vivian said. "You look less defeated. Around the eyes."

Her father appeared a moment later, wearing a suit and tie. "Hi, Dad," Selene said. "Did you come from work?"

"The airport. I was at a conference in the Quad Cities."

"Robert likes any excuse to get away from me," Vivian said tartly. She sat down, then asked, "Seleney, where's Kevin?"

Here we go. On to the first in the series of bombshells she was about to drop. "Oh, um, we broke up."

Vivian gasped. "Why?"

"It wasn't working."

Her mother's eyebrows climbed toward her hairline. "What do you mean? Poor Kevin must be devastated!"

"You dumped Kevin?" Cass asked eagerly, interrupting Vivian as she entered the room with Evan. "I knew you'd wise up one day."

"Did he cheat on you? I'll kill him," Evan said after he sat down. Vivian reached out to smooth his shaggy brown hair, but he pushed her hand away.

"No. We just grew apart," Selene said. She took a deep breath. "Our breakup actually has to do with the reason I wanted to see everyone tonight."

Vivian glanced at the menu. "Couldn't we have gone someplace less... foreign? Like a nice steakhouse?"

"Don't start," Selene's father said. "Isn't it enough that our daughter wanted to take us out?"

"I was only making a suggestion—"

"Nothing is ever good enough."

"That's rich coming from you," Vivian replied.

Evan turned away from his sparring parents to grin at his twin. "So, Cass. Bigfoot versus Mothman. Who would win in a fight?"

The "versus" game was one that Selene had made up when they were children to distract them during arguments. Not missing a beat, Cass said, "It's a toss-up. Bigfoot has stealth, and Mothman can fly. Though of the two, Bigfoot seems stronger."

"Yes, but can he see in the dark?" Evan asked.

Selene wondered if she'd ever get to tell them the truth about Bigfoot, Mothman, and the other Aurelian queens, but her anxiety was too high to chime in. The splintered conversations continued until Selene blurted out, "Listen to me! I'm leaving Nashville. Tomorrow."

Silence fell over the table.

"Excuse me?" Cass said after a moment.

Selene smoothed her hands across her lap. "I'm moving away."

"Where?" Her father asked.

"To an eco-village. I've applied to join a community, and was accepted."

"What the hell is an eco-village?" Evan asked.

"It's an intentional community that works for ecological sustainability," Selene said.

"Like a cult?" Evan asked.

"No, but I'll be living off the grid. No computers, TV, or cell phones."

"Are you serious?" Cass cut in.

Selene looked at her sister then down at her hands. "I know it's... abrupt. And odd. But I've thought a lot about it, and this is what I want. I just need a change. A big one."

"Where is this place?" her father asked.

"The Pacific Northwest," Selene lied. She had chosen an area the furthest away from Nashville, well outside of driving distance. "I-I'm not allowed to say where specifically. It's a private community, and they don't want visitors."

Her father's mouth was open. Cass's face was hard and suspicious. Evan was running a hand across his forehead, looking confused. Her mother was deathly pale.

Cass crossed her arms. "If you're off the grid, how are we supposed to get in touch with you? What if there's an emergency?"

"I'll come home periodically to visit. To check in," Selene replied.

"So you're cutting yourself off from us completely? Why would you do this?" Her mother asked. Her lips were pressed together so tightly it made her lipstick bleed.

"I'll be back to visit," Selene repeated. "I'm not sure when, but you can count on it."

"What's this secret eco-village called?" Cass asked.

"Azuresong Pastures," Selene replied, borrowing the name of Brunie and Eldridge's farm.

Cass pulled out her phone and began typing the name into a search engine. The server brought their drinks, and Vivian quickly downed her cocktail.

"Why would you want to hurt us this way?" Vivian asked loudly.

Selene felt herself shrinking into the chair, reverting to childhood patterns. "I'm not trying to hurt anyone," she said. "I love you all, but this is something I have to do."

"I think it's kind of cool," Evan said. "I'll miss you, but you deserve to have an adventure."

Selene smiled. "Thank you."

Cass gestured with her phone. "Strange how I can't find anything about it online."

"As I said, it's very private."

Her sister gave her a long look then asked, "Selene, will you do me a favor before you go?"

"Of course. What is it?"

"See a psychiatrist." When Selene started to protest, Cass cut her off. "I'm serious. Ever since we went to Rugby, something is very off with you. I'm worried."

Her mother whined, "Doesn't anyone care about my feelings here?"

"Please don't be upset, Mom. You're going to be okay," Selene said.

"Don't patronize me."

"Vivian... " her father warned.

"Why aren't you trying to stop her, Robert?"

Her dad shot Selene the same pleading look he always did when her mother's moods amplified. It was a look that said *control her, will you?*

Selene twisted her fingers together. "I know this is hard, and I'm sorry. I'm not trying to abandon you. I just want to lead my own life."

"It sounds bizarre to me," her father said. "But I've never known you to do anything without good reason. If this is what you want, I'm sure you've thought it through."

"I have, Dad."

Vivian pointed a pink-nailed finger at her. "Selfish. You're a selfish, spoiled girl, and that's all there is to it."

Selene felt like she'd been slapped. Her mother's reaction was expected, but the pain of her accusation cut deeply. She thought about the girl in the photo. Why was it Selene's responsibility to fill the emotional needs of everyone but herself?

The ache of guilt burned away as a rush of anger filled the space. The feeling was so strong it frightened her at first, then she let it wash over her like baptismal water. A shadow moved toward her, and she dismissed it with a finger. Instead of feeling victimized by her mother's manipulation, Selene felt a commanding sense of power.

She was done being needed.

Looking around the table, she said, "Dad, Evan, thank you for your support. Cass, I appreciate your concern. You're right, I haven't been the same since Rugby. I've realized I'm not happy with my life the way it is now. So I'm changing it."

She faced her mother. "Mom, I have spent my life catering to your needs. I am a grown woman, and if I want to move away, I can. You can't bully me anymore with guilt trips. I love all of you, and I will come back to visit when I can. But I *am* going. This is what I want."

She stood from the table and pulled two gift-wrapped boxes from her purse. She handed the first one to Cass. "I'm leaving you all of my jewelry and my laptop. There's also a large check in there; will you send it to Rugby's historic preservation fund? I'd really appreciate it." Cass accepted the box, nodding glumly.

Selene handed the other box to her brother. "Evan, I'm tired of seeing you drive around in that death trap of a car. I want you to have mine. Here are the keys and the title."

Evan stood to give her a big hug. Selene hugged him back, fighting the urge to sob. Quickly, she wiped her eyes and looked at her parents.

"Mom, Dad, I love you. Goodbye."

She left a wad of cash on the table to cover the meals and a generous tip. Then she walked out the door and didn't look back.

When she got back to the apartment, Selene took a moment to collect herself. All of her things were packed in boxes with a note asking Kevin to donate them, and she had tied up every loose end in her life she could think of. A mass email to her friends and colleagues broke the news of her major life change, but she still couldn't shake how badly things had ended with her sister.

Briefly, she considered sending her a letter explaining the real story, but Selene knew that was a bad idea. What would she even say?

Dear Cass, Just wanted to let you know that while we were in Rugby I actually traveled into another dimension, fell in love with a demon, and now I'm leaving to see him. Love ya!

Ridiculous. There was nothing she could do to fix this rift. She simply had to accept it as a casualty of her decision. Maybe one day she would be able to tell her the truth.

Donning a backpack full of essentials, Selene took one last look around her apartment. This was it. Ordinary Selene was long gone. She was Aurelian Selene now, through and through. It was time to claim it. She stood in the middle of the room, then pulled the traveler's stone from her pocket. Curling her fingers around it, she took a deep breath.

She pictured herself outside the gates of Queen Thema's castle. She imagined the sparkling white stone and arched windows. The sound of water rushing below the castle's bridge and the feel of mist swirling around her hair. She could practically smell the mint growing in the garden and hear Queen Thema's boisterous laugh.

And then with a tug deep in her belly... she was gone.

CHAPTER 48

S
am stopped sawing a long beam of wood to wipe the sweat from his forehead. The winter freeze was thawing in Snowmelt, and everyone was heartened by the first warm day of the season. Brunie sat under a tree, singing to herself while sewing the hem on a pair of blue-checked curtains. Eldridge was perched on a stump nearby, sanding pieces of wood.

For the past few months, Sam had been living in the loft of Brunie and Eldridge's barn. Since the plumbing was installed last week, they were working on other improvements to make the space more habitable. A set of windows had been added, shelves and cabinets were built, and now they were focused on flooring. The list of improvements to be completed was extensive but necessary for Sam's long-term comfort.

When Sam had arrived on Brunie and Eldridge's doorstep after months of waiting for Zaybris at the Goblyn castle, Brunie rushed to the attic to get his room ready. Sam told her not to bother. He didn't care if it was dusty or needed fresh bedsheets. All he wanted to do was sleep. He had finally admitted to himself that he had lost Selene forever, and when he wasn't having visions about his mate being tortured or killed, sleep was his only escape from the heartache and regret that plagued him.

But when he reached the top of the attic stairs, grief made him turn around. Memories of the passionate night he had spent there with Selene after the vampire attack were too raw. The pain had been more than he could bear. So he had retreated to the barn, sleeping on a bed of hay next to Rainsilver's stall until Brunie and Eldridge insisted they turn the loft into a living space. Though the renovations gave him something to focus on, Sam feared the emptiness he would feel once they were completed.

Sam took a drink from the jug of water Brunie had brought him. He pushed his hair back from his forehead, and the motion bumped his damaged horn, sending a shock of pain throughout his body. Although the healer at Queen Lilith's castle had worked magic on Sam's injuries, the new growth of his regenerating horn was tender.

He thought back to how Queen Lilith's remaining servants had been eager to assist him during his stay, and how all but a few vampires living at the castle were respectful to him. Waldron was especially rational for a vampire, and Sam felt he was genuinely concerned for Selene's safety. Their brief conversations about Queen Thema's search efforts turned more regular until they began to share a drink in the throne room nightly by the fire. Sam drank whiskey while Waldron sipped on donated Aurelian blood.

Through these talks Sam learned of Zaybris's obsession with Queen Lilith. Waldron believed this had something to do with her disappearance, but Zaybris would never speak of it. Sam cared little for stories of Zaybris's unrequited love for the Goblyn queen, but he did like probing Waldron about the habits and inclinations of human women. Though the vampire and Selene had been born in different centuries, Waldron had taught Sam much about the customs of her people. Sam was especially intrigued by the ceremonies of marriage. There was so much he wished he had learned about Selene. It made him more determined to find her and be the mate she truly deserved.

Since many of the rooms in the castle were small and Goblyn-sized, Sam made himself at home in the former royal chambers of Queen Lilith and plotted his vengeance. Her apartments were comfortable and decorated with the style and colors Sam would have chosen himself. Within her royal library, he found the law books she had created to govern the vampires, and he admired her shrewd but fair leadership style.

As the weeks turned to months, the determination Sam had felt when he arrived at the castle dimmed. It seemed that no one in the whole of Aurelia had spotted or heard anything about Zaybris or Selene's whereabouts. The queens offered rewards and sent out trackers, but their search efforts came up empty.

Finally, one bleak morning Sam resigned himself to the reality that Selene was gone. He wasn't going to see his mate again. She was lost to him forever, most likely drained to death or killed. Violently. Horrifically. Because he had failed to protect her.

Her last thoughts of him would have been bitter and ugly. He knew he had hurt her deeply and regretted every moment of their last conversation. Fate had given him a rare and precious gift, but he had wasted it by thinking only of himself.

He spent many nights considering what to do next. He could go back to his life as a guard for Queen Thema, but working in her castle was a lonely existence. He was fond of Thema and had respect for her close courtiers like Arkaya and Hollen, but there was no one there he missed enough to return to.

There were also none who knew who he truly was. Now that he had experienced being with someone who accepted him fully, he couldn't go back to pretending. He believed Selene's calming influence could control his demonic urges, but he was tired of acting as if he had none at all. He could be violent but also tender. Brutish, yet kind. She had allowed him to be each part of himself, and he had found it liberating.

Sam decided to spend his days with the only other Aurelians who knew him as well as she did. He bid farewell to Waldron and the others at the Goblyn castle and left to live with Brunie and Eldridge.

A satisfied groan from Brunie snapped Sam's attention back to the present. She stretched her wings, then said, "That's enough sewing for me today. Ah, look at the time. I should get supper on, shouldn't I?"

"What are we having, dearest?" Eldridge asked.

"I was thinking about a nice stew with lots of bread for dipping. Does that sound good?"

"Lovely," Eldridge said, smacking his lips.

Brunie tossed the completed curtain over her shoulder and turned to go inside. She had just reached the front door when a strange noise from the hills made all three of them turn.

It sounded like trotting horses, but there was also an odd whooshing tone, like the noise of a sled coasting down a hill. Sam shielded his eyes from the setting sun to see where it was coming from. At first, he couldn't see anything, but eventually, something large and egg-shaped crested over the hill.

"What is it?" Brunie asked.

Sam could make out four gray horses. They were pulling a glittering white carriage the size of a small house, but instead of wheels, it glided across the grass on curved runners. Gold flourishes decorated the windows, and the carriage door bore the image of two cats flanking a shield, the royal crest of the Malkina.

It was Queen Thema's carriage.

Sam's jaw clenched as the carriage drew closer. What could she want? He couldn't have been more clear in his letter to the Queen that he was finished working for her. Was she angry about his decision? Or did she expect to woo him back with riches and promises?

"Who is it, Samael?" Eldridge asked.

"It's the carriage of Queen Thema," he said tightly.

Brunie's wings trembled. Sam glanced worriedly at them both. The Harpy had never liked Queen Thema, and she hated unannounced visitors. Would she feel their humble home was inadequate to host a visit from a queen? Perhaps it was just a Malkina servant in the carriage sent to bring Sam some of his abandoned belongings.

Once the carriage reached the bottom of the hill, the driver signaled the horses to slow, and the gliding structure came to a stop. After a moment, the door opened.

A ginger-colored cat emerged first, trotting down the small stairs leading to the ground. Then the doorway was filled by Queen Thema herself. The evening sun made her silver breastplate shimmer as she stood at the top of the stairs looking out.

"Greetings, my friends," she called out across the expanse of grass separating them.

Sam set down his saw. "What are you doing here?"

Queen Thema gripped either side of the doorway and winked. "I've come to bring you a gift," she said, then turned her attention away from him. "You must be Brunie and Eldridge. I am Queen Thema of the Malkina. Truly a lovely farm you have. And Lady Brunie, I owe you my eternal gratitude! One of your extraordinary muffins came to me through the switch pouch, and it was the most delightful thing I had ever tasted. Do you mind if I brag to my sister Queen Aello of how I met the most skilled baker of all her subjects?"

The suspicion on Brunie's face was quickly replaced by delight. "Oh my, of course. If you wish, certainly! I have more muffins cooling inside if you'd like one."

"That would be divine," Thema replied. "It's been a long journey and—"

"What are you doing here, Thema?" Sam growled. "I told you my home is in Snowmelt now."

Queen Thema glanced inside the carriage and patted her upsweep of braids. "Forgive me. Samael, we miss you, but I'm not here to bring you back. I have something for you. I wanted to make the delivery myself. To make amends."

Sam could see through the windows that someone else was moving in the carriage. He assumed it was Arkaya but couldn't understand why she would want to see him.

As Queen Thema stepped down the stairs, Sam saw a face appear in the doorway behind her, which made his heart seize in his chest.

Selene.

CHAPTER 49

S am stumbled until his back pressed against the side of the
barn. His breaths came in bursts while his heart beat wildly
against his ribs. He blinked several times as he tried to recon-
cile what he was seeing. A honking sound came from his left, and he
saw that Brunie had burst into tears. Eldridge was hovering up and
down excitedly on his wings while Nim the cat licked his paw. Queen
Thema rested her hands on her hips, looking proud.

Sam's eyes raked over Selene hungrily.

It was her.

Not only was she alive, but she looked more beautiful than he
had ever seen her. Healthy, whole, and vibrant. The smile she gave
him was dazzling as she climbed out of the carriage. Was this truly
real?

My mate.

"Hi, Sam," she said softly.

The sound of her voice made his body start to tremble. He feared
he might collapse if it weren't for the barn supporting his back.

"You're alive," he breathed.

"Yes."

"How?"

She began walking towards him. "It's a long story."

"I can't... how is this... ?" Sam stammered.

She tugged at a cord encircling her neck. A shiny white stone was suspended from it. "The traveler's stone is mine now. Zaybris gifted it to me."

Sam's mind felt clouded, as if he couldn't absorb what he was seeing. His gaze snapped from the stone up to her face. "Where is Zaybris? Did he harm you?"

"He's in the Underworld."

"Dead?"

"No. After he grabbed me in the cave, he used the stone to take me to the Underworld."

His eyes widened. "Why there?"

"He was in love with your mother. That's why he kidnapped you. He did it just to hurt her, for revenge." She stopped to stand in front of him. Sam swayed as her familiar pomegranate scent washed over him. "Sam, your mother Lamia is actually Lilith, the Goblyn queen."

Sam's head jerked back at this information. Suddenly, he felt faint. He couldn't take in enough air. "What? How?"

"She fell in love with your father on Gaia and left Aurelia to become a demon. To be with him... and to give birth to you."

Queen Thema, seemingly unable to stop herself, called out, "That makes you my nephew!"

Sam swallowed. "Lilith is my mother?"

Selene nodded. "I met both of your parents while I was in the Underworld. They love you so much. And miss you. They tried so hard to find you but couldn't reach you in this realm."

Sam looked over at the queen's delighted face, then to Brunie's joyful tears and Eldridge's grin. He couldn't fully process what Selene had just told him; it was all too much at once. Sam's body tensed as Selene came closer. Suspicion began to claw at the elation he had felt upon seeing her.

"Is that why you're here in Aurelia? To tell me this?" he asked.

"That's one reason. But there are things we need to discuss." Selene said.

"I waited for you," he whispered. His eyes searched hers. "At the Goblyn castle. We all searched for you, and when I realized you weren't coming back, I wanted to die."

Selene's expression was wistful. "I'm sorry I didn't come sooner. I went home after I left the Underworld and Queen Thema told me I'd been away from Aurelia for nine months. For me, it was only nine days. The stone isn't enchanted to stop time as the portal did."

Sam rubbed his forehead, feeling confused. "You went home, yet you returned here?"

"Yes. I ended it with Kevin and told my family I was moving away. Then I used the stone to go to Queen Thema's castle. I wanted to see you."

"I was here. I didn't want to go back to that life."

"I know. The queen explained where you were and insisted on bringing me to you herself. We talked a lot on the way over here."

"Selene has forgiven me for using her as bait!" Queen Thema bellowed. "Haven't you, dear? And she's going to help me see my sister!"

Selene smiled and waved.

Eldridge cleared his throat. "Eh, Brunie, why don't we go inside to give Queen Thema a taste of your cloudberry muffins, shall we?"

Brunie wiped her shining eyes and nodded. "Yes, yes. Of course. Queen Thema, would you like to come in?"

"It would be my pleasure," Thema said loudly, then motioned for her carriage driver and cat to follow her. "Have you any milk?"

Sam watched them enter the cottage and then continued staring at Selene. It was difficult to believe she was real. His hands itched to touch her, but she seemed to be holding herself back from him.

"May I kiss you?" he breathed.

Her expression was tender, yet she said. "We need to talk first. Can we sit down somewhere?"

Feeling flustered, Sam ran a hand through his hair and motioned

366

inside the barn. Selene took a seat at the small table near Rainsilver's stall, and Sam sat across from her. His frantic heart pounded faster as he wondered if he was about to lose her forever.

She placed both palms on the table. Her expression was serious as she inhaled and blew out a slow breath. "Sam, being back home gave me a lot of perspective on who I am. In the past, it's been hard for me to identify what I want. Growing up, I wasn't allowed to explore those feelings, and it's held me back in ways I didn't realize."

Rainsilver let out a short neigh, causing Selene to glance at the horse and then back at him. "I have a lot to work on, but I want—"

"I'll give you anything!" Sam cut in. "Anything you want, it's yours,"

"Please don't interrupt me," she said.

"I'm sorry."

She held his gaze then said, "I want to be with you. I want to be your partner, your lover, and your friend. I want to learn *more* about what I want. With you by my side. But Sam, I need you to hear this. I'm not your therapy."

"My what?"

She shook her head slightly. "I guess that's not a term used in this realm. It means I don't want to be responsible for your emotional stability. When we were in the cave before Zaybris came, you told me you needed me to balance your instincts."

Sam winced. "I regret every part of that conversation. The way I lied to you. How you found out about Queen Thema's plan. The truth about Zaybris... "

Selene held up her hand. "Hold on, I'm still mad about all that, but we can move beyond it. What we can't move past is that you don't 'need' me to manage your instincts."

Sam's forehead creased. "You are my fated mate. It is natural for you to calm me."

"No. Ultimately, you have to learn to calm yourself."

Sam leaned back, trying to understand her meaning. He wanted to sing when she had said *I want to be with you*, but he knew he had to tread carefully at that moment. "My love, I have been trying to calm myself for over twenty years. Yet I've never felt more in control than when I'm with you."

"I'm glad you feel that way, but I'm not the solution you think I am."

"That first time at the Padu when I was about to lose control, it was your touch that brought me back. It was our bond."

"It may have played a part, but I believe the fated mate bond helps us develop new strengths from each other."

"How so?"

"I've been more in touch with my anger since being with you, and I feel like I'm not such a pushover anymore. You helped bring that out in me, and I'm grateful. Maybe I bring out the calm you already have inside of you."

He rubbed his chin, considering. Was it foolish of him to assume that claiming his fated mate would solve all of his problems? Once, it was unthinkable that he would release his burning desire for vengeance against Zaybris. Yet, he had made peace with his defeat. He had also assumed his demonic instincts would run wild without Selene, but he had kept control. Even when he believed she was dead.

He looked into her eyes and saw yearning there. She wanted to be with him. Yet she would not accept being anything less than an equal partner. In a flash, he understood her plea. She believed he only valued her for her calming presence, not for who she was.

"Selene, I didn't say I need you because I want you to balance my instincts," he said slowly. "I said I need you because I love being with you."

He stood up and came around the table toward her. Bending to one knee, he took her hands and said, "I need you because I'm in love with you. I need you because I don't ever want to leave your side."

Selene's face bloomed into a smile.

He kissed her knuckles. "You don't have to help me manage my instincts. You don't have to be anything to me but yourself. I'm sorry for lying to you and betraying your trust. I have spent countless nights thinking of what I should have done differently. I will never stop regretting how callous I was with your feelings in my plans for our future. It was agony to be without you."

Her eyes sparkled. "I missed you too. Everything in my life back home felt so meaningless. I saw how I've always tried to be what other people needed, but I've never done that for myself."

Sam reached out to stroke a lock of hair that had escaped her bun. "I want you to be the person *you* need for yourself. And I want to be the type of mate you want. The one you deserve."

She cupped his cheek and said, "Thank you, Sam."

"Please stay. Let me prove it to you," he said. "I love you."

Her smile widened. "I love you, too." Dropping her face close to his, she kissed him.

When her lips met his, it was as if lightning had struck them both. Instantly, his arms banded around her, pulling her off the chair. Tremors reverberated through his body, sending shock waves of feeling to every nerve. He palmed the back of her head, and she straddled his waist.

Without warning, the shadows came bounding toward them from every direction. They surrounded them both, cocooning them in tingly mist. He continued to kiss Selene, reveling in her taste. The feel of her tongue dancing against his. The warmth of her body pressed against him, and the scent of her hair and skin. The shadows grew and intensified until he realized it wasn't mist surrounding them... it was magic.

The mating bond.

Her words and kiss had made it shimmer over them both like the sparkle of starlight. He felt a pull in his chest as the connection snapped into place. The ache of loneliness that had followed him his entire life was replaced with a powerful sensation of belonging. Then as quickly as they came, the shadows dispersed.

Selene pulled back to look into his eyes. Her expression was awed and gratified. He stared at her for a moment, then closed his eyes, absorbing the magnitude of what had just happened.

"I think I just claimed my mate," Selene said, smiling.

He nodded and squeezed her to him tighter. Now that the mating bond was truly in place, he understood Selene's point about their strengths complementing each other. He brought fire and ferocity to her while she gave him peace and restfulness. The feelings of elation after he believed he had claimed her in the cave were nothing compared to what he felt at that moment. It was bliss. Joy. Peace. Satisfaction. Fulfillment.

They kissed again for several moments, and although Sam was grateful for the privacy Eldridge and Brunie had given them, he was anxious to get more private with her in his newly appointed room. Keeping her legs wrapped around him, he cupped her thighs and stood.

"I built a room for myself upstairs, but we don't have to live there," he said while climbing the stairs to the loft. "We can build a house of our own or go back to Queen Thema's. I want to go wherever you go."

"Sam, we don't have to stay in Aurelia."

Gently, he laid her on his bed then frowned. "What do you mean? Do you wish to go back home to Gaia?"

"No. I want to visit there, of course. But… " Selene began to twirl the traveler's stone between her fingers. "We have a lot more options now."

His eyebrows rose. "I see."

"You know how I've always wanted to travel."

"I remember. Where would you like to go first?"

The way her blue eyes sparkled made Sam feel weightless. Complete. Smiling up at him, she said, "Let's go to the Underworld."

～

THE END

Thank you for reading! If you enjoyed this book, please consider leaving a review on the platform of your choice. Reviews help an author so much by encouraging readers to take a chance on a new book.

And don't miss Sam and Selene's continuing journey the next book in the Shadows of Aurelia series, *To Dwell in Shadows*, featuring Cass and Hal's story.

THE SEVEN SISTERS OF AURELIA

Queen Aello of the Harpies
Sacred animal: Bird
Often known on Gaia as: Mothman, Swan Maiden, Mother Goose

Queen Cebna of the Nereid
Sacred animal: Fish
Often known on Gaia as: Mermaid, Grindylow, Kappa

Queen Delphine of the Drago
Sacred animal: Snake
Often known on Gaia as: Chessie, Loch Ness Monster, Champ

Queen Keebee of the Lycah
Sacred animal: Wolf
Often known on Gaia as: Barghest, Beast of Bray Road, Michigan Dogman

Queen Lilith of the Goblyns
Sacred animal: Bat

Often known on Gaia as: Ahool, Jersey Devil, Olitiau

Queen Thema of the Malkina
Sacred animal: Cat
Often known on Gaia as: Ozark Howler, Wampus Cat, Black Beast of Exmoor

Queen Yerena of the Vowa
Sacred animal: Bear
Often known on Gaia as: Bigfoot, Fouke Monster, Skunk Ape

ACKNOWLEDGMENTS

I have many people to thank for helping me bring this little book to life, but I first want to share how I came to write it. Several years ago, I attended a retreat for writers of creative non-fiction, but I left knowing I had to write this book. When Jennifer Louden, the retreat leader, gave our group the journaling prompt, "The thing I keep *not* writing because it doesn't feel okay but just won't leave me alone is... " I froze. It felt as though I had been punched in the gut. I knew exactly what my "thing" was. It was the story I had daydreamed about for years—the one about a woman who travels to another dimension and falls in love with a demon.

Yet I had never put it on paper because it didn't feel okay. Why? For all the reasons people make up when doing something big and out of their comfort zone. I didn't have time, I didn't write fiction, I wouldn't make any money, nobody would read it, it was too hard, etc.

But that story just wouldn't leave me alone. Tentatively, I began to entertain the idea of writing down a few notes and learning more about the romance genre. And when I finally mustered the courage to start writing, the words poured out of me. I kept going and going until the story-that-wouldn't-leave-me-alone started competing with my work responsibilities. I didn't have the mental space to commit myself to the book fully and knew something had to give. If I was going to give this fiction thing a real shot, I needed to cut out everything else.

And that brings me to my first expression of gratitude to my husband, Grant. When I told him I wanted to quit my job to write a book, he didn't tell me I was being silly or irresponsible. He simply said we'd make it work. And we did. I was terrified that making writing my full-time job was a mistake, but I am lucky enough to have a partner who believes in taking risks. Grant, I am so grateful for your investment in me and support of my unconventional path. Even though we couldn't fulfill your dreams of being a romance novel cover model, I appreciate how much you believe in my writing.

Bethany Seabolt, I have crossed oceans of time to find a friend like you. If Sam and Selene have a fairy godmother, it's you. You have been their biggest fan from day one, and I don't know if I would have continued writing this book without your ongoing encouragement. You have been there for me as a reader, an editor, a friend, a romance fan, and even a buffer when I get my feelings hurt by someone's criticism. There's no one I trust to know what good romance "catnip" is more than you.

Thank you to Susannah Felts, who sparked my return to writing with her classes in the upper level of a coffee shop before co-founding The Porch as a place for writers to connect. All of my most cherished writing friends I met through Porch classes, including my critique group, which we named "The Porch Pals" after a few cocktails and much giggling. The Pals have been monumental in my work by cheering me on, giving me tough love when I needed it, and pulling me through many crises of confidence. To Brad Buchanan, Peako Jenkins, Krissie Mulvoy Williams, Jason Maynard, Joy Ramirez, and Megan Roggendorff, you're the best. Thank you also to Katie McDougall, the Porch's other co-founder, who gave me the encouragement I needed to keep writing this book during her Foundations of Fiction class.

To beta readers, Pam Hinkle, Caryn Kelly, Kirby Lewis-Gill, and Alice Peterson, thank you for pointing out the sticky spots of this book, which helped me create a much better version than the one you read (I hope). And just when I thought this book was the best it could be, Jen Prokop blew my mind with so many good suggestions and tweaks to turn up the heat. Your feedback helped me zero in on themes from my subconscious that weren't yet fully formed, and I love the results.

Thank you to Julia Dobbins, Jonathan Lewis-Gill, and Brandon Ross for indulging me one night in pretending to be literary agents (complete with index cards of mock interview questions) when I was practicing for a pitch event. Shout out to Ellen Margulies, copy editor and fellow 90-Day Fiancé fanatic, for fixing all of my ellipses and comma issues. Thank you to Music City Romance Writers for events that helped build my romance writing muscles and Charissa Weaks for answering all my newbie-author questions.

To Sandy Spencer Coomer at Rockvale Writers' Colony, thank you for sharing your beautiful space, which gave me the peace I needed to complete my final edits. I also owe much to the historic village of Rugby and its incredible history. During every research trip I made to Rugby, I always ate at the Harrow Road Cafe and wanted to pay it tribute in this book since it was regretfully destroyed by fire in 2020.

Lastly, I want to thank my parents. I hate that my dad did not live long enough to see this book published. However, I am grateful that he never read the sex scenes! Dad always believed in my writing and made me feel like I could do anything. He would have been thrilled to see this book on his bookshelf. To my mom, thank you for instilling a love of reading in me and introducing me to romance novels. Your devotion to the *Outlander* series sparked my imagination for fish-out-of-water storytelling, and you have always been supportive of everything I do. I am proud to be your daughter.

About the Author

Photo by Wilde Company

Avalon Griffin writes paranormal fantasy romance with unique characters, far-away settings, and a healthy dose of heat. When not writing, she can be found traveling the globe in search of kitschy roadside attractions, off-beat museums, and cryptozoology legends. She lives in Nashville, Tennessee with her husband, an ungrateful house cat, and a rowdy crew of feral cats. To keep up with her, visit www.avalon griffin.com.

 instagram.com/avalon_griffin
 facebook.com/authoravalongriffin